Praise for *The Ni...*

"You will find yourself falling in love with eve... with bated breath just to see in which direction... end you'll find yourself not being able to go a m... journey and glorious storytelling of Tiffany Reisz."

—*RT Book Reviews,* ...

"This time-travel romance is swoon-worthy and lovely. Reisz is a powerful writer who hits all the high romance you can ask for, while creating a fascinating yet believable plot that makes us believe that love can conquer all, even time and death."

—*Kirkus Reviews*

"The perfect summer read for historical romance fans."

—*Barnes & Noble Reads*

"If you love romantic time travel and stories about eternal, never-quieting love, then you must absolutely pick up *The Night Mark*."

—*LitStack*

"An aching meditation on grief and loss… It's chock-full of symbolism and, most importantly, hope."

—*Heroes and Heartbreakers*

Praise for *The Bourbon Thief*

"A dark, twisty tale of love, lust, betrayal, and murder…this novel is not one to be missed."

—*Bustle*

"[Reisz's] prose is quite beautiful, and she can weave a wonderful tight story."
—*New York Times* and *USA TODAY* bestselling author Jennifer Probst

"*The Bourbon Thief* isn't just good, it's exceptional. The story captured my imagination; the characters captured my heart."

—*Literati Literature Lovers*

"Reisz fills the narrative with rich historic details; memorable, if vile, characters; and enough surprises to keep the plot moving and readers hooked until the final drop of bourbon is spilled."

—*Booklist*

"Beautifully written and delightfully insane… Reisz vividly captures the American South with a brutal honesty that only enhances the dark material."

—*RT Book Reviews*, Top Pick

"Impossible to stop reading."

—*Heroes and Heartbreakers*

TIFFANY REISZ

THE LUCKY ONES

mira

mira

Recycling programs for this product may not exist in your area.

ISBN-13: 978-0-7783-3116-2

The Lucky Ones

For questions and comments about the quality of this book, please contact us at CustomerService@Harlequin.com.

www.MIRABooks.com

www.BookClubbish.com

Printed in U.S.A.

To Andrew Shaffer and Jenn LeBlanc...we'll always have Cannon Beach.

THE
LUCKY
ONES

"…the companions of our childhood always possess a certain power over our minds which hardly any later friend can obtain."

—Mary Shelley, *Frankenstein*

CHAPTER 1

Louisville, Kentucky, 2015

All Allison wanted was for this conversation to be over. That and she hoped the heavy gray clouds would part and the sun would appear. It could go either way today—sun or rain. She stood at the kitchen window, peeling old white paint off the sill as she waited for the Kentucky sky to make up its mind. Meanwhile, sitting behind her at the table, her lover, Cooper McQueen, gently ruined her life.

Then, a small mercy—the clouds split wide open. The sun shone bright enough to momentarily blind her. She exhaled in her relief. Allison had always loved the rain. She could forgive McQueen for leaving. She would never forgive him if he'd ruined the rain for her.

"She's pregnant," McQueen said. "She's due in April."

"You're happy about it," Allison said, working another strip of paint off the edge of the frame. She felt a silly sort of triumph when it came off in one long white ribbon.

"Cricket," he said softly, apologetically. "Look at me."

Allison wanted to walk out right then, walk out and never

look back. She should have, she knew. Instead, she turned around and faced him. He'd just ended it and here she was, still obeying his every command.

"I'm sorry," he said.

"It's all right, McQueen," she said, shrugging. "We knew this would happen eventually. Not you getting some strange woman you picked up in a bar pregnant, I mean. But…"

"But…" He sat back in the chair.

"You are happy about it, though, aren't you?" she asked. "You can be honest with me. I'd appreciate it."

She was lying. She was lying through her teeth. She didn't want him to be honest with her. She wanted him to lie to her, lie as hard as she was lying to him. She wanted him to tell her he wasn't happy about it at all, that he didn't want to end it, that his hand had been forced, that if given the choice he'd throw caution to the wind and marry Allison tomorrow, even if it did cause a scandal, even if it meant his kids might never speak to him again…

"Yes," he said. "I'm happy about it."

"I'm happy for you, too, then."

Another lie.

Allison had sensed that morning that today was going to be the day. Instead of calling her to let her know when he'd drop by—for sex, of course, there was no other reason he ever called her—he'd called instead to tell her he had some mail of hers he was bringing over and a pair of earrings he'd found in his bathroom drawer.

"She has her own money. She's thirty-seven. A little bit more age-appropriate than you," he said. A joke. He was trying to make her laugh and, damn him, it worked. But it was a very small laugh. Her lover—or, she supposed, ex-lover—was Cooper McQueen, who was very possibly a billionaire if one got creative enough with the accounting. He was also forty-five to her twenty-five. She'd been his mistress for six years, although she'd known him for seven. The worst part of it all was what a cliché the whole tawdry thing was. At eighteen she'd gotten a job working for McQueen as his daughter Emmy's weekend babysitter.

"Congratulations," Allison said. He was trying to spare her pain by not admitting how thrilled he was to have child number three on the way. He and his wife had divorced after two kids, and he'd confessed to her a long time ago that he always felt someone was missing from the family. Not her. She wasn't family. She was an employee.

"It's going to be an adventure," he said, his voice neutral.

Going to be… He was already seeing the future with this child, with this woman. There was no talking him out of ending things. It was already done and over. Now if she could only get through the rest of this conversation without falling apart. She'd gone six years as the secret mistress of a very wealthy man without falling apart once in his presence. She hated to ruin her streak.

"Does she know about me?" Allison asked. An important question.

"I told her," McQueen said. "After she told me."

"She asked you to get rid of me, didn't she?"

"No, in fact. She said I could be in the baby's life if I wanted to keep you, but I couldn't be in hers if you were still in the picture. For the kid's sake, I thought we should try to make it work."

"You should, yes," Allison said. Even she couldn't deny he was doing the right thing—finally.

"She told me to tell you she was very sorry," McQueen said. "And she means it. She didn't know about you. This isn't personal."

"No, of course it isn't," Allison said. "What's her name?"

McQueen paused before answering as if weighing Allison's motives in asking. "Paris. Paris Shelby."

"Tell Ms. Shelby I appreciate that. And I understand." Allison paused. "Must be special. You kept me through three girlfriends."

"I'm crazy about her," McQueen finally admitted. It was a knife in her heart. A small knife, but serrated. It did damage.

"And you're sane about me," she said.

McQueen sighed heavily, too wise to retort. He was a handsome man—tan, tall and lean with a twentysomething's libido. But there was no denying he had crow's-feet around his eyes, hair more salt than pepper and, on those rare occasions when they were together in public, people always gave them that "daughter or girlfriend?" look. She wouldn't miss that. She needed to think of other things she wouldn't miss, but she kept coming up empty-handed.

"Your rent's paid through the end of the year," McQueen said. He removed an envelope from the box and showed her the receipt inside. "I would have given you the place, but I don't own the building. And if you want all the furniture, it's yours. Anything you don't want to keep, you can sell." A surge of relief flooded through her body. She wasn't married to the place, but she liked having a roof over her head. And it was a very nice apartment—a corner unit on the second floor of a Colonial Revival mansion in historic Old Louisville. McQueen had it furnished with an antique sofa and chairs, plush rugs on the polished wood floors and a luxurious king-size bed. Furnished for him, of course, not her. But she was relieved he wasn't kicking her out. She had nowhere else to go.

"I appreciate the grace period," she said.

"If you need more time, please ask for it." He smiled and took out a smaller envelope. "And I've written you a letter of recommendation."

Now that did make her laugh, loud and hard.

"Recommending me for what?" Allison asked. "Is there an employment agency for rich men looking for mistresses?"

He wrinkled his nose in disgust. "You weren't my mistress. It's so..."

"True?"

"Melodramatic. This was always a friendly business arrangement."

"I see. So you're not dumping me, then. You're firing me."

Allison turned away from him, back to the window and the peeling paint. Outside a knot of college students, a couple of them in red University of Louisville T-shirts, walked past the house, sweating in the sun. One girl linked arms with her boyfriend. Two other guys lightly punched each other's arms over a joke. They must have been at most four years younger than her, if that. And yet they looked like children. Happy children. Beautiful, happy children. All children should be that happy.

"I'll send someone to repaint," McQueen said. "I want to make sure you get the security deposit back."

"I can paint it myself."

"I'll send someone."

"It's my responsibility now, right?"

"Yes, but—"

"And I'm not," she said.

"Not what?" he asked.

"Your responsibility. Not anymore."

"That's going to take some getting used to," he said.

She turned back around and dug her hands deep into her jeans pockets. He never liked her to wear jeans. Or slacks or sweatpants. Skirts and dresses were his preference—or the lingerie that he bought her. One tiny rebellion, wearing jeans today. And yet she'd topped her outfit with his favorite blouse of hers—the sweet white eyelet lace top that made her look like a pretty hippie lost in time—and worn her hair down and loosely curled the way he loved.

"Get used to it," she said. "I already am."

McQueen ignored that and reached into the box again. He pulled out a canvas bag with something inside it the size and density of a brick.

"What's that?" she asked, narrowing her eyes at the bag.

"Fifty thousand dollars. Cash."

Allison's eyes widened.

"It'll tide you over until you can get a job," he said. "Or help you through grad school. I know you so I'm giving you an order—do not blow it all on books or give it all away to total strangers with sob stories."

She ignored that last part. If he was giving her money, she'd do whatever she damned well pleased with it. She'd buy a whole damn bookstore to spite him if she wanted.

"Fifty thousand dollars," she said. "You must feel really guilty, McQueen."

"I do feel guilty," he said with pride. "I paid you not to work after you graduated so I could have you when I wanted you. Three years is a big gap on your résumé."

"I'll tell them I was working for you as a professional kept woman. The name of Cooper McQueen goes far in this state."

"I would prefer you give them the letter of recommendation instead. It says you're a very good personal assistant."

"Emphasis on the 'personal'?" She picked up the bag, weighing it in her hand. "I thought it would be bigger."

McQueen raised his eyebrow. "Not a sentence I hear often."

She glared at him, tight-lipped, not amused.

"Five hundred Ben Franklins don't take up a lot of space," he said. "Don't believe everything you see in movies. Even one million won't fill a briefcase, unless it's all in ones."

"And you're giving it to me out of the goodness of your heart?" she asked.

"I am. You should know, my lawyer tried to tell me I should get you to sign an NDA before I gave you the money. I told him to shove it."

"An NDA? He wanted me to sign a nondisclosure agreement for sleeping with you?"

"I pay the man to protect me," McQueen said. "My daughter's ex-babysitter talking to the press about how I slept with her at the tender age of nineteen might hurt me a little. You know I want to run for governor one of these days. But I'm not making you sign anything. I trust you. I have always trusted you. The money is yours free and clear. I want you to take it. You're only hurting yourself if you don't."

"I shouldn't accept it," she said. "It'll let you off the hook too easily."

He smiled at that. He knew his own faults, which was one of his few virtues.

"But I'm going to take it," she said.

"You earned it."

"I did," she said. "But not because I put up with you the past six years. I earned this much just for putting up with this conversation."

He lowered his head and exhaled loudly.

"You don't make it easy on a man," he said. "You could say thank you. Most girlfriends don't get severance pay after a breakup."

"I'm not your girlfriend, remember?" She put the money into the box. She saw her earrings. She saw the rent receipt. She saw the letter. She saw two thick envelopes.

"What are those?"

"One's your mail. The other's...they're the pictures."

"Our pictures?" she asked.

He slowly nodded. "You have any idea how much it hurt giving those pictures up?"

"How much?"

"A lot. I came this close to keeping them." He held up his fingers a hairbreadth apart.

"They're pornographic," she said, glaring at him.

"They're beautiful. And you're beautiful in them. And I don't look too bad myself."

"What about running for governor someday?" she asked.

"That's the only reason I gave them back to you," he said.

"You seem sadder about losing them than losing me."

"Cricket, please…"

"Don't call me that anymore," she said, closing her eyes. "I did everything you asked me to do—in bed and out. Everything. I never asked for anything from you. I never complained. I never…" She never made a scene. She never cried in front of him. She did all his favorite tricks.

"We had six good years," he said.

"Good for you. I was nineteen. Do you feel bad about that at all?"

"Let me ask you this," he said. "Do you?"

"You want me to absolve you."

"I want you to be honest with me," he said. "Did I take advantage of you? If I did, then tell me. Or did you want it as much as I did?"

"I was nineteen," she said again.

"You weren't drafted into the army. You had sex with an older man who paid your rent and your bills and gave you diamonds for Christmas. You knew what the deal was when I offered it to you. I've told my fair share of lies to my fair share of women," he said. "But I never lied to you about us. Did I?"

Allison would have argued except it was true. Of course

he never lied to her. Lovers lied to protect the loved one. No love to protect meant no need for lies.

"No, you never lied to me."

McQueen met her eyes for a split second before glancing away, a guilty look on his face.

"So this is it?" she asked. "The end?"

"I'd like to have sex with you before I leave," he said.

Allison stared at him, incredulous.

"Yes, and I'd like to marry a knight-errant and raise rare-breed cats with him in our castle by the sea," she said.

"I'm taking that as a 'no' to breakup sex," he said.

"Safe to say that's a 'no.' We had sex yesterday," she said. "Twice."

"That wasn't breakup sex," he said. "And don't give me that look. This is your own fault." McQueen pointed at her, shook his finger.

"My fault? My fault?" Allison was laughing in utter amazement at the sheer gall of the man.

"Your fault. You've been trying for years to make me a better man," he said. "Give more money to the poor. Be nicer to my employees. Don't date girls my daughter's age. Well, maybe your guilt trips finally started to sink in a little. I don't call you Jiminy Cricket because you wear a top hat and tails."

"You are unbelievable," she said.

"Allison," he said, "I am sorry about this. I truly am."

He held out his hand to shake.

"Six years of my life," she said, "and it's going to end in a handshake."

"You already said no to breakup sex," he said.

Another hard truth. So she took his hand. As soon as her hand slipped into his he pulled her gently to him and held her close.

"You bastard," she said even as she wrapped her arms around his shoulders.

"Thank you for always being there for me, Allison. You are smart and lovely and kind—when you aren't furious at me—and I'll miss you."

"I hope you and your new lady and the baby are very happy together," she said.

"I hope so, too."

A knot formed in her throat. A vise clamped down onto her chest. One tear escaped her eye before she could capture it, lock it up and throw away the key.

"You know what the stupid thing is," Allison said, speaking to stave off the building panic. "I don't even like you very much."

McQueen chuckled. She felt his chest rumble against hers. She'd miss that, too.

"I mean it," she said. "You're arrogant and entitled and you do whatever you want, consequences be damned, and you're...you're..."

"Rich," he said. "That's the word you're looking for."

"That's it," she said.

"If you don't like me, why are you so upset?" he said, his tone teasing, and any other day they'd be in bed together already.

"Because I'm going to miss not liking you."

He pulled her a little closer, a little tighter. He kissed her cheek, her forehead and then, at last, let her go. She hated herself for letting him be the one to let go first. Once he was gone, she would be alone, completely alone. No family. No friends. A woman on call day and night for a powerful man didn't get to make friends. She hated him and never wanted to see him again. She loved him and never wanted him to leave her. But she didn't cling to him when he pulled away, and she counted that a victory.

"If it makes you feel any better," McQueen said, his hands still on her face, "this wasn't an easy decision."

"Weird," Allison said. "It doesn't make me feel any better."

McQueen raised his hands in defeat. "I'll go."

She swallowed again. "Bye."

"Don't forget there's some mail for you in the box."

"Anything important?" She never got mail at McQueen's address.

"It's a package from Oregon. No idea why it came to my house."

"Oregon?"

She glanced in the box at the padded envelope. Sure enough, it was postmarked Clark Beach, Oregon. And the name on the return address read *Roland Capello*.

Allison gasped, then clapped a hand over her mouth in shock.

"Allison?" McQueen had been retreating during the conversation but now he rushed to her. "Honey, what's wrong? You look like you're about to faint."

"It's from my brother," she breathed. "This is from my brother."

McQueen stared at her like she'd grown a second head in the past three seconds.

"Your brother?" he repeated. "I've known you seven years. You never told me you had a brother."

Allison looked at him with tears in her eyes.

"That's because…I don't."

CHAPTER 2

McQueen sat her in a chair and poured her a tumbler of bourbon, which Allison nearly dropped. She'd almost fainted. Truly fainted. She wasn't a fainter. She'd never been a fainter. But seeing that name on that envelope had nearly sent her falling to the floor. If McQueen hadn't been there she might have passed out cold.

"Drink," he ordered, and she took a sip. It hit the back of her throat and set fire to her brain.

"Whew. That's strong." Too strong, but it stopped her hands from shaking.

"That's panic-attack bourbon," he said. "Hundred-ten proof. Feel better?"

"I feel like I'm going to faint but now it's for a totally different reason."

"We'll take that as an improvement." Gently he removed the glass tumbler from her hand and set it on the side table. "Now, tell me what's going on?"

"Why?" She met his eyes with confusion.

"Why? Because I say, 'Hey, you have a package from Oregon,' and then you nearly faint on me?"

"I'm not your responsibility anymore, remember? We had that talk."

"Soon as I walk out that door," he said, pointing at the white door with the white knob, "it's over. Not until then."

"It's no big deal. Don't worry about it."

"Who's Roland Capello? Don't say he's your brother. I know he isn't."

Allison didn't want to tell him the whole sordid story, but she didn't want to fight with him about it, either. McQueen had a strong personality and an even stronger will. Better to tell him and get it over with.

"He was my brother," she said. "Once. A long time ago."

"How was someone once your brother? Stepbrother?"

"Adopted," she said. "Me, I mean. Sort of. It's complicated."

"Here. Drink more. You'll feel less complicated in no time."

He pressed the glass into her hand and she took another sip. Rough stuff but the buzzing in her head distracted her from the wild beating of her heart.

"You told me your mom died when you were seven, right?" McQueen said. "Car accident?"

"Drunk driving," Allison said. "She was the driver. I didn't know that until I was a lot older. I guess people didn't want me blaming her for dying. I didn't have any relatives around. Mom had moved us from Indiana to Oregon for a boyfriend but they split up. When she was gone, they stuck me in foster care. I was in one of those group homes with a bunch of girls. They were older and mean, and I was tiny and scared all the time. Then one day this man showed up in a big black car and took me home with him. Dr. Capello. He's a very famous philanthropist and neurosurgeon."

"Never heard of him."

"Well, he's famous in Oregon the way you're famous in Kentucky."

"So, pretty damn famous, then," McQueen said. Allison ignored that.

"Dr. Capello inherited a fortune from his parents and I think he had his own money, too."

"I never met a broke neurosurgeon."

"He was known for helping needy kids. I think in the beginning he did pro bono surgeries and that sort of thing. But at some point he became a foster parent. He took in a bunch of kids."

"An Angelina?"

Allison smiled. "Yeah, an old, male Angelina."

"How old?"

"Very old. Fifty, I think."

McQueen, age forty-five, gave her a dirty look.

"I was one of the kids he took in," she said. "Lucky me."

"And Roland?"

"Him, too. Except Dr. Capello adopted him," Allison said. "I haven't heard from him since I left The Dragon. That's why I was so surprised."

"The what?"

Allison smiled behind her glass of bourbon. "The Dragon— that's what the house was called. You know how beach houses have funny names? Sandy Soles and Blue Heaven or whatever? Dr. Capello said we lived at the edge of the world and on old maps that's where 'there be dragons.' And the house was big and green with shingles like scales. It kind of looked like a dragon when you saw it from a certain angle."

McQueen nodded his understanding. "So you lived there with a bunch of other foster kids. Was it as bad as I'm imagining?"

"It was paradise," she said. "Xanadu."

"Xanadu?" McQueen repeated. "Like the movie?"

"Like the poem," she said. "'In Xanadu did Kubla Khan /

A stately pleasure-dome decree...' I used to have it all memorized. Anyway, it was lovely there."

She couldn't sit still anymore so she put her glass on the table and stood up. She went to the bookshelves that lined the walls and started searching for a book, not because she wanted to read it, but to find something she'd slipped inside it long ago.

"You know that's crazy, right?" he said.

"What? Didn't everyone live in a magical beach house with a famous doctor as a kid?"

"Cricket." McQueen hated sarcasm as much as he hated when she wore jeans.

"I know it sounds nuts," she said. "I do, but it seemed normal at the time. I was seven, though. I still thought Santa Claus was real. Of all the kids, Roland was the one I was closest to. He was older. He was nice. I just... I never thought I'd hear from him again. That's all."

McQueen leaned back in his armchair and steepled his fingers. He did this when he was thinking. She had a feeling he was thinking, *That's not all.*

"What aren't you telling me?" he asked.

"That I want you out of my apartment right now," she said casually, without malice and without much truth, either. She ignored him as best as she could as she studied her shelves.

"About your brother. Usually when nice people send me mail, I don't almost lose my lunch."

"I'm done talking about this with you."

"I'm not done listening."

"Well, there's nothing more to tell."

"We've been sleeping together for six years, Allison. I know when you're faking it with me. You're faking right now. You went white as a sheet when you saw his name on that envelope. That's not like you. You are not a drama queen. You don't overreact. When we were mugged in Milan, I was the one who puked afterward, not you. There is something you're not telling me, and I'm not leaving until I know what it is."

"You're being nosy."

"I care," he said.

"You have an interesting way of showing it," she said. She'd found her book at last, but didn't open it.

McQueen sighed. He beckoned to her and she walked to him, sitting in front of him on top of the coffee table between his knees. He leaned forward and took the book from her hand and put it aside. He raised her hand to his lips, kissed her knuckles, before turning her hand over. He caressed her palm with his fingertips, a sensual touch but also comforting.

"Did something bad happen to you in that house?" he asked, meeting her eyes. If she'd thought for one single second that McQueen was prying out of curiosity or nosiness or because he felt entitled to her secrets, she would never have answered. But the man who'd asked that question wasn't McQueen the rich jerk who was dumping her, but McQueen the scared father who'd burn the world down if anyone hurt his children.

"Dr. Capello didn't molest me if that's what you're asking."

McQueen took a heavy breath, relieved on her behalf.

"That's what I'm asking," he said. "So nobody hurt you, then?"

"I didn't say that."

"Tell me what happened."

"It's not—"

"Tell me what happened and I'll leave."

"You promise?"

He carved an invisible *X* on his heart with his finger. "Once I know you're okay, I'll go."

Allison hadn't thought about her old life with Dr. Capello and his kids in a long time. She tried not to think about them, she certainly never talked about them and she never ever in-

vited memories into her mind. They came sometimes, however, uninvited, creeping like ants through a crack in the wall.

"You wouldn't be this freaked out if it was really that good
there," McQueen said.

"I'm not freaked out," she said, maybe a lie, maybe not. She
was just…surprised, that's all. "You'd be shaky, too, if your
brother contacted you out of the blue after thirteen years."

"True. Because I don't have a brother, even an almost-
brother. You do."

Allison released his hand and picked up the book she'd
found, an old copy of Shaw's *Pygmalion*, the pages highlighter-
yellow from her days as an English major in college.

"Allison?"

She gave in.

"The last summer I was there, someone in the house maybe
possibly pushed me down the stairs."

"What?" McQueen said, eyes wide with fury.

Allison shrugged, said nothing.

"An accident?" McQueen asked.

"So I was told."

"But you don't think it was an accident?"

Allison held the book to her chest.

"My great-aunt was seventy when my mom died. She was
living in southern Indiana. That's why I went to live with Dr.
Capello instead of her. But I still called her once a week to
check in. The day of my fall—or whatever it was—someone
apparently called her, pretended to be me and told her that there
was a killer in the house and I needed her to come get me."

McQueen started to speak.

"Before you ask," Allison said, "I don't know who it was
who called or who pushed me—*if* someone did push me.
When I fell, I hit my head so hard I don't even remember
falling. I don't remember waking up in the hospital. I don't

remember much of anything from around that time. What I do remember is that I was living at The Dragon, happiest kid on earth, and then I was in Indiana later that summer, living with my aunt in her tiny apartment."

"That must have been a hard hit," McQueen said. "What did the police say?"

"There wasn't even an investigation," she said. "There was no evidence other than the phone call, and everyone chalked that up to my aunt being old and hard of hearing, maybe even confused. Everyone but me. That woman could hear a pin drop and she had all her faculties intact to the day she died."

"No witnesses?" McQueen asked. Allison ignored the urge to roll her eyes. He was talking like a cop.

"Nobody came forward that I know of."

"Kids can be really violent," McQueen said.

"Not these kids," Allison said.

"Then who did it? Someone did something or you never would have had to leave."

"I'm telling you what my aunt told me when I started asking her why I was with her and not with the Capellos anymore. Apparently Dr. Capello was the one who found me at the foot of the steps bleeding from the ear. He said he was too panicked to do anything but scream for someone to call 911. If it had been an accident I'd like to think whoever it was would have admitted to it. But nobody 'fessed up. Not even when my aunt flew out to pick me up and take me home with her. When I went to live with her, she wouldn't let me contact the Capellos. She thought… She didn't know what to think. And the Capellos never contacted me, either, after that. Probably because my aunt told them not to. Thirteen years of radio silence. Until today." She glanced over at the table where the package from Roland still sat, unopened.

"So you never called? Never visited?" McQueen asked.

"I wanted to when I was a kid and then a few years passed and the whole thing kind of felt like a good dream with a nightmare ending. When I was old enough to go back on my own, I just…didn't. If they'd sent me even one birthday card, I might have. But they didn't."

"I can't believe you never told me any of this," he said, shaking his head.

"You never asked. You never wanted to know, did you? Then you'd have to think of me as a real person," she said. McQueen had the decency to look ashamed of himself.

"You still could have told me."

"You still could have asked," she said. "Anyway, doesn't matter. Ancient history. I'm over it all."

"Except you aren't," he said. "Except you see the name Roland Capello on that envelope and you turn white as a ghost. You take a book off the shelf and hold it so tight for some reason your hands shake." He took the book from her hands. "Except you…" He flipped through the book and found a page marked by a photograph, which he pulled out. "Except you keep a picture of your old family pressed in the pages of that book."

Allison swallowed. "Except all that," she said.

McQueen was staring at the photograph he'd taken out of her book. Allison didn't look at it. She didn't have to. She saw it in her mind's eye. There were three kids in the picture— all three in red hoodies. One boy with dark blond hair that fell past his ears, one girl with hair so red it was almost orange and one boy with black hair straight as an arrow. They all held sparklers in their hands and in the background of the photo was the ocean, vast and gray.

"Roland?" McQueen asked, pointing to the one with black hair.

"That's Deacon. Roland's the dirty blond," Allison said. "The girl's Thora. Dr. Capello gave us those red sweatshirts.

He said it made it easier for him to find us on the beach when there were big crowds."

"Sweatshirts on the beach?"

"It was Oregon," she said.

"And where are you in this picture?" McQueen asked.

Allison pointed to the left side of the photograph that had been torn away.

"There," she said. "I don't know who has the other section. I found this in my suitcase when I unpacked at my aunt's."

"So there were four of you?"

"No, there were others," she said. "But they were fosters, like me. There was an older girl named Kendra. And a boy about my age or a little older named Oliver. A few others but they didn't stay long. Roland, Thora and Deacon were the three kids Dr. Capello adopted."

"Did he want to adopt you?"

"I think so," Allison said. "But he didn't."

Allison took the photograph out of McQueen's hand, slipped it back in the pages of the book, walked over and put the book back on the shelf.

"There, I told you everything. Now you can go."

"Not until you open the package."

"Why do you care?"

"What if this Roland guy is writing to confess to the crime?"

"Roland was sixteen by then, almost seventeen. He had a summer job in another town. He wouldn't have been home at the time. Trust me, I thought about this a lot after I left them."

"So you aren't over it."

"I was twelve living with an elderly woman in a retirement community. Not like I had much else to do."

"Then maybe Roland knows something and is finally coming clean." McQueen stood up and followed her to the kitchen.

"Maybe he is," Allison said.

"Open it."

"I will." Allison turned to face him. "Soon as you're gone."

"Cricket..." He put his hands on her hips.

Allison touched his face, his five-o'clock shadow that always came in about an hour early every day.

"Goodbye, McQueen," she said, taking his hands by the wrists and removing them from her body.

His shoulders slumped in defeat before he straightened up again and picked up his keys off the table and shoved them in his pocket.

"All right," he said. "You win. But do me a favor, okay?" He went to the door. "Keep in touch."

Allison opened the door for him and he started to walk out. Then stopped. Then turned back. She knew it was coming and she knew she could stop it. She didn't.

He took her face in his hands and kissed her lips, a long lingering kiss, a kiss she returned. The kiss was a bad idea, a terrible idea, but at least it gave her the chance to pull away first.

"I always knew I'd regret getting involved with you," Allison said.

"Then why did you do it?" he asked.

"Because I knew I'd regret not getting involved with you even more."

He laughed and that was a shame because McQueen had a good laugh. Too good. He kissed her again.

"One more time," he said against her lips. "Maybe that'll make you feel better."

Allison let him take her into the bedroom.

She didn't want it, but she needed it.

Anything was better than being alone.

CHAPTER 3

Last times were no time for anything fancy. McQueen stripped her naked, put her on her back in the bed and kissed every inch of her like he was kissing every inch goodbye. Allison sighed with pleasure when he entered her. It was either sigh or cry and she refused to give in to her tears again. McQueen kissed her neck and said into her ear, "And to think I always thought I was the first rich son of a bitch to take you in from the cold."

"Oh, you were," she said, almost smiling. "Dr. Capello wasn't a son of a bitch."

Dr. Capello was, in fact, an angel. At least, that's how she'd once thought of him. Until age seven, Allison had lived in a little town called Red, where even the trees in spring were a dull shade of brown. High desert, they called it, past the Cascades, which might as well have been a sky-high wall for how well they trapped the rain on the other side of the mountains. Although Allison's teachers had said they lived an hour's drive away from mossy green forests and three hours from the ocean, she had never believed them. The whole world was high desert to her until that day the man with the brown beard came to the house where they'd taken her because she had nowhere else to go.

Allison lived in the single-story house with siding the color of desert sand, and shared a room with three other girls, all of them older. Older and terrifying. All three of them resented the intrusion of a "little girl" into their tween kingdom. It was 1997 and she had no idea who those boys were in the posters on the wall and not knowing who the Backstreet Boys were was apparently enough of a crime to render Allison unworthy of friendship or even basic kindnesses from anyone but Miss Whitney.

She'd gone to find Miss Whitney that day, because one of the girls—Melissa, the biggest one who called all the shots—had slapped Allison for daring to sit in the wrong chair. Allison had taken her tearstained red face to Miss Whitney's tiny office in the hopes of being allowed to hide there and read all day. Miss Whitney had let her do that a time or two. Apparently Allison was "adjusting poorly" and suffering from "profound stress," and she needed a "more nurturing environment." Allison wasn't sure what all that meant, but she'd heard Miss Whitney saying that on the phone to someone the day before. What Allison really wanted was her mother back, but Miss Whitney had reminded her—kindly and more than once—that her mother was never coming back. They'd been trying to find her long-gone father instead, or another relative for her to live with. No luck yet, except an aunt deemed too old to handle a seven-year-old girl.

The first time she'd seen the man with the beard he'd been hugging Miss Whitney in her office. Allison stood in the doorway and stared at the man who was tall and dressed in what looked to her like blue pajamas. He patted Miss Whitney's back very hard as he hugged her, which made Miss Whitney laugh and wince, wince and laugh.

"My God," the bearded man said as he pulled back from the hug. He'd seen her lurking in the doorway. "Is this her?" He turned to Miss Whitney, his brown eyes wide.

"That's her. That's our Allison."

Immediately, he squatted on the floor to meet Allison eye to eye.

Allison took a step back, afraid she'd broken a rule.

"It's all right," the man said, and his beard split apart in a big smile that showed a row of bright white teeth. "Don't be scared."

"I'm not scared," Allison said. "Are you?"

He grinned at that. "Surprised. You look a little like another girl I used to know."

"I thought the same thing when I saw her," Miss Whitney said. "Cousins at least. Should I not have called?"

"No, no…" the bearded man said. "It's fine."

"Why are you wearing pajamas?" Allison asked the bearded man. She knew they were pajamas because the pants had a drawstring on them like her pajamas. Zipper meant outdoor pants. No zipper meant indoor pants. That's how her mother had explained it.

The bearded man laughed and it was a nice laugh and he had nice eyes. Nice, not like pretty, but nice like kind.

"These are called scrubs," he said. "They're not pajamas. Doctors wear them."

"Are you a doctor?" Allison asked.

"I am."

"Is somebody sick?"

"You tell me," the bearded man said. "You don't look too good."

"I got hit."

"Hit?" the bearded man said, and looked up at Miss Whitney.

"Melissa?" Miss Whitney asked.

Tears welled up in Allison's eyes again and she nodded.

"I'll be back," Miss Whitney said with a put-upon groan.

"You go jerk a knot in Melissa's tail," the bearded man said. "I'll get Allison here back in working order."

He stood up straight and Miss Whitney patted him on the arm as she left the office. They were alone together now, Allison and the bearded man.

"Does it hurt?" he asked, his hand on his chin.

"A little."

"It's okay if you cry," he said. "I can tell you want to."

"Katie said I shouldn't cry."

"Why not?"

"They don't want you if you cry too much."

"They?"

"People who take kids home with them," she said.

The bearded man cupped his hand by his mouth and whispered, "I don't mind if you cry. No skin off my rosy nose."

That made her feel better, so much better she didn't want to cry anymore.

"Let's go find a bathroom," he said.

Allison showed him where it was. He put her on the counter, wetted a washcloth and pressed it to her cheek.

"How's that now?" he asked. "Better?"

"Lots."

"Fantastic," he said. "Another patient cured. That'll cost you two bits."

"What's a bit?"

"I have no idea," the bearded man said. "Used to hear it on TV all the time—shave and a haircut, two bits. Never did figure out how much two bits was."

Allison looked around, saw a tissue box and ripped two pieces off one tissue.

"Here," she said, holding them up in front of his face. "Two bits."

"Are you sure?"

"You said you didn't know what they are," Allison said. "So how do you know those aren't bits?"

The bearded man looked at the two tissues in his hand, stuck his lips out and nodded.

"You're a very smart little girl," he said. "I accept your payment. And I give you a clean bill of health. Now tell me, what's going on with you and this Melissa?"

"I sat in her chair. She didn't like that."

"And she hit you?"

Allison said nothing.

"You know," the man said, "sometimes kids learn to hit from their parents. Their parents hit them and then they don't know any better."

"I know not to hit," Allison said.

"That's because you're so smart," he whispered again. A whisper, then a wink. She didn't know why he was whispering. Everyone in the house was a shouter. Melissa shouted and the other two girls shouted and Miss Whitney shouted at them all to stop shouting. Allison didn't shout. She cried. She hid. She slept. But she never shouted.

"How's the patient?"

Allison turned to see Miss Whitney coming into the bathroom.

"She's on track to make a full recovery," the bearded man said. "If we can keep her out of the path of slappers."

"That's not going to happen in this house," Miss Whitney said with a sigh.

"No word on the father?" he asked.

"No father on the birth certificate. Sole living relative is a great-aunt who would take her if nobody else turns up. But she's seventy, lives in Indiana, and she's been sick."

The bearded man harrumphed. Allison hadn't ever met her great-aunt, a lady named Frankie who lived really far away, though she'd seen Christmas cards from her.

"I gotta figure something out here," Miss Whitney said. "Allison weighed forty-seven pounds when she got here. Yesterday she weighed forty-two. One month."

The bearded man harrumphed *and* whistled this time.

"Let me talk to her," he said.

"You are talking to me," Allison said.

"She's very bright," the bearded man said to Miss Whitney.

"Told you so. Reads on a fifth-grade level. Eats like a toddler." Miss Whitney patted Allison on her knee. "Sweetheart, this is a good friend of mine. Vincent Capello. He's a brain surgeon. We used to work together at a hospital in Portland. He was nice enough to come all the way out here to check on you. Brain surgeons usually don't make house calls, so you should feel very special."

"She is very special," the man said. Allison grinned, happy to have someone being nice to her for the first time that day. She was still sitting on the bathroom counter. She wasn't tall enough to be able to jump down without help yet and the bearded man, the doctor, had left her up there.

Miss Whitney left her alone again with the man who didn't do anything at first but tug his beard hairs.

"Do you like it here, Allison?" he asked.

Allison's mother had taught her not to complain, ever. Not so much out of politeness but because it never helped anything.

"I like Miss Whitney," Allison said.

"She is a very nice lady." The man nodded in agreement. "Do you like the girls here?"

Allison didn't answer.

"Allison? Do you like the other girls here?"

"I'm not supposed to say."

"Why not?" The bearded man furrowed his brow.

"If you can't say something nice, you shouldn't say anything at all."

He laughed.

"I guess I have my answer. You have quite the moral compass, young lady," he said. "Adults could learn from you."

She smiled broadly. She didn't know what a moral compass was, but she knew a compliment when she heard it.

"Miss Whitney says you aren't eating. Want to tell me why?" he asked.

Allison had dropped her chin to her chest. "Not hungry."

"Does your stomach hurt?" he asked.

She shook her head.

"No?" he said. Allison stopped talking and hoped he would, too.

"Have you ever seen the ocean?" he asked her. That was not the question she'd been expecting.

"No."

"You know what it looks like?"

"I saw pictures," she said.

"We can do better than that." That's when he plucked her off the counter and set her on her feet. He took her by the hand and led her out to the back porch. There was nothing back there but a slab of concrete where a few old chairs sat looking at a yard of scrubby dirt backed by a hill of scrubby dirt. Everywhere she looked out there she saw nothing but scrubby dirt.

"See all that?" the doctor said, pointing from one end of the hill to the other.

"I see dirt," she said.

"Okay. Now imagine everything you see is water," he said.

Allison's eyes went wide. She stared at the dirt and in her mind's eye it started to change color from brown to gray to blue. The hills turned to waves, the raw wind became an ocean breeze and the concrete slab they stood on became a raft, bobbing and floating on an endless sea.

"I see it," she said, grinning up at him.

"That's the ocean," he said.

"It's lovely," she said.

"Lovely? Yes, it is lovely, isn't it?" he said, laughing. "That's where I live, you know. On the ocean."

"In a boat?"

He laughed again. "No, in a house. But the house is right on the beach and you can see the ocean from almost all the rooms."

Allison couldn't imagine that. She never even looked out the windows in this house. Nothing to see but dirt out the back windows and other sand-colored houses out the front.

"Can you swim in it?"

He stroked his beard. "You *can* swim in it. Might not want to. It's kind of cold, but my son swims in it a lot."

"You have a son?"

"I have two sons," he said, smiling with pride. "And a daughter. They're all kids like you. Some bad things happened in their lives so now they live with me in my house by the ocean."

"Is it pretty?"

"The ocean?"

"The house."

"If I told you it looked like a dragon, would you believe me?"

"No," she said, laughing. That was the silliest thing she ever heard. "Dragons have wings. They have fire in their noses."

"I promise it looks like a dragon."

"You're lying."

"I'm not," he said, and looked hurt. Then he grinned. She liked him so much when he smiled like that. "It's a sea monster, I swear."

"I know a water poem," she said. "Do you want to hear it?"

"I want to hear your poem. Go for it."

Allison recited for him.

"The sun was shining on the sea,
Shining with all his might:
He did his very best to make
The billows smooth and bright—
And that was odd because it was
The middle of the night."

The man laughed heartily, a Santa Claus laugh, though he didn't have a Santa Claus belly.

"That's wonderful, Allison. Did you learn that in school?"

"I taught it to myself," she said. That was true but she didn't tell him why she'd taught it to herself. He'd probably laugh at her. "Can I come to your house and see the ocean for real?"

He squatted down low again so they were the same height, and while he wasn't smiling with his mouth, he was smiling with his eyes.

"I *would* take you to see it," he said, "but we have a rule at my house—everybody has to eat every single day."

She gave that a good long think and then made up her mind.

"If I could see the ocean, I would eat," she said.

"You promise?"

"I promise."

"Every single day?"

"Every single day."

"Good," he said. He stood up again. "It's a deal. Let's go get you packed."

"You mean it?" She couldn't believe it, but she couldn't believe this smiling man who wore pajamas to work would lie to her, either.

"I mean it."

She raced to her room and found her suitcase. She didn't have much to pack but one suitcase of her clothes and one bag of her books. Miss Whitney hugged her for a long time and kissed her cheek and told her she was a lucky little girl, because she was going to a wonderful home. Over Allison's shoulder, Miss Whitney winked at Dr. Capello. When Allison started out the door, her small hand in Dr. Capello's big strong hand, the other girls did nothing but wave half-heartedly from the couch where they sat playing a dumb video game on a too-small television.

The next thing Allison knew, she was sitting in the shiny smooth back seat of a big black car. A fancy car, fancier than any one she'd ever seen, and they were driving through the desert.

The big black car started up a hill, except it wasn't a hill because hills weren't nearly this tall. The man with the beard—he told her to call him Dr. Capello for now—told her it was actually a volcano named Mount Hood, but she didn't believe him. She'd seen volcanoes in her science book. They had fire coming out of the top and they didn't have trees everywhere. Then they were going down the other side of the big mountain and it was green, green, green everywhere she looked. The desert had turned into a forest so green and big she expected to see the Jolly Green Giant from the TV commercials wander onto the road and wave as they passed by. She was looking for him when something hit the car window hard enough to make her jump.

Water, a big fat drop of it.

"Just rain," Dr. Capello said. "It'll be raining at home, too." That morning she'd woken up in a desert and now she was being taken to a place where it rained so hard it rained on the ocean.

"What's your son's name?" Allison asked.

"Which one?" Dr. Capello asked from the front seat.

"The one you said swims a lot."

"That's Roland. He's twelve."

"Is he nice?"

Dr. Capello kept his face forward but even looking at his profile she could see him smile.

"Let me tell you a little something about my son," he said. "Roland Capello is the nicest boy in the world."

"You're smiling again," McQueen said as he quickly dressed. Allison was still in bed, still naked. Let him leave her this way. Let this be the last image of her in his memory. "Told you that would help."

She rolled onto her side and watched him put on his shoes.

"It helped, all right," she said, and kept it to herself she'd been lost in the past the entire time he'd been inside her. He stood up.

"You'll be okay?" he asked.

"I'll be fine," she said, already feeling the first stirrings of panic again. "I am fine."

He bent over the bed to kiss her lips, and she gave him her cheek instead. He didn't argue.

On his way out of her bedroom, he paused and looked back.

"Will you let me give you one piece of advice?" he asked.

"Do I have to?" she asked.

"I have been on this earth twenty years longer than you."

"All right, tell me," she said.

"When distant relatives contact you out of nowhere, it's never good. Never. *Never*," he said.

"Never?"

"Never. They either want money or they want something from you more valuable than money. The more I think about it, the more I think you should let me take that package down to the Dumpster."

"This was my family, McQueen."

"Was," McQueen said. "Thirteen years ago and they haven't contacted you in all that time? What's the lady's name who opened her box and screwed us all over?"

"Pandora?"

"Right." He pointed at her and nodded. "Don't be like her."

"You're telling me that's Pandora's padded envelope?" Allison asked.

"Pandora's box sounds a lot better," he said. "I have to go. Meeting in half an hour. You'll at least think about it?"

"I'll think about it," she said. "Have a good life."

"Yeah," he said. "You, too, darlin'."

She waited for him to leave. He didn't.

"I never thought it would end like this," he said, still looking at her. "I've been waiting six years for you to get shed of me. I thought any day now you'd tell me it was over, that you'd met someone, that you'd fallen in love."

There was nothing safe Allison could say to that so she said nothing at all. McQueen waited. She kept her silence. He turned and then, at last, he was gone.

The door shut behind him and Allison sat on the bed, her chin to her chest. She didn't cry. She wanted to but she couldn't find her tears. What she wanted was a shoulder to cry on but she had none. The last shoulders in her life that weren't her own had just walked out of the door.

She was twenty-five and college-educated. She had a roof

over her head and she had money. She had food and she had
clothes. She had a car and she had a letter of recommendation
from the wealthiest man in the state she could use to get a job
pretty much anywhere. She was fine. She was fine. She was
fine. She told herself a thousand times she was fine.

She wasn't fine.

She was alone.

Alone on her bed, she was a seven-year-old girl again, staring at the front door waiting for someone to come through it
and knowing, deep down, that no one ever would.

Her worst nightmare. She was all alone.

Or was she?

Allison grabbed her robe, pulled it on and went into the
kitchen again. She stood by the table, looking at the envelope.
Allison told herself she was doing it to spite McQueen, but
even she knew she wasn't telling herself the truth.

She picked up the envelope and ripped it open.

CHAPTER 4

Inside the envelope she found a letter. Before she lost her courage, she unfolded it and read.

Dear Allison,

What to say? I'll be quick. It's been thirteen years and I know I should leave you alone but you've been on my mind a lot lately so I'll get to the point fast. Dad is dying. Stage five renal failure. He doesn't know I'm writing you. I didn't want to get his hopes up. Fact is, he's always missed you. Any time your name comes up, you can tell he's full of regret. So am I. If you have it in your heart to come see him one last time, I'd be forever grateful. If you don't, I don't blame you. But if you do come, we're still at the old house, and you're sure to find one of us here day or night. Dad's determined to die at home in his own bed, and we're going to do the best we can to honor his wishes. If you want to come, all I ask is please come soon. He doesn't have long.

There's so much more I want to say to you, but I'll end here. I've taken up enough of your time.

Roland

P.S. Found this while digging through the attic. If you read
as much now as you used to, you probably want it back.
P.S. #2. I think about you every time it rains.

A humble letter, humble and polite. Humble and polite
and adult. It wasn't until Allison read that letter that it hit her:
Roland Capello wasn't sixteen anymore. What sixteen-year-
old boy says things like "I've taken up enough of your time"?
What sixteen-year-old boy talks about stage five renal failure? What sixteen-year-old boy knows anything about regret?

In her mind Roland had been forever sixteen. Tall and thin
with long coltish legs covered in light blond hair. Board shorts,
ripped and faded T-shirts, hair long enough he could tuck it
behind his ears. Wraparound sunglasses like Bono's, worn up
on his head more often than over his eyes to hold his hair back.

Allison had to walk away from the letter for a few minutes
simply to recover from the simple realization that as much
time had passed for Roland as it had for her. She was thirteen
years older and so was he. Roland's birthday was in July. Roland, eternally lanky and lean and sixteen, was now thirty.
A grown man. And here she was, twenty-five and freshly
dumped. Adults now, both of them.

She stood in the middle of her living room and breathed
through her hands. When she looked up, she was jarred by
her surroundings—the gray walls and the mullioned window
and the red sofa with its intricately carved oak arms. For a split
second she'd been back in the past where the walls were floor-
to-ceiling windows instead of floor-to-ceiling bookcases and
outside the door there was ocean, not asphalt.

Still shaking, Allison walked back to the table and the package and the letter. Dr. Capello was dying. She wasn't ready to
deal with that yet so she turned her attention instead to whatever it was Roland had sent her. She pulled it from the pad-

ded envelope and removed the newspaper wrapped around it. And as soon as she saw it, tears scalded her eyes.

It was a book, of course, a battered old yellow paperback with a winged centaur on the cover and three children riding on its back. *A Wrinkle in Time* by Madeleine L'Engle.

"Oh, Roland…" she breathed. "You remembered."

She sat down because she couldn't stand anymore. Allison slowly flipped through the book. The pages had grown so soft and supple with age it felt like she was holding not a book but another hand in her hand. She opened it to the middle and pressed her face into the pages. She inhaled the scent of paper, ink and glue, and if they could make a perfume that smelled like old books, Allison would wear it every day of her life.

Roland had read this book to her. He'd read it to her the first night she'd spent at The Dragon. Not the whole thing, of course, but the first few chapters while she sat on his lap in the big blue reading chair with the other kids in the house gathered around on the rug, and she was in charge of turning the pages.

She'd loved him for letting her turn the pages.

And when Allison flipped to the final page of the book she wept openly. Written on the inside back cover in cornflower blue crayon were two words—*Allison Capello*.

"All right, this is how we do it," Roland had said, taking her onto his lap and wrapping his big hand around her tiny hand. "*C* is an *O* and it's trying to touch its toes but it can't quite reach. And *a* is a little *o* with a line on the right side to keep it from rolling away. Make another little *o* for the *p* and put a long line on the other side. That's its tail. *P*'s have straight tails. *E*'s have eyes. See? It's looking at us and smiling. And *l* is a straight line. Do it again. Two *l*'s. And then one more *o* and there you go."

Roland had taught her how to write her name. Not Allison

Lamarque, the name she had been given, but Allison Capello, the name she'd coveted.

Allison put the book back onto the table next to Roland's letter. She'd faced the existence of the letter and survived.

Now she had to deal with the content.

Dr. Capello was dying.

How was that possible? She'd joked that Dr. Capello was old but only to insult McQueen. He was never old to her. When they played frisbee on the beach, he played the hardest. When they cooked hot dogs on the campfire, he ate the most. He was always good for a piggyback ride up and down the halls. He didn't read bedtime stories to them. They read bedtime stories to him. "One more page," he would say, pretending to pout, and they'd roll their eyes and tell him it was time for him to go to sleep.

He worked, yes, but still made as much time for them as he could. He chose his cases carefully, picking the poorest and the sickest kids to bless with his talent. He didn't have to work at all, as Dr. Capello had inherited a fortune from his parents, a fortune he spent helping kids, especially his own. Being taken away from that family had hurt worse than losing her mother because at seven, Allison hadn't understood quite how long a time "never again" really was. By twelve, she was starting to have an idea. By twenty-five, she knew. And what she knew was "never again" was too damn long.

And now Roland wanted her to come back.

Allison knew she shouldn't go. There were great reasons not to go back. Someone had tried to get rid of her and they'd succeeded. Maybe it was a prank, maybe it was something more sinister, but she couldn't deny someone wanted her gone.

Then again…

She had fifty thousand dollars in cash on her kitchen table.

She had nothing to do and nowhere else to go.

She had freedom to go anywhere she wanted, which she hadn't had since the first night she'd spent with McQueen.

McQueen would tell her not to go. He'd tell her it wasn't safe, and he'd tell her she owed them nothing. He'd tell her not to open up an old wound. He'd tell her to take the money and run. And all that was good advice.

But.

McQueen had dumped her an hour ago, so why the hell should she give his opinion any weight? She shouldn't. She wouldn't. She'd do what she wanted to do and no one could stop her. There. Finally, Allison found one good reason to be happy that she was a free woman now.

After all...it would only take a few minutes, right? A few minutes, an hour tops. She could fly out to Portland, rent a car and make a vacation of it. She could drive the 101 all the way down the California coast if she wanted. She'd pop in to see Dr. Capello. It wouldn't be fun, but it wouldn't be awful, either. A one-hour visit to her childhood home followed by a nice long overdue vacation to celebrate her newfound freedom... Why not?

She knew seeing Dr. Capello again, and seeing him dying, would break her heart.

But as her heart was already broken, Allison had no excuse not to go.

So she went.

CHAPTER 5

It wasn't until the wheels touched down at Portland International Airport that Allison realized she had never really believed she would go back. For two days, she'd been running on adrenaline, powered by the need to keep thoughts of the breakup at bay. Yet once she was in Oregon, the frenzy of energy disappeared and it took everything she had to disembark and collect her luggage. When the lady at the rental car counter asked her what brought her to Portland, Allison had been too dazed to think of a decent answer.

"I have no idea," she said, and the lady looked at her with a mix of confusion and sympathy. She didn't ask Allison any more friendly, prying questions after that.

The city was as green as she remembered and the rivers that bisected Portland still as blue. She took the highway to an exit that read Ocean Beaches and wondered how anyone managed to drive past that sign without immediately turning onto it and heading straight for the ocean. Very quickly the shining city faded behind her and lonely farms and hilly pastures popped up along the road. But soon enough those were gone, too, replaced first by patches of trees and then by full forests with branches so verdant and thick they formed an archway over the road, like soldiers forming an honor guard.

As she neared the coast, the clouds grew heavier, denser, stranger. The forests turned dark and eerie. In sunlight, the low-hanging mossy branches would look innocuous. At dusk, they looked like skeletal fingers pointing at her, the moss like skin falling off the bone.

Allison nearly jumped out of her seat when she banked around a curve and saw a fiendish grinning red-eyed face glowering at her from the side of the road. Once her heart slowed, Allison laughed at herself. During her flight to Portland, she'd reread *A Wrinkle in Time*. The villain in that book was a man with glowing red eyes who tried to get the three brave children to submit to him and allow him total control of their minds. She was glad McQueen wasn't there to see her jump at the sight of someone's stupid joke. Someone had nailed red safety reflectors to a tree trunk in the shape of eyes and a monstrous mouth. That was all.

When Highway 26 met the famous coastal 101, Allison turned south toward the cape. She'd spent the evening before online, reading everything she could about the Oregon coast and deciding where she would go and what she would see after she made her obligatory stop at The Dragon to pay her respects to Dr. Capello. It was a vacation, Allison told herself. No pressure. Just fun. If she were going to come all the way to the other side of the country, she might as well make an adventure of it.

Except, as her drive took her closer and closer to her old home, her sense of adventure left her and low-level panic took its place. Her heart beat rapidly and she had to stop at one of the highway's scenic viewpoints simply to catch her breath. She leaned against the long stone wall and gazed down at the ocean. It had been a long time since she'd seen the Pacific Ocean. Panama City Beach it was not. The waves were white-capped and hitting the beach hard, and she knew those blue-silver waters were like the siren's song—lovely, yes, but ice cold and deadly. The scenic marker warned that what she was looking at wasn't simply a nice ocean landscape, but the notorious Graveyard of the Pacific. Ship after ship after ship had gone down in those waters. No wonder Dr. Capello had called his house The Dragon. Allison imagined all it would take was two steps forward, and she'd fall off the edge of the world into oblivion. To think she used to swim here. Well, if she'd been brave enough and stupid enough to swim in a graveyard, surely she could be brave enough and stupid enough to go home for an hour.

Calmer now, Allison got back into her car and headed south toward Cape Arrow. The whole place wasn't much more than a collection of pretty beach houses on a hillside overlooking the ocean. It was an isolated, lonely sort of place, and Dr. Capello's house was the most isolated of them all, a mile farther down from the cape and situated on a solitary spit of land amid deep tree cover. She didn't know the street names and the GPS wasn't helping. She turned it off and let memory alone guide her to the correct turn.

Then, at last, after thirteen years, there it was.

Allison pulled in, stopped and got out of her car at the end of the long winding drive that led from the highway down to the beach. The eight-foot-high wrought-iron gates that stretched across the entrance of the driveway were open, but then again, they always had been. Iron and seawater were a bad combination and the gates were so rusted she doubted they could ever be closed again. She stepped through the gates to where the trees parted. Long ago she'd stood right here with Dr. Capello as he showed her the house, her new home, for the very first time.

"See it?" he'd asked her. "You see the dragon?"

She'd rolled her eyes, too smart for her own good at that age.

"It's a house," she'd said. A big house, yes. A tall odd house with blue-green shingle siding and a sort of square turret on top, but still...a house.

"Don't look at the house," Dr. Capello had said as he knelt down next to her. He pointed to the ocean. "Look there. Look at the water. You'll see the house out of the corner of your eye. And then tell me that doesn't look like a dragon."

She'd taken a heavy breath, the breath children took when adults insulted their intelligence. But she'd done it, anyway. She'd gazed far past the house onto the ocean. She saw the whitecaps of the waves, the water running up the beach and running away again. And there in the corner of her eye, she saw a dragon.

He was sitting up, this dragon, prim as a cat with four paws daintily placed together, a straight back and his head—the square sort of turret room on top—held high. The green rain-drenched shingles were his scales and the shimmering windows his wings and the gray deck his tail wrapped around his feet. Looking at the square turret, she could make out the back of its head, which meant the dragon, too, gazed out at the ocean, just like she did.

"I see it..." she had breathed. "I see the dragon."

Dr. Capello had laughed softly. "In the winter, when we use the fireplace, smoke comes out of his nose."

"Is it dangerous?"

"Oh, very. It wouldn't be a dragon if it wasn't dangerous."

"He's lovely." So lovely the dragon was, she couldn't help but try to get a closer look. She turned her gaze from the water to the house and in the blink of an eye...

"He's gone," she had said.

"Well, that's what happens when you look too close at magical creatures. You can only see them when you aren't looking at them."

"That's silly."

"That's magic for you." Dr. Capello lifted his hands as if to say he didn't make the rules. "It's wonderful but fragile. You have to be very gentle with it."

Although she was twenty-five and knew better, Allison couldn't help but look for the dragon where the house stood. As she'd done eighteen years earlier, she gazed out at the water, letting the house hover in her peripheral vision. At first nothing happened. She saw a house and nothing but a house. All the magic long gone. As she was about to give up, get into her car and finish her drive, she saw it. For a split second, she saw the shingles transform into shiny scales and the wrap-around porch turn into a tail and the windows on the third floor shimmer like silvery wings.

Maybe there was a little bit of magic in the old house yet.

Allison's heart ached looking at the house that had once been her home. She wanted to drive away right then and never look back. She'd told no one she was coming for that very reason. And yet she got back behind the steering wheel and drove down, down, down the winding road to the house. She parked the car where Dr. Capello had always parked his. No cars were there today. She got out and walked the flag-stone path to the side door, which was the family's entrance. She took a breath and rang the doorbell. When there was no answer, she knocked. When there was no answer again, she walked out onto the deck. The house was as close to the beach as it could be without being on the beach itself. The beach that day was deserted. It seemed no one was at home.

Allison didn't know what to do. Roland had said some-one was always at the house, but it seemed she'd come at the

one time no one was there. Maybe she was too late. Maybe
Dr. Capello was already gone. Regret tasted like copper in
her mouth and she almost wept with disappointment. She'd
tried so hard to tell herself she'd made this trip to clear her
conscience, but the tear she shed was proof she'd come here
wanting more than to do her duty to a nice man who'd taken
care of her a long time ago.

She'd really wanted to hug her Dr. Capello one more time.

A sound echoed from the side of the house and Allison spun
around, suddenly alert and afraid. It was a sharp loud sound
followed by a soft sort of grunting noise. Then she heard it
again. Then again.

She walked around the deck to an arched wooden door
that, if she remembered correctly, led to Dr. Capello's wild-
flower garden, something her aunt Frankie had always called
an "oxymoron," like "bad children."

Quietly and carefully Allison unlatched the gate and pushed
through the door. Ten yards away, a man stood with his back
to her, chopping firewood. He wore a yellow-and-black-
checkered shirt and he was tall and broad-shouldered with
blond hair pulled into a short ponytail at the nape of his neck.
He lifted the ax with ease and brought it down with precision.
Another log was sundered and the two pieces fell on each side
of the tree stump.

The man went for another log to split but stopped. He stood
up straight and turned around. He must have seen her out of
the corner of his eye. He let the ax blade fall into the stump
and it stayed there embedded in the wood even as he walked
away from it and toward her.

He took one step forward into a shadow cast by the tree,
and when he stepped out of it again, the man had turned into
a twelve-year-old boy. Gone were the jeans and flannels, the
big shoulders and strong forearms, and in their place stood

a lanky boy of twelve wearing black basketball shorts and a T-shirt with cut-off sleeves.

Allison remembered...

She remembered the first moment she saw him on the deck, Mr. In-Charge-Because-Dad's-Gone. She and Dr. Capello stood under his big black umbrella. The hard rain had turned into a light drizzle. She remembered thinking how funny it was that the boy was on the deck lounging in a chair like he was sunbathing in the rain. Rainbathing?

"Roland?" Dr. Capello had said. "Come meet Allison. Allison, this is my son Roland."

The boy with the stick legs so long she wondered if he could even see his feet slowly rose from his deck chair and walked over to her. Roland wore sunglasses with water droplets on the lenses. He shoved them up on his head to hold his damp hair out of his face. The boy looked at her for a very long time and then at his father.

"It's all right," Dr. Capello had said, and she wasn't sure if he was speaking to his son or to her. "Go on. Say hello to Allison."

"Hey, Al," he said, smiling. Allison stepped back away from him so far she'd bumped into Dr. Capello's legs. She had no idea who these people were, where this house was. She wanted her mother or Miss Whitney. She wanted to be anywhere but here.

"Hey, hey," the boy had said. He had his elbows on his knees as he squatted, and even in her panic she admired his balance. "Don't be scared."

"She's tired," Dr. Capello had said. "And probably hungry."

"Are you hungry?" Roland had asked. "I make a good grilled cheese."

She shook her head no.

Roland had glanced up at his father as if looking for guidance, but Dr. Capello hadn't done or said anything. He simply waited like he was watching a TV show, but she wasn't sure what the show was—*The Roland Show* or *The Allison Show.*

"Will you help me with something?" Roland had asked her then. "I'm supposed to read the bedtime story tonight. I need someone to help me turn the pages. Can you do that for me?"

Bedtime story? She hadn't had a bedtime story since her mother died. Slowly, Allison had nodded. She could definitely turn pages in a book.

He held out his hand, and it was a nice hand, not the sort of hand that she could ever see slapping a little girl for sitting in the wrong chair. She put her hand in his, and before she knew it, he'd stood straight up and swooped her into his arms. It was so sudden, she'd been shocked into laughing. And he'd smiled at her and carried her into the house. She'd clung to him tightly the whole way, pressing her nose to his hair. He'd smelled like the rain. After that, Allison didn't remember ever crying for her mother or Miss Whitney again.

Allison took a step forward and Roland, the man, not the boy, caught her up in his arms. She felt the warm flannel of his shirt against her cheek and the hardness of his broad chest against her breasts. She was seven again in his arms, and safe again in his arms, and home again in his arms. And when was the last time she'd felt all three? Here. With him. Thirteen years ago.

"I knew you'd come back," he said.

She looked up at him. "I came back."

Still holding her by the shoulders, he stepped back and looked at her face, and she wondered if he was trying to see the girl in the woman or the woman in the girl.

"You're beautiful. When did that happen?"

She blushed. "I didn't realize it had."

"It did." She made a horrible face at him. "Stop that," he said. He nodded. "Better."

"What's this?" She lightly tugged on the chin hairs of his almost-beard. "You going full hipster on me?"

"Not trying to grow a beard, I swear," he said. "This is what happens when I go two days without shaving."

"God, you're old."

He sighed heavily. "Remind me why I invited you here again?"

Allison grinned. "What are you doing out here? Who needs firewood in September?"

"Ah, you know how it is. We get about one month a year when the trees dry out enough to collect and chop firewood," he said.

"I heard grunting sounds. I'm glad it wasn't what I thought it was."

"Nah," Roland said. "Now if it had been Deacon…"

"I didn't need to hear that," Allison said.

"You and me both."

Roland smiled and it was a smile she'd never seen before. She remembered all his smiles. As a little girl a little bit in love with him, she'd counted up his smiles and cataloged them. He'd had six smiles. One—that laid-back, lazy, too-cool-for-school smile.

Two—the half smile, bottom lip out in casual agreement, and a knowing nod.

Three—the full smile with the wink of gentle "Dad'll never catch us in the cookie jar" mischief.

Four—the sudden and slightly insane smile given the second Dr. Capello's back was turned, the one to trick her into laughing and trick Dr. Capello into asking, "What's so funny?"

Five—the back-flat-on-the-beach-baking-in-the-sun sleepy smile.

And her favorite, smile number six—the secret smile and a jerk of the head to follow him outside or upstairs. Wherever he was going, she would go, too, even if it was just to the deck to do homework alfresco.

The smile her gave her now was a new one, one she'd never seen him wear before, but it was already her new favorite.

Four hours too late but she thought she might have an answer for the lady at the rental car place who'd asked her what brought her to Oregon.

Maybe it was him.

CHAPTER 6

They sat on the deck in the white Adirondack chairs where they used to do their homework, boards across their laps as desks and black beach rocks on their papers to keep them from blowing away. The front section of the deck was flat with no railing, so they could sit and look at the ocean without anything in their way. The setting sun had lit the sky on fire and the red tendrils of flame stretched from the horizon to the back of the world where it was already night.

"Where is everybody?" Allison asked after settling down in her chair. Roland set his chair close enough to hers that their shoulders brushed.

"Who is everybody?" he asked.

"You know. Everybody?" she said. "Dr. Capello. Thora. Deacon. Oliver. Kendra."

"I forgot how long you've been gone. Kendra and Oliver left the same year you did. Their families took them back. Haven't talked to either of them in years," he said.

"That's too bad," she said. She didn't remember them very well but she remembered liking them both. Kendra had been a reader like her, and Oliver, though quiet, had been a sweet little guy. "But I guess they were happy to get to go home."

"I guess," Roland said.

"What about the Twins?"

"Deacon and Thora are good. They still live here. They're with Dad at the hospital tonight."

"How's he doing?"

Roland shrugged. "He's okay for a dying man. He had some tests run today and they wore him out, so they admitted him for the night. Famous brain surgeons get lots of attention at small-town hospitals."

"I bet," she said. An awkward silence descended. Allison wasn't sure what to say next. She didn't want to ask questions about Dr. Capello's illness that Roland didn't want to answer, but maybe he needed someone to talk to. Maybe he needed someone to talk to about anything but that.

"He's got two weeks," Roland said, interrupting her nervous train of thought. "If that."

"Jesus."

Roland nodded, tight-lipped and blank-faced. No more smiles.

"Should I go to the hospital to see him tonight?" she asked. "Or should I come back tomorrow?"

"Come back? Aren't you staying?" He looked at her in confusion.

"I hadn't planned on staying. I'm taking a long vacation," she said. "I'm starting in Astoria and driving down to...well, until I get tired of driving or I hit Mexico."

"We have plenty of guest rooms," Roland said. "You can stay here."

"Or I can go see Dr. Capello tonight and get out of your hair."

"You're not in my hair. Plus, it's late. And he'll be home tomorrow morning. You really want to leave already?"

Allison pulled her legs into her chest and wrapped her arms around her knees, resting her head on her arms. Something about this house made her feel like a kid again, a scared kid.

"I can stay a few minutes," Allison said.

Roland nodded again, rested his head against the back of the chair and stretched out his long legs in front of him.

"I didn't get you into trouble, did I?" Roland asked. "Mailing you at your boss's company address?"

"My boss? Oh," she said, flushing pink. "My boss. No. Not in trouble."

"I wasn't stalking you, I promise. Just Googling. I found your name in an article about some big hotel grand opening. Said you were Cooper McQueen's assistant and you planned the party?"

Allison tensed. McQueen was not a topic she wanted to discuss.

"Sort of," she said. "It was a temp job. I don't, ah, I don't work for him anymore." McQueen's real personal assistant had been sick one week, and he'd sweet-talked Allison into taking over managing the guest list. At the party, a society reporter had cornered her and asked her what she did for Cooper McQueen. Since the truth would have been unreportable, Allison had lied through her teeth.

"I'm glad the package got to you, anyway," Roland said. "Couldn't find an address for you anywhere. You're a little off the grid, kid."

"I'm, ah, sort of subletting," she said, not ready or willing to tell Roland the truth yet. Or ever. "The apartment's not in my name. I'm glad I'm not too late."

"Never too late to come home," Roland said, and squeezed her hand.

They fell into another silence but this one far less awkward, more companionable. Maybe it was because he was still holding her hand. Maybe it was because she was getting used to this tall handsome man who shared her former brother's eyes and smile.

"So...anything new with you?" she asked. "Married? Kids?"

He shook his head slowly. "No wife. No kids."

"What about Deacon and Thora? Either of them married or anything?"

"We're all on our own out here. What about you?"

"Free as a bird," she said.

Allison waited for him to say something else, more small talk, more catching up, but he didn't seem in the mood for it.

"Let's walk down to the water," Roland finally said.

"I don't know about that. Are you going to throw me in like you used to?" she asked.

"Do you want me to?"

"Not while I'm wearing suede boots."

"Got it. I'll take off your boots, then throw you in. Come on," he said, standing. He held out his hand to help her up and she took it. He dragged her to her feet with ease, and she followed him down the deck steps to the beach below. The wind whipped through their hair, clean and cool, as she and Roland strode across the sand, Lawrence of Arabia in blue jeans. The water rushed up the shore. Allison danced backward away from the wave but Roland let it hit him, and the water turned his brown boots to black.

"Can I ask you something?" he said, and went on before she could answer. "Is it my fault that you never came back after you left?"

"Your fault? Why would it have been your fault?" she asked.

Roland looked at her, a long look, almost a guilty look,

and all of a sudden it came back to her, a memory she'd either forgotten or repressed.

From her first day in this household, she'd been treated like the baby of the family. The youngest child, the smallest, she'd fit into that role like she was born for it. Thora did her hair. Deacon walked her to class. Roland carried her on his back or his shoulders when they went anywhere because her legs had been too short to keep up with the older kids. But time passed and by her twelfth birthday, she and fifteen-year-old Thora were sharing clothes, even bras.

It was the first week of June in her last summer at The Dragon. Allison had turned twelve the month before, and Roland had one more week left of his sixteenth year. A heat wave had hit and they were all miserable. Like every other house on the Oregon coast, it didn't have air-conditioning, and Dr. Capello had taken the kids to the state park nearby where they could hide from the heat in the cool of the damp, dense forest. But Roland was going to start his summer job as a waiter at Meriwether's the next day and had wanted to stay home. And if Roland was staying home, so was Allison.

They were out on the deck in the hopes the ocean breeze would give them some relief from the stuffy house. Roland stripped out of his shirt but the heat was still too much for him, so there was nothing left to do but throw himself into the ice-cold ocean. Allison followed him out to the beach where they'd both stripped to their underwear. Roland went straight to the water, not even pausing once to acclimate himself to the cold. She ran in after him, watching him dive like a dolphin into the lively waves. He stood up in the waist-high water to push his hair out of face and that's when she'd noticed something about him she'd never noticed before. His biceps. Of course she'd known he had biceps. Everyone with arms had biceps. Even she had biceps, though her body was too soft to see any definition. But Roland had them. And triceps. Deltoids. All those muscles they'd studied in PE. Except in gym class, the muscles had looked like raw meat, but on Roland they were like...art. Like beautiful works of art, and when you saw beautiful works of art, you were supposed to stare at them, weren't you? So she had stared.

She'd stared at the water running down his arms and over his shoulders as he stood up. She stared at the lingering droplets on his stomach and had this strange strong urge to lick them off him, which was bizarre because nothing tasted much worse on the tongue than ocean water. Deacon always called it "whale piss." She'd stared so hard she hadn't noticed the wave until it had knocked her under. Roland grabbed her quickly and pulled her out of the water and into his arms. Without thinking, she'd wrapped her arms and legs around him like she'd done a hundred times before, and he'd carried her out of the ocean. He dropped down onto the soft sand, her still in his arms.

When they hit the sand she'd had to straddle him or fall over. So she'd straddled his hips. And then she'd stayed there. There was no reason for her to stay on top of him as long as she did, and there was no reason for him to let her sit on top of him for as long he did. There was no reason for her to wrap her arms around his shoulders, and there was no reason he should let her kiss him. But she did and he did.

Allison had kissed him a million times before but this kiss was different. It wasn't a pucker-upper sort of kiddy kiss, but she opened her lips a little against Roland's and he must have, too, because she remembered feeling his breath inside her mouth. Some sort of instinct made her move a little on top of him. It wasn't much, a mere shifting of her hips against his hips and then a second hard shifting after that. Roland moved once under her, then winced like it had hurt, though it hadn't hurt at all when his hands lightly scoured the backs of her thighs. It lasted an eternity. It was over in two seconds. Without a word, he'd lifted her off him, dumping her onto the sand, and rolled onto his side away from her.

Lying there, under the hot sun, she told herself she was shaking and quivering because of the wave that had knocked her over. She willed Roland to face her and say something. When he didn't, she'd rolled over toward him. She'd studied his long lean back, the line of his spine, the smooth skin caked with sand. With her fingertips she counted his ribs—one, two, three, twelve on the left; one, two, three, twelve on the right. It had never felt wrong to touch him before and yet it did now. And yet she still did it. Until he stood without warning and started back to the house.

"Better get cleaned up before everybody gets home," Roland had said. He wasn't looking at her as they walked. His head was down, his eyes on his feet.

"Okay," she'd said. She'd agreed without argument, though there was literally no reason to get cleaned up before everyone got home. Nobody would have cared that they'd dunked themselves in the ocean. That wasn't against the rules. But there was one ironclad rule in the house, and that rule was that the boys should never touch the girls and the girls should never touch the boys. Not touching like hand-holding or playing tag. But *touching* touching. Kissing and touching. Grown-up sorts of touching. And that's what she and Roland had done on the beach. They'd broken that rule. *She'd* broken that rule.

Allison had grabbed a sandy stiff beach towel off the deck and wrapped it around her before heading to the deck door.

"Allison," Roland had said. Usually he called her "Al" or "kid." Why all the syllables all of a sudden? She'd looked at him, towel clutched to her body, and waited. "No more white T-shirts in the water, okay?"

Allison had flushed red to the roots of her hair. She'd stammered something along the lines of "Oh, right," and then fled into the house. In the bathroom, she'd locked the door behind her before looking in the mirror. Deacon's old T-shirt she'd thrown on so thoughtlessly clung to her body, the outline of the most private parts of her body showing through. If she could see it, Roland had seen it. Allison had brothers. She understood what had happened.

As an adult, she knew it was hardly breaking news when a sixteen-year-old boy got an accidental erection from an adolescent girl in a white wet T-shirt squirming on top of him. As a child, however, she'd been mortified, ashamed and grief-stricken, like she'd broken something between them that could never be fixed.

"I can't believe it…" she breathed. "I'd forgotten all about that day. Completely forgotten."

At the water's edge they stood side by side, precisely in the same spot where it had happened. He'd brought her there to remember, and she had remembered. The memory—so long forgotten—hit her like a wave, and like a wave it left her cold and shaking and wet.

"I always worried it was… I thought that was the reason you didn't come back." The solemn, stricken look on his face hurt her worse than hate would have.

"God, no." She waved her hands in denial. "No, Roland, absolutely not. What happened that day… No, that was not why I haven't come back before, I swear. I can't believe you thought that."

His shoulders slumped in obvious relief.

"I was sixteen and you were twelve," he said.

"Nothing happened," Allison said. "Nothing. Yes, I freaked out afterward but that was from embarrassment, not… I don't know, trauma?"

"I know what a kid freaking out looks like. This was different," Roland said.

"Was it? I don't remember much after that day," she said, realizing as she said it that that day, that incident, was the last thing she remembered from her final summer at The Dragon.

"What *do* you remember?"

"I remember the wave hitting me," she said. "I remember you carrying me to the beach and not letting me go even after I was safe. I remember kissing you and, after, you telling me not to wear white T-shirts in the water anymore. I remember running to the bathroom to cry. After that day, it's all a blank. But that's... I'm sure that's because of the fall. I'm the one who was grinding on top of you, not the other way around."

"I might have done a little grinding," he said, wincing.

"It was, like, three seconds," she said. "And I was on top." She'd hoped the joke would bring back his smile but it didn't.

"You really don't remember anything after that?" he asked.

She shrugged. "Nothing," she said. "What did I do?"

"You blanked me. Completely. I tried to talk to you about it, to make sure you were okay, and you wouldn't say a word to me. You'd hide in your room when I was around."

"Sounds like a very typical twelve-year-old-girl reaction to extreme humiliation."

"I hoped that's all it was, but I never knew for sure. When Dad said your aunt was taking you home to live with her because of your accident... I don't know. I've never been able to shake the feeling it had something to do with me."

Allison couldn't believe she'd forgotten that day, that moment with Roland. Her first kiss. And with Roland of all people. What other lovely and terrible memories had her head injury stolen from her?

"No, of course that wasn't it."

"Then what was it? Why did it take Dad dying to get you

back here?" he asked. He still looked equal parts relieved and confused.

"You don't know?" she asked.

"Here's what I know. You and I were alone at the house. The 'incident' happened. You stopped talking to me. I'm at work a couple days later, and Deacon called and said you fell down the stairs and you were going to the ER. Next thing I know, your aunt showed up and told Dad she was taking you home with her. I told him we had to stop her, but Dad said we had to let you go. What I don't know is why you didn't come back on your eighteenth birthday. Or nineteenth. Or anytime between then and now."

"There's a lot more to it than that. Dr. Capello didn't tell you about the phone call?"

Roland looked at her, wide-eyed and baffled. "What phone call?"

"Roland... I thought you knew," she said. "Someone called my aunt. It was right before my... Before I got hurt. Who-ever called her, they pretended to be me. They told my aunt someone in the house was going to kill me. And then, bam, next thing she hears I'm in the hospital with a head injury."

Roland rubbed his face and shook his head. "Dad said you fell. That's all he told us. So who the hell called your aunt?"

"I don't know," Allison said. "My aunt said it sounded like me, but she also said the person cried the entire time on the phone, sounded hysterical. I've never figured it out." She knew it had to be one of the kids in the house but she could never picture any of them betraying her like that for any reason.

"Why would anyone pretend to be you? Why would they say those things? I know none of us would do that," Roland said. "I was at work. And Deacon and Thora were devastated when you were gone. I'd never seen either of them cry so hard. Thora screamed at Dad to find a way to force your aunt to give you back to us. Deacon tried to talk Dad into buying you back from your aunt. I cried. Kendra cried. God, even Dad cried when he thought no one was looking."

The thought of them all weeping for her, mourning her, broke Allison's heart all over again. Had she lost her family over a dumb prank gone wrong? Or had something truly sinister happened? Both seemed impossible to believe.

"I cried, too," Allison said. "But Aunt Frankie wouldn't even let me talk about visiting. No letters. No phone calls. I guess she told Dr. Capello you all weren't allowed to contact me, either."

"Dad said something about your aunt not wanting us to call you. But he said it was because she didn't want you getting homesick or trying to run away or something. He never told us... Why would he never tell us about that?"

Roland stepped back from the water and sat on the sand. She sat next to him.

"I can't believe Dr. Capello didn't tell you about the call," Allison said. "I thought you knew."

"Do you really think someone tried to kill you?" Roland asked. "Not by accident, I mean?"

"It doesn't make much sense but...something bad definitely happened and then I never heard from you or your dad or anyone again. That's why I didn't come back before. Whoever wanted me gone got what they wanted." Allison forced a smile. "See? Not your fault at all."

Roland rolled onto his back and lay in the sand. Allison stayed sitting upright. She didn't really want sand all over her black T-shirt or in her bra.

"I want you to know I never forgot about you," Allison said. "I would have come back if I hadn't been too scared to. Sometimes I dreamed about..."

Roland took her hand again and twined his fingers within hers, hers within his, and rested their joined hands on his chest.

"Tell me what you dreamed of," Roland said.

She smiled and looked up at the gray late-evening sky. The first stars were peeking out from behind the dark curtain of night, and she was alone on the beach with the first boy she ever loved, holding his hand with no witness but the ocean.

"I dreamed you'd come and find me," she said.

"Why me?"

"Wishful thinking," she said. "You were always my favorite."

"Favorite sibling?"

"Favorite person. Ever. On earth. I was a little in love with you. And maybe a little in lust…"

Roland did a double take.

"What?" she said. "Twelve-year-old girls think about sex. News at eleven."

"I'm stunned. Stunned, I tell you," he said.

Allison tried to punch him in the arm, but he caught her hand before she could make contact and then held it a moment before suddenly letting it go as if he realized he was doing something he shouldn't.

"You can hold my hand," she said teasingly. "I'm not going to jump on you and start grinding again."

"Too bad."

She went to punch him again, and once more he ducked and caught her hand, and with one impressive show of strength he swooped her up into his arms and carried her to the edge of the water.

"No, no, no! Don't you dare!" She screamed and laughed and laughed and screamed.

"You're going in the drink," he said.

"I'm wearing suede!"

"Fine," he said with a sigh, and then dumped her on her feet on the dry sand. "But only because of the suede. You probably need a dunk in cold water. Not that it helped last time," he teased.

"It's not my fault you were so sexy at sixteen. I lost my head. I won't do it again, I promise," she said.

"Good." He pinched her nose. They were having the conversation they should have had thirteen years ago. Better late than never.

"Unless you want me to do it again," she said, grinning.

"Behave, twerp. I'm…unavailable."

"Ten minutes ago you told me you weren't married and you had no kids," she reminded him. "And don't call me twerp, jerk."

He laughed and her heart danced a little in her chest. She was too happy. Happiness like this scared her.

"This is…a little different."

"Now I'm intrigued," she said, more nervous now than curious.

"I'll tell you, but you have to promise you won't act weird after I tell you," he said. "Everyone acts weird after I tell them."

"I will not act weird," Allison said. "Promise. I'll tell you my weird thing if you tell me your weird thing. Deal?"

"Deal," he said. They shook hands to make it official.

"Now tell me."

"Before I came back here to help take care of Dad, I was living…in a monastery," he said.

"You were living in a monastery? Okay. Why?"

He smiled at her, almost apologetically.

"Same reason anyone who lives in a monastery lives in a monastery," he said. "I'm a monk."

CHAPTER 7

"Holy shit."

That was either the most wrong thing for Allison to say or the most right. She couldn't be sure.

Roland lay on his back on the sand, hands twined behind his head, and quietly smiling. He must be used to reactions like that. One didn't normally suspect ruggedly handsome men of about thirty to be monks. At least, she didn't. She laughed but it wasn't a happy sound. Fifteen minutes ago it seemed like the only things that had changed since she left were their heights and weights and ages. But as Roland lay there on the sand waiting for her to say something else, something not stupid... she realized everything had changed. Absolutely everything. She had no idea who this man was.

"I didn't know monks were, you know, still a thing," Allison said, trying to hide her shock behind flippancy.

"We're still a thing," he said.

"It's just... I've never met a monk before."

"Have you ever been to a monastery?" Roland asked. "Because that's the best place to meet them. Often the only place."

"You're laughing at me."

"A little. But quietly and on the inside."

"You're really a monk. An actual real-live monk."

"I really am. I belong to Saint Brendan's. It's a couple hours down the coast."

Roland's choice of verb stung. He wasn't a *member of* Saint Brendan's. He didn't *live* there. He *belonged* to them. A tiny part of Allison had once thought he belonged to her. A bigger part of her once dreamed she belonged to him.

"So what's it like being a monk?" she asked, talking over the pain. "Can you work miracles? Recite a Bible verse? Sing a monk song? Monks sing, right? They sing and swing that smoky ball thing?"

"Don't take this the wrong way, kid, but you were born to be the baby sister."

"Hurtful," she said, shaking her head. "Very hurtful."

"I shocked you, didn't I?" he asked. He rolled up off the sand and looked intently at her.

"Yeah," she said with real feeling. He had shocked her, and like an electric shock, it had hurt. "I could probably shock you, too, if I wanted. Which I don't."

Why should she care if he was a monk or not? It was an interesting job, yes, but what did that have to do with her?

"A monk," she said again. "That wouldn't have been in my top one hundred guesses. Are you currently a monk? Or an ex-monk?"

"I'm a monk on abbot-authorized medical leave."

"So you're planning on going back? I mean, after your... When you can?" she asked, and she wanted him to say, *No, of course not.*

"That's the plan," he said. "Though I'm trying not to think about it. The longer before I go back, the better."

She nodded. "Right."

"Are you upset?" he asked.

"Why would I be upset?"

He turned his gaze to the ocean waves. "Same reason Dad was upset. You think I'm wasting my life on a fairy tale. You think it's medieval. You think I'd be happier doing a thousand other things with my life..." Allison could tell he'd heard those arguments a thousand times. "Dad's not religious. He worships science. I broke his heart when I joined."

"It's none of my business what you do with your life," Allison said. Roland looked at her, furrowing his brow as if she'd said something wrong.

"That's the sort of polite thing strangers say. We've got too much history to be polite strangers."

"What can I say? Roland, I was an English major. Most people thought I was throwing my life away on that, too. I'm not going to judge you."

"No vows of celibacy and poverty with being an English major," he said.

She chortled a dramatic, mocking chortle. "Oh, trust me— English majors and poverty go back as far as monks and celibacy."

"Are these fake diamond earrings, then?" He tugged her earlobe and she batted his hand away, still playing the part of the annoying baby sister.

"These were a gift," she said. "I couldn't afford them on my own. I spend all my money on books." It was McQueen who'd bought all her jewelry and her clothes including the ones she was wearing—suede boots, designer jeans, a leather jacket that cost McQueen as much as a small used car and La Perla underwear. If she were trying to pass for a starving artist, she wasn't doing a very good job of it.

"I can believe that," Roland said. "We'd have to take your book out of your hand to get you to eat. You loved them more than anything."

"You don't become an English major because you love books. You do it because you *need* books. It's a codependent relationship."

He grinned. "Very poetic. Spoken like an English major."

"Why did you become a monk?"

"Guess for a similar reason you were an English major. I didn't love God, but I needed God."

"I didn't even know you were religious."

"In my own way," he said. "The monastery hosts concerts all summer. Dad would take us to them sometimes if he liked the composer they were showcasing. We met a few of the monks and… I don't know, I liked them. I liked being there. I felt safe there. When I made the mistake of joking with Brother Ambrose about how much I liked it there, he invited me to a discernment weekend. They recruit hard."

"Looking for a few good monks, huh?"

Roland smiled. "They gave me some books to read, too. One of them was by a Cistercian monk, Thomas Merton."

"He's the Kentucky monk, right? I know that guy. I mean, not personally. I think he's dead."

"For a few decades," Roland said. "Anyway, in his book he said the true self was the spiritual self. I didn't know who my true self was. I thought maybe if I figured out who my spiritual self was, I'd know."

"Did you find your true self?" Allison asked.

"I found out who I'm not," Roland said. "And I found a little peace, which was more than I had before I went in." He turned his face to her and smiled. "So that's why I must politely ask you not to jump me. Now it's your turn."

Allison quietly panicked. How on earth could she tell Roland she'd been a billionaire's mistress for six years now that she knew he was a monk?

"Nothing nearly that interesting," she said, brushing the

question off as nonchalantly as she could manage. "I haven't been a nun, that's for sure."

Roland let it go and sat up again, and Allison almost reached out to brush the sand off his back. But she didn't touch him, didn't even want to. Everything was different now. He might have her old big brother's face and eyes and smile, but this man sitting next to her was a complete stranger. A few minutes ago, she'd tried to punch him and he'd caught her hand—like when they were kids. And he'd swooped her up and pretended to throw her in the water—like when they were kids. But he was playing the part of the Old Roland for her and she was playing the part of the Old Allison for him. That might have worked except neither of them were very good actors. She'd made a mistake coming back here. She'd made a terrible mistake. She realized she'd come home to find her old family and her old family didn't live here anymore.

She was as alone here as she'd been in her apartment right after McQueen had left her.

She'd come all this way for nothing.

"Well," Allison said, standing up and dramatically brushing the sand off her clothes. "I should run along."

"Allison?"

"It's late. I didn't mean to stay this long."

"You're really not staying here?" he asked. "Not even for a night?"

"Tourist season's over. I can find a hotel easy." Allison stood up and wiped the sand off her pants. "I'll stay the night in Astoria and run by the hospital tomorrow morning."

"Do you want to at least see the house again before you go?" he asked.

For his sake, for the sake of the hurt he was trying to hide, she decided to humor him.

"All right," she said. "It would be nice to see the house one more time."

In silence, they walked back to the deck, and at the side door took their sandy shoes and socks off and left them on the rack in the mudroom. She hung up her jacket, as well, and saw windbreakers and flip-flops, umbrellas and heavy winter coats. Something for every season on the coast. Roland stripped off his sand-covered checkered flannel and hung it up on a hook. Underneath he wore a plain white T-shirt that hugged his strong shoulders. She grinned to herself at the sight.

"What?" Roland asked.

"What's a monk doing with big shoulders like yours?"

Roland laughed, almost blushed, modest as a monk.

"We carry the cares of the world on our shoulders," he said. "It's our version of resistance training."

Roland opened the mudroom door to the house and said, "After you."

She paused before passing through, a small pause, but Roland noticed.

"Don't worry," he said. "No one else is home."

"Sorry. It's a little weird coming back here," she said. "Been a long time."

She wasn't scared of Roland, though he was a stranger now. And she wasn't scared of anyone who might be lurking in the shadows waiting to jump out and throw her down the stairs. What scared her was the ache in her chest, the ache of longing for this house, this family, even though she knew better.

Allison stepped gingerly through the door into the foyer. Glancing around, she saw that little had changed since she'd left. There was the sunroom with the floor-to-ceiling windows. And she saw the same long ebony table with the wooden benches in the dining room—the perfect table for a family of eight. Roland led her down the hall and she saw the kitchen, which was much like she recalled except in her day the walls had been yellow and now they were painted red. Big kitchen. A family kitchen. Not fancy. Not formal. There were even drawings still hanging on the fridge. Allison walked over to inspect them. One drawing was of a series of brightly colored fish, all of them with human hairstyles. The Roland fish had long blond hair, the father fish had brown wavy hair and a gray beard, the Deacon fish had black hair sticking in all directions and the Thora fish had wavy hair the color of the setting sun. At the bottom of the page in a child's hand was written *The Fishpellos*.

"I did that," Allison said, staring at the Allison fish with the curly brown hair. "I was...nine? Eight?"

"Something like that," Roland said. "My hair was never that long, though. You made me look like Bon Jovi. I mean, if he were a fish."

"There's nothing wrong with looking like Bon Jovi," she said. She had added on to the drawing as the years passed and kids had come to the house and stayed. Oliver had a blond bowl cut so Allison had drawn him with a fish bowl over his head, while she'd drawn Kendra's beaded braids as rainbow stripes. Even the cat, Potatoes O'Brien, got the Fishpello treatment. He was, of course, a catfish.

"Yours looks like you," Roland said. "Got the nice pouty fish lips." He made a fish face, mocking her rather thick bottom lip. McQueen had been a fan of her little lip bow, too.

Allison half laughed, half groaned. "I cannot believe this thing is still on the fridge. It's so stupid."

"Dad thought it was the cutest thing ever. He missed you, you know," Roland said. "We all missed you."

"Missed you, too," she said quietly. "Didn't realize how much until I got your letter."

"I should have written you a long time ago," he said. "I

talked to Dad about you sometimes. I asked him once if he thought it would be okay to look for you. He said if you wanted us, you'd come back on your own. But you didn't. I told myself you forgot about us. Better than thinking you hated me."

"Don't move," she said.

"What?"

"Just…stay here." Allison walked back to the mudroom, grabbed her bag off the hook and pulled out the photograph that she'd kept with her for thirteen years and four moves. She took it back to the kitchen where Roland stood waiting, back against the fridge.

"Here," she said, and handed him the photograph. "Proof I never forgot."

He took the picture from her and stared at it. Then he turned and put it on the fridge with a magnet. Then he took his wallet out from his back pocket and removed a photo of his own. It was the missing section of her picture, the torn-off part. With another magnet he put the two halves of the photograph together. Now it was complete. Allison in Roland's arms, Roland standing next to Deacon standing next to Thora and all of them holding their sparklers together so that the four glowing tips became one.

"You gave me the picture?" Allison asked.

"I guess you really don't remember anything from that time," he said. "You were in the hospital and I wanted to go talk to you. Dad had told us you were going home with your aunt when you got discharged so I knew it was probably my last chance to clear the air with you. I waited until after dark and I snuck in to see you."

Allison looked at him, stunned.

"You were asleep," he said. "So not a big surprise you don't remember that. But I talked to you for a long time, anyway. Probably my first confession."

"What did you confess?"

"I said..." Roland paused. His eyes darkened. "I said I was sorry about what happened between us. I said I wished I'd been at home so I could have helped you when you fell. I said I hoped you'd get to come home to us soon. But if you didn't, I wanted you to have this picture of us until you could come home again."

Allison blinked and hot tears fell.

"I wondered where this picture came from," she said. "I thought your dad put it in my suitcase."

"I wanted you to remember us," Roland said. "I should have given you the whole picture but I wanted to remember you, too. Monks don't carry wallets but I had that picture of you in my prayer book until I left." He paused and seemed to be deciding if he should say what he said next. "I prayed for you."

"You did? What did you pray?" she asked, deeply touched. Had anyone else ever prayed for her?

"Nothing big. That you were happy. That you were okay. That you'd come home someday," he said. "And here you are."

She touched the photograph where the torn seams met. Seeing the two halves of the picture together again made the old wound in her heart, the one left when she was taken away, ache a little, but the good kind of aching, the kind of aching that meant the wound was healing.

"I'll stay the night," she said, smiling through her tears.

"You will?"

"Why not?" she said with a resigned sigh. "One night won't kill me."

CHAPTER 8

Roland insisted on going out to her rental car to bring in her luggage. While he was gone she wandered around the downstairs. The house was neither grand nor intimidating but the signs were everywhere that Dr. Capello had money and lots of it. She'd learned how to spot money from McQueen. His house was beautiful and big but minus obvious ostentation. The really rich people, McQueen had said, are rich enough they don't have to prove anything. A millionaire will keep a wad of cash in a gold-plated money clip in his Armani suit pocket. A billionaire will show up in jeans with a couple twenties in his faded leather wallet. Now Dr. Capello, she knew, certainly wasn't a billionaire, but he had enough money he didn't have to prove anything to anyone. Yet the signs were there. The paintings on the walls weren't prints but originals with familiar-sounding names inscribed in the bottom right corners—Rex Whistler, Grant Wood, even one O'Keeffe. The furniture was heavy, handcrafted and hand-carved. Nothing from IKEA here. As a child, she hadn't had the eyes to appreciate the decorative woodwork, the antique mantel clocks, the stained glass transom windows, but her well-trained adult eyes saw it all. She was amazed that a man with Dr. Capello's wealth had become a doctor when he could easily have lived off his inheritance. Even more amazing that instead of getting married and having biological children, he'd adopted kids out of foster care. McQueen would never have taken in a needy kid. Not unless she was over eighteen and he was sleeping with her.

Roland returned with her suitcase in his right hand and her overnight bag on his left shoulder.

"You okay going upstairs?" he asked.

"I'm fine, I promise," she said as he led the way. The house was three stories high, and when she'd lived there, all the kids slept on the second floor. Dr. Capello's office and bedroom took up the entire third floor. They started up the stairs, and Allison clung to the carved banister railing as she followed Roland up.

"I hope Dr. Capello doesn't have to climb these stairs as sick as he is," she said.

"He's been doing it," Roland said with a touch of awe mingled with annoyance. "Insisting on it. I don't know how much longer he'll be able to keep that up. We'll probably put a bed in the sunroom when he can't make it to the third floor anymore."

"It's been slowly progressing?" she asked when they reached the landing.

"Very slow until recently. Dialysis isn't working anymore. He's had too many infections to qualify for a transplant. Last week he threw in the towel. They say kidney failure is one of the most peaceful ways to go. Small blessing. Very small." He pointed down the hall. "This way."

The second floor had been the kids' kingdom during her time here. In her last months here, six kids had divided up four bedrooms and two bathrooms. The girls—Thora, Kendra and Allison—slept on the east side of the house, which Dr. Capello called the sunrise side, and the boys—Roland, Deacon and Oliver—slept on the west side, the sunset side. The boys got the ocean view but the girls got the bigger rooms. A fair trade, Allison remembered thinking.

"Where am I sleeping?" she asked. The second floor looked markedly different than she remembered, which made sense. The kids weren't kids anymore. No reason for Technicolor paint jobs and skateboards in the hallway, Batman movie posters and swimsuits and towels hanging over the shower rod to dry.

"Over here," he said, leading her to the corner sunset-side bedroom.

"This is your old room," she said.

"Yeah, now it's the guest room."

"Where do you sleep?" she asked as Roland opened the door and turned on the light.

"For the past couple of weeks, on a chair in Dad's room."

Allison walked in and put her bag down on the bed. The room was in a corner of the house with two windows—one facing north to the sparse woods and the other west to the ocean. The ocean-view window was half open to let in the sea breeze, and she was pleased to see a window bench had been added with white cushions and navy blue pillows; a pair of binoculars for bird-watching hung on a hook. She could see herself sitting in that cozy spot and reading all day.

Roland's old wooden slat bed was gone, replaced with a full-size brass bed with a cream-colored quilt and sea-blue sheets and pillows, a dark blue rug and framed Ansel Adams landscapes on the walls. It was lovely, if a bit generic, like a bed-and-breakfast's best room.

"Very nice," she said, hiding her disappointment that so much had changed.

"Thora's been taking care of the house," Roland said. "She

handled the remodel up here about five years ago. Dents in the walls, scuffs on the floor. There was even barbecue sauce on the ceiling on Deacon's side of the room."

"Wait, barbecue sauce?"

"I mean, we hope that's what it was," Roland said. "We didn't ask."

"I can't believe this was your room," she said, sitting on the bed. "It doesn't smell like feet."

"That was Deacon's fault," Roland said.

"Liar. I remember your running sneakers. Dr. Capello threatened to call in the hazmat team to decontaminate your closet."

"Dad."

"What?"

"You keep calling him 'Dr. Capello.' He was your dad."

"He *was* my dad," Allison said. "And you were my brother. You still feel like my brother?"

Roland stood in the doorway, not quite out, not quite in. Even as a boy, he'd had a habit of blocking doorways, filling the frames, reaching up and holding on to the top of the molding to stretch his arms and back.

"I don't know what I feel," he said.

"He never did officially adopt me like he did with you and Deacon and Thora," she went on. "I was just a foster kid he took in."

"You weren't *just* anything. He loved you."

"I know he did. And he was wonderful to me. That's why I'm here. I owe him at least this much. A lot more probably."

"He would say you don't owe him anything."

"Well, I do. I loved Aunt Frankie, I really did. But she was seventy-five when I moved in. And it was only me and her and her bridge partners on Tuesday and Sunday nights. Then she was gone and that was it for real family. I almost wish I hadn't been so happy here. Maybe I wouldn't have missed you all so much."

Roland had watched her the entire time she'd been speaking. She didn't look at him, and gazed instead at the moon dancing over the water.

"You aren't happy, are you?" Roland asked.

"What?"

"Since the second I saw you, I've been trying to put my finger on what's different about you now. I mean, other than you're older and taller and prettier."

She let the "prettier" pass without comment.

"And you figured it out?" she asked.

"Think so. You're sad. You never used to be sad. Even when you first came here, you weren't sad. Scared, but not sad."

She walked over to him in the doorway and let him see her face, her dry eyes, the smile she didn't have to force around him.

"I'm a little sad," she said. "But don't worry. Sad's the weather, not the climate."

"Are you sure?" he asked, his voice softer, almost a whisper. She could believe then he'd been a monk. Such a voice surely had God's ear.

"More mad than sad," she said. "It's not fair, you know. I should have grown up in this house." She turned away from Roland and went to the north-facing window.

The windowsill did double duty as a bookshelf. Old books lined the ledge, novels they'd read in school, tattered paperbacks with pencil markings and yellow highlighting on the pages. *Flowers for Algernon, The Island of Dr. Moreau, Frankenstein, Dr. Jekyll and Mr. Hyde.* All of Deacon's twisted sci-fi favorites.

"You think you get used to it, to losing people you love. I lost my mom," she said. "Lost you all. Lost my…"

"What?"

"My aunt," she said hastily. "She died a year after I started college."

Roland nodded but the skeptical look remained.

"You should get used to it," Allison said. "But you never do."

"I don't think you should get used to it," Roland said. "You'd have to be pretty heartless to get used to something like that."

"I wish I were heartless some days."

"Don't," he said, and he said it so sternly and sharply she looked up at him in surprise. "Don't ever wish that."

He held her gaze and didn't look away, didn't let her look away. She couldn't remember ever seeing him so serious, so solemn.

"You have a good heart," he said. "A lot of people don't. You shouldn't wish a good heart away."

"You're such a monk. I was being jaded. Ignore me."

"Twenty-five is too young to be jaded."

"I have my reasons."

Roland waited, sitting on the windowsill. He didn't need to ask—she didn't want him to. And yet she suddenly felt the urge to reveal everything.

"I got dumped," Allison said. "Two days ago."

Roland's eyes widened.

"Two days?"

She shrugged. "It happens."

"How long were you together?"

"Six years."

Roland looked equal parts amazed and horrified. "Six? That's longer than a lot of marriages."

"This was *nothing* like a marriage."

"It wasn't serious?"

"It was very serious," she said. "Hard to explain. But, if you're glad to see me, you should be grateful to him. I wouldn't have been able to come out here if he hadn't ended things."

"Well, I am glad."

She threw a pillow at him.

He caught it deftly and tossed it back onto the bed.

"I mean—I'm not glad you got dumped. That's brutal. Especially after six years. But definitely glad it brought you here. And you have a free pass to be as jaded and bitter as you want to be."

"Thank you. I'll take it," she said. "Now if you'll excuse me, I'm on Kentucky time, which means it's two hours past my bedtime."

"Tired?"

"A little."

"*Tired* tired or tired of me?" he asked.

"Definitely not tired of you. But I am tired. And if I keep talking I'll talk about things I don't want to talk about."

"Then I'll let you sleep. I'll crash in Deacon's room tonight since Dad's not here. It's the one right across the hall. If you need anything, knock."

"Same here."

They said their good-nights and Allison took a quick shower to get rid of the last of the sand before putting on her pajamas. They were cotton—white shorts and a camisole top—and covered enough skin she wouldn't feel strange walking around the house in them. She lay in bed and turned off the light—a milk glass lamp with a blue glass shade—and tried to sleep. While her body was exhausted from the time difference and the travel, her mind wouldn't shut off. Roland a monk. Dr. Capello dying. Kendra and Oliver long gone. Mc-Queen living his new life with his new lady and the baby on the way. Her brain spun like a roulette wheel, and no matter what number it landed on, she lost.

After half an hour, she switched on the lamp again and went to her suitcase to look for a book to read. None of the ones she brought made for good bedtime reading. They were too serious, too scholarly. She needed a comfort read. She got out the copy of *A Wrinkle in Time* Roland had sent her and started reading it again for the second time that day. She didn't get very far, two whole pages, when she heard a soft tapping on her door.

"Come in?" Allison said.

"Someone wants to see you," Roland said, pushing the door open. He was in his pajamas, too. Plaid pants, bare feet, sleeveless T-shirt. He'd shaved, the lack of stubble making him look five years younger. And in his arms he held a cream-colored cat.

"No way," she said. "Is that Potatoes O'Brien?"

"It's just Brien now," Roland said. "We dropped the Potatoes O. I caught him lurking outside your door like a creeper."

Roland carried the cat over to the bed and sat down with him.

"Can I pet him?" she asked. "Or will he scratch me?"

"Brien doesn't scratch anybody," Roland said. "He's a pacifist. See?" He lifted Brien's paw and it hung in the air before he dropped it down to his furry belly again. "Pathetic. Grow a spine, man."

"He's sweet," she said, grinning as she petted the old boy, happily sinking her hands into his soft warm fur. "And old. How old is he now?"

"Dad got him for Deacon for his tenth birthday, I think," Roland said. "He was a kitten so…about eighteen. But the vet says he's healthy."

"Hi, Brien," Allison said. The poor cat blinked sleepily. "You remember me? I remember you."

"I remember you," Roland said.

"I wasn't talking to you," she said, trying to hide her smile. As she petted and scratched Brien, Roland looked at her.

"What?" she asked. "Do I have something on my face?"

"You look really young without any makeup on," he said.

"Well, you look almost sixteen again now that you shaved off your scruff."

"Don't take this wrong way, but this all feels really weird to me," he said, narrowing his eyes at her. "What about you?"

"I was kind of thinking the same thing. One second you're like a total stranger to me," she said. "The next, it's like I never left."

"Exactly. One second you're this sophisticated twenty-five-year-old woman in diamond earrings and fancy suede boots. The next, you're an obnoxious ten-year-old driving me up the wall again."

"Who do you like better?" she asked.

"I missed the obnoxious kid. I'm enjoying getting to know the lady in suede. You sure you can't stay longer?"

Allison propped herself up on her pillow and looked at him.

"I'm staying tonight, for old times' sake. See Dr. Capello tomorrow. But after that, I think I should move on. It doesn't have anything to do with you, Roland. I want you to know that." He'd been so kind to her, so brotherly, so honest with her since she'd arrived, she hated to tell him this had to be it.

"I won't take it personally when you leave." Roland set Brien down on the floor and the cat sashayed out of the room, tail in the air, off no doubt to find his favorite sleeping spot.

"Never occurred to me Brien would still be around. That makes me happy," she said, smiling contentedly.

"I saw your light on. Thought I should check on you. But you're good so... I'll go and let you sleep."

"Wasn't sleeping." She spun her finger by her ear. "The hamster on the wheel in my brain is refusing to stop running," she said. "I'm reading to him in the hopes he'll conk out." She held up her book, *A Wrinkle in Time*.

"I remember when we read that together," he said.

"First night I spent here." She held the book out to him and waved it. He took the bait.

He jerked his thumb, indicating she should move over to make room. He lay down next to her and propped himself up on the pillow. Unlike her, he hadn't showered, and she smelled the sea air on his skin, salt and sweat. She wanted to press her nose to his neck and inhale but managed to control herself.

Roland opened the page and read the first sentence.

"'It was a dark and stormy night,'" he read. After that one sentence, he stopped. He closed the book, sat up and turned around to face her.

"Roland?"

"I lied to you about something," he said.

"What?" She rolled up. They were knee to knee on the bed, like they were kids again, telling stories and secrets. What had he lied about? Did he know who'd tried to get rid of her thirteen years ago? Did he lie about being a monk? Had he lied about his father's medical condition? What was it that made his eyes so clouded and his face so solemn?

"I lied when I said I wasn't glad you got dumped. I am," he said.

"You are? Why?"

Roland kissed her.

CHAPTER 9

The kiss was quick, but so was lightning. And it struck Allison the way lightning strikes the beach, rendering sand into glass in an instant of natural alchemy. She counted one breath between the first kiss and the second. The first kiss was his. The breath was hers. The second kiss was hers, as well.

She wound her arms around his shoulders and dug her fingers into the soft hair at the nape of his neck. Before she knew it, he'd lifted her into his arms, into his lap. She wrapped her legs around his lower back and he wrapped his arms around her waist without breaking the kiss. She couldn't break it. If she broke it, then one of them might come to their senses. Roland kissed her like he'd spent the last thirteen years waiting to have the chance again.

It was a powerful kiss, possessive and consuming. Tongues met and mingled over and over. His large hands dug into her hips, dragging her flush against him. This wasn't a kiss anymore. She knew kisses. This was foreplay.

In an instant, she was that twelve-year-old girl again, feeling these strange, terrifying desires all for the first time. Her heart raced, her blood pumped; she ached between her legs and moved against him to ease the aching. It didn't work. Thirteen years ago Roland had pushed her off him when she'd moved on him like that. Not this time. This time he rolled her back onto the bed. She'd been waiting for it from the moment their lips had met. With one arm around her waist, he lifted her and shifted her so that she lay directly underneath him. He bent his head and kissed her again, slowly lowering himself on top of her. She felt how hard he was against her and it was the shock she needed to snap out of the fog of lust that surrounded them.

"Roland..."

He lifted his head and looked down at her. When she didn't say anything more, he twined a lock of her hair around his finger, brought it to his lips and kissed the tip. Then he let it go and touched her shoulder instead. He slid a finger under the strap of her camisole top and pulled it down her arm until he'd bared her breast. Allison's whole body, inside and out, was beset with flutters. Heart flutters, stomach flutters—every nerve inside her fluttered.

Roland lowered his head and took her nipple in his mouth and sucked it deeply and slowly and for a very long time. She caught his hair in her hand again and held him to her chest. He'd been the object of her first fantasies and she'd wanted him to be her first. That hadn't happened, but now she had the chance and the choice to let him be her second. She wanted that and he clearly did. Was it wrong? Maybe. But she wasn't going to worry about that now. Plenty of time for second-guessing later.

Allison let him undress her completely and watched without comment as he took his clothes off. He had an impressive body—muscular arms, stomach, thighs. And if there was any part of her that still thought of him as a kid, it was long gone by the time he joined her on the bed again.

She reached for the lamp to turn it off and he stopped her with a hand on her wrist. It shocked her into awareness again, and she looked at him in confusion.

"Leave it on," Roland said softly, though it was clearly an order and not a request. "I want to watch you."

There was a world of difference between the statements "I want to see you" and "I want to watch you," and Allison felt that difference right in her core. The first was flirtatious, a compliment. The second would scorch the earth to bare rock and the smoke would smolder for days if you let it. Allison let it.

Oh, no, they were definitely not kids anymore.

He parted her legs with his knees and pressed two fingers inside her. His hands were large, his fingers thick and long and rough from work. The slow penetration was pure erotic pleasure. As he explored inside her, stroking her carefully but deeply, her head fell back. She noticed for the first time that hanging from the ceiling was a green glass dragon, with its delicate wings spread wide. The window had been left open a crack and a cool breeze snuck inside and set the dragon to flying. Beautiful, it was all so beautiful.

"It feels so good inside you," Roland said into her ear. "Too good. Makes me forget things."

"Like you're a Brother and I'm your sister?"

"Yeah," he said. He almost smiled, but didn't.

"I've already forgotten both."

Though she knew she shouldn't, she couldn't help but compare him to McQueen. McQueen had sex the way other men went on morning jogs. It was physical. Exertion plus release equaled a happy, healthy Cooper McQueen. He paid for the use of her body the way other men paid for gym memberships and personal trainers. He used her; he used her well and often. His pleasure was paramount, hers was peripheral. She'd never minded, even enjoyed it if she were honest with herself. But it was different with Roland. The way Roland touched her, looked at her, held her... This was important to him. This mattered.

Roland moved over her slowly, kissing her breasts again and her stomach, before lying between her open legs to kiss her inside. He murmured a sound of approval at the first taste of her.

And he was in no hurry, either. He lingered between her thighs, licking and kissing and opening her until she was nearly out of her mind with impatience.

"Roland," she said, and that was all it took. He rose up and crawled over her, nudging her legs wider with his knees until he rested into the cradle of her thighs. Slowly he pressed inside her, inching in, turning the tumblers one by one until they were locked together, locked and joined, joined and coupled. He pressed into her again and she wrapped her legs over his hard thighs. She lifted herself against him to tell him she wanted this as much as he did. As much and more.

For those first few taut moments of penetration, Roland didn't kiss her. Allison lay back on the pillow and he held himself up on one arm over her, and they simply watched each other.

"You okay?" he asked. She nodded. "This isn't too weird, is it?"

"Nah," she said, smiling up at him. "It's just weird enough."

His knuckles grazed her cheek. She felt simultaneously aroused and sleepy. Now that they were over the initial awkwardness, it felt perfectly natural having Roland inside her body. They fit. They fit so well she wondered if this was how it had to be. She had to leave as a child so she could come back to him a woman. Thirteen years ago, a moment of awkward fumbling had left them both miserable and ashamed. Now as adults, there was nothing in their coupling but pleasure, utter pleasure, and no pain or shame at all.

Roland lowered himself onto her again and kissed the

breath out of her. When she tried to run her fingers through his hair, he caught her by the wrist and pressed it into the bed. His hands were large and powerful, but gentle, too, so that it didn't feel like he was holding her down, but simply holding her. She turned her head and kissed his inner bicep, a long, lingering kiss that left him panting, lips parted and eyes closed. He was so beautiful. For a second she was that twelve-year-old girl again, discovering for the first time how beautiful her eldest foster brother was, how handsome and strong. She needed him like she'd needed him that day, and he put up no fight when she pushed him on his back and sat astride him.

She sighed his name and he lifted his head to smile at her, pleased with her pleasure. This was a new smile, too, an erotic smile. Allison licked the hollow of his throat as she moved her hips in a slow oval. The breath he took stole hers. She should have come back years ago.

"That was obscene," Roland breathed, his head falling back on the pillow.

"Sorry," she said, grinning and unrepentant. "I've waited a long time to do that."

"What else have you waited a long time to do?"

"So much," she said. "This..." She traced the lines of his shoulder blades with her fingertips. "And this..." She scoured his stomach with her fingernails from neck to hip. "And this..." She lifted her hips into his as slowly as she could, making him feel every inner muscle that held him inside her and surrounded him with heat. He said something that might have been "God help me," but she couldn't tell. All she knew was that it was good so she did it all again. She moved harder against him, faster, and Allison gave herself up to him, let go, surrendered entirely. She came first, lost in waves of pleasure and happiness, and he came shortly after, shuddering in her arms and breathing her name.

It was over. She knew it was over when Roland turned off the lamp and the room was plunged into darkness. But he didn't leave. She'd expected him to leave, but instead he lay on his side and pulled her back against his chest.

He kissed the back of her neck and pulled her a little closer. They were silent for a few seconds before Allison thought to ask him a question she'd had ever since she'd received his letter.

"Why do you think of me when it rains?" she asked, wondering if it was for the reason she remembered.

"You don't remember? I guess it didn't rain much where you grew up," he said. "And rain out here right by the ocean can be loud. Whenever it rained, and the wind was blowing, it shook the whole house. So you would come crying to me, asking if you could sleep in my bed."

Allison grinned. She recalled those autumn storms, those winter squalls and the wind wild enough to make you wonder if you would wake up in Oz. Sometimes they could only tell the day from the night from the color of the rain—gray by day, black at night. And in January the ice would come and frost The Dragon so that his green scales shone like silver.

"I don't know why me," Roland said. "But it had to be me. Not Dad, not Thora, no one but me. And you'd always fall asleep about five minutes after I let you in bed with me. And then I'd pick you up and go put you back in your own bed. Every single time it rained. Finally when you were about ten you grew out of it."

"You want to know a secret?" she asked.

"Of course."

"I was never afraid of the rain."

"You want to know my secret?" Roland asked.

"Sure."

"I always knew that."

CHAPTER 10

Roland fell asleep in seconds, it seemed. Allison listened to his steady breathing, so peaceful and contented. She envied that contentment.

Carefully she eased out from under Roland's heavy arm and went to the bathroom to clean up. She was on birth control so she wasn't worried that they hadn't used a condom. She never kept any on her, and she doubted a monk, on medical leave or otherwise, would, either. Roland, a monk. Roland, her first love. Roland, her former brother. The whole thing was so utterly surreal that she couldn't bring herself to go back to bed yet. That would mean treating what had happened as nice and normal, and she wasn't yet sure if it was either of those things.

She slipped back into her pajamas and snuck out of the room. In the quiet, dark house, she tiptoed down the stairs and walked out onto the deck. Calm hit her at the first kiss of night air. The breeze blew through her and over her, tickling every inch of her bare skin. Her toes tingled in the cool of the night and chills passed through her, delicious chills like the gentle touch of a handsome stranger. She leaned against the deck railing and stared out at the water, breathing in the air, breathing out her confusion. With the vast horizon shrouded in darkness, it seemed so much smaller, like her own private ocean. She was tempted to walk out onto the beach and go wading. The ocean was always warmer by night, wasn't it?

She went to the steps and started to walk down.

"Leaving already?"

She turned around and saw Roland coming out the deck door.

"I was thinking about going to the water."

"You've been gone too long," he said. "You need a flashlight or you might step on something."

"A rock?"

"A jellyfish."

"Oh," she said. "I should wait till morning, then."

"Not a bad idea," he said. He'd thrown on his pajama pants again but he was shirtless, and she fought off the urge to wrap her arms around him and steal his body heat.

"Are you okay?" he asked, shutting the deck door behind him and walking over to her. She returned to the deck railing and resumed her night watch.

"Seems I'm not supposed to sleep tonight," she said.

Roland stood next to her, his elbow touching her elbow at the railing.

"I saw you out here," he said, "in your little white pj's with your hair down, and I remembered something."

"What?" she asked.

"Why I believe in a loving God."

She grinned.

"You're too nice to me," she said.

"Not possible."

"Possible," she said. "I don't know if I deserve it."

"You sound more like a monk than I do," Roland said. "I think you're being a little hard on yourself. We had sex. People do that sort of thing. Monks, too, even though we're not supposed to."

"Do they?" she asked. "You're my first monk."

"Ah…when I left," he said, "my abbot gave me a long sex talk."

"Like the birds and the bees?"

"More like the 'You're young and taking care of a dying parent is stressful. You're probably going to have sex while you're back out in the world. Don't let it become a wall between you and us. Sin should always be a bridge that brings you back to God, not a wall between you and Him.'"

"You had a nice abbot."

"He's a very wise man," Roland said. "He also told me to be honest with whoever I'm with. Don't raise expectations, that sort of thing."

"I'm not expecting a marriage proposal."

"You can be honest with me, Allison. Don't let me being a monk put a wall between you and me. If you have something to tell me, tell me."

"I keep thinking you're going to judge me."

"If I wanted to judge people all day I'd either be a priest or get a Facebook account," Roland said. "I didn't do either."

A night breeze blew past, and she shivered. She wanted to ask Roland to put his arms around her to warm her up, but she didn't. They were strangers again. He'd been inside her not half an hour ago and now she couldn't even ask him to hold her. She and McQueen had been willing strangers, especially during sex. She'd played her role and he'd played his and the unspoken agreement was to never peek behind the curtain. And she'd never wanted to peek. But with Roland she did. She wanted him behind the curtain with her. She didn't want to pretend anymore.

"If you weren't a monk this would easier," she said.

"Even if I were the judgmental type," Roland said, "I don't have much of a leg to stand on after tonight."

"Good point," she said, dropping her head between her arms to hide her smile.

"Are you thinking about him? Your ex?" Roland asked. He sounded serious now. It was so strange to hear his voice like that.

"I'm thinking about you," she said. "And him. How to tell you about him."

"Just tell me."

"I lied to you, too," she said at last.

"About what?"

"McQueen."

"What? Cooper McQueen? Your boss?"

She nodded.

"He wasn't my boss."

Roland stared at her, wide-eyed in surprise. "Cooper McQueen…the billionaire investor guy? You were his girlfriend for six years?"

"No. We were sleeping together," she said. "For six years. But I wasn't his girlfriend."

"Then what were you? Secret wife?"

"Secret mistress. His bought and paid-for secret mistress."

Roland turned his head quickly and looked at her through narrowed eyes.

"Told you so," she said. He was clearly stunned. No words necessary.

"A mistress?" Roland said.

"Or a kept woman. I've called myself that a few times."

"So…that's still a thing? Kept women?"

She laughed. She hadn't expected to laugh during this conversation.

"Yeah," she said. "Kept women are still a thing. Where there are men with money and women without it, it'll be a thing."

Roland waved his hand to indicate she should keep talking.

At first the words didn't want to come out, but then eventually everything started to spill. Finally she managed to look Roland in the face. He didn't seem to be mad, though he didn't seem all that happy, either.

"You expected better of me, didn't you?" she asked him.

"I expected better *for* you," he said. "There's a difference."

"Is there?"

"Obviously you and I never had a normal brother-sister bond," he said.

"Obviously," Allison said.

"But I always loved you," he said. "I don't like the thought of you being trapped in a tower by some rich guy using you for sex."

Allison smiled wanly, her laugh hollow and cynical to her own ears. She felt older than Roland then. He seemed so innocent to her, this noble-hearted monk. He had no idea what her life had been like with McQueen.

"I wasn't trapped except by choice. I have could left him if I'd wanted to. And I'm not ashamed of my relationship with him. I'm not comfortable talking about it with people but...but I know I should have told you about it before we slept together."

"I'm glad you didn't tell me first. I might not have slept with you otherwise."

"Ah-ha. Judging. I knew it."

"No, it's not that, I swear," he said, raising his hands in surrender. "I mean... I wouldn't want you to think I came to your room because I thought you were, you know, *easy*."

"I'm not easy at all," she said. "McQueen's handsome and a billionaire. Fact is, I'm quite difficult."

Roland held up two fingers.

"What?" she asked, eyeing those two fingers.

"I'm pretty difficult, too," he said.

"Wait. I was your second?" she asked, pointing at herself.

He nodded. "Wow. So it was me and someone from a long time ago?"

He nodded again.

"Hope it was worth the wait," she said.

He nodded again, slowly, and with his eyes wide open.

"I feel very honored to be your second," she said.

"And I'm honored to be your rebound monk," Roland said. "I'm not anywhere close to being a billionaire."

"It wasn't really the money, you know," she said. "The money made it possible but...truth is, I didn't want to be alone. I needed someone in my life. McQueen was definitely better than nothing."

"I thought he had a girlfriend. In the article where I found your name...he definitely had a girlfriend."

"Oh, he did," she said. "And he had me, too."

"You deserve more than that," Roland said.

"Maybe," she said. "But in fairness to McQueen, he made it very clear from the beginning what I was going to be to him. I was in his life to provide sex on demand. Girlfriends had their own lives. Girlfriends could say, 'Not tonight, dear, I have a headache.' My job was to be the girl who never had a headache. I was a luxury purchase, and the luxury was that I was there when he wanted me, and when he didn't, I simply ceased to exist. I was—" she blew on her fingertips "—a ghost."

"A ghost in love," Roland said.

"He called me Cricket," she said. "How can you not fall in love with someone who calls you Cricket?"

"Why Cricket?"

"Our first trip he took me on was to New York. I was twenty, summer before my junior year of college. We went to a Broadway play and it was a nice night so we walked back to the hotel. We passed some homeless people and I told Mc-Queen he should give them money. He said being with me was like having his own personal Jiminy Cricket. I was his conscience."

"It sounds like he cared about you."

"You're being nice."

"He kept you for six years," Roland said. "He must have cared about you a little bit, anyway."

"Maybe. Not that it matters one way or another. It's over. He met someone and they had a one-night stand. And, bam, she's pregnant. So goodbye to me."

"Ouch," Roland said, wincing dramatically.

"Yeah, ouch," she said. "But it's the right thing to do. There's a kid involved now so…" She took a shuddering breath, wiped her own tears before Roland could. "It's for the best. I had to put my whole life on hold for him. No job. No boyfriend. The girl in the tower is a romantic image to anybody *but* the girl in the tower."

Allison felt the tears threatening to come again and she blinked and blinked until she'd blinked them away. Roland stood between her knees, his hands warm on her bare thighs. She covered his hands with hers and looked at their entwined fingers.

"So that's it," she whispered. "The story."

"Is it the whole story?" Roland asked.

"When he walked out the door two days ago," Allison said, "I was seven years old again waiting for my mom to come home from the drugstore where she'd gone to get me some cough syrup. It should have taken thirty minutes. Two hours later she still wasn't back. I just… I walked around the apartment calling for her like a lost dog or something. Like she'd hear me calling and come back." Allison blinked more hot tears from her eyes. "She never came back. I barely remember her, but I still hate being left alone."

"Is that why you're here? You didn't want to be alone?"

"Probably." She realized as she said it how cold that sounded. "Sorry."

"You don't have to be sorry. If Dad wasn't dying, I doubt I would have had the guts to write you, anyway. I'm glad I did, though."

"Even knowing who you just slept with?"

"Especially knowing who I just slept with," he said, smiling.

She playfully but not-terribly-gently elbowed him in the ribs.

"I deserved that," he said. "You okay?"

"I will be." Allison shrugged, pretending she was fine already. "You know what's funny? His new lady told him that I couldn't be in the picture anymore. That's what she said. I was never in the picture. Except the sort of pictures you shred and then burn the negatives after."

"Negatives, huh?" Roland said.

"McQueen doesn't trust the Cloud with his dick pics."

Roland laughed. At least one of them could laugh about it.

"If it helps, you're in our pictures," Roland said. "Lots of them. They're up in Dad's office."

"You're sweet," she said, then laughed tiredly.

"What's funny?"

"Oh, thinking about the things we let rich men get away with. McQueen's girlfriends knew about me. I mean, they didn't know my name, where I lived, but they all knew he had someone on the side. He warned them. And they let him get away with it. Never would have happened if he'd been a mailman or a mechanic."

"Look at Dad," Roland said. "You think a normal man, a poor guy, would do what he did? He could literally walk into a foster home, snap his fingers and walk out with a kid." He raised his hand and snapped his fingers like a diner rudely summoning a waiter. "When a rich man does it, it's philanthropy. When a poor man does it, they call the cops on him."

"Dr. Capello helped people. McQueen helped himself," Allison said. "Must be nice, though."

"Being that rich?" Roland said.

"Yeah, so rich you can snap your fingers and get someone to come home with you just like that," she said. "Think it would work for us?"

Roland looked at her before raising his hand and snapping his fingers in the air twice. Allison grinned and crooked her finger at him. He wrapped a strong arm around her waist and pulled her away from the deck railing, leading her by the hand into the sunroom.

"Hey," he said, once they were back inside the house. "What do you know? It does work."

"Roland Capello," she said, running her hands up his bare arms to his shoulders. "You really are the nicest boy in the world."

"Am I? Back at the monastery it's compline. I should be at night prayers." Allison looked into his eyes. He didn't have bedroom eyes, not like McQueen did. Roland had hallway eyes—labyrinthine hallways made of marble and lit by torches resting in iron sconces. She could wander those shadowy hallways forever and never once feel lost.

"You are nice," she said, sliding her fingers slowly down his broad chest and over his tight stomach. He shivered at her soft touch and she smiled at his shivering. Her Roland, a monk. A sweet, gentle, tenderhearted monk and who'd been with two girls in his entire thirty years. She would have to teach him a few of the things McQueen had taught her.

"Very, very nice. But guess what?"

"What?" he asked as he brushed his hands through her hair.

Allison dropped down onto her knees, but not to pray.

"I'm nice, too."

CHAPTER 11

Allison awoke the next morning and found herself alone in the bed. The sheets were cool next to her. Roland had been gone for some time now. Bracing herself to meet the sunlight, she opened her eyes and saw a note lying on the pillow next to hers.

Good morning, sunshine—
I'll be at the hospital all morning with Dad. Deacon and Thora will probably be back by noon. Make yourself at home.
    Thank you for last night. If you want a kept man, I promise my rates are very reasonable.
Love,
Roland

P.S. There are no secrets in this house. Be prepared for Hurricane Deacon. Once he finds out, we will not hear the end of it.
P.S. #2. I wasn't kidding about you being in our pictures. Go look in Dad's office on his desk.

She smiled at the letter. She was glad there didn't seem to be any lingering awkwardness in his words. Roland had never been the dramatic sort. And Deacon? Oh, she could handle Deacon. She kind of liked the thought of being teased for sleeping with Roland. She'd never been teased over a guy before. Her one serious adult relationship had been with Mc-Queen, and he'd been a secret.

After her shower she made herself a small breakfast of yogurt and toast. Apart from Brien, who was asleep on the sunroom sofa, she was alone in the house. For a few minutes she wandered around downstairs, letting the memories of her time here wash over her. Loud family dinners in the dining room. Playing charades in the sunroom after sunset. Dr. Capello helping her with her science project in the kitchen. They'd made a volcano, a mini Mount Hood. Happy memories, all of them. She found more happy memories on the second floor. Thora doing her hair for her—a French braid one day, pigtails the next. Deacon and Roland swinging her in a blanket while she yelled, "Faster! Faster!" She and Kendra reading on the deck while out in the ocean, the boys trying to impress them with their pitiful attempts at surfing.

Allison walked from bedroom to bedroom, growing younger as the memories teased her into smiling, tickled her into laughing. Warm memories, sunlit memories. Memories that made it almost impossible for her to reconcile the beauty she'd found in this house with the ugly way it all ended. She'd known nothing but love here, nothing but kindness. But someone must have left a door open a crack and evil had snuck in when no one was looking.

Allison climbed the stairs to the third floor, where she knew Dr. Capello's office waited. These were the stairs, the ones they'd said she'd fallen down, which meant she'd been on the third floor for some reason. Yet, she couldn't think of why she'd be up here. This floor had been mostly off-limits to the kids since Dr. Capello kept his office there—medical records, computers and other expensive equipment. But if they were sick and had to stay home from school, Dr. Capello would let them upstairs to spend the day with him. He had a couch in his office and Allison remembered dozing off a fever under a blanket, waking to read or watch his small portable TV while he worked on whatever it was he did back then.

Was that why she'd been up here that day? Had she been sick? It was summer, so there would have been no school to miss. Maybe she snuck up here? Did someone lure her upstairs for the sole purpose of pushing her down? Or had she fallen completely by accident and the phone call to her aunt was something entirely unrelated? If it weren't for that call, Allison would be sure the fall was an accident. But she couldn't pretend it hadn't happened. She'd been betrayed twice in this house—first by whoever had hurt her, and then by Dr. Capello when he let her go without a fight. Allison stared down the steps, trying to trigger a memory—anything about that moment, that day, that week.

Nothing. If she had any memories of that time, they were locked up in a vault in her brain, and she'd long ago lost the combination.

Allison gave up trying to remember. She turned from the stairs and wandered down the hallway, opening the door to Dr. Capello's office.

She smiled as she stepped inside. Dr. Capello had truly snagged the best room in the house. It was spacious and airy, with bright white walls and windows looking out on the ocean. Her favorite was the massive bay window with the padded window bench perfect for a child to lie on for reading or napping or watching the waves. Dr. Capello had a beautiful old boat of a desk, weathered gray wood with a three-masted ship carved onto the back and sides.

A map hung behind the desk, over a decorative fireplace. At least in Allison's memory it had been a map, the old-fashioned ink and parchment sort with dragons lurking along the far edges. But her grown-up eyes now saw it for what it was—a skull. A map of the skull with parts of the brain labeled like countries. At the very core of the skull, there she saw the pen-and-ink dragons. How strange. Why would there be dragons inside the human brain? She'd heard of the "lizard brain" but never the dragon brain. She'd have to ask Dr. Capello about it.

Allison walked around the desk and that's when she found what she'd come for. Photographs, a dozen of them in plain black frames, sat on Dr. Capello's desk in an array that spanned twenty years or more.

On the far right corner of the desk was a picture of the five of them—Dr. Capello, Thora, Deacon, Roland and her. It had been taken on the back deck with the sun and the ocean behind them. A summer picture, they were all in shorts and T-shirts. Allison grinned at the sight of her tiny self in Roland's arms. She was the shortest one, which meant Roland had to hold her up so that more than just the top of her head would be in the picture. She couldn't quite remember when that picture had been taken. She slipped the photograph out of the frame and read the back.

July 30, 1997—the kids and me with our new addition, Allison.

The picture had been taken one month after she'd come to The Dragon, and she looked happy and healthy and at home. One of the family already.

Next to that picture Allison found a photograph of orange-haired Thora and black-haired Deacon playing tag on the wet sand. Thora and Deacon—otherwise known as "the Twins." They weren't related, Deacon and Thora, but they were the same age, had the same birthday by coincidence and were inseparable. For a long time, Allison had simply assumed they were twins despite looking nothing alike.

As the photos progressed from right to left, the children in the pictures aged from kids to preteens to teenagers to adults. Somewhere around the middle section, the teenage years, she and Kendra and Oliver disappeared from the pictures. Only Roland, Deacon and Thora were in the photos on the left of the desk. Allison knew where she'd gone—home to live with her aunt. But what about the other two? Where were they now? In the three farthest pictures she saw Thora, as a beautiful young woman, in a pretty strapless prom dress with Deacon and Roland standing next her and beaming like proud papas. Another photograph showcased Deacon and Thora in their graduation robes and caps, grinning awkwardly at the camera. The picture next to that one was of Deacon on a Kawasaki motorcycle, looking terribly dashing in a leather jacket, his black hair wild from wind.

One picture held her eye longer than the others—Roland, about age twenty-four or twenty-five, stood in front of a chapel wearing the black robes of a Benedictine monk. He wasn't smiling in the photograph, but he didn't look sad, either. Pensive? A little. Maybe lonely, too? Or not. Maybe that's what she wanted to believe. It wasn't as jarring as she thought it would be to see him as a monk. He looked like himself, only younger, his hair an even lighter blond, still parted down the center and tucked behind the ears like she remembered so well. In the photograph she spied an eyebrow piercing—an endearing mix of medieval and modern, just like Roland himself. Curious to see when this picture had been taken, she slipped the photo out of the frame and read the back—*Brother Paul*, it said, *2009*. But that wasn't all she found. Hidden behind the picture of Roland in his black robes, Allison found another photograph.

The second photograph was of four very young children. She recognized three of the four—Roland, Deacon and Thora—but the last boy she'd never seen before. He had olive skin and dark eyes. She imagined his hair was dark, too, but she couldn't see it since he wore a bucket hat with Clark Beach emblazoned on the front. On the back of the photograph it read:

The kids meet their new brother, Antonio Russo, age eight. February 1995.

New brother? She didn't remember any of them mentioning a boy named Antonio. He must have been another foster child Dr. Capello had taken in who'd come and gone before Allison had arrived. It appeared the picture had been taken in the sunroom. She recognized the big white couch and the windows behind them. All of the kids wore big cheesy grins in the photograph, all of them but Antonio, who stared blankly at the camera.

Allison put the photographs back exactly as she found them. She made a mental note to ask Roland later who Antonio was. During her time at The Dragon, a handful of kids had come for a week or two each before being placed with relatives. Maybe that's what had happened to Antonio. They had thought he'd stay for a long time but a relative had been found to claim him. These things were sad but they happened in the system. The question was…why was the photograph with Antonio hidden behind another picture? It wasn't like Dr. Capello couldn't afford another frame. She'd ask Roland about that, too.

As Allison was leaving the office, she noticed a framed newspaper article on the wall by the door. The photograph in black and white was of flip-flops, seven pairs of them, all lined up in a row, and the headline read The Lucky Ones— Sick Kids in Oregon Find a Hero in Dr. Vincent Capello and a New Home in a House Called The Dragon. It was a profile of Dr. Capello and his work as a philanthropist and foster father, dated 1998. Allison hadn't seen it before, or if she had, she'd been too young to remark on it. Intrigued, she began to read.

The call came on a random rainy Wednesday when Vincent Capello was scrubbing out after surgery—a child with a brain tumor that left the boy partially blind.

"The president for you," Dr. Capello was told, "on line one."

"President of what?" he'd asked.

"The country," the nurse said.

It seemed Dr. Vincent Capello was then President Clinton's top pick to replace the outgoing surgeon general. The call was brief and polite, with Capello turning the offer down in under two minutes.

"It was an honor to be asked," Capello said of the position. "But I had kids to take care of."

Allison laughed in surprise. She'd had no idea Dr. Capello had once been offered the surgeon general's post. And he'd turned it down for his kids? Amazing. She kept reading.

Vincent Capello and his children live in picturesque Cape Arrow, in a grand old house that was built as a gift from a man to his beloved wife and later became the scene of her murder.

Allison paused. Murder? She'd never heard this story about The Dragon.

In 1913, wealthy timber baron Victor Courtney purchased one hundred acres of pristine coastal land and began work on the beach home his wife, Daisy, had longed for since leaving her old-money Boston family to marry the upstart Oregon millionaire. Work was completed on the house in 1921 and Victor and Daisy moved in shortly after. No expense was to be spared as the house was built to satisfy Daisy's every whim—a Victorian turret, a library of first editions on solid oak shelves, a sunroom, a drawing room, a formal dining room, servants' quarters and ocean-facing windows galore. At first, the Courtneys were happy in their new home, but a few months later their troubles began.

"My grandmother Daisy had always been cheerful, they say," Capello said on the day of our interview. "And she loved her daughter, my mother, doted on her, and she wanted many more children. But she miscarried shortly after they moved into this house. Then miscarried again a year later. She fell into a deep depression. Friends said she changed completely and could be found day and night, rain or shine, walking the beach and weeping, talking to herself and her lost children.

"My grandfather had a temper, though it was more bark than bite. But after moving into the house, he changed. He became brutal, even violent. He raged at servants, sometimes beating them, even beating my grandmother, which they say he'd never done before. The abuse was bad enough my grandmother sent my mother away to boarding school back East. It likely saved her life."

The rages became legendary in their small coastal community. People speculated the Courtneys were cursed or the house haunted, and the suffering couple was called cruel nicknames by locals—Crazy Daisy and Vicious Victor. Victor blamed his own troubles on his wife. He had her subjected to brutal psychological treatments—unregulated drugs, water "cures" and even high-voltage electroshock therapy. Nothing worked to alleviate her depression. When the news came that Victor and Daisy were found dead in an apparent murder-suicide, no one was much surprised. The house remained in the family but laid abandoned for decades until the Courtneys' only grandchild returned to it in his midthirties.

"It was morbid curiosity that brought me here. I wanted to see the old pile my mother talked about but refused to visit. I knew I'd inherit it eventually and wondered what I'd be getting myself into. Sell it? Knock it down? I was planning for the worst when I drove out here. My mother blamed this house for killing her parents. My grandfather had named the house Xanadu, but behind his back everyone called it Courtney's Folly," Capello said. "All up and down the coast you can still hear people telling ghost stories about the house. I was in medical school at the time and had a very good feeling it wasn't a ghost that caused my grandparents' troubles. I sent in contractors who tested the paint, tested the pipes. My grandparents weren't insane and they weren't bedeviled by ghosts or demons." What they were, Dr. Capello's testing found, was ill. Very ill. "They both suffered from lead poisoning, which has both physical and neurological side effects. Unscrupulous builders had substituted poor quality lead pipes for the higher quality copper pipes my grandfather had ordered. My feeling had been right. The house did kill them but not for the reason everyone thought."

That discovery lead Capello on a quest to restore the house and his grandfather's reputation in the community. The three-story estate has half a dozen bedrooms, just as many bathrooms and sits directly overlooking the beach. "I stood on the old deck and saw a family of five splashing in the water. One of the kids ran over to me and asked if I lived in the house. I told her no and her face fell. She said that was too bad, because the house was 'so cool' because to her it looked like a green dragon from a distance. I'd never noticed that before, but then I couldn't stop seeing it like that."

And so it began, Dr. Capello's quest to turn a house haunted by death and darkness and rumors of madness into the ideal family home. The old pipes were replaced, of course, and all the lead-based paint removed or painted over. Capello had inherited two fortunes when his parents passed away—his mother, who despite her wealth spent her life teaching English literature in underprivileged schools, was heir to the Courtney lumber money, and his father, David Capello, had invested heavily in pharmaceutical stock that paid off handsomely in the 1980s. The hardworking surgeon is now a very wealthy man, though you couldn't tell from looking at him. He wears scrubs at work and old khakis and sweatshirts at home.

"I'm a dad," he says of his attire. "We don't dress to impress around here. We dress to make a mess." This, his eldest child says, is one of Capello's many "dad-isms."

Capello explains he was the sort of man married to his work, but always longed for children. As Capello dreamed that first day at Courtney's Folly, the house is now full of children. Seven, at the moment, and all of them taken from the foster care system.

"My grandparents' story taught me we have a long way to go to understanding and treating the causes of violent behavior. When I decided to bring foster children into my life, I knew I would help the kids no one else wanted, kids with behavior problems that made them 'unadoptable.' Every child's fate is up to the luck of the draw. I won the lottery of birth—wealthy parents and a happy life. These kids lost it. All I want to do is share my winnings with them."

But it's how some of these "unadoptable" children ended up in Dr. Capello's life that is, perhaps, the most incredible story. He even spoke of meeting one of his foster children through his medical practice. The boy, he explained, was diagnosed with a brain tumor, which Dr. Capello was scheduled to operate on. This same child also had extensive behavioral problems, including a compulsion to harm children and animals. Remarkably, once the tumor was removed, the child's sight was restored and his behavior improved by leaps and bounds. Capello continues his research in this area, however, hoping to show how extreme behavioral issues are sometimes the result of trauma on the brain (from a tumor, for example) and are, in fact, treatable with surgery.

Some of the children he fosters stay for a week or a month. Others stay with him longer. Capello has officially adopted three of his foster children and may adopt more in time. "Seven at the most," Capello said. "My van won't hold more than that."

Friends in the Department of Health call Capello a natural, a born foster father and even a magician. Katherine Grant, head of DHS's foster care placement program agrees, saying, "If I had a hundred Vincent Capellos I could save every troubled child in this state. We send him our tough cases, the ones we despair of being able to help. Every lion comes back a lamb. Either there's something in the water out there, or he's working miracles."

Ask Capello his secret to helping these children through their issues and he'll answer with one word: "Love."

Soon the legendary surgeon, nicknamed "the Man of Steel" for the strength of his hands, a boon to any surgeon, will retire to become a full-time foster father. "Surgery is a young man's game, and I'm not a young man anymore."

His children are counting down the days until Dad no longer has to leave at five in the morning and come home exhausted from the hospital. The sooner, the better, they say, agreeing, "Dad really is getting too old for that stuff."

The once-abandoned and seemingly haunted house is a palace now. A children's palace. No longer is it called Courtney's Folly but The Dragon, a perfect name for the green-shingled gentle monster of a home that lurks at the edge of the map. When Dr. Capello is working, which is more often than he likes, three local women take turns acting as nannies to the brood—cooking and cleaning, driving the kids to school and helping with homework. But more often than not, you'll find Dr. Capello here alone with his children, which is exactly the way he wants it.

Today seven pairs of flip-flops sit by the deck door. Every room is brightly painted and lovingly decorated. There are toys and books and beach towels everywhere you look. Anyone watching Dr. Capello grilling hot dogs on the deck while his children play in the sand can't help but envy them. From being dealt a bad hand to holding a full house, these kids are indeed very lucky to have found a doctor, a father, a savior and a hero in Vincent Capello. But don't try telling that to him.

"No, no, no," Capello said to this remark. He pointed at himself. "I'm the lucky one."

CHAPTER 12

Allison read the article beginning to end twice, and by the time she finished, she had to wipe a tear off her face. She'd never known any of that about Dr. Capello's family or the history of The Dragon.

It sounded like Dr. Capello, calling himself the lucky one, though she would have argued with him if she could. She'd been miserable in that group home before a man in blue pajamas had brought her to this magical house. If her luck hadn't run out, she could have stayed here her whole life. Maybe she would have been in all the pictures on the desk.

Allison left the office and walked down the third-floor hallway, seeing the house now with new eyes. Daisy Courtney had walked this same hall Allison walked. Did the floor creak under Daisy's every footfall as it did for Allison? Did Daisy bathe in the same pedestal bathtub Allison had that very morning? Allison couldn't picture it. To her this was The Dragon, a children's home. Impossible to imagine two very ill and troubled people haunting these hallways and dying in these rooms. What room had Daisy died in? What room had Victor? Allison didn't want to know. She could understand why Dr. Capello hadn't told her the history of the house and his family. Madness, violence, miscarriages, poison water and a weeping woman walking the beach at all hours hardly made for a cozy bedtime tale for children. Even as a grown woman, the story disturbed her deeply.

On the third floor there were only two other doors. The first was the door to Dr. Capello's bedroom, which must have been the library in Victor and Daisy's day. Built-in oak bookcases lined the walls and a bench sat in the bay window, a perfect spot for reading. As a child she'd paid no attention to Dr. Capello's books. These weren't storybooks—no pictures or conversations, as Alice in Wonderland would have complained. These were medical books, many of them clearly valuable antiques. She ran her fingers over the red and black leather bindings, took random tomes off the shelves and examined the elegant pen and ink drawings of human organs and veins, muscles and bones and parts of the brain. They smelled like heaven—or like old books, which was her version of heaven. Dr. Capello had a vast collection of books on child psychology, brain development, personality and behavior disorders. One would have thought he was a psychologist and not a neurosurgeon based on his bookshelf. But the article on the wall had made clear Dr. Capello believed most behavioral issues had medical causes. Made sense to study both physiology and psychology, she supposed.

The bed stood in the arched alcove by the big window like it always had and next to it sat a leather armchair covered in an old blue afghan. Allison felt a deep and troubling tenderness as she took the afghan off the chair and folded it neatly. This was where Roland slept when he was on night watch with his ailing father. A book about famous inventors lay on the side table. She picked it up and turned to a dog-eared page. "All that was great in the past was ridiculed, condemned, combated, suppressed—only to emerge all the more powerfully, all the more triumphantly from the struggle." The quote was from Nikola Tesla, and it must have resonated with Dr. Capello as he'd underlined it in blue pen.

Allison placed the book back on the table where she'd found it. She pictured Roland reading it to his father at night. She wished Roland were here so she could kiss him again. Bad thought. Dangerous thought. She didn't need to feel this intensity of affection for Roland so quickly. She was leaving today, after all.

Wasn't she?

Allison left the question behind her as she walked into the hallway and shut the door to the bedroom behind her. Directly across from Dr. Capello's bedroom was the door to the attic. From the very first time she'd seen the house, with the square sort of turret sticking up from the top, she'd wondered what delights were in that room, but the attic had been mostly off-limits back then. Roland had said in his letter to her that he'd found her copy of *A Wrinkle in Time* up there. Maybe more of her old things were up there. She reached out for the doorknob, but the second her finger touched it, a jolt of electric shock ran through her arm. Nothing too painful, and yet she stood there in a daze as if it had stopped her heart. She remembered something. What was it? Something about the attic. Something she needed to know.

Closing her eyes, Allison touched the doorknob again. The static shock had dissipated, but when she tried to turn the knob she found it locked. Odd. It had made sense to lock up the attic when they were children, but there were no children in the house anymore.

Allison tried the door one more time. It was an old house; doors swelled and hinges rusted. No, it was definitely locked. A key lock, too, which meant somewhere there had to be a key. Allison stepped away from the door, intending to check the key hooks in the kitchen, when she felt her phone vibrating in her back jeans pocket.

When she saw who was calling she almost didn't answer, but she longed to hear a familiar voice.

"Yes, McQueen?" she said as she started down the stairs. She tried not to sound annoyed when she answered, but she didn't try very hard.

"Where the hell are you?"

The worry in his voice caught her by surprise.

"What? Where am I?" she asked as she walked down to the second floor. "Where are you?"

"I'm home where I belong. You aren't. I sent a painter over to your place and your neighbor told the guy you'd packed up and left on a long trip."

"Well, there's your answer," Allison said. "I packed up and left on a long trip."

"You didn't tell me you were leaving."

"I don't have to tell you anything anymore."

"I'm trying to do you a favor here," he said.

"I told you I would take care of getting the place painted," she said. "Not my fault if you refused to hear a word I said."

She went down the second set of steps and walked into the sunroom. If she had to have this conversation, she would do it in a room with an ocean view to distract her.

"I heard. And I told you I'd take care of it," he said.

"I haven't changed the locks," Allison said with a sigh. "Give the painter your key."

"I gave you my key," he said. "It's in the box."

"Sorry," she said. "I'm in Oregon. I'm not going to fly back for a housepainter."

"Oregon? What are you doing there?"

"Visiting the Capellos."

McQueen fell silent for a few seconds. Allison braced herself.

"Allison…"

"I opened Pandora's padded envelope."

"This isn't funny."

"No, it isn't," she said. "It's not funny at all. The reason Roland contacted me is because Dr. Capello is dying. He thought I might want to see him before it was too late. I did, so here I am. The end."

"Not the end. Not even close. Someone in that house tried to kill you. You shouldn't be there."

"It was thirteen years ago."

"So was my divorce. You don't catch me at my ex-wife's house, do you?"

"First of all, your ex-wife wouldn't let you in her house. Second, none of this is any of your business, McQueen."

"We're friends, aren't we?"

"No."

"Cricket—"

"I told you not to call me that anymore. And shouldn't you be out buying nursery furniture or something instead of interrogating me?"

"I have plenty of time to interrogate you and buy nursery furniture."

"I'm a little busy, however, so I'm going to go."

"Busy? Doing what?"

"Sitting on a couch staring at the ocean. I'm swamped."

"Are you going to stay mad at me forever?" he asked.

"Forever? It's been three days. And as a matter of fact, I'm not mad. However…I don't think we need to be talking to each other. Do you?"

"I think if you're in a house with someone who wants to kill you, we probably should stay on the line."

"I'm alone in the house," she said. "And I feel very safe here. Roland gave me quite the welcome home last night."

"Big party?"

"We slept together," she said.

That admission had the desired effect of silencing McQueen for a good long time. She spent those beautiful seconds grinning and watching the waves dance up the beach. They seemed happy today, happy for her.

"You had sex with Roland?"

"Twice."

"You had sex with your brother?"

"It gets better. Or worse, depending on how Catholic you are. He's a monk."

"Monk? Black robes and bad haircuts? That kind of monk?"

"He wears jeans and flannels and he has very nice hair. But yes, he is a monk. He left his abbey a few months ago to take care of his dad."

"You had sex with your ex-brother who is now a monk."

"It was surprisingly good," Allison said. "You would never have known he was a monk."

"Did you do that just to hurt me?" he asked.

McQueen was silent again for long enough Allison stopped enjoying it.

"No," she said. "Not *just* to hurt you."

"Dammit, Allison."

"McQueen, you really give yourself too much credit. You called me. I didn't call you. You ended things. I didn't."

"Six years. You can't ask me to stop worrying about you overnight after six years."

"You don't have to worry about me," she said with an exaggerated groan.

"I don't? You're in a house where you almost died and

you don't know who did it or why, and I'm not supposed to worry?"

"I know what I'm doing."

"I'm not sure that you do."

"McQueen, need I remind you I was nineteen when we had sex the first time. You treated me like an adult when I was still a kid. Now I am actually an adult, and you're treating me like a child. If your next sentence isn't an apology, I'm hanging up and this is the last call of yours I'm ever taking."

Knowing McQueen and his congenital inability to apologize, she fully expected this to be the last time they'd speak. Seemed McQueen was still capable of surprising her.

"You're right," he said at last. "I'm sorry. I'm sorry for taking you to bed too young. I'm sorry for making you put your life on hold for me. And I'm sorry for treating you like a child when I know you're as smart and capable as they come."

"Thank you," she said. "Apology accepted."

"But one more thing, please?"

"Are you going to say something sexist and patronizing again?"

"Probably. But give me this one."

"Fine. Go on."

"Please, Allison, please be careful."

The pleading tone in his voice wriggled through the chinks in her armor. Since her aunt died, he'd been the closest thing to family she'd had. He'd helped her buy a car. During a hard winter, he'd rented her a hotel room when the pipes in her old building froze. When Allison contracted pneumonia her senior year in college, he'd made sure she had the best medical care money could buy. If they'd still been together when this had happened, he would have paid her way out to see Dr. Capello, paid for her hotel room and paid for her way back.

While he was never there for her when she wanted him, he was always there for her when she really needed him.

"It's just…" she said, no longer angry. "I think I'm starting to remember things."

"What?" he asked. "Remember what?"

"Remember things I need to remember. Something important. I'm almost there, I think, like when you're trying to remember a word and it's on the tip of your tongue? It's like that."

"Do you want to remember?"

"One of my old drawings is still on the fridge. Maybe if I knew what happened, why I had to leave… I don't know—"

"If you knew why you had to leave, you could stay?"

"I'm not thinking that far ahead."

"You're a terrible faker," he said.

"Okay, maybe I am thinking that far ahead. Might be nice to spend Christmas with someone."

"We always celebrated Christmas together."

"On the twenty-seventh," she said. "Never on Christmas Day. You were always with your kids on Christmas Day."

"Cricket, I—"

"I know. You're sorry. But you shouldn't be. Not about that. Christmas is for family, and I was never part of your family."

"And Roland is?"

"He used to be."

"So you're planning on staying there awhile, then?"

"Long enough to see Dr. Capello."

"All right," he said. "Have it your way. But if you decide to stay longer, check in with me every now and then so I know you're alive."

"If you insist."

"I insist," he said. "And let me know if anything weird happens, okay?"

Allison heard something outside. She looked up and saw someone standing on the deck. A man in black. All black. Black jeans, black boots, black sleeveless T-shirt, black hair and black tattoos all the way up and down his arms.

"McQueen, I've gotta go."

"What's up?"

"Something weird happened."

CHAPTER 13

By the time Allison had slipped on her shoes and made her way out to the deck, her mysterious man in black had seated himself on one of the lounge chairs with sunblock on his nose, one leg crossed over his knee and a book in his hands. All in all, he was doing a fine impression of a California beach babe baking in the sun. He ignored her as she came to stand in front of his chair. He merely turned a page in his paperback without giving her a second glance.

"Hello, Deacon," Allison said.

He pushed his sunglasses down his nose to look at her before pushing them up again to resume his reading.

"Hi, sis," he said.

"What are you reading?" she asked.

"Book I picked up at the library this morning," he said. "Little ditty called *Flowers in the Attic.* Ever read it?" He looked up at her and grinned as manically as the Joker. Allison glared at him.

"Ohh…" he said, shuddering. "You give a good death stare. Almost better than Thora's."

"Roland is not my brother. I am not his sister. We are not flowers nor are we in the attic," Allison said.

"True, but *No Flowers in the Beach House* doesn't have quite the same ring to it," he said, and tossed the book back over his shoulder, where it landed on the deck in a flurry of bent pages. The book lover in her died a little inside. "Walking funny today?"

"That's a very crude question."

"He hasn't gotten laid in years. Plus he's six feet tall and weighs two hundred twenty pounds. I'd hate the big behemoth if he weren't my brother. I can't break one-eighty wet with boots on. Maybe I need bigger boots." He held out his leg to show off his motorcycle boots.

"I'm fine," she said. "Thank you for asking."

"Did you have fun last night?" he asked as he pulled his legs in to make room for her to sit down on the lounge chair. "He definitely did. Grinning like an idiot all morning. Which is kind of weird in a hospital, but hey, Nero diddled while Rome burned, right?"

"Deacon?"

"Yes?"

"I hate you."

"Aww... I love you, too." Deacon reached out, grabbed her and pulled her down into his lap. To make it even worse, he started to rock her back and forth. "Our little girl's all grown up."

"So much hatred. Burning, burning hatred."

"Be happy, poopsie," Deacon said. "You got the good monk to stay up after his bedtime for something much more fun than praying. You must be a miracle worker."

"Roland warned me about this," Allison said with sigh. "You, I mean. He warned me about you. He should have warned me way more."

"You have to let me enjoy this. If men had hymens his would have grown back by now."

"Can you take the sunblock off your nose?" she asked. "It's getting on my shirt."

"You're no fun." He pushed her off his lap, and wiped the sunblock off with the corner of his beach towel. All at once it struck her how handsome a man Deacon had grown into. Not handsome, she reconsidered, but beautiful. Like many people on the West Coast, he had some Asian ancestry, which had blessed him with high cheekbones, elegant dark eyes and thick eyelashes sooty as cinders. A striking man. If someone put him in a Tom Ford suit and sent him down a runaway, he'd be America's next top male model.

"You're pretty, too," he said.

She narrowed her eyes at him. "How did you know I was thinking you were pretty?"

"I assume that's what everyone's thinking." He winked at her.

"You're a menace," she said, rubbing her forehead. Deacon was so easy to love and yet she also wanted to strangle him. But with love. But also strangling. In a loving way.

"Allison, baby," he said, suddenly serious. "It's okay. This isn't a big deal. People have sex. It's normal."

"Thank you."

"I mean, it's not normal to have sex with your big brother who also happens to be a monk, but who wants to be normal? I don't."

"You were almost helpful. Almost. So close and yet so far..."

Deacon laughed and it was a lovely laugh.

"I know he's not your big brother," Deacon said. "I tease because I love. Glad you're back. Are you?"

"I was until the wildly inappropriate questions about last night."

"You can ask me some wildly inappropriate questions if it'll make you feel better," he said. "Hit me. I have no secrets."

"Why is the attic locked?"

"Except that."

She glared at him again.

"What do you want in the attic?" he asked.

"Roland said he found one of my old books in the attic. I thought more of my stuff might be up there," she said, and hoped he bought it.

"Dad keeps some medical equipment and files up there now. If you want to see it, I'll show you. You'll regret it, though."

"I'll regret it?"

"Damn skippy, you'll regret it. Not even joking, sis. You still want to go?"

"More now than ever."

"You're my kind of girl," Deacon said. He stood up and she found he'd grown nearly as tall as Roland. She experienced a moment's vertigo when she realized the last time she'd seen him they'd been the same height.

She followed him into the house and up the first and second flights of stairs.

"So," he said, "I have to tell you the truth."

"About what?" Allison asked. They went into Dr. Capello's office where Deacon dug around the desk drawers until he found a key on a plastic tag.

"The reason I came to see you."

"Which is…?" She already regretted asking.

"Roland. You. You and Roland."

"There really is no me and Roland. We spent one night together. We're not planning the wedding yet."

"Thora and I don't want to see him get hurt. I love the

man," Deacon said. "I can't help but be protective of him. He's…a little out of practice with women."

"I didn't plan last night."

"I'm sure you didn't," he said as he unlocked the attic door. "I mean, if you were going to plan on sleeping with one of your former siblings, it would have been me, wouldn't it?"

"Not Thora?"

"Oh…" he said. "I like the way you think."

He opened the door and reached way up to pull the cord on the light. Deacon immediately headed up but Allison stayed at the foot of the steps.

"Are you coming up or are you going to stand there checking out my ass all day?" Deacon asked, looking over his shoulder and down at her. He stood at the top of the steps, holding on to the railing on either side. Twelve hardwood steps between them. She'd counted. Enough of a push and anyone could break their neck on these steep narrow stairs.

"I was trying to remember something," she said. "And check out your ass."

She'd made the joke to cover her nervousness, but Deacon noticed.

Deacon turned around, faced her. "It wasn't me," he said.

"What?"

"Whoever pushed you down the stairs, it wasn't me. And you didn't fall down the attic steps, anyway," Deacon said. "It was the third-floor stairs you fell down. I know because Thora and I ran into the house and saw you on the second-floor landing with Dad kneeling over you. You don't forget a day like that. You don't forget the day you saw your father scared shitless for the first time."

Allison couldn't speak. Deacon spoke for her.

"Roland told us you thought someone might have pushed you on purpose and that's why your aunt came and took you from us," Deacon said. "If you think that's what happened, I believe you. But it wasn't me or Thora."

"You would say that, wouldn't you?" she said. "I mean, if you did do it." Roland was the only Capello she felt completely comfortable around. He wasn't home the day of her fall. No way he had anything to do with it.

"Good point," Deacon said.

"That doesn't comfort me," she said.

"Sorry. I'm too honest, I guess."

"Can I trust you?" Allison asked.

"I hope so. But in case you don't…"

Deacon stuck his hand in his pocket and pulled something out. He tossed it down to her. She caught it, poorly, but still caught it.

"Mace? You carry mace with you?" Allison asked.

He shrugged. "Pepper spray. It's for you. Lot of psychos out there, you know. Now are you coming up?"

She did go up the stairs.

But she kept the pepper spray in her hand.

The attic smelled of years and dust and must, but it was a pleasant sort of smell, comforting, like old books. Everywhere she saw boxes, many of them with RC written on them. Roland must have stored all his things up here when he went to the monastery. There were also old wooden filing cabinets, steamer trunks and unmarked boxes sealed with layers of tape.

"See?" he said. "You're safe with me. Come on. I'll show you the freak show."

"The freak show?" Allison asked as she tucked the pepper spray into her pocket.

Deacon pointed at something. All Allison saw was a large white sheet draped over what she assumed was a huge stack of boxes.

"We cleaned out Dad's office after he retired and put everything up here. Including his 'collection.'" Deacon pushed the curtain aside and Allison stared, wide-eyed, at three dark wood glass-front cabinets. She looked at Deacon, who said nothing but waved his hand as if to say "you asked for it, here it is." She leaned in and peered through the glass. Inside on beds of midnight blue velvet lay various metal objects in strange, fascinating and grotesque shapes. They were not shiny, not polished, not gleaming. These were old things, tarnished things, some with rust on them that on second look revealed it was not rust at all.

"What the hell is all this stuff?" Allison asked, intrigued and horrified by the macabre display in front of her.

"What do you do when you have too much money, too much free time and not enough good sense?"

"I don't know," she said.

"That's a bone wrench," Deacon said, pointing at an F-shaped steel object about ten inches long. "Don't ask me why you'd need to wrench a bone, but that's what it is. And that thing next to it that looks like a wine bottle corkscrew is, in fact, a trephine."

"A what?"

"A trephine? It's, um, for drilling holes in the skull."

"Oh, gross," she said, wincing.

"I know, right? This is the best one, though," Deacon said as he pointed out an object that looked something like a wooden rolling pin with a rounded tip and split down the center.

"What is that thing?"

"You can't guess?" he asked.

"Please tell me that's not a wooden dildo."

"Close. It's a speculum," he said, grinning.

"Made of wood?"

"It's been sanded and shellacked."

"You're kidding me, right?"

Deacon grinned maniacally. "It's got a leech applicator, too."

"Oh, my God." Allison covered her mouth with her hands and laughed in disgust and horror.

"I wasn't kidding about the freak show," Deacon said.

"Dr. Capello collects this stuff? By choice? On purpose? No one is making him?"

"This is medical history right here." Deacon waved his hand, indicating the cabinets. "Insanely gross and fucked-up medical history. We've got a tonsil guillotine here. A set of forceps as big as your arms here. And, oh, this little guy is a gold-plated eyelid retractor. Are you ready to puke yet?"

"A tonsil guillotine?"

"Chop, chop," Deacon said.

"Yes, I'm ready to puke."

"I told you you'd regret it," Deacon said.

"I need to sit down," Allison said, mostly kidding. Deacon had warned her, after all. As gross as the stuff was, she found it pretty fascinating. Fascinating *and* gross.

Deacon threw open a large steamer trunk and pulled an old quilt out of it, tossed it on the floor and sat down cross-legged. Allison sunk down next to him.

"Dad is weird," Deacon said.

"I had no idea."

Deacon laughed. "Blame his grandparents," he said.

"Vicious Victor and Crazy Daisy?"

"Yeah. Dad found a bunch of his grandparents' stuff up here in the attic when he came back the first time. Including some of the stuff they used on her. Including..." Deacon crawled to one of the cabinets and pointed at the object inside. "That ice pick."

"Ice pick?"

"Up the nose and into the prefrontal lobe," Deacon said.

"Didn't work very well. Supposed to make her less moody. Instead she was pretty much catatonic after that."

Allison shuddered at the sight of the thin metal rod and its tapered tip. She couldn't stop thinking about how it had once been shoved into a suffering woman's brain.

"That wasn't in the article I read," Allison said.

"The one on Dad's wall? Trust me, there's a lot that's not in that article," Deacon said, rolling his eyes. "But you know what they say—don't let the facts get in the way of a good story. A catatonic woman being choked to death by her own husband as a sort of mercy killing is a bit much for the Lifestyle section of your friendly neighborhood newspaper."

"He choked her to death?" Allison said.

"Choked her with his bare hands," Deacon said. "Then he blew his brains out with his pistol. Fun story, right?"

"And Dr. Capello wanted to keep all that old medical stuff of hers?" Allison asked. "I think I would have thrown it all away."

"It's part of his family's history," Deacon said. "Plus, collecting antiques is like getting tattooed. You tell yourself you're going to keep it small and simple and then a year later..." Deacon held out his bare arms to show off his tattoos, stylized Chinese black dragons that twined from his back over his shoulders and all the way down his arms.

"Your tattoos are much nicer to look at than a giant wooden speculum with a leech applicator."

"That's the nicest thing you've ever said to me," Deacon said.

"I'm going to be thinking about the giant wooden speculum on my deathbed."

"Um...how are you planning to die, sis?"

"Up here," she said, "puking to death."

"Poor Allison," he said. "I warned you."

"I'm fine. Horrified but fine."

"There's more he's got locked away."

"I don't need to see it."

"Not even his collection of Civil War–era amputation saws?" Deacon asked. "Some of them still have dried Confederate blood on them. He's even got Daisy's old ECT machine. It's pretty cool-looking…"

"I'm good, but thanks, anyway."

Deacon laughed and she smiled at him.

"Good to see you again, Deac," she said.

He narrowed his eyes at her and nodded.

"You've been gone too long," he said.

"I had my reasons."

"Roland gave me the rundown. I'm not going to lie—I have no idea what happened the day you fell or who did it. But I do know this—I had nothing to do with it and neither did Roland or Thora."

"You're sure?"

"You don't forget the day your sister almost dies," Deacon said. "I remember that day the way people remember where they were when Kennedy was shot. Roland was at work. And Thora and I were outside together when we heard Dad screaming for help. If she knew anything she would have told me. She tells me everything."

"Everything?"

He nodded again. "We work together, you know."

"What do you do?"

"We have a shop in Clark Beach. I'm a glass artist and Thor runs the business."

"A glass artist? Are you serious?"

"Totally. The studio's called The Glass Dragon, our home away from home. You can come see it, watch me work, if you want."

"I'd love that. Wait..." Allison remembered something. "There's a glass dragon hanging from the ceiling of my room. Did you make that?"

"I did."

"It's beautiful. I thought it was an antique."

"All me."

"Where'd you learn how to do that?"

"I have a great-aunt and -uncle in Shanghai—they're my mother's relatives," Deacon said. "They both work at the big glass museum there. After I graduated high school, I needed to get away but college wasn't for me. I went there for a few years and they taught me glass-sculpting. Came home a couple years ago, and Dad helped me set up the shop."

"Very cool," Allison said, impressed. "Your dad must be really proud of you."

"He is," Deacon said. "He's proud of all of us."

"Even Roland? He said your dad hates that he joined the monastery."

"He does hate it, although he knows Roland was happy there. He's proud Roland turned out so well despite the monastery. I swear, when Dad first got sick, it crossed my mind that he was faking how serious it was to make Roland come home. He wasn't. Wish he was, but..." He shrugged again.

"Why did your dad hate Roland being in the monastery so much?"

"He's a humanist. All religions are cults to him. And Catholic monks? Oh, my God, you would have thought Ro joined the Taliban. Science is Dad's religion. He thinks religion is bad for humanity. It makes people think some big guy in the sky is going to solve all their problems. Dad took us to the monastery because they had good summer concerts. That's it. None of us ever dreamed Roland would join."

"Do you have any idea why he did it? Seems so drastic," Allison said.

Deacon puffed up his cheeks with air and then blew it out hard.

"He'll probably tell you he was called, whatever that means," Deacon said. "Thor and I think it's because of Rachel. Dad, too, although he wouldn't say that out loud."

"Rachel?"

"She was Ro's sister," Deacon said. "Biological sister."

Allison was stunned. "What? I had no idea he had a biological sister."

"Not surprised. He never talks about her. Nobody talks about her."

"Nobody?"

"*Nobody,*" Deacon said, nodding. "Seriously, I only found out about her by accident. When I returned from China and moved back in, I came up here and started digging in boxes, looking for my stuff. Ended up in one of Roland's boxes. Found a photo of a little girl. I thought she was you at first till I got a better look."

"Me?"

"Straight brown hair, brown eyes, gap teeth."

"Sounds like me."

"I turned the picture over and it said, *Roland, age eight, Rachel, age five.* Freaked me out. I took it to Dad. He said Rachel and Roland were the first two kids he ever fostered."

"That wasn't in the article, either," Allison said.

"That article's a puff piece," Deacon said. "They were trying to recruit more people into being foster parents. Talking about a dead kid doesn't really sell people on the program."

"A dead kid? What happened to her?"

"It's pretty horrible," Deacon said, wincing. "She and Roland were playing on the beach and Roland buried her in sand. The sand sort of caved in, and she was smothered to death."

Allison was speechless.

"Unfortunately, it happens," Deacon went on. "About once a summer we hear a story about some kid dying or nearly dying on the beach," Deacon continued. "Sand shifts and gaps open up and you sink down. Dad says Roland's always blamed himself. He told me to put the picture back where I found it and pretend I hadn't seen it, for Roland's sake. So I did."

A little girl, dying under Roland's care. It all sounded so terrifyingly familiar. She could still feel the wild pounding of Roland's heart against her chest as he held her and carried her out of the water.

"I just… I had no idea," Allison finally said.

"Anyway, Dad doesn't think Roland should blame himself for what happened to Rachel. And he doesn't think Roland should punish himself, either."

"And that's what your dad thinks the monastery is?"

"He might be right," Deacon said. "You know what they call the little rooms monks sleep in? Cells."

"God, poor Roland," Allison said.

"He buys his Catholic guilt in bulk at Costco," Deacon said.

"You know, this actually makes sense," Allison said, pointing at him. The pieces were slowly clicking into place. "When your dad came and got me out of the group home they'd put me in, the lady who ran the place, Miss Whitney, she said something about me looking like someone. And the first time I met Roland, Dr. Capello watched us really close like he was… I don't know. Like he was watching to make sure Roland was going to be okay with me."

"Dad loves fixing broken kids," Deacon said. "When I came here, I was really upset because—" Deacon paused "—because of my cat back home."

"What about your cat?"

"He was dead," Deacon said, his voice flat. "So Dad got me Brien. Dad would do anything for us. Replace a dead cat..."

"Replace a dead baby sister?" Allison said, shivering despite the stuffy heat of the attic.

"A very Dad thing to do," Deacon said. "Fixing broken kids is what he does. Or tries to do. Anyway, Dad's going to be thrilled when he finds out you and Roland hit it off."

"Don't get him excited," Allison said. "I'm leaving soon."

"Sure you are," Deacon said. "Dad's gonna pull out all the stops to get you to stay. If it means getting Roland out of his prison cell, he'll try anything."

"Do you want me to stay?" she asked. If he had lied to her, if he knew something about her fall or the phone call, then surely he wouldn't want her to stick around. She searched his face, looking for guilt, but didn't see any.

"Stay?" Deacon said. "I wish you'd never left." He seemed sincere, truly sincere, for the first time since he showed up on the deck.

"I should have come back sooner," she said. "Now it feels too late, you know?"

"Never too late. Shit," Deacon said, jumping to his feet.

"What?" Allison looked around in confusion. Gravel crunched. A car door slammed in the distance.

"We're not supposed to be up here," Deacon said, grinning like a little boy with his hand caught in the cookie jar. "Dad moved his medical files up here so technically it's off-limits. At least, we pretend it's off-limits until the three of us want to smoke up here."

"Smoke?"

"Not cigarettes," he said, and winked at her.

Allison followed Deacon down the stairs and she watched him put the keys back into his father's desk drawer, the second from the bottom. When she saw the photographs on the desk again, she remembered something.

"Hey, who was Antonio?"

"Who?" Deacon asked.

"I saw his picture," she explained. "When I was looking at all the pics of us. Antonio Russo? Does that name ring a bell? He was nine, lived here before me."

"Oh, yeah," Deacon said, his brow furrowed. "Antonio. Tony, I think he went by. I think he stayed a week. Had lots of behavior problems so he had to get a new placement. Come on. I can't wait to see Dad's face when he sees you."

Deacon's enthusiasm seemed genuine but so had his confusion when she'd mentioned Antonio Russo's name. Had he really forgotten one of his foster brothers? Probably. She had friends in elementary school whose names she didn't remember anymore. And that had been a long time ago. Maybe Roland remembered more about Antonio.

Allison and Deacon walked out to the landing. Allison stopped at the top, looked down and felt her heart lift like a balloon.

"'The sun was shining on the sea, / Shining with all his might,'" sung a warm gentle voice from below. "'And that was odd because it was…'"

"'The middle of the night,'" Allison said.

He stood at the bottom of the stairs, smiling up at her and waiting. In his eyes she saw that same old kind and shining light she remembered from the first day she ever saw him.

She started down the stairs, slowly at first and then faster, until she was practically skipping down to the bottom. When she reached the final step, Dr. Capello opened his arms and she stepped into his embrace. Once she was there, wrapped in his warmth, she forgot it had been thirteen years since she'd been taken from this house, thirteen years since she'd seen this man, thirteen years since she called this place home. She'd even forgot he wasn't her father anymore, so when she found her voice to speak again, she said what she'd said a thousand times before.

"Hi, Dad."

CHAPTER 14

As soon as Dr. Capello was in her arms, Allison regretted the force of her greeting. His shoulders were thin and bony, sharp as stainless-steel cutlery wrapped in a paper napkin. He smelled like a hospital, like Lysol and medicine. She started to ease up on her embrace, and he whispered, "Not yet, doll face. I've waited a long time for this." So she clung to him, for his sake and hers, because she'd waited a long time for this, too.

"Missed you," Allison whispered.

"Missed you more," he said.

She pulled back from the embrace to look at him, at this man who should have been her father had the world worked out according to a child's wishes and not adult rules and whims. He looked mostly the same as she remembered, except in negative. The hair Allison remembered as brown with streaks of gray was now gray with streaks of brown. His tan skin was now sallow and his brown beard now white as snow. Only the eyes were untouched by time. Bright brown eyes, full of mischief and full of joy, just like she remembered.

"It's good to have you home again," he said.

He patted her face and she grinned, happy as a child.

How she had loved this dear old man…how she had missed him. She'd missed his whiskers against her cheek. She'd missed the way he patted her back when he hugged her, rough and tender. She couldn't recall a single instant when he'd lost his temper with them, or raised his voice in anger. When he did yell it was, "Be careful, kids! Watch each other!" as they ran from the house to the water. And they were careful because they loved him and never wanted to hurt him. Oh, Deacon talked with his mouth full. Roland forgot his homework. Thora made messes. Allison hated taking baths and would cry when anyone gave her a cross look. For all that, they'd been a happy family, if a bit mismatched and ragtag, and all thanks to this one lovely man who gave the best hugs in the world.

"Look at you," he said, shaking his head and smiling. "You were a cute kid, but you're a stunner now."

"Stop it. You're such a dad."

"I swear, seeing you come down those stairs gave me an extra six months to live."

"Then I'll go back up and come down again," she said.

"I wish that worked," he said.

"Surprised?"

"You're lucky I didn't have a heart attack when my eldest told me you were here," he said, shaking his head. "Never. I never dreamed… Hoped, yes, but never dreamed."

"I dreamed," she said. "But never hoped."

He kissed her cheek again.

"How long are you staying?" he asked.

"I have to get on the road sometime today," she said. "But no rush."

He didn't seem to like that answer but he didn't argue with her about it, either.

"You been swimming yet?" he asked.

"Swimming? The water's freezing."

"Never used to stop you kids."

"We swam in summer. Need I remind you today is the first day of October?"

"Hmm...how about wading, then?" he asked. "Will you go wading with me?"

"You got back from the hospital two seconds ago," she said, looking over his shoulder at Roland, who'd come in from the kitchen. Roland stood in the kitchen door, quietly smiling at the two of them. It was the first time she'd seen him since last night. He wore the same clothes as yesterday except he'd changed from a yellow-and-black flannel shirt to red and black. There was so much she wanted to talk to him about but that all could wait. It would have to.

"Is he trying to talk you into letting him go skinny-dipping?" Roland asked.

"It's on my bucket list," Dr. Capello said.

"Either get a new bucket or get a new list," Roland said.

"Do you really think we should go to the beach?" Allison asked him.

"I'm tired and I'm dying, but I'm not dead yet. And you better believe I'm going to spend as much time on the beach as I can before I go. With or without you, doll," he said.

He said it all so casually, as if being tired were as much his issue as his dying.

"All right," Allison said. "If Roland approves, we'll go wading. But just wading. You keep your clothes on."

"One of these nights when your backs are all turned..." he said as Roland helped him into a light jacket.

"I'd prefer it if we had as much time with you as possible," Roland said. "If you don't mind."

"No," he said. "I don't mind. I'll keep my clothes on. But only for you. And Allison. And anyone with eyes."

"Thank you. I appreciate that," Roland said. "Now you two go and have fun. Allison, don't let him in past his knees."

Dr. Capello sighed loud as the ocean breeze.

"How old are you now, Allison?" he asked as they walked to the deck door.

"Twenty-five."

"Stay that way, kiddo. Never, ever get old."

Dr. Capello certainly looked older and he looked ill, but Allison couldn't quite wrap her mind around the terrible fact that he was dying, and dying very quickly. He walked slowly, but steadily. The tide was out and the wet, bare sand was packed solid, which made for easy walking when they reached it.

"Now this is nice, isn't it?" Dr. Capello asked as they reached the edge of the water. That afternoon it was blustery and cool, but the sun was out and the water was a bright blue.

"It's perfect," she said. "You come out here a lot?"

"Every chance I get," he said. "Ten years ago, I was out here on a day like today and it was so damn beautiful I said to myself, 'Vince, you've done enough. You've done work you can be proud of. You've helped as many kids as you can. Time to call it quits and enjoy your family.' I quit working that very month. Maybe I should have quit sooner."

"I read the article on the wall in your office. You helped a lot of kids."

"I tried," he said. "I certainly tried. Failed with some. Succeeded beyond my wildest dreams with others. Did my best with the rest."

"No one can ask for more than that from a doctor," she said.

"You could," he said. "Couldn't you?"

She tensed, shrugged. She hadn't planned on having this conversation with him so soon, or ever.

"You did your best with me," she said.

"I failed you, doll. You and I both know it. You would have

been back here to visit years ago if I hadn't. It's all right. You can say it. I carry the guilt with me every day."

He seemed to want to clear the air between them and she admired him for not pretending everything was okay when it wasn't. Pretending things were good when they weren't was one of her talents. "I wanted to come," she said.

A gust of ocean wind blew hard into them, a taste of the chilly autumn days to come.

"Roland said you don't feel safe staying with us, even though he'd like you to."

"Would you feel safe here if you were me?"

"Probably not," he said. She appreciated his honesty.

"I don't know how it all happened. I don't know why. But it still scares me a little," she said. "Wish it didn't."

"Let me ask you this—what do you remember about that whole situation?" he asked.

"Not much," Allison said. "There's an entire week I'm missing in my mind. I remember everyone going to the park but me and Roland." She hoped she wasn't blushing. "After that…nothing much. Isn't there a name for that? When you forget stuff that happened before an injury?"

"Retrograde amnesia," he said. "I was afraid of that. You hit your noggin so hard it scared me, and I fixed kiddo noggins for a living."

"I kind of remember coming to in the hospital and my aunt being there. I'd never met her before, just talked to her on the phone. I definitely remember her telling me I couldn't come back here."

"I can't say I blame your aunt." He stuffed his thin hands deep into the pockets of his too-loose khakis. "But I shouldn't have let her take you. Not without a fight, anyway."

"Can I ask why you didn't fight for me?" she said, and then immediately regretted the question. This was an old man, a dear man, a dying man. Surely it was wrong to give him the third degree five minutes after reuniting.

"Fear," he said. "It's integrity's worst enemy. I was afraid your aunt would fight me for you. I was afraid she'd sue me. I was afraid the state might try to take the kids away from me for letting one of you get hurt so badly on my watch. Your aunt clearly cared about you. I knew you'd be safe in her hands, and I couldn't say for sure anymore you were safe with us."

"So you think someone did push me?" Allison asked.

"I think so, yes. And I even think I know who it was."

"Who?" Allison asked, forgetting in the moment Dr. Capello was old and ill and dying. "Why?"

Dr. Capello grimaced.

"Dad?"

"It's hard," he said. "I took an oath."

Allison understood. The Hippocratic oath. Doctor-patient confidentiality.

"Still..." he said. "I suppose it doesn't really matter anymore. I don't think you're here to have a little boy arrested for a thirteen-year-old crime."

"No, of course not. But if you know something..."

She waited, nearly holding her breath in her nervous excitement.

"You remember Oliver, don't you?"

"Of course," she said.

"He was a very troubled little boy."

"Oliver," Allison said. "I just... I mean, I believe you. You knew his situation better than I did."

"Try not to let it upset you," Dr. Capello said. "He was very young, and I doubt he knew what he was doing."

"But why did he do it?" she asked. "Do you know? I never... I know I never did anything to hurt him."

"Jealousy, I imagine," Dr. Capello said. "He worshipped

the ground Roland walked on and everyone knew you were his favorite."

"I was?"

"Then and now, it seems."

Allison glared at him. Dr. Capello raised his hand, wagged a finger.

"I see I hit a nerve," he said. "When I was a surgeon, I hated hitting nerves. Now that I'm retired, I hit them on purpose."

"Oliver," Allison said, refusing to let him goad her into talking about Roland. "You really think he pushed me and called my aunt? Seriously?"

"I think that boy had motive, means and opportunity. And you better believe he was capable of it. You certainly wouldn't have been the first child he'd hurt. He had problems even I couldn't... I tried, though. I did try everything. That's my one comfort about that boy is that I know I did everything I could for him. Sometimes you slay a dragon. Sometimes you cut off its head and three more grow in its place."

"It was Oliver?"

Dr. Capello exhaled slowly and gave the tersest of nods.

Allison had to turn away from him to collect herself. The article on the wall in Dr. Capello's office mentioned a boy he'd treated and fostered, one who had a tumor that grew back. Was that Oliver? It made so much sense.

"Doll?"

"I know this is going to sound awful," she said, "but I feel like a hundred pound bird flew off my shoulder. I wish I'd known this years ago." She turned back to him and gave him a trembling smile.

"I wish I could have told you," Dr. Capello said. "And it doesn't sound awful. It sounds human."

Allison wanted to laugh in her happiness and relief, but contained herself for Dr. Capello's sake. She knew. She finally knew what had happened to her. Oliver. Poor Oliver, she couldn't even be angry at him. He'd been ill, like Dr. Capello's grandparents. Not evil, but sick.

"Thank you for telling me," she said.

"You're welcome. But please, don't say anything to the kids about this. They don't know and it would upset them. Oliver went back to live with his family right after you left us," Dr. Capello said. "I don't want them blaming him for something he couldn't help. And they were heartbroken when you left us."

"Is that why you never told anyone about the phone call?"

Dr. Capello smiled and started walking again in the wet sand. In Roland's bedside note he'd left her that morning, he'd joked there were "no secrets" in this house. In one day she'd discovered three—the phone call, Rachel and now Oliver attacking her.

"You don't have children, right?" Dr. Capello asked.

"Not yet."

He nodded thoughtfully. "You remember the day I picked you up at Whitney Allen's group home?"

"Yeah, like yesterday," Allison said. "Why?"

"You and another girl at the house had tussled. Or rather, she'd tussled with you and you'd gone running with your tail between your legs."

"Yes, thank you very much for reminding me."

He patted her face again.

"You poor little thing. You broke my heart the second I saw you. Red-cheeked and trying so hard not to cry. Miss Whitney called me to see if I could do anything for you. She said she needed a doctor to make a house call, but I knew she was hoping I'd take you home with me. Don't be hurt by that. Whitney cared about you very much, but she had three other girls in the house—all of them older than you—and they had all finally started to get along. Then a little girl showed up who needed all of her attention and everything was chaos again. It's not easy balancing the needs of multiple kids from different backgrounds. It's like that old circus act—the man spinning the plates, keeping them up in the air, trying to let as few crash to the ground as possible. If I had told the kids that your fall wasn't a fall, that there'd been a call to say there was a killer in the house…well, you can imagine what kind of chaos that would cause. I needed my kids to love each other and trust each other and trust me, too. Can you understand that?"

Allison swallowed a hard lump in her throat. She could hear the note of anguish in Dr. Capello's voice, the note of pleading. He wanted her to understand the choice he'd made. And the thing was, she did.

"Makes sense," she said. "If it had been Thora and not me who'd been pushed and we didn't know who did it? I wouldn't have slept for weeks. I would have been terrified I was next."

"So you understand," he said, nodding. "Oliver left right after you, and I decided to keep it quiet instead of stir up the kids. Please believe me, there hasn't been a day that passed without me wondering if I did right by you. But I can see that you turned out better than I hoped."

"I don't know about that," she said. She helped Dr. Capello take off his shoes and socks and then removed her own. "I'm not doing much with myself. Between jobs."

"You know, a house on the ocean is a fine place to sit and think and figure out what you want to do with your life," he said.

"You think so?"

"I know so," Dr. Capello said. "That's what happened to me. I came here, stood on the deck, looked at the ocean, looked at a big family with kids playing in the water and I knew that's what I wanted. And then I went out and got it.

You'll get it, too, if you stay long enough. The water will tell you what to do." He pulled his khaki trousers up and waded into the water up to his ankles. "Heaven," he said with a happy sigh.

Allison followed him into the ocean, wincing at the sudden shock of cold water on her feet.

"I didn't think you believed in heaven," she said. "Deacon said you're a humanist."

"Junior's been gossiping, huh? Not surprised. That boy's a blabbermouth—God love him, someone has to," he said.

"We were talking about Rachel," she said. "And why she's the reason Roland's at the monastery."

Dr. Capello winced. "Sore subject."

"Sorry, forget I brought it up," she said.

"No, no, no." He waved his hand again. "Better to talk about it. I love my son. I want him to be happy. I simply would prefer he didn't devote his life to an institution that I consider to be an enemy of human progress out of some misguided guilt for a long-ago tragedy."

Allison's eyes widened. "Enemy of human progress? Those are some strong words."

"Too strong, I know," he said with a sigh. "But I'm a scientist. We can't count on the pie-in-the-sky man to fix our problems. Mankind causes its own problems. It's up to mankind to solve them."

"Maybe it helps Roland feel more at peace about Rachel."

"He's not going to bring her back into the world by taking himself out of it."

"He says he needs God," she told him.

"What he needs is a damn girlfriend," Dr. Capello said.

"Be nice," she said, chiding him as though she was the parent now and he the child. "You have to admit there's good reason for believing in God and heaven and hell, even if they aren't strictly real."

"Give me one good reason to believe in heaven or hell, I dare you."

"Evil?" she said. "Surely Hitler deserves to burn in hell, right? Rapists? Child abusers? Nobody wants them to get off scot-free."

"Spoken like a poet," he said. "Not a scientist. There is no such thing as evil."

Allison boggled at him.

"You're kidding, right?" she asked.

"There are evil acts, yes. I grant you that. Murder. Rape. Child abuse. Absolutely those are evil acts if by evil we mean 'harmful to the human race.' But they aren't caused by a red man with a pitchfork sitting on our shoulder. Take Oliver, for instance. He harmed animals, harmed children, lied about it without compunction or remorse. All the hallmarks of classic psychopathy. Was he evil? No, ma'am. He was sick. That's all."

"Is that what causes people to be psychopaths?" she asked. "Brain tumors?"

"Sometimes a tumor in the frontal lobe can profoundly affect the personality. Or lead poisoning in my grandparents' case. Most people who fit the criteria for psychopathy are simply born with it. They have atrophy in key areas of the brain—the limbic region, the hippocampus, et cetera. In layman's terms, they are born with broken brains. That's the worst hand any child can be dealt."

"So not actually evil, then?"

"Not evil. Sick. He was sick, and I tried to cure him. Didn't work but give it a couple decades and we'll have it all figured out."

"A cure for evil?"

"A cure for evil is possible," he said, nodding. "Mark my words."

"I'll mark them," she said. "And if you love me, you'll live long enough to tell me 'I told you so.'"

"I'll do my best, doll. Count on it."

He took her arm in his and they strolled side by side into deeper waters. The ocean was cool enough to make her wince but not cold enough to send her running.

Dr. Capello looked happy, contented, but there were moments, little ones, when she saw the fear hiding behind his mask. Once, he stopped, simply stopped, and let the water swirl around his feet while he stared and stared and stared out into the water. Side by side they watched the waves roll in and break, roll out and break again. His shoulders sagged.

"Is it hard?" Allison asked. "Dying?"

"It is," he said, nodding. "I wish I could say otherwise. But you've never heard of a happy person committing suicide, have you? I love my life. I love my children. I love my house. I love this ocean. I love every grain of sand under my feet. What's that old poem? Only a happy heart can break?"

"Almost," Allison said, and then recited the poem to him from memory.

"It will not hurt me when I am old,
A running tide where moonlight burned
Will not sting me like silver snakes;
The years will make me sad and cold,
It is the happy heart that breaks."

When she finished, Dr. Capello applauded. She gave him a little curtsy.

"Sara Teasdale," she said.

"The world needs people who can recite poetry from memory. My mother could, too. *Kubla Khan* was her favorite to recite. She loved those lines—'Where Alph, the sacred river, ran / Through caverns measureless to man...'"

"'Down to a sunless sea,'" Allison said, finishing the quotation for him.

"Ah, sweet memories. A thousand of them came running back to me with those words." He patted her face tenderly. "You are staying, aren't you? I know a very nice young man who'd be thrilled if you did," he said with a wink.

"You want me to stay so I can seduce Roland out of the monastery?"

"If you don't mind," he said. "I'd appreciate it."

"I do mind," she said. "That's terrible." She laughed despite herself.

"I love my son," he said. "And if I have to play dirty pool to make sure he's happy and healthy and living a good life, you bet I'll do it."

"What if he's happy in the monastery?"

"He's hiding in the monastery, punishing himself, and it kills me to know it. You really want that for him?"

"Well...no. Not unless that's—"

"You said you remember the day I met you at Miss Whitney's, right?"

"Right."

"You remember that you asked me to take you home with me?"

"I remember," she said, nodding.

"And I did, didn't I?"

"You did, yes."

"Well, now I'm asking you to return the favor. Stay here with us. A few more days, a week, a month."

"You're playing matchmaker. It's not going to work."

"It's working already," he said. "And yes, I am. Shamelessly.

Allison, I do not want to die knowing my son is going to spend the rest of his life in that prison of his own making. It makes me sick to my very bones to think of it. He had a childhood that broke his heart and mine, and I'm not about to let him spend the rest of his life punishing himself for something he did as a child. This is my final wish, doll. Will you help me?"

Allison swallowed a hard lump in her throat at the sight of the tears in Dr. Capello's eyes. He meant it. It did kill him that Roland had left the world for the monastery. How could she say no to this man, this dear old dying man who'd brought her home with him to his children's paradise? And now she knew who'd hurt her, so there was no reason not to, right?

"This is dirty pool," she said.

"I have no shame," he said. "I'll beg if I have to."

"Fine," she said. "I'll stay for a few days. But just for you."

He pulled her into his arms for a long hug.

"Just for me?" he said, his tone teasing.

"And Roland. Just a little tiny bit for Roland."

"Just for me and Roland?" he asked.

"Oh," she said, finally giving in. "Maybe for me, too."

CHAPTER 15

A name. She finally had a name, and it was such a relief. *Oliver*. And now that she thought about it, really thought about it, it did make a little bit of sense. She and Oliver had never been close, not the way she was close with Roland or Thora or Kendra. Even she and Deacon played together. But Oliver… He'd come here right after Christmas her last year at The Dragon, and they'd never bonded. While sweet, he was a solitary sort. He'd sit in the same room with her and Roland as they worked on homework or watched TV, but he never interacted much with her, never joked around. When she remembered him, what she remembered was his silence, his self-imposed solitude. Lonesome even in a house full of children. At the time she thought he was merely homesick, but depression often masked itself as anger and vice versa. Was he sad when he watched her and Roland talking? Or was he seething? Oliver had been smart, very smart, always bringing home A's from school. She could believe he was capable of planning a prank as elaborate as calling her aunt and faking her voice. It wouldn't be hard. Cry a lot, pant and scream. Make the call quick and hang up without answering questions.

So Allison had her answer.

Mystery solved. And now she had one very good reason to stay here—she wanted to—and no reason at all to leave. She had nothing to be afraid of anymore.

So why was she still scared?

Roland, of course. She wasn't close to being ready for another relationship. She'd been dumped all of three days ago. Staying here was a mistake. She knew it was a mistake. But it was an honest mistake because she honestly wanted to stay, especially now that she knew she was safe at her old home. At least her body was safe. When Roland smiled at her when she came back into the house on Dr. Capello's arm, she knew her heart was in mortal peril.

For lunch Roland served comfort food—tomato soup and grilled cheese—and she let herself enjoy every bite. She was a kid again for a few minutes, safe at home with her family with nothing to worry about. Deacon skipped lunch because of work, he said. Thora, he said, desperately needed him at the glass shop.

"Can I go with you?" Allison asked him as he made a quick pass through the kitchen to steal the sandwich crust off his father's plate.

"You want to see the shop?" Deacon asked, downing the toast in one bite.

"If no one minds," Allison said.

"Go," Roland said. "It's Dad's nap time, anyway." He was already steering Dr. Capello out of the kitchen, his large hand on his father's too-thin shoulder.

"See, doll?" Dr. Capello said. "That used to be my line. Never get old, Allison. Never get old."

"I won't, I promise," she said, watching as Roland followed Dr. Capello up the stairs.

"Did she let you skinny-dip?" she heard Roland ask his father.

"She didn't, damn her," Dr. Capello said.

"Good. If you get arrested for indecent exposure, we're leaving you in jail," Roland said. "I love you, but nobody needs to see that."

"You go skinny-dip," Dr. Capello said to him. "Since I can't."

"I'm trying to impress Allison," Roland said. "Cold water is no man's friend."

"Youth is wasted on the young."

"And wisdom is wasted on the old since you're clearly not using yours."

The back-and-forth continued all the way up to the third floor. Allison's eyes burned with unshed tears as she listened to the gruff and tender bickering between father and son. She was in danger in this house, but not from violence—unless it was the violence of her own feelings. This was a family, the one she'd wanted all her life. This was love in the rough— the coal, not the diamond. There was nothing pretty about a dying man leaning on a son who can't save him though he'd give his right arm to do so. Allison felt warmth all the way to her core. This moment was everything she ever wanted from McQueen but never got because she'd never asked. Allison hastily wiped a tear from her cheek but it was too late. She'd been caught in the act.

"Pathetic," said Deacon. Allison turned and saw him standing in the kitchen doorway shaking his head.

"I know," she said, wrinkling her nose. "But they're so cute."

"They're terrified," Deacon said. "And they're hiding it from each other."

That brought Allison back down to earth.

"It's so hard to believe," she said. "He's thin. He's old. But he seems okay."

"Dad's doctor told us kidney failure was a 'gentle' death. That's the word she used. *Gentle*. Gentle for who? The doctors? We don't want him in pain. But if he were suffering, at least we could tell ourselves dying would be a relief for him. A release from the pain, I guess. This way it feels like he's being stolen from us." Deacon looked past her as if he was too raw to make eye contact. "Remind me to die fast. I don't want anyone knowing it's coming. Not even me. Basically I want to be murdered. And I want it to make the news. National news. Postmortem dismemberment is a bonus."

"Which member?" Allison asked.

"Lady's choice. I assume it's a woman killing me. Thora, most likely."

It seemed it wasn't just Roland and Dr. Capello hiding their fears behind jokes.

"Well," Allison said, "best of luck with that."

"Thanks, sis. Ready?"

"Not quite." She reached into her pocket and pulled out the key chain can of spray he'd given her. She knew who'd hurt her. She didn't need it anymore. That she and Deacon could joke around like old times was proof she trusted him.

He raised his eyebrow but didn't take the spray out of her hand.

"Keep it," he said. "A welcome home gift."

"You're weird, you know that, right?"

"Stop hitting on me, Allison."

Allison and Deacon drove separately into town—he on his motorcycle and she in her rental car. She didn't blame him for wanting to take out his bike on these last good days before the rain started up. Once it got going, it might be next summer before they saw anything but steel-gray clouds again.

Allison followed Deacon all the way north to Clark Beach, the quaint little tourist town where Dr. Capello had taken them every Saturday to visit the library, get ice cream and look through the telescopes on the beach. Though it was October and the summer tourists were long gone, the streets were still lively with locals taking advantage of one of the last good days of the year to come to the coast, walk on the white sand and watch the puffins and terns playing on the enormous rock stacks at the edge of the water. So little had changed since Allison was last there she almost expected to see a bearded man in khakis and a cardigan walking down the sidewalk with four or five or six or seven kids behind him doing impressive damage to their ice-cream cones.

Deacon turned into a tiny parking lot next to a gray-shingled, two-story house. Over the glass front door hung a painted sign that read The Glass Dragon.

"This is my baby," Deacon said as she joined him on the sidewalk. The front window of the shop was filled entirely with one glass sculpture—a green-and-gold Chinese dragon, four feet high, five feet long and grinning with manic amphibious joy. The face was astonishingly expressive and the detail on the claws and the scales and the individual dots of color on its dappled skin took Allison's breath away.

"You did this?" she asked Deacon.

"You like it?"

"It's amazing."

"You want one?"

"Might not fit in my suitcase," she said.

"Get a bigger suitcase," Deacon said, leading her through the front door. Before Allison could look around the shop, she heard a sound—almost a gasp, almost a squeak.

Allison saw a woman walking toward her—fiery red hair,

tall and fiercely lovely. She grabbed Allison in a rough embrace that almost knocked the wind out of her.

"Good to see you again, too," Allison said to Thora, and though the words were slightly sarcastic, Allison was surprised by how deeply she meant them. Until she'd seen Thora again, she'd forgotten how much she'd missed her sister. While Allison had worshipped Roland and adored Deacon, she'd simply loved Thora. Her silly big sister. And Thora *had* been silly—a quirky, kooky kid through and through. She'd called Allison by a different pet name every day—Rascal and Rainmaker, Pilgrim and Tenderfoot. "Blow on my homework, High Roller. Luck be a straight A tonight," Thora would say as Allison dutifully blew on her assignments like they were dice. Thora did Allison's hair for her, helped her pick out her clothes for school, helped her buy her first bra, taught her how to shave her legs but told her she never had to if she didn't want to. Georgia O'Keeffe had been Thora's patron saint. Allison's first taste of feminism had come from Thora, and Allison was forever grateful she'd had someone so sweet to help her through those first harrowing days of puberty. Thora had been both a sister and a substitute mother to Allison, a crazy, wonderful woman who apparently still wore her hair in pigtails at the age of twenty-eight, and as she rocked Allison in her arms, both of them wept.

"Why are you back?" Thora whispered. "I never thought you'd come back."

It wasn't quite the greeting Allison expected, more stunned than happy.

"Roland asked me to," Allison said. Thora pulled back and held her by the upper arms. Thora's eyes were red-rimmed with tears as they searched Allison's face.

"I couldn't believe it," Thora said. "When they told me you showed up last night, I just... I couldn't believe it."

"Believe it," Deacon said. "That's her. I checked."

"You really thought you'd never see me again?" Allison asked.

Thora glanced over at Deacon and then met Allison's eyes again.

"You know, after all that happened," Thora said.

"All in the past," Allison said. Dr. Capello had hinted he'd prefer she not discuss Oliver with anyone. Even Thora.

"Good," Thora said and hugged her again.

"Come on, Al. Enough hugging. I want to show you the hot shop," Deacon said. He waved her through the small front room and then through an industrial-looking metal door. The second she stepped through the door, Allison was hit with a blast of heat.

"Wow, that's hot," she said, blinking. "I think my face melted."

"You get used to it," Deacon said as he stripped out of his leather jacket down to his sleeveless T-shirt.

"I thought the no-sleeves thing was because you like to show off your tattoos," Allison said. "I see now it has a practical benefit."

"No," Thora said, coming in behind them. "It's to show off the tattoos."

Allison took off her own jacket. She'd already started sweating.

"Truth," Deacon said, and Thora rolled her eyes. "This is the hot shop. Named because it is really hot."

"How hot?" Allison asked.

"Ninety," Thora said, glancing at a thermometer on the wall. "Ninety in the room. About a thousand in there."

She pointed at a large round floor-to-ceiling oven.

"A thousand degrees?" Allison repeated.

"Fahrenheit," Deacon said. "This is the crucible." He

opened the door to the oven and Allison saw an orange glow emanating from inside. "It's the reason our electric bill is four thousand dollars a month."

"You're kidding," Allison said.

"Good thing I make bank doing this," Deacon said as he grabbed a long metal pole and twirled it in his hands.

"What are you doing with that pole?" Allison asked, suspicious.

"This is the pipe," he said. "Not a pole. A pipe."

"Pipe. Got it."

"This—" he pointed at something that looked kind of like an open flame gas grill "—is the pipe warmer. The pipe is room temperature now, and we have to get it hot so the molten glass will stick to it."

He put the end of the pipe in the pipe warmer and turned it rapidly.

"How heavy is that thing?"

"Oh…twenty pounds or so?"

"So this is how you got the Popeye forearms," Allison said.

"You turn a twenty-pound steel pipe for hours every day for five years and you'll get pretty good arms, too."

"Don't stroke his ego," Thora said to her. "He's already impossible to live with. Artists. Can't live with them. Can't stuff their bodies in the crucible."

Allison laughed. The Twins were still the Twins, through and through.

"So, you run the shop?" Allison asked Thora as she took a seat far away from the action. The hot shop looked more like a mad scientist's laboratory to her than an artist's studio. Everywhere she looked, she saw large and dangerous equipment—steel pipes and blazing ovens, blowtorches and jars upon jars of color chips in every hue of the rainbow and then some.

"Yep," Thora said. "I do all the bookkeeping, the accounting, pay the bills, set up museum showings, arrange payment for the pieces he sells. Honestly, dealing with shipping his monsters is the hardest part of the job."

"Does he sell a lot?" Allison asked as Thora pulled a metal chair next to her.

"A lot," she said, nodding. "Last week we sold a pair of dragons like the one in the window to a hotel in Seattle. Sixty K."

Allison blinked. She had to sleep with McQueen for six years to get fifty out of him.

"Holy… Guess that pays the electric bill," Allison said.

"He pretends to be arrogant," Thora whispered, "but it's a cover-up for his modesty. He's becoming very well-known as one of the foremost glass artists in the world."

"That's fantastic," Allison said. "Our brother is a famous artist."

"No autographs, please," Deacon said, and winked at her.

Deacon finally pulled the pipe out of the warmer. "Come here, Al. I'll show you how to sculpt glass."

"Me?" Allison said, pointing at herself and looking around.

"You," Deacon said. "Come on. I taught Dad, I taught Thor, I taught Ro. I can teach you."

"Are you sure this is safe?" Allison asked as she crept from her chair over to the giant round furnace near the wall.

"Safe enough," he said. "Long as you don't do something actively stupid, we'll be fine."

"Okay, I'll stick to passively stupid. What now?"

"Gathering glass," he said, opening the small round hole to the crucible. As soon as that door opened, Allison felt her mascara melt and congeal. She stepped back, watching from a safe distance as Deacon inserted the pipe into the crucible and started to rotate it again. Standing up on her tiptoes she peeked in and saw a round blob of orange goo taking shape at the end of Deacon's pipe.

"What are we making?" Allison asked him.

"You wanted a dragon, didn't you?"

"It'll have to be a baby dragon," she said. "My rental car's a compact."

"I can make a baby dragon," Deacon said. "Go to the jars over there and pick out a color."

Allison eyed the jars and picked a blue halfway between sea and sky.

"Now what?" she asked.

Thora came over and took the jar from Allison's hand, opened it and spread color chips the size of Legos on a metal table.

"Step back a little," Deacon said as he brought the spinning orange blob of glass to the table. He dipped the ball into the color chips and they instantly melted into the blazing-hot glass.

"I'm going to do the hard part now," Deacon said. "But you're going to twist the tail. Ready?"

"For what?" Allison asked.

"To be impressed," Deacon said, grinning again.

"Ready," she said.

Deacon carried the blue blob on his pipe to a wooden stand. He grabbed giant metal tongs, dipped them into a bucket of water and before Allison could wrap her mind around his movements, he'd begun to spin the pipe and pinch the molten glass with his tongs. In seconds it seemed, the little ball turned into a vague lizard shape and then into a dragon with ears like a puppy and a scaly spine.

"That's so bizarre," Allison breathed. "You're pulling glass like taffy."

"Fun fact," Deacon said. "Glass isn't quite a solid or a liquid. It's its own weird thing."

"It doesn't seem right that you can do that. It looks so solid," Allison said.

"It's already solidifying," Deacon said. "Better make this quick."

He dipped his tongs back into the water bucket and then passed them to her.

"What do I do?" she asked.

"Pull and twist, twist and pull," Deacon said. "I'm talking about the glass, by the way."

Allison grabbed the dragon's tail with the tip of the tongs and did as Deacon asked, wincing as the glass stretched and turned and twisted.

"It's like a piggy tail," Thora said, kneeling at the stand to eye the creature. "He's very cute."

"He's supposed to be scary," Deacon said as he put on a large oven mitt. Using a wooden block he knocked the dragon off the end of the pipe and onto his gloved hand. "Maybe I can put some big teeth in his mouth."

"No, I like him cute," Allison said. And it *was* cute, this blue-green little beast with scales and claws and small enough to fit into the palms of her two hands. It was so cute she instinctively reached out to touch it. Thora immediately shoved Deacon so hard the dragon dropped out of his glove. When it landed on the floor, it didn't break, but merely splatted like blue pancake batter.

"Oh, shit, I'm sorry," Allison said.

"You okay?" Deacon asked, eyes wide.

"Fine, fine. Just…forgot it was still warm."

"Warm?" Deacon said. "It's nine-hundred degrees. You would have burned your hand off."

"So much for not doing anything actively stupid," Allison said, on the verge of tears. "I'm sorry. I didn't mean to break it."

"I can make another one in five minutes," Deacon said. "Can't make another Allison. Good reflexes, Thor."

Allison laughed that sort of relieved, terrified laugh of someone who'd dodged a bullet. But Thora wasn't laughing. She grabbed Allison and hugged her tight again.

"You okay?" Thora asked.

"I'm fine. Except I feel like an idiot," she said. "You saved me from a dragon. You should be knighted."

"Sisters protect each other," Thora said. "Right?"

"Right," Allison said, trying to smile through her shaking. Thora had shoved Deacon so hard he probably had a bruise on his arm.

After the almost-tragedy, none of them were in the mood to keep playing in the hot shop. Deacon and Thora quickly finished up their paperwork while Allison poked around the front of the shop where Deacon's premade items were for sale. Glass wind chimes, glass Christmas ornaments and her favorite—hourglasses filled with sand from Clark Beach.

She paused and studied one particularly strange glass sculpture sitting on a shelf—a skull with a large hole in the top.

"What's this?" she asked. "You make a boo-boo, Deacon?" Allison pointed to the hole the head.

Deacon stood up and turned her way, his hand resting on Thora's shoulder.

"Don't ask what that is," Deacon said. "Ask who."

"Okay," Allison said, happy to bite. "Who is this?"

"That's Phineas Gage," Deacon said. "He's the guy who got the iron rod shot through his head in the 1800s. I think he was a railroad worker."

"Oh, yeah," Allison said, eyeing the quarter-sized hole in the glass skull. "I remember reading about him in high school. He survived, right?"

"Sort of," Thora said. "He had a completely different

personality after the accident. He was nice and polite and hard-working before. After the injury, he swore all the time, couldn't hold a job very well. Dad said Phineas is the reason the science of neuroscience exists. People realized the personality is partly in the frontal lobe because of him. But don't be impressed by Deacon's nerdy art. He was trying to make a skeleton for Halloween. He popped a hole in that skull like a balloon, and then he pretended it was supposed to be Phineas Gage."

"Hush, wench," Deacon said. "I totally meant to do that."

Allison rolled her eyes and let them get back to work.

What a picture-perfect life they led—a successful art gallery and studio in a quaint and scenic coastal town steps from the beach and half a mile from dense old-growth forest. More than that, however, Allison simply envied Deacon and Thora because of Deacon and Thora. Thora sat at her desk, Deacon hovering behind her chair as they quietly planned the weeks and months ahead—a gallery showing in Vancouver, a seminar Deacon would teach at a local college in summer. They were a brother-sister dream team, good partners making a successful business together. Even after Dr. Capello passed away and Roland returned to the monastery, Deacon and Thora would still have this shop and each other.

"Done," Deacon said as he came out from behind Thora's desk. "Sorry that took so long."

"It's fine. I love your store," Allison said. "This place is like my dream come true."

"You want to own a glass studio?" he asked.

"Bookstore, but close enough."

"Why don't you head home and check on Dad," Thora said to Deacon as she switched off her computer. "I want to catch up with Allison."

Deacon gave Thora a quick questioning look but then it was gone again in a flash.

"Sure," he said. "See you two at home." He headed out the door. A few seconds later, Allison heard his motorcycle rev up and disappear down the road. Thora locked up and they walked to Allison's car together.

"I am sorry about almost, you know, burning my hand off," Allison said once they were inside her car.

"We have liability insurance," Thora said with a wave of her hand.

"Should I head straight home?" Allison asked. "Or do you need me to take some detours so you can drill me longer about Roland?"

"Ah," Thora said, wrinkling her nose. "Busted. Well, you better take a detour."

Allison headed south to Cape Arrow but didn't rush.

"There's not much to talk about," Allison said.

"You two did sleep together, right?"

"We're adults, and he's already told me he plans on going back to the monastery. I know what I'm doing." She hoped she did, anyway.

Thora nodded and stared out the car window as Allison drove.

"Was it weird to see him again?" Thora asked.

"It was," Allison said. "Good weird. I was pretty in love with him when I was a kid."

"Yeah, you were," Thora said. "Made me nervous."

"Nervous? Why?"

Thora shrugged. "You were both kids, but he was almost five years older than you. I didn't want you getting your heart broken."

"Not twelve anymore," Allison said.

"True," Thora said. "Thirteen years is a long time ago and you were what, twelve? Do you even remember us?"

"I remember the good stuff," Allison said. "Roland reading to us and letting me turn the pages. All of us playing Mario Kart and Deacon beating the pants off us every time. And you taught me to ride a bike."

"Right. In the school parking lot," Thora said. "You and me and Dad. We made the boys all stay home because they made you so nervous."

"They were too competitive," Allison said. "I wasn't trying to win the Tour de France."

"What else do you remember?"

"Oh, lots of things," Allison said. "What I don't remember is my fall and the days before it happened."

"You don't remember what happened before?"

"All gone," Allison said. "Nothing after the day, ah...you all went to the park and Roland and I stayed home. Why?" Dr. Capello had asked her the same thing, what she remembered before her fall. Same answer. Nothing.

"Just curious."

"Do you remember the day I fell?" Allison asked, trying to keep her eye on the winding highway and watch Thora's face at the same time.

"I remember hearing Dad scream. I ran out of the bedroom and saw Dad kneeling over you on the floor. It was terrifying."

"You ran out of the bedroom?" Allison asked.

"Yeah, I was in there...reading. Or something."

"You weren't outside?"

"No, why?"

"Deacon thought he remembered you were outside with him when it happened."

"Oh," Thora said. She smiled but it was a brittle smile, like it was made of thin glass. "Yeah, that's right. We were outside together."

Allison smiled, though her stomach tightened.

"Long time ago," Allison said. "Easy to forget things."

They drove on a little longer and Allison stayed quiet. She wanted Thora to do the talking. Thora hated silence, always had. Eventually she'd open up again and say something.

"I'm worried about you staying with us," Thora said.

"What? Why?" That wasn't what Allison had been expecting, not at all.

"Dad's dying. You don't want to be around for that, do you? I've lived with him all my life and I don't want to be around for it."

"Do you want me to go?"

"I'm…I'm very happy to see you again," Thora said. "I could cry I'm so happy. I thought… I was scared you were gone forever. But for your own sake, not mine, I think you'd be better off going. It's not going to be pretty."

"I won't overstay my welcome, I promise."

"That's not what I'm worried about."

"Then what are you worried about?" Allison asked.

"Oh," Thora said. "The usual. Everything. Roland especially. I'm my brother's keeper."

"And sister's?"

"Maybe," Thora said. She reached over and squeezed Allison's knee. "If you stay, I'll want to keep you."

"You wouldn't be the first person to keep me."

Thora looked at her out of the corner of her eye. "You have dirt to tell your big sissy?" Thora batted her eyelashes.

"If you want dirt, I got dirt."

"Good dirt?"

"Sex with a horny billionaire dirt."

Thora raised both hands and shook them in frenzied excitement.

"That's the best kind of dirt. Head south. I don't care if we end up in Big Sur, I gotta hear this," Thora said as she took off her cardigan to get comfortable. It was then that Allison noticed something hanging off the belt loop of her jeans.

A little can of pepper spray.

CHAPTER 16

When they arrived back at The Dragon, Thora disappeared upstairs into her bedroom and Allison did the same. It was a relief to be completely alone again. She'd gotten used to spending her days by herself, and she'd probably talked more in the past twenty-four hours than she had in the last few weeks combined. She hadn't asked Thora about the pepper spray. She'd never thought of coastal Oregon as a high crime area, but she couldn't blame any woman for wanting to have a little protection on her. Still…it seemed odd that Deacon would want both his sisters to carry pepper spray. What was he afraid of around here?

The quiet and the solitude didn't last long. Roland knocked on her door about an hour later, and by that time, she was ready for company again, especially tall, broad-shouldered, handsome company.

"Hey, you," she said as she let him into her room. "How's Dad?"

"Resting and reading," Roland said. "You?"

"Reading and resting." She sat on a white wicker rocking

chair in the corner of the room. Roland sat across from her on the bed.

"You had fun with Thora and Deacon?" he asked.

She considered asking him about the pepper spray but decided to keep that to herself for now.

"Did they tell you I nearly killed myself today?" she asked.

"What made you think touching nine-hundred-degree molten glass was a good idea?" he asked.

"It was cute."

"Third-degree burns, however, are *not* cute."

"True," she said, nodding sheepishly. "It was so odd, though. It looked like normal glass, but when it fell it was goo."

"The first time Dad sculpted glass with Deacon, he said it felt like messing with the brain again because it's not quite solid, not quite liquid and really dangerous."

"I can see that," she said, recalling how unnatural it felt to be able to pull and mold thick heavy glass like putty. "I promise to remain a spectator in the future."

"Please. Deacon's tattoos are half art, half covering up burn scars on his arms."

"Thora saved me," Allison said. "I owe her."

"She's a good kid," Roland said. "So...are you freaked out?"

"About almost burning my hands off?"

"About last night." He looked adorably young and uncomfortable sitting there on the bed, not quite meeting her eyes.

"Last night was lovely," she said, and stretched out her legs and rested her feet on Roland's thighs. "You freaked out by it?"

"I had a moment this morning when I woke up in bed with you. And you were there all naked and beautiful, and I thought, *Yup, gotta go to confession today.*"

She laughed. "Did you?"

"I'm keeping a list. When I have an even dozen, I'll hit up Father Larry for absolution."

"How many sins do you have on your list?"

"After last night, two more," he said.

"Need a hand reaching a baker's dozen?" she asked.

Roland raised his eyebrow at her.

"You're bad," he said, pointing his finger at her. "It's the middle of the day."

"Ever heard of a nooner? McQueen used to squeeze me in between his breakfast and lunch meetings. You can squeeze me in before dinner, can't you?"

"I'd rather take my time."

"You say such sweet things," she said. "But I know how wicked you are."

Roland's eyes widened. "What did you hear?" he asked. "Do I want to know?"

"Deacon said you, him and Thora used to smoke pot up in the attic."

Roland's head fell back in annoyance.

"That was years ago. *Years*," he said. "We haven't done that since I was a teenager."

"You sure about that?" she asked. "You're being awfully defensive."

"Not once in eleven years," he said.

Allison tapped her foot on his leg.

"Okay, maybe once," he said. "Right after I came home from the monastery. Deacon made me do it."

"That better be on your sin list for Father Larry."

"It is, promise."

"What else is on your sin list?"

"That's between me and Jesus."

Allison took her feet off his lap and stood up in front of

him. He put his hands on her waist and she wrapped her arms around his shoulders.

"Here," she said. "One more for your list."

She kissed him, a deep kiss but a quick one. When Roland returned the kiss, Allison pushed him onto his back.

It didn't take much more than that to convince Roland to squeeze her in before dinner. She crawled on top of him, but Roland rolled her onto her back. He stripped her clothes from her quickly but not quick enough for her. She unzipped his jeans and guided him into her before he even had time to take his flannel shirt off. He slowly moved into her and she groaned with pleasure. Roland buried his face between her breasts and laughed softly.

"What?" she said.

He lifted his head and put a finger over his lips.

"Dad's directly above us," he whispered.

"Oops," she said, wrinkling her nose. "I'll try to be quiet."

"Thank you," he mouthed, and started moving inside her again. She pressed her face to his chest, relishing the warmth of his body and the feel of his flannel shirt on her cheek, soft and well-worn with age and too many washings. But she wanted to feel his skin against her, so she quickly undid one button at a time while he braced himself over her, then pushed it down and off his arms.

He was good at being quiet while making love, and she wondered if that was simple discipline or embarrassment. McQueen had made her shameless, so it wasn't easy for her to stifle her moans and gasps, especially when Roland touched her throat the way she loved. A groan escaped her lips and Roland pressed his hand over her mouth. She giggled behind his palm and felt his laughter rumbling through his body.

"Shh…" he breathed into her ear, and she couldn't stop herself from giggling again. Roland pushed two fingers into her mouth and in an instant the room disappeared, transformed into another darker room. The blue bed was gone and she lay on a bare cot. The air was no longer light and cool and salt-scented from the open window, but hot and close and musty. And it wasn't Roland's fingers inside her mouth but something hard and cruel, shoved between her teeth.

Allison turned her head to gulp air and Roland rose up over her.

"You okay?" he asked, his eyes wide and worried.

"I'm fine," she said, panting.

"You don't seem fine."

"I think…I think I gagged on your fingers."

"Sorry, I'm sorry," he said. "I didn't mean to hurt you."

"No, it's okay," she said. "I'm fine now."

She kissed him to prove she was okay, but he didn't kiss her back at first. Had he seen the truth—that she'd been on the verge of full-blown panic? That she'd suddenly disappeared into what felt like an incredibly vivid memory? Eventually he returned her kisses and she relaxed underneath him. But the magic was gone from the moment. He came a few minutes later but she couldn't. Afterward she slipped on Roland's flannel shirt and rested her head on his chest.

"Okay, time to tell me what happened there," he said as he stroked her hair.

"I don't know."

"*Something* happened."

"I…" She rested on her elbow and met his eyes. "I had some kind of flashback or something."

"A flashback? Of what?"

"Nothing that makes sense," she said. "I was on some kind of cot, like a hospital bed, and someone was pushing something in my mouth."

"Do you remember what?" Roland asked. He searched her face as he spoke and she saw the concern in his eyes.

"It tasted kind of like...plastic?" she said, shaking her head as if she could dislodge a memory like shaking a Magic 8-Ball.

He took a moment to think. "You know, that could have been a memory of you being intubated in the ER after you fell," he said. "I've seen it done. It's horrible. It could traumatize anyone."

"That makes sense," she said. She closed her eyes and willed herself to remember it all again, but nothing new came back. Yet, it was undeniable that something about being in this house again was bringing memories to the surface she'd long ago forgotten or buried.

"It hit me when you pushed your fingers in my mouth. It's gone again."

"I'm sorry," he said. "But you moaned, 'Oh, fuck, Roland,' and, well, you know..." He pointed at the ceiling.

"I think your dad knows about us," she said in a stage whisper.

"True, but I'd like to be able to make eye contact with the man later."

"You're blushing," she said. "It's cute. Do all monks blush after sex?"

"Yes," he said. "Although most of us skip the sex and get right to the blushing." He kissed her forehead. "You okay now?"

"Better."

"How much better?" he asked, kissing her neck under her ear.

"Are you trying to have sex with me again?" she asked.

"You didn't come, did you?"

"You *are* trying to have sex with me again."

"Yes? No? Maybe?" he asked, kissing her cheek, then her lips and her throat and her chest.

Yes. Definitely yes.

After they finished, Roland stole his flannel shirt back, left her grinning on the bed and went to make dinner while she cleaned herself up. Her shower cleared her head and she regretted that she couldn't be more honest with Roland. She'd always played her cards close to the chest with McQueen but that was because of the nature of their relationship—the sex was professional, not personal. She didn't want to have that sort of distance with Roland. But what could she do? Deacon had begged her not to ask Roland about his sister, Rachel. Dr. Capello had instructed her not to tell anyone he thought Oliver was the culprit behind her "accident" and the phone call to her aunt. And what was there to say about Thora forgetting where she was when Allison had her fall? Allison couldn't even remember where she'd been when she fell—how could she expect anyone else to remember?

Still, she didn't like how many topics of conversation were off-limits in this house. Too many. But she'd only been home for a day. Not like she had any right to barge in while Dr. Capello was dying and make everyone miserable by dredging up ancient history. But there were things she needed to know. Since she couldn't ask, she would figure them out on her own. Luckily it seemed the house was on her side. So far she'd been here less than twenty-four hours and she already remembered more than she had in years. The kiss on the beach. The attic door. Roland's fingers in her mouth. What memory would the house offer up to her next?

At six, they all convened in the kitchen for dinner. It should have made for a pleasant meal, the five of them together again, making small talk about the weather, happy memories and Thora and Deacon's work at the gallery, but Allison sensed quiet tension. She was worried at first she was the cause of it, until she noticed that Dr. Capello wasn't eating but merely pretending to. Food moved on his plate but didn't disappear.

Allison said nothing, knowing it wasn't her place, but then Roland said, "Dad, you have to eat something."

"You know what they say," Dr. Capello said. "I only have to pay taxes and die. And I'm all paid up for the year."

"Dad," Roland said.

"Allison, would you please take my son for a walk on the beach? Or anywhere? Off a cliff maybe."

"Maybe I'll go back to the monastery where I'm appreciated," Roland said as he started to stand.

"And celibate." Deacon muttered the words but everyone heard him.

Roland looked at Deacon, glared at him, in fact, then slowly sat back down. Thora laughed so hard she nearly shot water out of her nose. Meanwhile Allison blushed like a monk. Embarrassing as it was, Deacon's snark was exactly what the dinner needed. The tension dissipated, and for the first time Allison felt truly back at home.

"Just for that," Dr. Capello said, "I'll try to eat something."

After dinner she and Roland did go for their walk on the beach while Deacon and Thora washed and dried the dishes.

"I'm going to be laughing all night at you sitting back down at the table," Allison said.

"When Deacon makes a good point," Roland said, "he makes a good point."

"Dad's really sick, isn't he?"

"I told you."

"I guess it didn't hit me until dinner."

"He's trying to act healthier than he is," Roland said. "He's good at pretending things are okay when they aren't."

"He seemed so...himself today when we were walking out here," Allison said. "Like nothing had changed in thirteen years." Roland took her hand in his and she was surprised by how much she liked it. She and McQueen had never done much in the way of hand-holding. There wasn't much chance to as they rarely went out in public together.

"I'm glad you had a good day with him," he said. "I hate to think how few good days are left."

"How are you holding up?" she asked, squeezing his hand.

He stopped walking and turned to face the water.

"I'm fine until I think about it," he said.

"I shouldn't have asked. Now you're thinking about it."

"I would like to be able to be not fine in front of you." Roland turned to her and she saw the tight line of his mouth, the hard set of his jaw, telltale signs of a man trying very hard to be strong when inside he was falling apart.

"You can be not fine with me all you want," Allison said.

"Thank you," he said, taking her face in his hands to kiss her.

She glanced up at the house and saw a face gazing down on them from a third-floor window.

"Wait—Dad's watching."

"Let him watch," Roland said, and kissed her, a kiss she returned, unable to stop from wrapping her arms around his neck. Eventually they broke off the kiss and started ambling along the beach again. A mile from the house stood the basalt caves they used to play in as kids.

"So Dad seemed okay today?" Roland asked.

"Pretty good," she said. "Tired, he said, but sharp as a tack. A little bit ornery, too."

"Ornery?"

"Is a Southern word."

"I like it. Ornery. I hope Dad stays ornery to the end."

"I'm sure he will," Allison said.

"What did you all talk about?"

"The past. The future. You."

"Did you ask him about your fall?" Roland asked.

"I did."

"And?" Roland asked.

"He made a very good point about why he didn't tell you all about that phone call to my aunt. He said he didn't want you all freaked out in the house, afraid of each other."

"Yeah, that makes sense," Roland said. "With so many kids in one house...the fewer reasons to fight, the better. And if we thought one of the four of us was to blame for you leaving, it would have been a bloodbath."

Allison furrowed her brow, stopped walking.

"The four of you? You, Deacon, Thora, Oliver and Kendra. That's five."

"You don't remember? Oliver's mom took him back home the day after our...you know. On the beach. And you fell or whatever a couple days later. By the time of your accident, there were just five of us."

Allison went cold.

"Oliver's mom took him back before I fell? You sure?"

"I helped him pack his stuff," Roland said. "He was upset with me because I hadn't gone to the park with them the day before. Your accident was after he left. I know because Oliver said he wanted to stay another week for my birthday, but his mom wouldn't let him. I know he left before your fall. I remember thinking how insane it was we lost both of you in the same week."

"That...that doesn't make any sense," Allison said.

"Why not?"

She didn't answer.

"Allison, why doesn't that make sense?" Roland asked again, his voice more demanding this time, almost scared.

"I...I'm not sure I should tell you," she said. "Your dad asked me not to."

"Tell me what?"

Roland looked so worried Allison knew she had to tell him. It wouldn't have been fair to keep him in the dark after she'd already said so much.

"Today when Dad and I were talking about what happened to me, he said he thought Oliver was the one who called my aunt and told her someone was trying to kill me. He said Oliver was jealous of how close you and I were."

"Dad said that?"

"He did. He said he couldn't swear it was Oliver, he didn't know for sure, but that if anyone was responsible for my fall, it was him. But...why— How would Oliver call my aunt or push me down those stairs when he wasn't even here?"

"He could have called her from his house, maybe?" Roland offered.

"True, but why try to get rid of me when he was already gone?" she asked, to him, to herself. "And even if he did call from his own house, he wouldn't have been there the day that I fell."

"Dad really mentioned Oliver by name?" Roland asked.

"He did. He said knowing what he knew about Oliver's background...that was his theory."

"Bizarre," Roland said, shaking his head. "This is not good."

"Because he lied to me?"

"Dad wouldn't lie about something like that. What scares me is that he's slipping. Mental confusion is a symptom of end-stage renal failure," Roland said. "But...he hasn't acted confused at all."

"It was thirteen years ago. People forget things, get dates mixed up." She thought of the conflicting stories from Thora and Deacon, realizing how hard it would be to determine whose version of events was closest to the truth.

"True," Roland said. "I mean, maybe I'm the one remembering it wrong. But still…"

"Maybe we could talk to Oliver. Ask him what he remembers. He might 'fess up if we make it clear I'm not trying to get him arrested for something he did when he was a kid."

Roland exhaled hard. "I have no idea where he is. We lost touch when his mother took him back. I think we got one letter from him and that was it. Parents don't want their kids confused about what family they belong to."

Allison understood that. Her aunt had been the same way.

"Do you remember his last name?" Allison asked. "Collins, I think?"

"Yeah, Oliver Collins."

"Come on," Allison said, turning to head back to the house.

"Where are we going?"

"To ask Mr. Internet where Oliver is."

"What if Mr. Internet doesn't know?" Roland asked as they walked as briskly as they could across the sand.

"It's okay," she said. "I have a backup plan."

CHAPTER 17

Sadly, Mr. Internet didn't seem to know anything useful about the Oregon "Oliver Collins." Allison scrolled through pages and pages of results on her phone, but none of the Oliver Collinses that turned up was the right Oliver Collins. Too young. Too old. Wrong country. Wrong face.

"I hate when Google fails me," Allison said with a sigh. They were back in her room, Roland on her bed and Allison in her wicker chair by the window. "Everyone should be on the internet. At least when I'm trying to find them."

"You're not," Roland said. "I had a hell of a time trying to find you online."

"McQueen likes his ladies to keep a low profile. I have a great Pinterest account, though. All book covers."

"Of course," he said. "You can't find me online, either. No computers allowed in our cells."

"It really was prison, wasn't it?"

"Not at all. Prisoners get conjugal visits," Roland said with a grin. He rolled onto his side facing her. "You said you had a backup plan to find Oliver?"

"I do, but you're not going to like it." Allison sat forward in the chair and tugged gently on a loose lock of Roland's hair.

"If it involves digging through Dad's medical records, I'm not going to do it," Roland said. "I won't stop you, but I won't be part of it, either."

"I doubt Oliver's current address would be in your dad's old files," Allison said. "I've moved three times in thirteen years. I'm sure he's moved at least once."

"Good point. What's the plan?"

"You maybe want to leave the room for this," she said with a wary sigh.

Roland narrowed his eyes at her.

"What are you going to do?" he asked.

"The thing is… McQueen has a whole company that does venture capitalism. They find start-up companies to invest in. But you don't invest in a company first without doing lots of background checks on the company founders. You don't want to accidentally give money to a con man or a sex offender. So McQueen has a couple of women on his staff who do nothing but dig up people's pasts."

"You're going to ask your ex…whatever to help us find Oliver?"

"I was thinking about it," she said.

"Okay," Roland said. "Call him, then. As long as his ladies on staff don't do anything illegal."

"Nah. They have all the databases that private detectives use. It won't be a big deal to get a phone number or address. I'm calling. Are you staying?"

"I can handle it," he said.

"All right. Here goes."

Allison made the call.

McQueen answered after two rings.

"Allison? This is a quite a surprise," he said.

"Hey," she said. "Sorry to bother you."

"No bother at all, sugar. What's on your mind?"

Sugar? She did the mental math—it would be right about eleven in Louisville right now. Good chance he was already on his third drink of the night.

"I need your help with something."

"Name it," McQueen said.

"Name it?" she asked.

"Name it and claim it. You're talking to a man sitting in a doghouse. Got nothing else to do in here."

"What did you do now?" Allison asked.

Roland eyed her with suspicion and amusement.

"I made the mistake of answering my lady love's questions about you."

"You said you already told her about me."

"I apparently neglected to inform her of your age at consummation."

"Oh...dear," Allison said in sympathy. "I guess she's mad?"

"She's not happy, that's for damn sure. I'm under orders to make amends."

"Should I write your girlfriend a letter of recommendation for you?" Allison asked. If Roland furrowed his brow any harder, she could put a pencil between the folds.

"That's not the worst idea I've heard all day. Now tell me what I can do for you," McQueen said. "I hope it involves the loss of a limb. That might appease the future missus."

"Roland and I want to find one of the kids who used to live here. Nothing came up when we Googled him," she said. "Can you help?"

"You and Roland, eh? Hmm...might do it for you. Not sure I'll do it for him."

"Be nice, McQueen. He's sitting right here."

"Put him on."

"What?"

"Put the man on the phone. I would like to talk to him."

"Oh, hell, no," Allison said in an exaggerated Kentucky accent.

"What?" Roland whispered.

Allison put her hand over the phone.

"He wants to talk to you," she said in a whisper.

Roland shrugged. "I'll talk to him."

"No," Allison rasped.

"Allison…" McQueen sang her name.

"Speakerphone," Allison said. "That's my offer. I want to hear what nonsense you tell him."

"Offer accepted," McQueen said. "Put the boy on."

Allison sighed heavily and hit the speakerphone button.

"All right, McQueen. Here he is."

"Am I speaking to Brother Roland Capello?" McQueen asked.

"You can call me Roland," Roland said, smiling at Allison, who was already rolling her eyes.

"And you can call me Mr. McQueen."

"Of course, Mr. McQueen."

"Oh, my Lord." Allison sighed.

"I understand you and Allison are seeing each other now?" McQueen asked.

"You understand correctly," Roland said.

"And you're a monk of the Benedictine persuasion. Do I also understand that correctly?"

"I'm on leave from the order," Roland said. "But technically, yes."

"This is weird," Allison said to them both. "This is very weird. This is weirder than the time I had sex with my brother who is also a monk."

"You mean two hours ago?" Roland said.

"I did not need to hear that," McQueen said. "Not enough bourbon in the whole goddamn world."

"You dumped me," Allison said. "You've obsessed about me more in the last forty-eight hours than you did in the entire six years we were together."

"I don't obsess about my big toe, either, but I sure as hell would if someone made me chop it off," McQueen said.

"How much have you had to drink tonight?" Allison asked. "You sound like Matthew McConaughey."

"I've had three shots of Knob Creek Single Barrel, one-hundred-twenty proof. We call that 'guilty conscience' bourbon in the trade," McQueen said. "It's not helping as much as I'd like. I best increase the voltage."

"Guilt is the soul's way of reminding you that actions have consequences," Roland said. "So says my abbot."

"I am a forty-five-year-old man with two grown children and a baby on the way with a woman I hardly know from Eve. Young man, I *know* actions have consequences."

Roland looked at Allison and mouthed, "Does he always talk like this?"

"I heard that," McQueen said. "Tell me, Roland, do monks drink bourbon?"

"We bust out the Maker's Mark on special occasions," Roland said. "Feast days, parties, anniversaries, days ending in *Y*."

"Hmm."

"McQueen, that's a good Kentucky bourbon," Allison said.

"Maker's is ninety proof," McQueen said. "But I suppose it's a decent enough breakfast bourbon."

Roland laughed again.

"Are you laughing at me, young man?" McQueen demanded.

"With you," Roland said. "I'm starting to understand why Allison stayed with you for six years."

"I could show you why she stayed with me for six years," McQueen said.

"McQueen, that's—"

"I was referring to my bank balance," McQueen said.

"That's not any less insulting," she said. "That's it. Chitchat is over." She took McQueen off speakerphone and shooed Roland from the room. He went, reluctantly. Very reluctantly. "Okay, we're alone again. Will you help? Seriously?"

"I'll help. What exactly am I doing?"

"I need the contact information for Oliver Collins from Oregon, about age twenty-six."

"And why am I hunting this boy down for you?"

"We think he might know something about my fall or whatever it was. We want to ask him a few questions."

There was a pause before McQueen answered and Allison hoped the man hadn't passed out on her.

"You really are planning on staying there with them, aren't you?" he asked.

"For now," she said. "But even so, I need to know what happened."

"I'd want to know, too. I hope you have the family I could never give you someday," McQueen said.

Allison swallowed a lump in her throat.

"I should hate you," she said. "I really should. Why can't I?"

"You know what they say...ours is not to wonder why. Ours is but to drink bourbon and rye."

"*They* don't say that. *You* say that, McQueen."

"Is that so? Then I am a very wise man."

She whispered a good-night and hung up before McQueen could say something else to make her remember why she didn't hate him. She texted him Oliver's name, his age and what little else she remembered about him—blond, blue eyes, from Portland. McQueen sent back a thumbs-up emoji. Message received.

She left her phone in her room and found Roland in the kitchen putting together what seemed to be a cocktail of pills into a tiny shot glass.

"Bourbon is better," she said.

"These are all Dad's," Roland said. "We've got Benadryl for the itching. A diuretic to help with swelling. A few others

I forgot what they do but they're very important, I was told. They'll add literally hours to his life."

She sat down across from him at the table.

"Sorry McQueen gave you the third degree. You handled it really well."

"I expected him to be, I don't know, more of an asshole," Roland said.

"He can afford to be nice. You were nice, too. Nicer than I would have been."

"I hate to say it, but I like him."

"He's a charmer."

"Seriously," Roland said. "I'm straight and even I was thinking, *Yeah, I'd sleep with this guy.*"

Allison laughed. "Now that is quite a mental picture."

"You still have feelings for him?" Roland asked. His tone was neutral but she could see a flash of nervousness in his eyes.

"I had feelings for us," she said. "I liked us. I was used to us. He ended it and it felt like the rug had been pulled out from under me. Turns out there's pretty nice flooring underneath."

She saw Roland trying not to smile. He didn't try very hard.

"I'll always care about him," she said, "but I'm not pining for him."

"That's good."

"Very good. I pined after you for years," she said.

"You did?" he asked.

"I was still a virgin at nineteen," she reminded him. "I think a big reason for that is a little part of me compared every boy to you. And they all paled in comparison."

"I'm not that wonderful," he said. "Really. I'm not."

"You were to me," she said. She watched for a moment as he added pills to the shot glass. "Deacon told me earlier today about Rachel. He asked me not to bring her up but I don't want it to be like that with us. You don't have to talk about her with me. I want you to know I know so there's no secrets with us."

Roland had looked up sharply at her when she said Rachel's name but he didn't seem to be angry.

"It must've been really painful to lose her in that accident. We don't need to talk about it. All I'll say about it is I'm very, very sorry," she said.

"You lost your mom. Everyone in this house lost somebody," he said.

"Everybody in this house found somebody, too," she said.

Roland smiled and said no more about it.

"I'll take those up to Dad if you want," she said.

"You won't talk about Oliver to him?" Roland asked.

"No."

"Good," he said. She kissed his cheek and started from the kitchen.

"It was my fault," Roland said softly, but Allison heard and turned around.

"What was?"

"Rachel dying."

"I had a cold. When my mother died, I mean. I had a horrible cough and I couldn't sleep, so Mom went out to the drugstore at midnight. She'd been drinking—not much, just enough to be tipsy and tired. But she lost control of her car. Knowing the area, she probably swerved to avoid a dog or a tumbleweed she thought was a dog. Was her death my fault?"

"Of course not."

"See?" she said, and kissed his forehead.

Roland took her hand and kissed it. She sensed he had more to say but all he said was, "Tell Dad I'll be up later."

"Of course."

She left him in the kitchen and went up to the third floor, where she found Dr. Capello shuffling around his bedroom in his green-and-blue tartan plaid bathrobe and matching blue slippers. Something about the sound of the slippers on the floor and the loose way the robe hung on his shoulders made him look even older than his years.

"Hey, Dad," she said from the doorway.

"There's my girl," he said, and waved her inside.

"Don't get excited to see me," she said, and held up his medicine cup.

He pursed his lips. "Did my eldest put you up to this?"

"I volunteered," she said. She hadn't done it to be nice, although she wouldn't tell Roland that. She wanted a chance to be alone with Dr. Capello again, to see if he said anything about Oliver.

"Talk about dirty pool," Dr. Capello said. "The monk knows I'll be nicer to you than him."

"You have to be nice to me," she said. "I'm armed and dangerous."

"I don't believe it for one second."

"It's true. Deacon, for some reason, gave me a can of pepper spray today." She pulled it out of her pocket and showed it to him.

"Ah," Dr. Capello said. "I'll be nice, then."

She shoved the pepper spray into her pocket again and came into the room.

"Any idea why he keeps spare cans of pepper spray around?" she asked him. "I noticed Thora carries it, too."

Dr. Capello nodded slowly. "It's not something I should be talking about."

"Why not? He's your son. You're allowed to talk about your children," she said.

"What did he tell you?" Dr. Capello asked.

"He said there are a lot of psychos around."

"He would know."

"What does that mean?" Allison asked. She sat in the big armchair by the bed. Dr. Capello's shoulders slumped a little.

"We have a rule in this house, if you'll remember, and it's a good rule. We don't talk about the past. The kids' pasts, I mean. No more than we have to. It's for their sake. Kids like them, they needed security, a permanent home. I never wanted them to think they'd ever have to go back to their old lives."

She remembered Dr. Capello telling her that when he brought her to the house the first time. He said all the kids in the house had been through tough times and she wasn't supposed to ask them about their old lives or their old families. None of them had asked her how her mother had died. She never asked them how they ended up at The Dragon, either. No reason to. They were all so happy here, none of them wanted to remember the pain in their pasts. None of them wanted to remember they were born anything other than Capello kids.

"I respect that," Allison said. "But they're not kids anymore, you know."

He waved his hand. "Bah. You all were born yesterday."

Allison sat back in the chair and said nothing, only waited.

Dr. Capello picked up his medicine cup and then put it down again without taking anything.

"His biological father," Dr. Capello said. "He's in prison. Two counts of aggravated assault, one count of murder. He'll die in jail if we're lucky. Let's hope we're lucky."

"That's horrible," Allison said. "Deacon's biological father killed someone?"

"Classic psychopath," Dr. Capello said. "I read his file. Liar, manipulator, glib, shallow, remorseless, I could go on and on. But don't listen to Deacon. There aren't a lot of them around. True psychopaths make up about two percent of the population. In prison it's more like…fifty percent. In politics, maybe ninety percent."

Allison smiled. "Well, thank God Deacon turned out so well despite his father," she said.

"Not God's doing," Dr. Capello said, then pointed at himself. "*My* doing."

She smiled. "Well, thank *you*, then. But that explains why Deacon's a little...paranoid, I guess?"

"He had a violent childhood before he came to me. It'll change a child," Dr. Capello said. "I hope that answers your question?" His tone implied that he'd prefer she dropped the subject.

"Yeah, it does. I wish it was a better answer."

"We all do, doll."

Her stomach knotted up at the revelation. Poor Deacon, growing up with a murderer as a father. Yes, that sort of thing would definitely change someone. Because of her mother dying after drinking and driving, Allison had been so cautious around alcohol she'd never once gotten drunk in all her twenty-five years. Not even McQueen could ever talk her into having more than one drink, even when she wasn't driving anywhere.

"Now," he said. "I'm going to bed before my eldest gets up here to hassle me some more."

"I'm not leaving until you take your meds," she said.

"It's hard to take them when you're nauseous."

"Not taking them will make it worse, though, won't it?"

"I'm the doctor here, kid. Not you." Dr. Capello eased himself down onto his bed. He seemed more fragile tonight. His eyes looked puffy and his skin more sallow. "You know what the awful irony is? My grandparents died in this house of lead poisoning. I did everything I could when I took over the place to make it safe and habitable. Yet, here I am, two generations later, poisoning myself to death."

"Poisoning yourself?" Allison helped Dr. Capello lie back on his pillows. She brought the covers over him to his chest.

"The kidneys clean poison out of your body. When the kidneys can't do their job anymore, the poisons stay in the system."

He patted the bed next to him and Allison sat at his side.

"Does it hurt?" she asked.

"It's not comfortable, but it's not quite pain, either. What hurts is the unfairness. To give your life in service to mankind and then...this."

"No, it's not fair at all," she said, reaching out to take his hand. He held hers in his and squeezed it. She took heart in the strength she felt in his hands. There was life in him yet.

"You know what else isn't fair?" Allison said. "You still have to take your meds."

"Ah, dammit."

"I know a man trying to change the subject when I see it."

"How about you recite me another poem?" he asked. "A good long one. An epic, maybe? *The Iliad*?"

"'Hateful to me as the gates of Hades is that man who hides one thing in his heart and speaks another.'"

"*Prometheus Bound,*" he said.

"'Such is the reward you reap for loving mortals.'"

"My mother would have adored you. How about *The Odyssey*?"

"How about you recite me a poem?" She stood up, crossed her arms over her chest and waited.

He chuckled a little, wagged his finger at her.

"Oh, that's your trick not mine. But I know one. If I can recite one poem, will I still have to take my meds?"

"Yes, absolutely."

"How about this?" he said. "I recite my poem and you keep that nagging monk out of my room so I can pretend for one night I'm a grown man."

"All right," she said. "Deal. Recite."

He smiled a little and tapped his temple as if trying to jar the poem free. He recited the poem to her.

"So much depends
upon
a red wheel
barrow
glazed with rain
water
beside the white
chickens."

Allison applauded. "William Carlos Williams. A classic. A very short classic."

"You know what it means?"

"An ode to a wheelbarrow?"

A deal was a deal. She watched as Dr. Capello took his pills one by one.

"Dr. Williams was a pediatrician," he said. "He wrote that while sitting at the bedside of a dying child." Dr. Capello blinked and in an instant tears were in his eyes. And hers.

"I never knew," she said. "Wonder why he thought of that."

"I'd say he was looking out the window and trying to think about anything other than the little child he couldn't save. All doctors keep a graveyard inside their hearts for those patients. That's why I like my view so much." He reached out and tapped the glass of his window, which looked out onto the ocean. "It comforts me."

"Looking at the Graveyard of the Pacific comforts you?" she asked.

"Of course it does," he said, gazing out his window at the dark shifting waters in the near distance. "Compared to that graveyard out there, mine's tiny. A doctor with children in his graveyard takes any comfort he can get."

CHAPTER 18

Allison left Dr. Capello in his bed and walked out into the hallway. Her talk with him tonight had been strange and revealing. She never would have guessed someone as sweet and funny and well-adjusted as Deacon seemingly came from such a violent background. Well, that explained the pepper spray. What explained Oliver? She wasn't sure about Roland's theory that Dr. Capello's memory was failing. She'd challenged him to recite a poem from memory, and he'd done it without breaking a sweat. And yet reciting one little poem hardly proved anything, right? Seemed far more likely Roland remembered the timeline of events differently than Dr. Capello did. Did it matter? Allison felt safe staying at The Dragon. Dr. Capello devoted his life to helping children, not hurting them. And Deacon had given her pepper spray to protect herself. Thora had saved Allison that very day from a severe injury. And Roland had asked her to come back, which is the last thing someone with something to hide would do.

Nevertheless, she wondered...

She was about to go downstairs when she noticed that the

attic door was ajar and someone had taped a note to the frame that read, *Family meeting at 10:00 p.m. Attic! This means you, Al!*

Family meeting? Why were they having a family meeting in the attic?

Allison carefully peeled the note off the door, closed the attic door behind her and headed up the stairs. When she reached the attic, she found everyone already present, including Brien the cat draped over Deacon's shoulder, dozing like a furry baby. This was to be an informal meeting, Allison saw. Everyone was in their pajamas—Thora was in a short white nightgown with a chic oversize ivory cardigan wrapped around her, while Deacon and Roland were both in plaid lounge pants and T-shirts. They'd uncovered some chairs and the old metal camping cot. It seemed all was in place, but for her.

"Well?" Allison said to Deacon. "I'm here. What's this about?"

"I call this meeting of the Capello brood to order," Deacon said. Allison sat on a pillow on the floor and rested her back against Roland's legs, the way she'd done as a kid on Friday night movie night in the sunroom.

"Someone tell me why we're having a family meeting," Roland said.

"Because I'm pretty sure we've all had a very hard week. And because it's been twenty years since the four of us got to play together, and...as our Allison has been living in Kentucky for way too long, I thought we should give her a very special Oregon welcome. As opposed to an organ welcome, which is what my brother gave her last night."

"God help me," Roland said, his head falling back.

"An Oregon welcome?" Allison asked.

Deacon held out a wooden box and opened the lid. Allison leaned forward to look in, then narrowed her eyes at him.

"Deacon…is that what I think it is?" Allison asked.

Deacon waggled his eyebrows.

"You on the Left Coast now, baby girl."

Allison stared at Deacon. Deacon stared at Allison.

"Please tell me one thing," she said. "That's not your dad's medical marijuana you stole, is it?"

"That hurts, sis," Deacon said. "Right here." He tapped the right side of his chest where his heart wasn't. "I'll have you know this is my own stash."

"So it's illegal?"

"Nope. It's legal here," he said. "Ready to pack up and move yet?"

"You don't have to do this," Roland said. Deacon put Brien down and walked the attic, opening all the windows.

"Yes, she does," Deacon said. "We're bonding. Aren't we, my twin?" Deacon chucked Thora under her chin.

"We're voting?" Allison asked.

"Gotta be unanimous," Deacon said. "Capello rules. What's your vote, Thor?"

"We're twins," she said with a wink at Deacon. "I vote how you vote."

"Well, we all know how I vote," Deacon said. "Brien?" Deacon said, holding out the box. Brien lifted his head to sniff and Deacon shut the lid. "None for you, cat. You're stoned enough as it is."

"Why is Brien stoned?" Allison asked.

"Ragdoll cat." Deacon put his box down and picked up Brien, then flipped him over, and the cat went limp as a noodle. "They have all the aggression bred out of them. They are, in other words, born stoned. Lucky bastards." He flipped Brien back over and put him on the chair again. Much like someone stoned, he didn't seem the least perturbed by what had just happened to him.

"I'm having what he's having," Thora said.

"Now you, brother…" Deacon said to Roland. "Yea or nay?" Roland started to protest and Deacon made a slashing gesture with his hand. "Shut it. Monks have been drunks since Jesus still walked the earth. Ever heard of anyone dying of a pot overdose? Ever heard of pot poisoning? Ever heard of a mean stoner? No, you have not. You're not allowed to get holier than thou less than twenty-four hours after jumping Allison's pretty little bones, so put that in your pipe and smoke it. Or skip the pipe because my rolling skills are second to none."

"I'm in," Roland said. "If it'll shut you up."

"No guarantees of that," Deacon said.

"And," Roland said, "we have to check on Dad every fifteen minutes."

"Now you, little sister." Deacon went onto his knees in front of her, his hands holding hers. "Would you do me the honors of riding with me and Mary Jane all the way to the top floor? Don't be afraid. We'll walk you through it. There's a first time for—"

Allison took a joint from the box, picked up the lighter and lit up.

Deacon's eyes widened. He blinked at her. He blinked at Roland.

"Marry her," Deacon said.

Thus the family meeting commenced.

"I'm really not much of a smoker," Allison said as she leaned back against Roland's legs.

"You sure about that?" Deacon took the joint from her.

"Like a few times in college," she said, feeling quite a bit less stressed out than she had in days. "I'm only doing it now because you're making me."

"Oh, yes," Deacon said. "We forced it on you."

"So rude," Allison said.

"She gets a free pass," Roland said. "She's recovering from a breakup."

"Ah, so this *is* medical marijuana for you, then," Thora said, blowing out an elegant smoke ring.

"Does it cure a broken heart?" Allison asked.

"No," Deacon said. "But that's what he's for." He pointed at Roland.

"I'll do my best," Roland said.

"I'm so proud of you for getting laid." Deacon wiped a fake tear from his eye. "It makes all my suffering worth it."

"Your suffering?" Roland demanded. "How did you suffer?"

"You broke my heart when you joined that monastery," Deacon said. "Speaking as one pretty man to another, you could have at least waited until you were old and ugly for that bullshit. A man is at peak pretty between twenty-four and twenty-nine. You wasted your pretty years. Now you're vaguely ruggedly handsome. It's a step down."

"I'd still fuck him," Allison said.

Deacon's jaw dropped. "Listen to that mouth." Deacon stared Allison down. "You kiss your brother with that mouth?"

"I do actually."

Then Allison crawled up into Roland's lap and kissed him. It wasn't long before she realized she was truly relaxed and enjoying herself for the first time in days. She'd had fun with Roland last night but it certainly hadn't been relaxing. The pot wasn't very potent and it didn't do much but make them all loose and giggly with the added benefit—no doubt Deacon's intention—of making her feel like one of them again. And it was all going very well until Deacon opened his mouth again.

"So. Allison," Deacon began, lifting his head off the floor, where he lay with Brien on his chest. Allison knew she was in trouble already. "A little bird told me that you had a special friend in Kentucky. Is that true?"

"What did you tell him?" Allison asked Roland.

"Nothing," Roland said. "I swear."

"He didn't tell me anything," Deacon said. "My wild Irish rose over there is the traitor."

Allison glared at Thora. "Traitor."

"I can't help it," Thora said, hiding her face in her cardigan. "He beat it out of me."

"I said, 'Thor, wonder if Allison had a boyfriend,'" Deacon said, "and then you spilled the beans."

"You asked the question very pointedly," Thora said.

"Beans everywhere," Deacon said. "Girl can't keep a secret to save her life."

"Not true. Unfair. All lies," Thora said.

Deacon hushed her with a snap of his fingers. "So, tell me," Deacon said to Allison. "I want the whole story."

"Fine," Allison said. "I was the paid mistress of Cooper McQueen, heir to the McQueen family fortune. Maybe McQueen should have made me sign that NDA, after all, for how many times I've told the story since we broke up. Anyway, for sex years he paid me for six. I mean, for six years he paid me for sex. Then he broke up with me and now I'm here sleeping with Roland."

"How was the sex?" Deacon asked.

"Top-notch," Allison said.

"Who's better? McQueen or my brother?"

"Your brother," Allison said. "He didn't have to pay me to sleep with him."

"The mistress and the monk," Deacon said, blowing smoke to the ceiling of the attic. "This is a buddy cop show waiting to happen."

"I think he's had enough," Allison said. Roland apparently agreed and took the joint from his brother's hand.

"Anybody else banging a billionaire around here?" Deacon asked.

"You should tell the story about when you made out with a guy," Thora said.

"That's a good story," Deacon said.

"You made out with a guy?" Allison asked.

"I did," Deacon said, grinning. "Went to this sake bar in Shanghai, met a super pretty guy from South Korea who looked weirdly exactly like Storm Shadow. He asked me about my work at the glass museum. I asked him what Snake Eyes looked like under the mask. Blah blah blah, fifteen minutes later we were making out in a back booth. Then we got kicked out, and I remembered I don't have sex with strange men. Especially if they might be working for Cobra."

"Okay, but when you say he looked *exactly* like Storm Shadow," Roland said, "do you mean—"

"I mean he wore all white, had two crossed swords on his back and he was literally a ninja," Deacon said. "I'm not sure if I'm bi or not but I'm definitely sure I'm a huge G.I. Joe fan."

"Lots of overlap on that Venn diagram," Thora said, making two circles with her fingers and bringing them together.

"Roland..." Deacon said, eyeing him meaningfully. "What about you?"

"Are you asking if I'm bi or if I'm a G.I. Joe fan?"

"I'm asking if, you know...during those long cold nights at the monastery, you found yourself someone to keep you warm in your lonely little cell."

"You didn't see the size of our beds at the monastery," Roland said. "There was hardly room for one, much less two."

"So what you're saying is...you fucked the other monks on the floor?"

"Right," Roland said, adorably deadpan.

"What about you?" Deacon said to Thora. "Any secret trysts you've never told me about?"

"You know all my secret trysts already," she said.

"If I know them, then they're not secrets," Deacon said.

"But if I tell them to you, they're not secrets, either," she said.

"I never thought of that." Deacon stared wide-eyed at the ceiling. He seemed to be having an epiphany. The entire time Allison watched this absurd exchange she was thinking, *This is my family. This is my family. This is my family.* And maybe it was the pot talking to her, but in that moment, she loved her family.

"This is just like *The Breakfast Club*," Deacon said. "Right?"

"It's almost midnight," Allison said.

"This is just like *The Very, Very Early Breakfast Club*," Deacon said. "Wait. We have to do the talent show, right? Talent show? They do a talent show in the movie. We should do the talent show?"

"What should we do, Deacon?" Allison asked him.

"I'm thinking a talent show." Deacon snapped his fingers. "Roland, you start."

"I have no talents," Roland said.

Deacon shifted his eyes left to right rapidly. "That's not what Allison said…"

"I said he had no talons."

Roland held up his hands. "It's true. I have no talons."

This was the pot talking.

"I would watch a show called *America's Got Talons*," Deacon said. "Anyway, talent show now. Make up something. Impress us."

Roland exhaled heavily and then stood up.

"Fine," Roland said. "How much do you weigh?" he asked.

"That's a personal question," Allison said. Roland stared.
"All right, one-twenty-mumble."

"Did you say one-twenty-mumble?" Deacon asked.

"That is my exact weight," Allison said.

"Thora?" Roland asked.

"One-forty-mumble."

"Deac?"

"One-seventy-mumble."

"Okay, then, you," Roland said. "Up."

"Me?" Deacon pointed at himself. "You want me?"

"I don't want you. But I'm going to use you." Roland laid
down, stomach to floor.

"What is happening here?" Deacon asked.

"Sit on my back," Roland said.

"This better not be a weird sex thing," Deacon said.

"It's not a weird sex thing," Roland said. "It's a totally normal sex thing."

Deacon sat down on Roland's midback, crossed his lanky
legs and waited.

Then Roland put both hands flat on the floor and lifted
himself in a perfectly formed push-up.

Thora and Allison applauded.

"This is it?" Deacon asked. "This is your big talent? You
showing off you can do a push-up with a man sitting on your
back? I could do that, please don't make me prove it."

"No," Roland said. "This is the talent."

Roland proceeded to do *twenty* push-ups with Deacon on
his back, the final four of them on his knuckles.

"This is humiliating," Deacon said. "I mean, impressive,
but humiliating."

"I'm enjoying the show," Allison said. Roland wasn't a
show-off, so it was quite a sight to see him putting his strength
on display.

"That's it. I'm out," Deacon said, clambering off his brother's back after Roland hit twenty. "Show's over."

He collapsed back down into the big chair as Roland stood up and dusted off his hands.

"Thanks, little brother," Roland said, smiling angelically. "Much obliged."

"So am I," Allison said as she reached for Roland's arms. The push-ups had made the veins in his biceps bulge out, and she planned on running her hands over them for the next ten hours or until she was no longer stoned out of her gourd.

Roland sat down on the chair and dragged her into his lap. Allison went willingly and happily. It was nice to feel like a girlfriend, part of a couple that other people knew about. No secrets here.

"Someone else go," Deacon said. "Thora, you do a thing."

"I don't have any talents, either," she protested.

"Now we both know that's a lie," Deacon said, then proceeded to poke her repeatedly in the arm saying, "Go, go, go," with every poke.

"Fine!" She stood up at last with a put-upon sigh. "Pot doesn't interfere with inner ear stuff, does it?"

"I have no idea," Deacon said. "But now you have to do what you were going to do."

"I really don't want to end up in the hospital." Thora took her cardigan off and tossed it to Deacon.

"I have never had a better idea in my life," Deacon said.

"Zip it," she said. "If you make me laugh, I'll fall over." Thora stood in the middle of the floor on the checkered rug and took a steadying breath. Then she raised her arms in the air and bent backward in a bridge.

"*Bravissima!*" Deacon said.

"One problem," Thora said from the floor. Her voice sounded strained and nasal. "I can't get back up."

Deacon hopped up and wrapped his arm under her lower back and lifted her back to a standing position. Once she was up, he spun her in his arms in a silly parody of a waltz. He spun her once more and led her back to the chair.

"Your turn," Thora said to Deacon. "What's your talent?"

"You've been smoking my talent for two hours. It's Allison's turn."

"I don't have any talents, either," Allison said.

"Enough with the false modesty, people, and fucking do a thing," Deacon said, fists in the air as if he were about to start a cartoon battle with them all.

"Fine. I can do a thing. I have some poems memorized. I don't know if that counts as a talent, really, or a skill."

"Recite!" Deacon said, and snapped his fingers.

With a sigh Allison rose and stood in the middle of the room on the rug, which had apparently become their stage.

"Let's see…" she said. "I've got *London* by William Blake. 'I wander thro' each charter'd street, / Near where the charter'd Thames does flow…'"

"No, boring, stop," Deacon said. "Better poem, please."

"Um…" Allison tapped her foot on the carpet. "'Because I could not stop for Death— / He kindly stopped for me…'"

"No death poems," Deacon said. "Don't you know any fun poems?"

"Fun poems?" Allison asked. "Well…maybe one fun poem."

"Bring it," Deacon said.

"A sonnet," Allison began. "From the—"

"No Shakespeare," Deacon said. "Don't you dare say Shakespeare."

"A sonnet," Allison began again, one decimal louder to get Deacon to shut his trap, "from the Earl of Rochester. Otherwise known as the most notorious libertine in history."

"Now," Deacon said, snapping his fingers and pointing at the ceiling, "we are getting somewhere."

Allison cleared her throat. She raised her hand like a poet of yore. She recited the poem.

"I rise at eleven, I dine about two,
I get drunk before sev'n, and the next thing I do,
I send for my whore, when for fear of a clap,
I spend in her hand, and I spew in her lap;"

"I love poetry," Deacon said with a sigh.
Allison continued.

"Then we quarrel and scold, 'till I fall fast asleep,
When the bitch, growing bold, to my pocket does creep;
Then slyly she leaves me, and, to revenge the affront,
At once she bereaves me of money and cunt.
If by chance then I wake, hotheaded and drunk,
What a coil do I make for the loss of my punk?
I storm and I roar, and I fall in a rage,
And missing my whore, I bugger my page.
Then, crop-sick all morning, I rail at my men,
And in bed I lie yawning 'till eleven again."

Roland, Thora and Deacon all applauded and Allison bowed.

"I knew I should have been an English major," Deacon said.

"I didn't learn that from my professors. I learned it from McQueen."

"I knew I should have been a rich guy's mistress," Deacon said.

"Why do you have poems memorized?" Thora asked her.

If she had been stone-cold sober, Allison wouldn't have answered the question. Or she would have answered it, but not truthfully. But that night in the attic with these strangers who were starting to feel like her family again, she was feeling safe enough to be honest.

"There was this girl, Katie, at the group home they sent me to after my mom died," Allison said. "She told me what to do to get adopted. She had five rules. Rule number one—don't cry. Nobody likes a crybaby. Rule number two—don't complain. Nobody likes a whiner. Rule number three—smile. Rule number four—don't ask for anything. Rule number five—learn a trick."

"Like memorizing poems?" Thora asked.

She shrugged. "Eighteen years later and I still can't break the habit," Allison said.

"How many poems have you memorized?" Thora asked.

Allison didn't want to answer. She did it, anyway.

"Hundreds," Allison said. "Hundreds and hundreds."

Roland stared at her before dragging her back into his arms.

"It's okay," she said, resting her head on his chest. She didn't realize she'd started crying until he'd held her.

"That's the saddest, sweetest, dumbest thing I've heard," Thora said. "You were a kid, not a puppy."

"It worked, though. I recited a poem to your dad the day he came to meet me."

"You did?" Deacon asked. "Not that poem, I hope."

"Lewis Carroll," Allison said. Roland wiped the tears off her face with the corner of his T-shirt.

"That explains a lot," Deacon said.

"What?" she asked him.

"Explains you." Deacon pointed at her. "You when you came here, I mean. For months you didn't break a single rule. Didn't talk back. Didn't fight. Didn't raise your voice. You walked on eggshells. Dad was scared to death you'd act like that forever. He knew you thought if you broke a single rule...you'd be out the door. First time you got in trouble for...what was it?"

"Fight over the TV," she said. "You wanted to watch *The X-Files.*"

"And you wanted to watch...what?" Deacon asked.

She coughed her answer. *"Powerpuff Girls."*

"No wonder we fought," Deacon said.

"You forgive me?" Allison asked him. Deacon reached out and pinched her nose.

"You can't blame a kid for being a kid," Deacon said. "Even if she is a dumb kid with terrible taste in TV shows."

Allison grabbed Deacon by his nose and pinched it. "Your turn. Put on a show and stop making me cry. And rolling a decent joint does not count as a talent."

She released his nose and he stood up. "I do have one talent," Deacon said as he took his place at the center of the rug. "One very special talent. One very special Oregon-themed talent..."

"Allow me to apologize in advance," Allison said, "for making Deacon do whatever it is he's about to do."

"Apologies accepted," Deacon said. "And now...drumroll, please."

No one gave him a drumroll.

Deacon lifted his shirt, stuck his stomach out and wiggled it as best as a guy who was five-ten and one-hundred-and-seventy-mumble pounds could.

Then he lowered his shirt and bowed.

"What the hell was that?" Allison demanded.

"The Truffle Shuffle!" he said.

"The what?"

"Oh, no, you didn't just say 'the what?' to the Truffle Shuffle," Deacon said with a sigh. "That's it. I'm getting the Oreos. I'm getting the Pringles. I'm getting the grape soda. We are going stay up and watch *The Goonies* until dawn." Then he picked up the roach he'd left in the ashtray.

Of course, that was precisely the moment when Dr. Capello appeared at the top of the stairs.

Deacon stood up straight immediately and put his hands behind his back. In unison, all four of them attempted to play it cool. Even Brien, who did a much better job than the rest of them.

"Dad," Deacon said. "You're…you're awake."

Dr. Capello stood in the doorway in his robe and pajamas.

"You okay, Dad. Daddy?" Thora said, her eyes too wide. Allison wanted to tell her to make her eyes normal, but she didn't seem to get the telepathic message Allison tried to send her through a series of intense blinks.

"I heard something," Dr. Capello said. "I smelled something."

"We're just, um, hanging out," Deacon said.

"Hanging in," Roland said. "Since we're in. In the house, I mean."

Allison pinched him. Nonstoned people did not say "hanging in."

"Allison?" Dr. Capello said.

"Ah, yes?" she said, her voice hitting a high note it had never hit before.

"What are you all up to in here?" Dr. Capello asked her.

"Oh, you know," Allison said. "We were doing a talent show."

"What's the talent?" Dr. Capello asked. "Who can stink up the house the fastest?"

"Dad," Deacon said. "Sorry. We were just—"

"Grounded," Dr. Capello said. "You." He pointed at Deacon. "You." He pointed at Thora. "You." He pointed at Roland. "And you." He pointed at Allison.

"I don't even live here anymore," Allison said.

"I'm thirty," Roland said.

"I don't want to hear it," Dr. Capello said. "Grounded. All of you. No television. No movies. No dessert for a week."

"A week?" Deacon said, horrified.

"You heard me. Now clean this mess up and go to bed."

"Yes, Daddy," Thora said. "Sorry, Daddy."

"Sorry, Dad," Deacon said, and Roland mumbled a "Yeah, sorry" of his own.

"Allison?" Dr. Capello prompted.

"Sorry, Dad," Allison said. He nodded his stern acceptance of their apologies.

Dr. Capello turned to leave and as he left Allison caught a glimpse of something on his face. The tiniest little hint of a smile.

A soon as he was gone, they all looked at each other and burst into laughter.

"Kids!" came Dr. Capello's voice through the door.

They went silent. Instantly.

Those approximately ten seconds after they stopped laughing and before they started laughing again—more quietly, of course—might have been the happiest ten seconds of Allison's life. In those ten seconds, Dr. Capello was still the patriarch of the house. In those ten seconds, he wasn't dying anymore. In those ten seconds, they were kids again. In those ten seconds, Allison feared nothing but getting grounded yet another week. And in those ten seconds, Allison felt completely and utterly and unconditionally loved and accepted and home. Her home. Her family. And she knew she was home, and she knew she was family, because at age twenty-five, her dad had grounded her for smoking weed in the house with her boyfriend.

Her boyfriend? No, but in that instant it felt like Roland was her boyfriend. Allison loved him. She loved him and Dr.

Capello. She loved Thora and Deacon and even silly old Potatoes O'Brien sleeping soundly on the cot. Even the house Allison loved and the quiet tide and the friendly ocean and the kissing breeze and the comforting clouds and the bright and laughing stars hidden behind them. If one could marry a moment in time, she would have married that one. That moment when the stars were laughing with her and not at her. That moment when the sand in the hourglass was on her side and the house was once again her home.

She and Roland crept down the stairs to her bedroom and crawled under the covers and all over each other, and they didn't part ways until dawn.

CHAPTER 19

One almost-perfect week came and went. If Dr. Capello had been well it might have been perfect. It took almost no time for Allison to settle back into the old family patterns, the old groove. In the morning she had breakfast with Thora and Deacon while Roland helped his father shower and dress. Thora and Deacon went to work, and Dr. Capello sat at his desk in his office and played at working while Roland slept. During Dr. Capello's nap time, Roland would take her to her room. As kids they'd blissfully wasted summer afternoons watching movies or drowsing on the beach. As adults they found better ways to spend their lazy afternoons together. She was woven so easily and so quickly back into the fabric of life at The Dragon that she hadn't noticed it happening. No one remarked on it. No one treated her like a houseguest. Perhaps the cord had never been broken between her and them. Perhaps all it took was one quick tug, one little stitch to weave her back into the fold. Allison even took up her old chores. Washing the breakfast dishes had been her job, which she did without complaint or even second thought. Her other chore had been straightening the toy room. As there was no toy room anymore, she replaced it with doing laundry.

She was halfway through folding a basket of towels on her eighth morning at The Dragon when her phone rang. The vibration rattled the whole couch and woke up Brien, who'd worn himself out battling with a pair of her underwear she'd let him play with and had fallen asleep against her hip. Allison, too, was startled by the call. She'd forgotten she was expecting one until she saw who was calling.

"McQueen," she said. "Did you forget about me?"

"No," he said. "Just took a little longer than I expected."

No jokes. No flirting. No drunken rambling. Something wasn't right.

"But you found Oliver's number, didn't you?" she asked, suddenly concerned by his serious tone.

"I found some contact information. I'll email it over to you."

"Thank you."

"It's for his parents," he said. "His mother is Kathy Collins. The guy she's married to now is her second husband, not Oliver's father. She kept her last name."

"No number for Oliver? He's around my age. I'd think he'd be on his own by now."

"Allison..." McQueen said, and from the tone of his voice Allison knew immediately the news was bad, very bad. "I don't know how to tell you this, but...honey, Oliver's dead."

Allison nearly dropped the phone.

"What? How?"

"Just after his fourteenth birthday," McQueen said, "he shot himself in the head."

"Fourteen? No way. That would have been right after he left here."

"I am so sorry." McQueen sounded like a father now, not

her irritating ex-lover. "When Sue told me what she'd found, I made her double- and triple-check before I called you with the news. But it's all true. I can give you his mother's phone number like I said and her address if you want to visit and pay your respects."

"Sure," she said. "That's... Yeah, send me that." She paused. "You don't know if there was a note or anything? Or a reason he gave?"

"That's not really Sue's area," McQueen said. "We didn't want to bother his parents by calling. Looks like the father cut out when Oliver was eight or nine, so I don't know if he could tell you anything. Mother's the best bet."

"Yeah, makes sense," she said, still dazed.

A dozen memories of Oliver flitted through her mind in that instant. Instead of playing tag on the beach with the rest of them, he'd sit for hours in the sun digging for shells. And she remembered the funny way he'd stick his tongue out in concentration while coloring. The way he'd randomly stand on his hands because he was a kid and he could.

"I wish I had better news," he said.

"I asked you to help."

"Is there anything else I can do?"

She shook her head, although McQueen wouldn't have seen it. She was too dazed to think straight. Except, maybe there *was* something.

"McQueen? Can I ask for another favor?"

"What is it?"

"Two more names," she said. "Can you get me their information?"

"What are the names?"

"Kendra Tate," she said. "And Antonio Russo."

"Other siblings?"

"Kendra came to the house a couple months before I left.

Antonio… I never met him. He came and left right before I did, but I still want to talk to him, anyway. Deacon said Antonio was one of the kids Dr. Capello couldn't help."

"I'll see what I can find for you."

"Thank you. Really, thank you."

"Of course. But, Allison?"

"Yes?"

"I don't like this."

"You don't have to help me if you don't want to," she said.

"No, I mean, I don't like hearing that a teenage boy killed himself a few months after leaving that house you're in."

"Do you think I like hearing it?" she asked.

"First you, and now this boy? I'm tempted to bring the police in."

"That's insane, McQueen."

"Insane? Someone tried to kill you, and this kid kills himself a couple months after leaving that house," McQueen said.

"I'm trying to find out what happened. And whatever did happen, children were involved. Young children, who probably didn't understand what they were doing. I'm not trying to put anybody in jail," she said. "I just want to know the truth so I can stop wondering what happened. That's all. And I really don't want anyone bothering Dr. Capello. He doesn't have much time left, anyway."

"I'm going to lose sleep at night over you," McQueen said. "And not for the reasons I used to."

Allison sighed heavily.

"Look," McQueen said with a sigh, "I'm not telling you to leave. I wouldn't dare tell you what to do. But where there's smoke there's fire, and if I were you, I'd keep my mouth and nose covered."

Allison wanted to argue with him, but she was afraid he might have a point.

"I'll be safe," she said.

"Better be."

She got off the phone with him and a minute later had the email. She found Roland in the side yard chopping wood again. It was warm that day, surprisingly so for October on the coast, and Roland was just in jeans and a T-shirt. For a couple minutes, she stood far back and watched him work. It amazed her how he made it look so easy as he raised the ax, brought it down, split the wood in two. His grip was strong and his swing fluid and fearless. This was not a man who worried about chopping off a toe. She took great comfort in Roland's strength and size. He was the sort of man one instinctively ran to when scared or in trouble. A human umbrella, a living breathing shelter from the storm. McQueen had never done anything more physically taxing than lift weights at the gym three times a week with his trainer. If he could see Roland right now, he wouldn't worry one bit about her. With Roland with her, she would be safe.

Roland finally noticed her presence. He took his safety glasses off and set his ax aside.

"You looking for me?" he asked.

"More firewood? Still not cold out," she said.

Roland sighed. "What can I say? It's good stress relief. I was the wood chopper at the abbey, too. Wonder who they suckered into doing it now that I'm gone."

"You had to chop wood at the abbey?"

"We ran a working farm," Roland said. "Grew most of our own food. And we had sheep and a few cows. We also brewed our own beer. It helps pay the bills."

"Your own beer? Hipster monks. You even have the man bun."

"It's just a ponytail."

"You're so Oregon," she said, smiling. "I was wondering how a monk got your bulk."

"Throwing hay and chopping wood every day for eight straight years is a good workout. Now, what's wrong? You look upset."

"McQueen called me back. Finally."

"He found Oliver?"

"Yes and no."

"What does that mean?"

Allison told him everything while Roland listened in silence.

"Roland?" she asked when he hadn't responded at all.

He ran a hand roughly through his hair.

"Shit," he said, followed by a few more choice words. "He's sure about all this?"

"He had his assistant triple-check it. He didn't want to freak us out without reason. That's why it took so long to get back to us." Allison took a step toward him but didn't touch him. He didn't seem ready for that yet. "What do you think we should do?"

He exhaled heavily.

"You said his mom's in Vancouver?" Roland asked.

"Vancouver, Washington," she said. "Not Canada."

"That's two hours away," Roland said. "Right across the bridge from Portland."

"You really think we should go knocking on her door?"

"We'll call first, but we should go, too. You can hang up on a call but it's a lot harder to slam a door in someone's face. Especially your face."

"Do you want to come with me?" she asked.

"No," he said. "But I will. I want to know why I never knew my brother killed himself. That's something we should have known. And it wasn't like with you. He seemed fine when they took him home."

"Do you think they told your dad when he died?" Allison asked.

"If Dad had known, he would have told me."

"You sure?" she asked. "He didn't tell you the whole truth about why I left."

Roland shrugged. "I thought I was sure."

"You want to ask him?"

"If he weren't so sick I might," Roland said. "He barely slept last night. He's in a bad mood this morning already. I don't want to risk upsetting him."

"Yeah, I wouldn't want to tell a dying man one of his foster kids killed himself, either," Allison said. "You think he'll be suspicious if we went away for a day?"

"Let me handle that," he said.

She went to him and kissed him.

"I needed that," he said.

"Me, too. I was doing laundry when McQueen called. I was folding your underwear."

He laughed. "You don't have to do my laundry."

"I threw yours in with mine. I kind of like folding your underwear," she said. "Is this what a real adult relationship feels like?"

"I don't know. I've never been in one."

"Me, neither. I'm enjoying it," she said. Shared work, shared sorrows, shared joys...she could get used to living like this.

He kissed her again. "Don't tell my abbot but...so am I."

Roland offered to make the phone call to Oliver's mother. He'd met her once and had been closer to Oliver during his time at The Dragon than anyone else. Meanwhile Allison returned to the house and changed out of her yoga pants and sweatshirt into her jeans, brown leather boots and her fa-

vorite burgundy wraparound cashmere sweater. She hoped
it was appropriate for paying condolences to a total stranger.
As she'd finished putting her hair up in a twist, Roland came
into the bathroom.

"Well?" Allison asked.

"I got his mom on the phone. She said we can come by
this evening for a few minutes. She remembered Oliver telling her I was his best friend."

Allison smiled weakly. "That's sweet. How did she sound?"

"Not very happy to hear from me, but it sounds like she's
never very happy to hear from anyone. I think she's depressed.
Can't blame her for that."

"She say anything else?"

"She said Dad did know. She called him right after it happened."

"He knew?" Allison wasn't as surprised as she wanted to be.

Roland nodded. "I couldn't get much more out of her. She
said we could talk about it this evening."

"Did you tell Dad we were leaving?" she asked.

"I told him I wanted to get you out of the house and take
you to Portland on a real date."

"What did he say?"

"He said, 'There's five hundred dollars in cash in the top
drawer and don't you dare show your face until morning.'"

"I take it he approves?"

"You could say that."

Thora agreed to come home and watch Dr. Capello while
they were out. She said she'd watch their dad day and night
as long as they brought her Little Big Burger from Portland.
An easy promise to make and keep. Allison and Roland got
into her rental car and headed east down the tree-shrouded
highway that linked the city to the coast.

"I'll never get over how green it is here," she said as they drove in and out of shadows.

"It's not going to stay green much longer if it doesn't start raining. We're overdue."

Roland wasn't looking at her but staring out the car window. She saw the reflection of his face in the glass and his expression was grim.

"You're worried about your dad," she said.

"He tells me everything," Roland said. "I'm the oldest. I've always been the one in charge when he was away. I've always been the one he told the bad stuff to, even when he didn't tell Deac or Thor. It doesn't make sense he'd keep this from me."

"He is very protective of his kids."

"I get not telling me when I'm sixteen or seventeen or even eighteen. But I'm an adult," Roland said. "I can handle bad news now."

"I'm sure he has his reasons. Medical confidentiality, maybe?"

"He did operate on Oliver. Maybe that's it."

"I wish I remembered Oliver better," she said.

"He was with us about six months," Roland said. "Came after Christmas, left in June."

"Killed himself in October," she said. "I can't imagine why... And at fourteen?"

"Teenagers do risky things," Roland said. "Maybe he didn't even kill himself on purpose? Maybe he was just playing with a gun."

"Maybe," Allison said. "Although McQueen called it a suicide, not an accident."

"We'll see what his mom says. She'll know."

"Do you really think it was an accident? Or are you just hoping that because you're Catholic?"

"Catholics aren't fans of suicide," Roland said. "But I don't believe in a God who would send a troubled child to hell for one bad decision. I believe in a God who says, 'Suffer the little children to come unto me.' Santa Claus is the guy with the nice and naughty list for children. Not God. Not my God, anyway."

Allison thought that was possibly the loveliest thing she'd ever heard him say, and she put her hand on his knee and squeezed it. Roland smiled, lifted her hand to his lips and kissed it, and though she wasn't much of a believer, she said a little prayer that maybe there was an abbey out there that would be short one monk come Christmas.

Afterward, they drove across the bridge into Washington. They found the house without too much trouble—a small blue bungalow that had seen better days. It seemed Kathy, too, had seen better days. It was a shell of a woman who answered the door—thin and pale with sunken cheeks and sunken eyes surrounded by dark circles. Though Kathy didn't smile once when they introduced themselves on the porch, Allison didn't find her unfriendly—simply too worn out to contort her face into an expression she wasn't used to wearing.

"Thank you for seeing us, Mrs. Collins," Allison said. "We're really sorry to bother you."

"Kathy, please," she said. She pointed to a faded floral print sofa in a cluttered living room. Allison and Roland sat and Kathy took her seat on the matching ottoman. "You were with Oliver when he lived at that house?"

"We were," Allison said. "Oliver left about a week before I did actually. He did leave in June of 2002, right?"

"Right, that's right." Kathy nodded. "My husband, Oliver's father, left me when Oliver was eight. He couldn't be in the same house with him anymore. I lost my job after that, and nobody in the family would help me with Ollie. He was too much. I couldn't do it anymore. Had to let the state have him."

"Too much?" Allison asked. "You mean he had behavior problems?"

"That's a way of putting it."

"Most of us did," Roland said. "Until Dad helped."

"Well, your dad certainly tried," she said, and Allison saw Kathy try to smile. She didn't do it, but she got closer than she had before.

"Can I ask what sort of behavior problems he had?" Allison said. She'd never pried into people's private lives like this before and it felt as strange to her as smiling probably did to Kathy.

"You don't know?" Kathy asked Roland.

"We had a rule at the house," Roland said. "Dad's rule. Don't talk about the old life. He wanted us kids to get past our pasts."

"There are some things in your past you can't ignore," Kathy said. "That was Ollie's trouble even after your father helped him. I guess you don't know that he...he killed my baby."

Allison couldn't manage a response to that. She looked at Roland, whose eyes were wide but who also remained silent in the face of this news.

Kathy dragged a ragged hand down her face. She seemed more exhausted than sad at this point. "He threw his baby brother, Jacob...he threw him against the wall. Killed him."

Allison gasped, covering her mouth with her hand in shock. Kathy had spoken the words in monotone, without flinching, barely blinking. In her hands she clutched a rolled recipe magazine. As she spoke she twisted the magazine until the pages ripped, then folded it over and twisted it again.

"Jacob cried a lot," she said. "So, I had to be with him all the time. Ollie was very jealous. But that wasn't Ollie's fault. Your father—" she nodded at Roland "—he explained that

Ollie had a problem here..." She tapped the side of her head. "A tumor. Made him act out."

"Dr. Capello operated on Oliver, yes?" Allison said, composing herself.

"I called his office because some lady at child services said Dr. Capello was a miracle worker with kids like Ollie. And we needed a miracle. He agreed to see Ollie and he fixed that tumor. Didn't even charge me a dime. And it was..." Kathy paused, waved her hand like she was waving a magic wand. "Night and day after."

"What do you mean?" Allison asked.

"Oh, before Ollie was a hard kid to live with. He lied all the time. He stole all the time. You couldn't punish him. He'd laugh it right off. And he'd mess with your head, too. He'd... play games. Ugly games. One second he'd kiss me and say, 'Mommy, I love you, I love you, I love you...' and soon as I said I loved him back, he'd stab me in the arm with a fork."

Allison felt her stomach roil. Kathy held out her arm to show an old scar, an inch long, pink and white and ugly.

"He'd never been a normal boy," Kathy said. "Not since he was born. Never cried much. Your father, he said that was a bad sign. Crying meant a baby was feeling what he was supposed to feel. And he was always like that, even as a boy. Too quiet. Intense. Like a time bomb, you know. But after the surgery, he wasn't like that anymore. The first week when he was in the hospital, he barely talked at all. Just ate and slept. One afternoon he asked for a Sprite and I got him a Sprite and he said, 'Thank you, Mommy.' And I waited for him to turn on me, but he didn't. He just drank his Sprite. Then a couple days later he said he was sorry for what he did to Jacob. He'd never..." She pursed her thin lips. "He'd never apologized before for anything in his life. Not even stabbing his own mother in the arm. I wanted to take him home, but your dad said Ollie needed time away to really heal. The house, me, everything would remind him of what he did. He needed a new start. So he went to live with you all at that house. Maybe I should have left him there. Bringing him home sure didn't help, but I wanted my son back. I wanted...I wanted both my boys back. But I'd take what I could get."

Her voice was hollow and wispy as a reed.

"I know this isn't any of our business," Allison said. "And I'm sorry for asking, but can you tell us about how Ollie died? Why he died? He was our brother for a little while. We just... We were so shocked to find out."

"I think it's my fault," Kathy said.

"I'm sure it's not," Allison said.

"I don't know about that," Kathy said. "Before the surgery, Ollie couldn't care less about what I was feeling. When I brought him home from your house, he was like a..." She snapped her fingers, searching for a word. "Like a sponge. Whatever I was feeling, he'd soak it all up. And I was pretty low then. Depressed. Cried a lot. Ollie would cry with me, and even after I stopped, he kept right on crying. Every day he'd tell me he was sorry about Jacob. One day, he just got too sorry to go on. A neighbor kept a shotgun in his garage. Ollie found it." Kathy looked at Roland. "I shoulda listened to your dad."

"What did he say?" Roland asked.

"He said I ought to leave Ollie with him," Kathy said. "But he was my son. And I wanted my boy back."

Kathy dropped her chin to her chest. She hadn't cried the whole time they'd been talking. Allison had a feeling she was cried out and then some. Slowly she raised her head.

"That's all I have to tell you," Kathy said. "Hope that's what you wanted to hear."

"I never want to hear about kids suffering," Allison said.

"We weren't trying to be nosy. The thing is, someone tried to hurt me when I was living there at Dr. Capello's house. I fell down a flight of steps and hit my head. Dr. Capello said he thought it might be Oliver who'd done it. I guess he did have a history of hurting his siblings."

"Not after that surgery," Kathy said. "No, ma'am. He wasn't that same boy at all. Not even close."

"Are you sure?" Allison asked. "I'm not here to point fingers, but with Oliver's past—"

"It wasn't Oliver, I'm telling you. After he came home, he stepped on my foot by accident and burst into tears. Cried for so long he made himself sick. Whatever your father did to him, he wasn't able to hurt a fly afterward."

"Do you remember when you brought him home with you?" Allison asked.

"Yes, it was, ah, a Friday. It was June 28. I remember because that's my wedding anniversary. I didn't want to be alone on that day."

"I'm asking because…before my accident, someone called my aunt. They told her someone in the house wanted me dead. Oliver went home with you before I fell, so I know he didn't push me," she said. "I didn't really think it was him who hurt me, anyway, but I thought…maybe he made the call from here?"

"Back then we only had one phone," she said. "And it was in my bedroom. I can't swear he didn't make any calls, but I…I just don't think Ollie had anything to do with this. Believe me, I have no illusions about who and what my son was. Before that surgery, he would have pushed his own grandma down the stairs and laughed if she broke her leg. I tell you that without batting an eyelash. But after… Whatever your father did to Ollie, it fixed him."

"I know one of Dr. Capello's patients had a tumor removed but it came back. Was that Oliver?" Allison asked.

Kathy shook her head. "It never came back, no. In fact, not only did the operation fix him, it, well, I think it fixed him too good. Poor boy went from feeling nothing to feeling everything. But what choice did I have? If your father hadn't found that tumor, he would have been in juvenile detention for sure. Hell, he probably would have been on death row by eighteen, anyway."

"You did the right thing," Allison said, and she meant it. She wanted to reach out to touch Kathy's hand, but held back. "I can't think of any other parent doing any different. We..." She glanced at Roland. "We wish we'd known what happened when it happened. We could have paid our respects to him."

"Well," Kathy said, putting the magazine she'd been shredding down at last. "It's all right. I didn't have a funeral. I couldn't bear to watch them bury another one of my babies."

"We are sorry," Allison said. "Oliver was always sweet."

"That's nice of you to say," Kathy said.

She still didn't smile.

CHAPTER 20

Back in the car, Allison realized she hadn't heard Roland speaking for what felt like hours.

"Roland?"

Allison took his hand in hers. He didn't take it in return. He let her hold on to him but that was all.

"Roland?" she said again. "You're so quiet." He'd barely said a word in the house with Kathy. It seemed he'd lost his ability to speak.

"Sorry," he said finally. "Just taking it all in."

Allison pulled out of the driveway and drove aimlessly around the neighborhood, not sure where to go or if she wanted to go anywhere yet. She just wanted to move.

"I read that profile of Dad that's on his office wall," she said. "I thought when it said he took in kids who had problems...I thought that meant temper tantrums and attention span problems and impulse control issues. I didn't think it meant he took in kids who'd killed other kids." Allison realized what she was saying and who she was saying it to. "You know, killed kids on purpose. Not like with you and—"

"I know what you mean," he said.

She smiled apologetically.

"Doesn't it seem dangerous, bringing a kid like that into a house with other kids?"

Roland shrugged. "You heard the lady. Oliver had a brain tumor and Dad fixed it. Dad told me all kinds of horror stories about people with tumors and cysts and what it does to their behavior. One man had a tumor in his prefrontal cortex. He went from being a nice normal family man to trying to seduce his twelve-year-old stepdaughter. They took out the tumor and he went back to normal. Just like that." Roland snapped his fingers. "And you know about his grandparents."

"Dad's? Yeah, lead poisoning turned a normal man into a murderer."

"And he committed suicide after he killed his wife," Roland said. "You can't blame people like that for their actions. They're sick—they aren't doing it on purpose."

"I know," Allison said. She took a long breath. "At some point we have to talk about why your dad lied to me about Oliver."

"I know," Roland said. "I know we will. But not yet."

At least he wasn't trying to convince her or himself that Dr. Capello was just confused anymore. After their talk with Kathy Collins, it was apparent Dr. Capello hadn't been truthful with her or with Roland. But why lie?

"When you're ready," Allison said, and squeezed his hand. It took a minute but Roland finally squeezed her hand back.

Allison found the interstate and bridge, and with Roland's help navigating, they were soon back on their way home.

"We were supposed to stay out all night," Allison said, noting the time on the clock. Not even nine yet, though it was already dark.

"Dad said he didn't want to see us until morning," Roland said. "Didn't say we had to stay out all night."

"Good point. We'll just be very quiet..."

That wouldn't be a problem for Roland. He'd been quiet at Kathy's, quiet after, more quiet than he usually was. She wondered if he was mourning Oliver. She wondered if he was praying for him. She wondered if he was angry or scared or both.

"What are you thinking about?" Allison asked, unable to take the silence any longer.

"Ah, it doesn't matter," Roland said, looking out the window.

"It matters a lot. It matters to me."

He put his hand on her thigh again.

"I'm thinking about Dad. How hard it must have been for him to save a kid's life, and give that kid a home, and then find out that kid threw away that life he worked so hard to save."

"Do you think it means something that Oliver shot himself in the brain?" Allison asked.

"I think it means he was very depressed," Roland said. "But maybe he was trying to put a bullet into the thing that was causing him all his pain. I know I should be feeling bad for his mom, and I do, but I keep thinking, *Poor Dad*. To lose a patient is bad enough but to lose one like that..."

"Dad talked to me about the graveyard," Allison said.

"The graveyard?"

"He said every surgeon carries a graveyard inside them. And all the patients they've lost are buried in it."

"It's a lot to carry around with you," Roland said. "And he lived with us, too. He was Dad's son for a few months. No wonder he didn't tell us about Oliver. It probably broke his heart."

"I'm sure it did," Allison said. "He always liked things to be nice and happy at the house. He tried, anyway."

"We all had such shitty childhoods," Roland said. "He

was just trying to make up for that. You were happy with us, right?"

"I was as happy to be with you then as I am now."

"So…?"

She turned and gave him a quick grin. "Very happy."

They drove on longer in silence, but the tension had disappeared and now it was a companionable sort of quiet. Roland moved his hand a little higher up her thigh.

"You can ask me what I'm thinking about again," Roland said.

"I think I can guess." She patted his hand and playfully took it off her thigh and placed it on his. "Driving here."

"Sorry."

"You are not." She laughed, when suddenly the magnitude of the day hit her like it hadn't before. Hit her hard. "Oliver shot himself."

"Yes, and…?"

"He was fine at the house with us."

"Or he was pretending to be," Roland said. "Brain surgery can have some odd outcomes. Dad says issues can pop up years after operations. Maybe something like that happened with Oliver."

"I guess so. But now I want to talk to Kendra and Antonio even more."

"Kendra and Antonio?" Roland sat up straighter in the seat. "What about them?"

"I asked McQueen to get me their addresses, too."

Roland shook his head and she didn't know why.

"What?" she asked.

"I wish you wouldn't talk to her."

"Why not? I always liked her. I think she liked me."

Roland went quiet for a few seconds before answering.

"Remember when I told you that you were my second?" Roland said. "She was my first."

Allison almost ran off the road.

"Kendra? She was your girlfriend?"

"Yeah. Sort of. I mean, we didn't really date. You don't have to date when you're living in the same house."

"When did this happen?"

"A few months after you left. I was seventeen. She was fifteen. I'd feel weird about it if you saw her. Kendra probably would, too."

Allison would, too, but that didn't matter. The timing, that was what mattered.

"A few months after I left… Any chance she was in love with you while I was there?" Allison asked.

"Allison, Kendra wouldn't push you down the stairs because of you and me."

"That's not an answer to my question."

Roland said nothing. Then Allison thought of something.

"Did you tell her what happened that day? On the beach?" Allison asked.

Slowly Roland nodded.

"Why did you tell her?"

"I didn't mean to but she knew something was wrong. She's very intuitive. She could tell I felt guilty. This was the day after it happened and you were acting so weird and I guess I was acting weird, too. I had to tell someone or I'd go nuts."

"What did she say about it?" Allison asked.

"It was thirteen years ago," he said.

"Was she upset?"

"No, not with me."

"But she was upset with me?" Allison asked. "Angry?"

"Scared," Roland said. "But not mad. Although I think she said we were being 'stupid.'"

"If she was half as in love with you as I was," Allison said, "and you told her that you and I had fooled around, what do you think she would feel?"

"I don't think she was in love with me at the time," he said. "She never said she was."

"I never said I was, either," Allison said. They drove a few more miles before she could speak again.

"What exactly did she say when you told her?" Allison asked.

"She reminded me of Dad's rule about us, you know, not doing that sort of thing with each other."

"I remember that rule," Allison said.

"Kendra said that was the sort of thing that got kids kicked out of group homes. Dad wasn't going to kick me out—I was adopted—but he might kick you out, she thought. She was worried about you, not me."

"Is that all she said?"

"She told me to make sure it never happened again. That's all."

"And you're just telling me this now?" Allison asked.

"Trust me, if you knew Kendra the way I did, you would know she wouldn't push you or anyone else down the stairs. Or call your aunt and terrify her. That's not like her at all."

"Was it like Oliver to kill himself?"

Roland didn't answer.

"Do you know where she is?" Allison asked.

"I don't know her address. Long time ago I asked Dad if he ever heard from her, and he said as far as he knew she was fine and well and living in Olympia. Works at home doing something in computer programming. There's really no reason to bother her."

Allison wasn't sure about that.

"Now you're being too quiet," Roland said after they'd

driven for about another fifteen minutes in silence. "What are you thinking about?"

"I was thinking about that day. You told Kendra but nobody else, right?"

"Right..."

"And Dad didn't tell you Oliver killed himself. No one told me about your sister, Rachel, until Deacon did a few days ago. And Dad didn't tell you all about that phone call to my aunt. And he didn't tell you all that my fall might not have been an accident. On top of all that, Deacon and Thora said they were together when my fall happened, but Deacon said they were outside and Thora said they were inside, which means one of them or both of them aren't telling me the whole truth. That's a lot of secrets in one house, isn't it?"

Roland said nothing.

"Just has me wondering," Allison said.

"What?"

"What else are you all hiding from each other? And from me?"

"You don't have to sound so suspicious," Roland said. "There's a big difference between keeping secrets and wanting your privacy. None of us—me, Deac, Thor—we don't ask each other about what happened to us in BC times."

"BC?"

"Before Capello," he said. "We don't want to talk about it. We don't want to pry. None of it is secret. It's just...private."

"I respect your right to privacy, but I think there are some things I deserve to know."

"You're right, you do. If I thought for one second Kendra did it, I'd tell you. We broke Dad's rules, me and her, and so we've never told anyone we were a couple. That's private," he said. "Not some deep dark secret."

"What if Dr. Capello knew?"

"What?"

"What if he knew about you and Kendra? Possible?"

"Possible, maybe," Roland said. "We didn't tell him, but that doesn't mean he didn't figure it out. We were sleeping together sometimes while he was one floor above us. Deacon could have found out and blabbed. Or Thora even. Why?"

"Follow me here," she said, excited because the pieces were clicking into place. "The day after I came here, I told your dad I didn't feel safe staying at the house because I didn't know who'd hurt me. He wants me to stay for, you know, reasons."

"Me," Roland said.

"You."

"And because he loves you and missed you."

"That, too," Allison said. "So he needs to tell me something to get me to stay. He says it was Oliver. Why? Oliver's dead. Not like we can get a dead person into trouble. It's safe to blame Oliver. And your dad wouldn't want to tell me it's Kendra because I'd ask why she did it and then he'd have to tell me about you and her. He knows she hurt me out of jealousy, but he doesn't want me to go after your ex-girlfriend for something that happened so long ago. Does that make any kind of sense to you?"

"I suppose," he said. "It's logical."

"And my aunt thought it was me calling her. That means it was very likely a girl. So that leaves Kendra or Thora."

"It wasn't Thora," Roland said. "It's just so hard to picture Kendra doing that." He rubbed his forehead as if the very idea of it gave him a headache.

"She was a young girl in love. Girls in love do dumb, risky things—for example, kiss your big brother on the beach even though you're twelve and he's almost seventeen."

"You have a point there," Roland said.

He sounded resigned, as if the force of her reasoning had finally overwhelmed his objections.

"I do get why Dad would keep it a secret from me," Roland said at last. "I mean, if Kendra did do it, I would go and talk her about it. But Dad, he wants us to move on, to heal, to let go of the bad stuff we can't change. Sometimes there's just...too much bad stuff to ignore." His voice sounded more bitter than she'd ever heard it. They drove in silence again for a few minutes before Allison asked a question that had been on her mind since learning Roland and Kendra had once been together.

"Will you answer one more question for me, please?" Allison said, trying not to sound as frustrated as she felt. "Is there anything else you're not telling me? Anything at all I should know that you're keeping from me?"

For a painfully long moment, Roland said nothing. Allison lived and died in that silence.

"Yes," Roland finally said.

Allison's heart jumped in her chest a little. Her hands gripped the steering wheel tightly.

"Are you going to tell me what it is?"

"Do you really want to know? It'll change things between us. Really change them."

"Yes," she said. "I want to know."

The long terrible silence came and went again.

"I think I'm falling in love with you," Roland said.

Allison took a long hard breath.

"Yeah, that does kind of change things."

"Told you so."

"When were you planning on telling me this?" Allison asked.

"I wasn't," he said, almost laughing, though it was clear he found none of it funny. "You asked."

"True," she said, and blew out a long breath. "I asked."

By ten they arrived back home at The Dragon and in the dark it looked even more like its namesake than it did by day. The uneven outline of the house loomed tall, strange and humpbacked in the moonlight. The Dragon seemed sad to Allison, slumped almost, like the poor thing had heard about Oliver and bowed his old head in sorrow and in respect.

She and Roland had said almost nothing to each other since his declaration of—well, not of love but of *almost*-love. What could she say? She'd been in a relationship for six years before she came home. Could she trust her feelings for Roland? She adored him. Every time she looked at him with his father she felt a deep and deepening tenderness for him. She loved bringing him tea at night when he was reading to Dr. Capello. She even liked folding his underwear, especially when she had to fight Brien over them. These were all novel experiences for her. As an adult, she'd never been a girlfriend, only a mistress. She'd never folded McQueen's underwear. She never brought him chamomile tea at bedtime. With Roland she felt love, but was it love for *him*? Or for the idea of him and home and family? If that love was real, was there any difference?

Allison thought about the moment McQueen had left her two weeks ago, the moment he'd finally walked out the door and out of her life. She remembered the sorrow and the panic. Then she tried to imagine Roland leaving her, walking out the door to return to his old life at the monastery. She couldn't. If there was leaving to do, he would let her do it first. And for a girl who'd been left behind more times than she could count, that felt like real love to her.

Roland started to go into the house and she reached out to stop him, touching his arm, holding him by his sleeve.

"Roland," she whispered.

"What's wrong?"

"I'm falling in love with you, too."

He narrowed his eyes at her.

"Are you sure?" he asked.

"Let's see... I've been home, oh, nine days? No, of course I'm not sure. I'm insane and so are you."

He laughed, which she appreciated.

"It's not like we're strangers," he said.

"No, but it's not like we know each other, either. But I do know this...when I was here as a little girl, I would pray for rain, because that was my excuse to go crawling into bed with you. I'm twenty-five now and I don't need an excuse. But I still keep hoping it rains. Does that mean I'm in love with you?"

"Close enough," he said, and moved to kiss her. She put her hands on his chest.

"You're a monk," she said. "You do remember you're supposed to go back to the monastery, right?"

"Not tonight," he said.

He took her in his arms then and kissed her in The Dragon's long shadow. It was a passionate kiss, hard and hot and sensual. He paused and whispered against her lips, "Maybe not ever."

Allison took his hand and led him into the house and up the stairs, quietly, very quietly so no one would know they were home yet and dare to interrupt them.

Inside the bedroom that had once been his, then hers and now was theirs, Roland shut the door behind them and locked it. Allison was already undressed by the time they reached the bed, and Roland was already inside her by the time her head hit the pillow. Before, all the times they'd been together, it had felt like they were making love. And that's what she would have called it, and that's what it was. But now they'd admitted they did love each other, or almost did, and for the first time it felt like Roland was fucking her. He held her down on the bed, hands on her wrists, which he'd pinned over her head.

His thrusts were rough and she had to work to keep up with him, and what delicious work it was. She came faster than she'd known she could and even came a second time when he let go inside of her. She understood the difference between the times that had come before and this one. Before there was always the chance Roland would go back to the monastery. He'd been holding back with her because he knew it would end eventually, and he didn't want to risk doing anything he regretted. He'd been on his best behavior. Not anymore.

Truth was, she liked this Roland even better than the other one.

And she told him.

His chest moved in silent laughter as she lay across his body. They were both sweating together, breathing together, dripping wet together.

"When the beautiful girl you're crazy about tells you she might be in love with you, it makes you a little wild," he said. "Not too wild?"

"The perfect amount of wild. I didn't know you had it in you."

"I believe, technically, you had it in you."

She grinned and kissed his chest.

"I love it in me," she said. "Feel free to have it in me again anytime. Or right now."

"Thirty-minute nap," he said. "Then we go for episode two of *Wild Kingdom*."

"Take your nap. I'll wake you."

He kissed her forehead and rolled over. She went to the bathroom, and by the time she came back, he was already breathing the rhythmic breaths of deep sleep. Men.

She looked at him and his long muscular back and remembered how she'd seen it, as if for the very first time, that day at the ocean's edge when they'd crossed a line a foster brother and sister shouldn't cross. Maybe it was for the best, really, that she'd left and gone to live with her aunt. Maybe it was for the best that years passed between that day and this one. Instead of her thirteen years away from this place acting as a wall between them, the time apart had become a bridge, the path from what they had been to what they could be.

The room was stuffy from the day's heat and fragrant with the scent of sex. She cracked the window, and when Roland didn't wake from the sound, she pushed it all the way up.

Not tired enough to sleep, Allison sat in the window bench. She thought about reading but there wasn't quite enough moonlight to read by and she hated reading on her phone, but that was fine by her. She watched the water instead, watched it shimmering in the glowing deck lights. She wondered at the strangeness of the day, how it had begun with death and ended with sex. But was it that strange? Her best night with McQueen, the one night she cherished most in her memories, had come when she'd returned home after attending her aunt's funeral. McQueen had surprised her with his kindnesses during that difficult time, hiring a car to take her there and bring her back, sending a spray of roses, orchids and lilies to cover her aunt's casket. He'd even been waiting at her apartment when she arrived. He'd wanted sex from her, of course, but that night she'd wanted it from him even more. She'd spent three days in the company of death. And sex was almost the opposite of a funeral. A funeral said "life ends." Sex said "life goes on." No wonder she and Roland had fallen on each other like wild animals tonight. After learning one of their own had taken his life, they'd needed the reminder they were still alive.

Allison was almost asleep in the window seat when she thought she saw something moving on the beach. People? An animal? She took the old binoculars off the hook and trained them on the patch of beach just beyond the deck. She didn't see anything at first, but then the binoculars picked up a red flame. A bonfire on the beach. Someone was having a cook-out. This late at night? Well, why not? It was a nice night, warm and dry. She saw the burning logs. She saw the dancing sparks. She saw a square beach blanket next to the fire and one person lying on it.

Her eyes adjusted to the dim light. No, it wasn't one person on the blanket but two. Two people, one on top of the other. Allison knew she shouldn't be looking but there was something about the couple that made it impossible for her to look away.

The woman on top had hair the same color as the fire.

The man underneath her had black tattoos on his naked arms and chest.

Allison slowly lowered the binoculars and turned her head from the scene as if she could still see it.

Now she knew one more secret hiding in this house.

CHAPTER 21

Allison pulled on her jeans and Roland's flannel shirt and went down to the sunroom. She turned on a lamp, pretended to read a book and waited. Five minutes later she heard the deck creaking, the sound of people climbing up the staircase from the beach. Outside the French deck doors, Deacon and Thora paused, wiped their feet and brushed sand from each other's clothes. They came inside and saw her, smiling like nothing in the world was different.

"You're home early," Thora said. "Did you bring my burgers?"

"In the kitchen," Allison said.

"Didn't Dad tell you all not to come back until morning?" Thora asked.

"He did, but we didn't feel like staying out all night."

"Don't tell Dad you disobeyed an order," Deacon said. "He's in a horrible mood."

"What's wrong?" Allison asked.

"Kicked me out of his room when I tried to make him take his meds," Thora said. Allison could tell she'd been crying, too.

"He used to never lose his temper with us."

"It's not really his fault," Thora said. "The poisons in the bloodstream mess with the brain. He's been a lot testier. Then again, it could just be the fear talking."

"Was he really bad?" Allison said.

"He wasn't any fun, that's for sure," Thora said. "I had to go for a walk on the beach to calm down."

"Feel better now?" Allison asked.

"Much," Thora said.

Allison nodded. "Good."

"I'll go check on Dad," Deacon said. "You going to bed?"

"In a few minutes," Thora said. "Good night."

"Good night," Deacon said.

He was almost all the way out of the room when Allison said it.

"Guys, I know, by the way."

Deacon froze, then slowly turned around. Thora's eyes widened slightly.

"Know what?" Thora said.

"I was sitting in the window in my room," Allison said. "I thought I saw something on the beach. I got out the binoculars. I promise, I thought it was just, I don't know, an animal or something at first. I didn't mean to snoop."

Thora said nothing. Deacon said nothing.

"It's okay," Allison said. "It's really okay. I just didn't want to not tell you all I knew. Seems like there's enough secrets in this house without me keeping any extras lying around."

"If I'd known you were watching," Deacon said, "I would have put on a better show."

"I didn't watch," Allison said. "I saw. And then I immediately stopped looking."

She was speaking very calmly but her heart was pounding in her chest and her stomach was tight.

"Does Dad know?" Allison asked.

"No," Thora said. "At least, we've never told him."

Deacon sat on the white overstuffed chair opposite her on the couch. Thora sat on the arm of the chair.

"You remember his rules," Deacon said. "We were scared he'd separate us if he knew."

"So you have been together a long time?" Allison asked.

"Since we were fourteen," Thora said. By lamplight, Allison could see the soft blush on Thora's face. "Are you angry?"

"Why would I be? I mean, it's kind of surprising," Allison said. "We used to call you the Twins."

"Because we're the same age," Deacon said. "Not like we look much alike."

"I keep thinking I should have known. How did I not know?"

"We always tried to be careful," Thora said.

"And come on, I was fourteen," Deacon said. "Not like it lasted much longer than two minutes, anyway."

"You got much better with age," Thora said.

"I couldn't have gotten much worse."

"That's true," Thora said, then flinched. Deacon had apparently pinched her at that remark.

"Does Roland know?" Allison asked.

"Yeah," Thora said. "We finally gave in and told Ro when we were eighteen. We asked him not to say anything to anyone. Legally, we are siblings."

"How did Roland take it?" Allison closed her book, done now with any pretense.

"He handled it better than I thought he would," Deacon said, now rubbing Thora's back. "Apparently he and Kendra were a thing for a very short time. So he understood. He didn't like that we were keeping it a secret from Dad, but he got it."

"You don't think Dad would be okay with it now?" Allison asked. "I mean, you all are what? Twenty-eight? And he's happy about me and Roland."

"No offense," Deacon said, "but you aren't one of us."

Allison wasn't offended, but it still stung. No, she wasn't one of them. She could have been, maybe, but fate had other ideas for her.

"Dad tried really hard to make us into a perfect family. And we tried to be a perfect family for him. We really did. Deacon even lived with family in China for years to get over me."

"Didn't work." Deacon looked up at Thora and winked. "But we did try for Dad's sake. He's done so much for us—treated us, took us in, adopted us, gave us everything we ever wanted and needed. He never asked for anything in return. Maybe he'd be okay with me and Thora together, but we're not going to stress him out now."

"We don't want to hurt Dad."

"I get it," Allison said.

"Are you sure you aren't angry?" Thora asked her.

"I'm sure I'm not angry. I know what it's like to be in a relationship you don't know how to talk about," Allison said. "Can I ask if that's what you two were doing when I fell?"

Deacon and Thora looked at each other. Thora nodded.

"We were in my room," Thora said. "Doing exactly what you think we were doing. I was upset about something and Deacon was trying to make me feel better."

"I'm sorry I lied," Deacon said. "I was protecting Thora. It's what I do."

Allison smiled at them. "I feel silly. I should have known," she said. "At the studio, you were invading Thora's personal space big time."

"He's allowed," Thora said.

"And your two rooms, those are the two with the Jack and Jill bathroom, right?" Allison asked.

"Connecting doors," Deacon said.

"Guess we won't be needing separate bedrooms much longer," Thora said.

"I'm still sleeping in my own room," Deacon said. "You steal the covers."

"You kick."

"Because you steal the covers!"

Allison couldn't help but laugh.

"You two are cute," Allison said.

"We are," Deacon said, nodding slowly. "Extremely adorable even."

"Thanks for being cool about it," Thora said.

"I'm cool," Allison said.

"You are, you rascal." Thora came over to the couch, bent down and kissed her on the cheek. Deacon applauded. They both looked at him and glared.

"Sorry," he said. "I'll show myself out. Better make sure Dad's okay."

"I'll go," Allison said. "He's still on his best behavior with me."

"You sure?" Deacon asked.

"If he needs something I can't do for him," Allison said, "I'll get Roland. Good night."

"Night, sis," Deacon said. They left the room but two seconds later Deacon stuck his head back in.

"What?" Allison said.

"Told you there were flowers in the attic."

Allison made like she was going to throw her book at his head and he ducked out again, laughing. Allison switched off the lamp, when something Deacon had said earlier suddenly struck her. She raced from the sunroom to the stairs to stop them before they disappeared for the night.

"Hey," Allison said in a whisper when she found them heading upstairs.

Deacon waited while Allison ran up to meet them.

"Did you say Dad treated you?" Allison asked him, her voice low.

"Yeah, of course," Deacon said. "Where do you think we met him? At a bar?"

"You and Thora both?" Allison asked.

"Us both."

"I had an astrocytoma," Deacon said. "Thora had a dermoid brain cyst. We were charity cases. Dad brought us home after to recover. We never left. Why do you ask?"

"Just curious," Allison said.

"He saved our lives," Deacon said. "Whatever we have to do to repay him for that, we'll do it. Even lie for years and years."

"You're a good son," Allison said. "Good brother, too."

Deacon kissed her on the cheek and went off to bed. Allison climbed the steps to the third floor. It was quiet. She heard nothing but the wind and the ocean and the creaking of the floors under her feet. She hoped this meant Dr. Capello was sound asleep. She went to his bedroom and saw it was dark inside, no lights on at all. She crept over to the bed and started when she saw it was empty. Slept in, yes, but abandoned. Where was Dr. Capello then? She walked over to the door to the bathroom and rapped her knuckles on it lightly.

"Dad? You in there?"

No answer.

"Dad?"

She turned the knob and found the bathroom empty, as well.

"Dad?" she called out a little louder and heard nothing. She would have to find Roland. Dr. Capello must have snuck out.

What if he was hurt? What if he had gone off somewhere on his own to die like an animal? All sorts of horrible thoughts raced through her mind as she ran from the bedroom. It was then she noticed a faint light coming from under the door to the attic. She turned the knob and found the door unlocked. The stair lights were on and she heard someone shuffling about above.

"Dad?" she called out as she started up the stairs.

"I'm up here, doll," Dr. Capello called back.

Allison took a huge gulping breath of utter relief.

"You scared the hell out of me," she said.

"Sorry," he said. "Had to do something up here."

She turned the corner at the top of the stairs and found Dr. Capello standing in his robe and slippers by the big wooden filing cabinet. At his feet was a metal wastepaper basket, and although every window in the attic had been opened, it didn't completely erase the scent of smoke from the room.

"What are you doing?" she demanded. She looked down into the metal trashcan and saw the remnants of burnt paper.

"Something I should have done a long time ago," he said. "I don't want you kids having to clean up after me when I'm gone. These old medical records should have been destroyed when I retired. Just never got around to it."

"It's midnight and you're burning papers in the attic," she said.

"I was hoping to get it all done before any of you kids noticed and sent me back to bed."

"Can I help you?" she asked.

"I'm afraid this stuff is all confidential."

"You know there's such a thing as a paper shredder, right?" Allison asked. Dr. Capello opened the top drawer of the cabinet and pulled out a sheaf of files, five inches thick. It made a thud on the top of the filing cabinet.

"You can put shredded papers back together," he said. "Burning them is the best way to get rid of them. And I already know the smoke goes right out the windows. A few rotten kids of mine like to come up here to smoke pot when they think I'm not paying attention."

"I know nothing about that," she said, batting her eyelashes.

"I'm sure you don't. My littlest angel girl would never do anything like that, would she?"

With her finger Allison drew a halo over her head. Dr. Capello chuckled and got back to burning. It was a little odd, burning the old medical files. Seemed so drastic. And smelly. Then again, just a few days ago she'd put the photographs McQueen had taken of them together plus the negatives into a metal trashcan and dropped a match on them and watched them burn. She'd had to do it fast before she chickened out. They'd been mementos of her six years with McQueen but they were also so explicit she couldn't bear the thought of anyone anywhere in the world getting their hands and their eyes on them. Was Dr. Capello as embarrassed by his medical files as she'd been of her pornographic pictures? What on earth was a bunch of children's medical files that a simple paper shredder wouldn't have sufficed?

"You really should be in bed," Allison said. "I'm saying that because I know Roland's going to ask me if I told you to go back to bed."

"You did. I'll vouch for you. You just sit over there and make sure I don't faint. I'm feeling okay today but we know that won't last. Gotta do it now."

She pulled a white sheet off an old chair and sat down in it. She warily eyed the cabinets along the south wall, the ones that held Dr. Capello's "collection." How strange that a man as normal and kind as Dr. Capello kept such a gruesome collection.

"What's on your mind tonight, doll?" Dr. Capello asked.

"Can I ask what's up with all the creepy stuff?" Allison said.

"What creepy stuff?" he said as he tossed a few more pages into the metal basket.

She pointed at the cabinets.

"That's not creepy stuff," he said, sounding affronted.

"You have a speculum made out of wood. With a leech applicator."

"All right, that one may be a little creepy," he conceded. "But those objects over there were created to save lives. Even two hundred years ago, surgeons were drilling holes in the head to relieve the pressure on swollen brains."

"Did anyone survive these surgeries?"

"More than you would think. Less than you would like."

"What are you doing with it all?" she asked.

"A few of the pieces were here in the house when I inherited it. My grandfather hired doctors from all over the world to treat my grandmother, bought every machine, every treatment, every pill and potion money could buy trying to bring her around. I imagine he thought if he could heal her, he'd somehow magically be all right again himself. Where you see 'creepy,' I see lives saved by brave pioneers. I see surgeons trying to help others as best they could given their limited understanding of anatomy and physiology and psychology. In a hundred years people may look back on my own work in horror the way so many of us look back on medicine from the past. I hope they show me the same mercy I show the doctors of past decades and centuries."

"I'm sure they will," she said.

"It's good to see where we've come from. This creepy stuff is living medical history. Someone has to take care of it. It's all been cataloged. My alma mater is getting it when I'm gone. Unless you want it?" he said with a raised eyebrow.

"No, thank you. I know it was used to help people, but they can have the saws covered in Civil War soldier blood. I'm good."

"Your loss, kiddo."

He turned back to his work but stopped and looked over at her with a furrowed brow again. "Didn't I tell you not to show your face until morning?"

"It's after midnight," she said.

"Doesn't count. There are hotels in Portland, you know. Nice ones."

"Oh, we got a hotel room. We rented it for an hour."

He gave her a dirty look. "And this is the girl I want for my monk of a son?"

"I told you not to match make," she said.

"Can't help it," he said as he tossed some more papers in the basket and dropped a match in. "I need something to think about other than my impending demise."

The papers in the files must have been old because the match caught quickly and fire leapt up. In short order they turned black and gray and shrunk to mere ash.

"You'll be happy to know then that your son and I are crazy about each other. And I have a pretty good feeling a certain monastery is going to be short one monk by Christmas."

"Is that so?" Dr. Capello asked, leaning on the filing cabinet and grinning broadly at her.

"That's so. We had a long talk tonight."

"Excellent news."

"Thought you'd like that," Allison said.

Dr. Capello looked up at the ceiling and heaved a sigh, his eyes closed. For a moment, it seemed he was a man of prayer expressing intense gratitude and relief. She forgave him the lie about Oliver. This was a man who wanted nothing but to see his children happy.

"It gives me peace." He placed his hand over his heart and patted it twice. "A lot of peace."

"Good," she said. "It's making me a nervous wreck but as long as you're happy…"

He laughed. "You'll be sticking around then? Even after I kick the bucket."

"Oh, can we not talk about that, please?"

"Let's say I get hit by a bus tomorrow and that's what does me in. Would you, even when I'm a greasy spot under a bus wheel, stick around here?"

Allison exhaled heavily. Fair question.

"Probably," she said. "For a little while, anyway. All my stuff's back at my apartment, and I've got no idea what I'd do out here, but maybe I could find a job in Astoria or Clark Beach. Know anyone who needs a professional poetry reciter?"

He grinned at her. "I have a better idea. Come down to my room with me."

"You're done playing with matches?"

"All done," he said as he dumped a bottle of water into the wastepaper basket to extinguish every last spark of flame. "I want to show you something."

Allison waited for Dr. Capello to go down the stairs but he waved her down first.

"Go slow," he said. "These old legs are getting weaker by the minute."

She went as slow as she could, step by step, Dr. Capello right behind her in case he stumbled, his hand on her shoulder to steady himself. At least his grip was still good and strong. The Man of Steel wasn't done for yet.

They went into his bedroom. Dr. Capello paused in the center of the plaid rug and tugged the hairs of his beard.

"Now, where'd that laptop of mine go…" he said.

She saw it. It stuck out from under a throw pillow on his bed. He sat in the armchair and she gave him his computer.

"What are you going to show me?" she asked.

"Hold your horses, I'm pulling it up. There." He turned the laptop around and showed her a photograph on the screen. "Like it?" he asked, smiling like a child.

It was a gray shingle building, one-story with a wide, white front porch and a picture window painted with the words *Clark Beach Books.*

"It's a bookstore," she said. "I like it already."

"You want it?"

Allison's eyes went wide.

"What?"

"Would you like to own a bookstore in Clark Beach?"

Allison stared at him. "Is this a trick question?"

"No. Especially since I already know the answer. The owners were planning to sell and retire in four years. They'll happily get out a little early for the right price. I can give them the right price."

"You can give them the right price," she said, her voice dull to her own ears. She couldn't believe what she was hearing.

"I bought Deacon and Thora The Glass Dragon. And Roland's inheriting this house. Gotta give you a building, too. Fair is fair."

"Not fair," she said, waving her hand. "Deacon and Thora and Roland are your children."

"And you were my child for over four years."

"Yes, thirteen years ago."

"And now you're back, doll. And you're going to stay here with my son. And if you're going to stay here with my son, I want you to have a job that gives you as much joy and satisfaction as my work gave me—as you kids gave me. You told

Deacon owning a bookstore in a little town like Clark Beach is your dream? Well, here you go, dream come true."

He nudged the laptop forward, and Allison stared long and hard at the photograph. It was a beautiful little building. It even had a porch swing where people could sit and read in good weather. She had that fifty thousand dollars from McQueen burning a hole in her suitcase. That would be enough to live on while she got the bookstore up and running.

"You can change the name," Dr. Capello said. "Anything you like. Allison's Books. Oceanside Bookstore."

"Pandora's Books," Allison said.

Dr. Capello nodded his approval. "It's two blocks from the ocean," he said. "And right next to an ice-cream shop."

"You're trying to seduce me."

"It's working, isn't it?"

"This has to be insanely expensive," she said.

"I can afford it. And it's not like I need money where I'm going."

"Your kids may need it." The upkeep on The Dragon alone would be a huge figure.

"Yes, and you're one of my kids," Dr. Capello said. He leaned forward and took her hand in his and held it gently. "Let me do this for you. If it hadn't been for my negligence, you would never have had to leave. Let me make it up to you. And on top of that—for years I've been nursing a broken heart over my son joining the monastery instead of finding a nice girl. All I ever wanted for him was to find someone to love him, someone he can love and have a normal, happy life with. You've made a dream of mine come true. Let me return the favor."

She was tempted to say yes right then and there. So tempted. But she couldn't quite bring herself to do it. Not yet. Not without talking to Roland first. Allison would never forgive herself for taking financial advantage of an ill and elderly man, no matter how lucid he might seem.

"Can I think about it?" she asked.

"You can, but don't take too long. I don't have much more time. I'd like to see you settled here and happy before I move along."

She looked at him and he shrugged.

"No use pretending."

"Whatever I decide," she said, "thank you. This is the kindest thing anyone has ever offered to do for me."

"The kindest thing you could do for me is accept it."

"I'll get back to you about it quickly," she pledged. "I... It's just a lot to think about, never going back to Kentucky, owning my own small business."

"No denying it'll be work. But maybe you can talk a certain ex-monk we know into helping out. He's great at heavy lifting."

Allison came off the bed and wrapped her arms around Dr. Capello's thin shoulders and held him for a good long time.

"Thank you, Dad."

"My pleasure, doll face. Now you get to bed, and I'll get to bed."

"Great idea." She helped him to his feet and made sure he was comfortably situated before she turned off the light and left him alone in his room. When she emerged into the hallway, she saw she'd left the attic light on. A moment's paranoia sent her heading back up the stairs to double check that Dr. Capello's trash fire had gone out completely. He knew what he was doing apparently, because the fire was dead, completely, though a light smoky smell remained in the room. Out of curiosity, Allison opened the top filing cabinet drawer. The key was in the drawer lock, but now that the drawers were empty, Dr. Capello hadn't locked it up. There was nothing left in it at all but empty hanging folders. She flipped through them and found nothing. Not until she came to a file folder near the very back. Dr. Capello had missed one small scrap of paper stuck to the bottom of the file. In plain type at the top of the page was written "Pre-Op Instructions." Underneath in Dr. Capello's slanted and angular handwriting were words Allison found legible and yet utterly incomprehensible.

Operation: Partial hippocampectomy.

Patient: Larsen, Roland J., age 8

Date: 8-8-93

Time: 7:00 a.m.

Anesthesia: General.

They were medical notes to an anesthesiologist named Dr. Penn about an upcoming operation. An operation on an eight-year-old boy named Roland J. Larsen. An eight-year-old boy named Roland J. Larsen in the year 1993. Which meant that eight-year-old boy named Roland J. Larsen was now thirty years old.

Dr. Capello had operated on Roland. Her Roland. It had to be him, didn't it? It's not as if "Roland" was a very common name. It wasn't a huge surprise to her that Dr. Capello had operated on him. He'd operated on Deacon and Thora and Oliver. But why wouldn't Roland tell her he'd been operated on? And what was the operation for? There was medical jargon at the bottom of the page that was beyond her. Dr. Capello could translate it for her but he'd been burning these records. He wouldn't be pleased if she admitted to nosing through them. And if Roland had wanted her to know, wouldn't he have told her already?

Too many secrets in this house.

So many they were starting to feel like...

Lies.

CHAPTER 22

The bed was empty when Allison woke up the next morning. Try as she might to wake up before Roland, he was still on monastery time and always got out of bed at five in the morning.

But that was fine by her, as she didn't know what to say to him yet. There was a note on the pillow that said, *You forgot to wake me up, sleepyhead. Tonight. Love, Roland.*

She would have smiled if she could have but she didn't have it in her. There were too many unknowns now. Too many secrets. She wasn't going to be able to rest easy until she had a few more answers to her too many questions.

It was late enough in the morning that Allison had a good feeling Deacon and Thora had already gone to The Glass Dragon, but not so late that Roland and Dr. Capello would be downstairs yet. If she could time it just right, she could leave the house without having to answer any awkward questions about where she was going.

She dressed in her leggings and boots, her wraparound sweater and jacket, and without stopping in the kitchen for breakfast or coffee, she walked out the front door.

Once in her car, she took off, driving up the hill to the highway. Immediately her phone began to buzz. She ignored it until she reached the first scenic viewpoint area and pulled in and parked.

Where are you going? You disappeared.

He must've heard her car tires on the gravel when she left. Of course he'd wondered where she'd run off to. Allison thought fast and replied a few seconds later.

Your father offered to buy me a bookstore in Clark Beach. I need to think about this, go see the place.

Thank God it was just a text message. She wasn't sure she could pull off a lie like that face-to-face. It seemed Roland bought it.

Why am I not surprised he wants to buy you a bookstore? I love that crazy old man. Have fun in CB. Call me if you need to talk about it. Bring me back ice cream! Pralines and cream or chocolate, not picky. Just nothing mint.

Allison sighed with relief that he hadn't called her bluff.

Mint, it is, then. See you tonight.

Roland replied with a heart. She replied with a heart in return and hated herself for the deception. No mint, he said, like nothing was happening and nothing was wrong. She wanted to believe that. She truly did. Roland was wonderful, handsome, funny, sexy, kind. She didn't have to nag him to do the bare minimum of decent behavior like she had to with Mc-

Queen. Roland just did it on his own, without prompting. He left his life at the monastery to take care of his father. He'd been nothing but understanding with her about McQueen. He'd gone with her to Vancouver on her wild-goose chase to find out if Oliver had been the one to push her or prank-call her aunt. Roland cooked her breakfast. He made her coffee. He made her happy when, by all accounts, she should be miserable and heartbroken after the end of a consuming six-year relationship. Back home he was alone with Dr. Capello helping him bathe and dress and eat and make it through one more hard day without thinking too much about how the days left could probably be counted on two hands. Roland wasn't just nice, he was good. He was a good man. But she couldn't let her feelings for him cloud her judgment. McQueen had warned her where there was smoke there was fire. And she'd seen the fire herself last night in the attic. Nothing left to do but search out the source of the flame.

Maybe—she hoped and prayed—there was a perfectly good explanation for why Roland hadn't told her he'd been a patient of Dr. Capello's. Maybe. But she wasn't going to wait around for him to volunteer any information. She would find it out for herself if she could.

And that meant seeing Kendra.

Roland had said she lived in Olympia, Washington. It was a heck of a drive, but she could do it in one day if she didn't dally. And she was in no mood to dally. She gave the ocean and the beach below the scenic viewpoint the most cursory of glances before getting back onto the highway. The ocean would wait. Her questions could not.

She thought of nothing but those questions during the three-hour drive to Olympia. McQueen had confirmed Kendra's address, and she headed straight there, not even bothering to stop for breakfast. The thought of Roland, her Roland, lying to her had killed her appetite. She had no idea how she was going to face him tonight when she came back to The Dragon. If she went back. Depending on what Kendra revealed today, there was a good chance Allison wouldn't be going home. She'd even brought the money McQueen had given her just in case she decided to run for it.

She was too nervous to call before showing up at Kendra's house, so Allison prayed that she would be there when she arrived. Sure enough, when Allison found the house in the Olympia suburbs, a little red Mazda that looked about Allison's age sat in the driveway. A light was on in the window. Kendra seemed to be home.

Allison took a few steadying breaths after parking her car. She hated bothering people. Hated it. But, she told herself two and then three times, Kendra had been her sister. They'd bonded over books, with Kendra nearly as much of a reader as Allison. Kendra had even let Allison read the books that she'd been assigned for school. Kendra had been a sophomore when Allison had been in the seventh grade. Allison was supposed to read stuff like *The Call of the Wild* by Jack London— yawn—while Kendra got to read exciting writers like Kurt Vonnegut and Toni Morrison. And they had something else in common now, too. They'd both been with Roland. The only two women on earth who could make that claim.

Unless he'd lied about that, too.

Allison got out of her car.

She walked to the front door of the little brick bungalow and rang the doorbell. It was a cute house with everything in good repair. The paint was new. The lawn was well-maintained. Not surprising. Unlike the rest of the kids, Kendra had always made her bed without prompting from Dr. Capello. She'd said made beds just looked prettier. Allison stiffened in nervousness as she heard footsteps approaching the front door. There was a pause, which sounded to her like the unfastening of several locks, and then the door opened.

It was Kendra who stood across the threshold—Allison recognized her at once. She was taller, of course, but not much taller. The braids with rainbow-colored beads were gone and now she wore her hair in natural curls. But those were the same large brown eyes behind her glasses and the same pretty face with the same full lips and the tiny mole on the bottom one, a beauty mark Allison had always envied.

"Can I help you?" Kendra said.

"Kendra," Allison said with a nervous smile. "You probably don't remember me. My name's Allison. We used to live together with Dr. Capello in Oregon."

Kendra's eyes widened behind her glasses.

"I shouldn't talk to you," Kendra said.

"Why not?"

"I'm not one of you," Kendra said, taking an uncertain step back as if she meant to shut the door.

"Well, technically I'm not one of them, either," Allison said with an awkward shrug. "Last week was the first time I'd seen them in thirteen years."

"So you didn't go back to them? You're not with them? Not one of the kids?"

"No. I promise. I'm not one of the kids. I left, too, remember?"

Kendra nodded slowly.

"What do you want?" Kendra asked.

This wasn't the happy reunion Allison had hoped for.

"I was hoping I could talk to you. That's all."

"Do they know you're here?" Kendra asked.

Allison instinctively knew "they" meant the whole family, the Capellos.

"I didn't tell anyone I was coming. Can you give me just a

couple minutes? Then I'll go, I promise. We used to play together on the beach, remember? You taught me how to make sand castles. Yours were palaces and mine were shacks."

"You weren't very good at it," Kendra said.

"No head for architecture."

There was a pause, a long one, and then Kendra stepped back again, but this time she held open the door to let Allison inside.

"You'll have to forgive the mess," Kendra said.

The house was even nicer inside than outside. It looked like a page from a Pottery Barn catalog. The walls were a soothing gray with white crown molding and white wainscoting. The brown sofa matched the brown-and-gray rug, which matched the rather generic abstract pictures hanging on the wall. It was all spotlessly clean and tidy.

"The mess?" Allison said as she followed Kendra to the sofa. "Where?"

Kendra sat down and faced her across the coffee table. Computer coding books were arrayed on it in neat piles, and Allison remembered Roland saying that was her area of expertise these days.

"I'm the mess," Kendra said, and gave her the faintest of smiles.

"Mess?" Allison asked. "You?"

"I— Just a joke," Kendra said. She turned her head, looked away and didn't look back. "Why did you come to see me?"

"Roland wrote me a letter a couple weeks ago. Like I said, I hadn't heard from him in thirteen years. He told me Dr. Capello was dying. Did you know that?"

She shook her head.

"I flew out to see him. I ended up staying longer than I intended. Roland and I are…we're involved."

"Oh," she said. "You always did like him." Kendra didn't show the slightest flash of surprise or jealousy or guilt.

"Dr. Capello operated on Roland, didn't he?"

"Better talk to him about that."

This was getting Allison nowhere.

"You remember why I left?" Allison asked.

"Someone in your family took you in," Kendra said. "After you fell."

"Right," Allison said. She thought about telling Kendra the whole story about the phone call to her aunt and Oliver and all of that, but she decided to wait and see if Kendra brought it up. It was hard to imagine this anxious and quiet young woman hurting anyone, but if she had a guilty conscience, maybe it would come out on its own.

"So, ah…" Allison continued. She hadn't really planned this far ahead. She'd make a terrible detective. "Since I got back I was just curious how everyone was. You remember Oliver?"

"I remember."

"Did you…" Allison didn't know how to say it. "Are you in touch with him?"

"No, why?"

"I was wondering if you knew… Oliver killed himself right after he left the house. Had you heard?"

"No," Kendra said. "But I'm not surprised."

"You aren't? Why not?"

Kendra shrugged and didn't answer.

"Do you know a boy named Antonio Russo?"

She shook her head again.

"He used to live with Dr. Capello, too," Allison said. "For a week or so. Before my time there."

"He dead, too?"

"I don't know. Why do you ask?"

"No reason."

Allison sighed, frustrated.

"Kendra, I'm really sorry for just showing up out of the blue. I'm trying to figure something out, and I was hoping you could help me."

"I don't think I can," she said. "I wish I could."

"Maybe if you told me a little more?" Allison said. "I guess we don't know each other very well anymore, but—"

"It's not you," Kendra said. "Don't think it's you. I'm not mad at you. You and me, we were good. It's... I can't talk about this."

Kendra finally looked at Allison again.

"I suppose they didn't tell you about me," Kendra said.

"Well, Roland told me you two used to be a couple."

"When we were kids," she said. "Just dumb kids."

Allison decided to try a new tactic.

"Someone maybe tried to kill me," Allison said. Kendra's eyes widened again. She sat up straighter.

"My Lord. Recently?" Her shock was as genuine as her question. Either Kendra had nothing at all to do with the fall or she was the best actress in the world.

"No, in the house," Allison said. "When I was a kid. My fall wasn't a fall, I don't think."

Allison told Kendra about the phone call, about Dr. Capello telling her he thought Oliver was to blame, how unlikely that was as Oliver had left before any of it happened.

Kendra listened intently, asking no questions. When Allison came to the end of the story, she looked at Kendra and with her hands open and her voice pleading she said, "Please, if you know anything at all, tell me."

"They told me you fell," Kendra said. "That's all I ever knew about it. Except... Roland thought you wanted to leave after because of him."

"You don't know anything else about it? About Roland? About Dr. Capello? Anything?"

Kendra took a long, slow breath before raising her hand and, with her index finger extended, indicated the roof of the house and the four walls.

"Dr. Capello bought me this house," Kendra said. "That's why it's hard for me to talk to you. I wish I could. I do."

"I'm sorry, I'm not following you," Allison said.

"There was an agreement. I can't break the agreement."

An agreement. Where had she heard something like that before?

McQueen.

"A nondisclosure agreement?" Allison asked.

Kendra paused, then nodded.

Allison inhaled sharply. Why would someone with nothing to hide make someone else sign a nondisclosure agreement?

"I like my house," Kendra continued. "I spend a lot of time in the house. I work from home. I don't go out very much. I freelance. If I don't work, I don't make money. Sometimes I'm too sick to work. I don't want to lose my house."

"It is a very pretty house," Allison said. "I wouldn't want to lose it, either."

Kendra looked at her with a deeply apologetic expression. It was the look of a woman who desperately wanted to talk but couldn't. Allison wouldn't force her to say anything for all the money in the world.

"Okay," Allison said. "I'll go. I'd hate to get you into any trouble."

"Thank you," Kendra said, standing up. Their little interview was apparently over.

"It was good to see you again," Allison said. "I have nice memories of you."

"If I knew something about your fall I'd tell you," Kendra said. "But I don't know anything to help you."

"I believe you," Allison said. "I just thought… Never mind. I won't ask."

She started to walk to the door but Kendra stopped her with a hand on her arm.

"You should use my bathroom first," Kendra said. "It's a long drive back."

"I don't have to go, but thank you."

"But you should try," Kendra said. "You should really try before that long drive."

Kendra looked her in the eyes as if trying to tell Allison something.

"You're right," Allison said, playing along. "I should."

"It's over here."

Allison followed Kendra to the bathroom. She switched on the light for her and pointed around.

"If you need hand lotion after you wash your hands," Kendra said, "there's some in the medicine cabinet. I hate dry skin."

"Me, too," Allison said. "Thank you."

Kendra left and Allison closed the door. After she flushed the toilet, she washed her hands and dried them on a hand towel. Allison opened the medicine cabinet to find the hand lotion. She stared in utter astonishment at the sight that greeted her.

Pill bottles. One entire shelf in the cabinet was lined with nothing but prescription pill bottles. There were over a dozen different medicines. Kendra was only three years older than Allison. How could one twenty-eight-year-old woman be on so much medicine? Allison scanned the labels. She didn't know what many of the pills were for but some of the names she recognized. One was a well-known and often-prescribed antidepressant. The other was an antianxiety pill. Allison pulled her phone out of her bag and took quick pictures of the labels on the bottles. She'd have to look them up later to see what they did. But Allison already had an idea why Kendra wanted her to see them.

A house. A nondisclosure agreement with a retired surgeon. And a whole row of prescriptions. It all added up to one hell of a malpractice suit. Dr. Capello had operated on Deacon and Thora and on Roland, too. And on Oliver. Which meant it was very likely he'd operated on Kendra. He'd operated on her and something had gone wrong. Kendra's family had sued or threatened to sue, and Dr. Capello had settled with money in exchange for Kendra, and probably her family, signing an NDA in order to keep it quiet.

When she finished taking the photographs, Allison quietly closed the medicine cabinet and went back out to the living room.

"I did have to go, after all," Allison said.

"Never hurts to try before a long trip. You used my hand lotion?" she asked.

"I did. It smells nice, like strawberries. I noticed all the medicine in your cabinet."

"Told you I was a mess," she said quietly.

"I'm sorry," Allison said. "I wish… I'm just so sorry."

"Do you have medical problems?" Kendra asked.

"No," Allison said. "I wasn't one of Dr. Capello's patients."

Kendra's lips were set in a firm, straight line. She nodded. "Lucky you." She managed a smile as Allison walked out the door. "Drive safe."

"Thank you," Allison said. "It was good to see you."

"You, too." Kendra stood in the doorway, her hand on the door ready to close it. "If you see Antonio, say hello for me."

She shut the door.

Allison stared at the closed door. Behind it she heard the locks engaging. Say hi to Antonio... Kendra had said she didn't know Antonio.

Another hint. If Allison had been on the fence about tracking down Antonio Russo before, she wasn't on it anymore.

Back in her car, Allison frantically typed in the names of the prescription drugs from inside Kendra's medicine cabinet. Nearly all of them were psychotropic medications—there were the pills for depression and anxiety, yes, but also OCD and mood disorders. There was an antiseizure medication, too, plus two different sleeping pills. Allison nearly wept as she read through the conditions the various pills treated. Kendra, sweet, nerdy, quiet, gentle Kendra, must have a legion of mental illnesses. And if Dr. Capello had settled a malpractice suit with Kendra or her family, that meant he was the cause of them.

Allison turned her car on and off again immediately.

She looked at Kendra's ancient Mazda in the driveway, at the house her former sister was scared to death of losing. Allison dug into her handbag and found the brick of cash McQueen had given her. He'd said not to give it to strangers with sob stories. He never said anything about giving it to family. She counted out ten-thousand dollars, wrapped it up in a ponytail holder, walked back to the house and shoved it through the mail slot. Then, before Kendra could find it and give it back, Allison drove away.

As Allison made her way to the interstate, she reminded herself that lots of doctors had unintentionally harmed patients. It didn't necessarily prove any kind of malice. It just happened. Surgeries were risky, and sometimes they had good outcomes, sometimes they had bad outcomes and sometimes there were lawsuits—that's what malpractice insurance was for. Dr. Capello himself had spoken with deep feeling of the surgeon's graveyard he carried within him, which contained every patient he'd ever tried to help and lost. Kendra's medical problems were heartbreaking, devastating, but they might not have had anything at all to do with Allison's fall or the phone call. Kendra was a very ill woman, but she didn't seem violent or aggressive to Allison at all. When Roland said Kendra was incapable of hurting her, he'd meant it, and now Allison believed him.

But still…

Allison stopped for gas. Before driving away she sent McQueen a text message asking if he had an address or phone number for Antonio yet.

She'd made it fifty miles down the road before her phone buzzed with his reply. She glanced at the message and wished she'd been smart enough to pull off the road before she'd read it. The message nearly caused her to swerve onto the shoulder.

Russo's been in a private mental hospital for fifteen years.

A private mental hospital?

This was getting worse and worse by the minute.

Allison saw a McDonald's just ahead, so she pulled in and parked. She rested her forehead on the steering wheel and breathed. Her phone buzzed again, another message from McQueen.

I have the address if you want it.

Did she want the address? No, of course she didn't want the address. She would rather eat glass than go to a mental hospital to see a man who'd been living there over half his life. There was no reason for her to go. Antonio had lived with the Capellos for such a short time, then he'd left long before Allison had arrived. It was absurd to think he'd had anything to do with her fall or the phone call. If she went to see him, that would mean she wasn't investigating her accident anymore. It would mean she was investigating Dr. Capello. And why would she do that?

Because her former sister was on fourteen different drugs and almost never left her house, and no one deserved that. That's why.

Allison texted McQueen back.

I want it.

CHAPTER 23

The hospital was in a suburb of Portland. Allison knew she could make it there and back to The Dragon before the end of the day. It would be very late when she got back, and it wouldn't be easy accounting for her whereabouts, but she couldn't worry about that now. She needed to see Antonio, and she might not get another chance like this.

Something had gone terribly wrong at The Dragon when she'd lived there, something much worse than one prank phone call and a fall that might not have been an accident. If she ever wanted to move past this, she'd have to learn the truth. She plugged the address into her phone's map and headed east.

She survived the drive on coffee and determination. By late afternoon, Allison was nearing her destination. As soon as she took the exit off the interstate, she knew she was in money country. The houses were large and hidden behind high walls and old trees. The streets were clean, the sidewalks were in excellent repair and the children she saw getting out of school were being picked up by well-heeled parents and nannies who drove shiny SUVs. McQueen had said Antonio was in a private hospital. Those didn't come cheap. She found her way to the road, which seemingly led straight into a forest. Once she passed through the outer perimeter of thick tall trees, she saw she was driving not through a forest but a park surrounded by forest. The signs that warned her not to drive more than eight miles per hour weren't the ordinary black-and-white metal sorts on every city street in America, but elegant wooden signs, painted in cheerful colors.

The winding path went on so long, Allison wondered if she'd ever find the hospital. Then she saw it, the prettiest hospital she'd ever seen. It looked like an old English manor house. The exterior was gray stone with dark wood support beams here and there, possibly decorative. It was a three-story hospital, far wider than it was tall. She counted twenty windows in the top row, and that was just the front of the building. She could tell it stretched on far back into one or two other wings. The lawns were extensive and neatly manicured. People in regular clothes walked the paths in the park. The only signs that this was a mental hospital and not a posh private home were the abundance of people in wheelchairs and the dozen or so security guards keeping a close eye on the people taking their afternoon strolls.

Allison found the visitor parking section and went through the front doors to find the reception desk. Even inside, it looked like a luxurious private home. Everywhere she looked she saw comfy armchairs, cozy rugs, fireplaces and fine art on the walls. Soothing classical music played in the background. Was this a hospital or a boutique hotel?

Yet for all its surface beauty, nothing could completely disguise the building's purpose. A woman in a white robe sat silent and still in a wheelchair that was parked near a window. With glazed eyes she gazed out at the park. From behind a heavy set of double doors Allison heard a low hopeless keening. A patient suffering? Or a heartbroken visitor?

Tucked away in the corner of the lobby was a grand U-shaped desk with a woman in a crisp white nurse's uniform, a stack of files at her elbow.

"Welcome to Fairwood," the nurse said from behind the desk. "How can I help you?"

"My name is Allison and my foster brother is a patient here. I was hoping I could see him. Antonio Russo."

The nurse's eyes widened slightly, as if Allison's request was unusual. Then she politely held up her index finger to indicate this would take a moment before she disappeared into another room.

The nurse returned shortly, wearing a smile.

"I apologize for the wait," the nurse said. "He's never had any visitors before, so I was under the impression he wasn't allowed any. But he is, I've been assured, so we'll have an orderly come and take you to him. I'll just need to see your ID and have you sign in."

Allison had to sign more paperwork than when she'd bought her car. She barely read the forms she signed. They all seemed to be full of legalese. She had no intention of suing the hospital if a patient up and decided to throw a punch at her. She wasn't scared of sick people. If she'd been living in a hospital for fifteen years like Antonio, she might feel like throwing a punch or two herself.

A young orderly in blue scrubs arrived shortly thereafter and led her through double doors into the main wing. She'd thought that behind the doors she'd find where the money ran out and the elegant lobby would reveal itself as a front for the cold, metal-barred institution she'd been expecting. But it wasn't the case. Even behind the ward doors, it looked like a five-star hotel. The floors were dark wood and freshly polished. Windows let in light and the few rooms she could see into looked homey and warm. No bare cots in sight.

"This place must be expensive to stay in," Allison said to Michael, her orderly escort. He gave her a tight smile.

"I'm just glad I work here," he said. "I couldn't afford to live here."

"I guess it's where rich people go when they get sick?"

Michael nodded, then lowered his voice. "Rich or important," he said. "Safe to say we don't take Medicaid."

Allison had to wonder how Antonio's family was able to pay for a place like Fairwood. She knew from personal experience rich kids didn't go into foster care. At least, none of the kids she ever met in the system came from wealthy families. If the kid had money, there was a relative somewhere willing and ready to take them in. Did the same person who paid for Kendra's house pay for Antonio's stay here? Was that person Dr. Capello? Allison hated to think so, but she couldn't deny it was the most likely answer.

Michael led her through another set of double doors into a narrower hallway and another wing.

"It's quiet in here," she said, glancing around. The silence was far more eerie than the noises of the other wards.

"This is the wreck ward," he said in a low voice.

"Rec ward? Like recreation?"

"No, with a *W*. Wreck. Surgical wrecks. Mostly PVS patients."

"PVS?"

"Persistent vegetative state. *PVS* sounds nicer than calling them vegetables. *Wreck* doesn't sound very nice, either, but that's what the docs call them."

"So Antonio's considered a wreck?"

"Yeah, you didn't know? You're his sister, right?"

"Foster sister. I haven't seen him in a long time." She hoped Michael wasn't good at spotting lies. "Is Antonio...is he a PVS patient, too?"

"Tony? No. He's here because something went wrong during a childhood brain surgery. Doc either cut too much out or didn't cut enough. His mind wanders a lot and he's got impulse-control issues now, which is why we have to keep him mostly sedated and in restraints. He's a sweet kid, really. Can't help himself. But keep a little distance from him, for your own sake."

"Okay," she said. "Thanks."

He pointed at a door, dark wood, like the hallway. Michael knocked, and when there was no answer he scanned a key card on a panel, opened the door and went inside ahead of her. Allison peeked in and saw Antonio lying on his side away from her in a hospital bed. The room was bare of knick-knacks or flowers or anything personal at all. Antonio wore gray sweats and white socks and what looked like cloth shackles on his ankles.

"It looks like a prison cell," she whispered to Michael.

"His room and board is paid for. No money left over for decorating," he said. "You can go in. He's awake."

"You sure it's okay?"

"Tony's good," he said. "Just remember what I said."

"Keep a little distance."

"That's right. Buzzer is by the door when you're ready to leave. I'd say no more than fifteen minutes with Tony. He might not stay awake for you that long, anyway."

"Is there anything else I need to know about him?" she asked. "I didn't know he was here until today. I don't want to upset him or hurt his feelings or anything."

Michael gave her a kind but almost patronizing smile.

"He says anything and everything on his mind. Don't take it personally. But as for hurting his feelings, he's been stuck here most of his life," he said. "And he's probably going to die in here. You can't hurt him more than life has."

Michael held open the door for her and Allison went inside. Nervously, she walked around the hospital bed until she stood three feet from where Antonio lay facing the open window.

"Antonio?" she said gently. "Tony?"

He was a normal-looking young man in his late twenties. A little pale from a life spent mostly indoors and a shaggy haircut that wasn't very flattering, but otherwise he looked like anyone she'd see out in the world. He slowly blinked his dark eyes as if trying to force himself to focus. His gaze wandered the room, darting here and there, into shadows and corners, before it finally settled onto her.

"Hi, Tony," Allison said again.

He grinned at her, which she hadn't at all been expecting.

"You're hot," he said.

She blinked a few times at that. Well, Michael had warned her.

"Thank you," she said.

"Or maybe you're not," he said. "I don't see many girls in here. Bar's pretty low. I'm desperate."

"I would be, too," she said. That got a smile out of him. "My name is Allison. I used to live with Dr. Capello and his kids. Like you did. I heard you were in the hospital. I thought I'd stop by and see you."

"Been here a long time," he said. His voice was as normal as his appearance. It seemed so unnecessary for him to be chained up and sedated, but it was clear there was something in his system keeping his mind and body in low gear, and he had the same sort of cloth shackles on his wrists as on his ankles.

"Yeah, I heard you've been here fifteen years. I would have come sooner if I'd known."

"Liar," he said.

She couldn't argue. "Yeah, maybe I am."

"Why are you here? You can fuck me if you want."

"That's not why I'm here."

"Shit."

Allison laughed.

"You came to stare at the wreck?" he said.

"No, that's not why."

"They say that," Antonio said. "They say people can't help but stare at train wrecks. But that's not true. If people wanted to stare at train wrecks, they'd come stare at me. Nobody comes to stare at me."

"You're not a train wreck," Allison said. "You seem like a nice person to me."

"You don't know anything about me." He twisted on the bed as if trying to get a better look at her. "You're not here to stare at me?" he asked.

"I want to talk to you. They say you don't get many visitors."

"No visitors."

"Do you hate it here?"

He turned his head a little as if trying to find a more comfortable position on his pillow.

"They're nice to me," he said.

"That wasn't my question," she said.

"Hotel California," he said. "Except you can't check out or leave."

"You like music?" she asked.

"The cleaning lady plays music when she comes in here, Seventies on Seven. Lots of Eagles. Who needs IV sedation when you have Easy Listening blaring in your ear?"

Allison laughed. "I'll try to smuggle some Beyoncé in for you."

"Please," he said. "Anything."

"Are you always in restraints?" she asked.

"There's a room," he said. "An exercise room. I get to walk in it."

"Do you ever get to go outside?"

"They take me out in the chair."

He nodded toward the corner of the room where a wheelchair was folded up near the wall.

"How's the food?" she asked.

"Okay," he said. "I bite my tongue so much I have trouble tasting food."

At her quizzical look, he clarified, "I have seizures. They have to put stuff in my mouth to keep me from biting it off."

"Stuff?"

"A bite guard. I'm special. Mikey says that's old school *Cuckoo's Nest* shit."

"Is he your friend here?"

"We talk about girls. We'll talk about you."

"Go for it," she said. "I'm sorry you have to be in here."

"Not your fault. Shit."

"What?"

"I'm falling asleep," he said. "I don't want to. Keep talking to me."

"I'll talk to you all you want," she said.

"Were you really in that house?" he asked. "With the doc?"

"Yes," she said. "A couple years after you were."

"What did he do to you?" Antonio asked.

"Nothing."

"Not nothing," Antonio said. "If you were in that house, he did something to you."

Antonio yawned again and Allison was terrified he'd fall asleep before she had any answers.

"Antonio? Can you tell me why you're here? You were injured, right? From a surgery?"

"I was..." Antonio yawned hugely.

"What?" she asked.

"Butchered."

The word inspired a visceral reaction in Allison. She felt it more than heard it.

"Butchered," she repeated. "Dr. Capello? He butchered you?"

"Tried to fix me," Antonio said, yawning again. She yawned, too, couldn't help herself. "Like a cat."

"Wait. He tried to fix you like a cat? Do you mean he neutered you?"

Antonio laughed. He had a nice laugh, a warm masculine chuckle. It was almost painful for her to keep her distance from him. This man, with a laugh like that, chained to a hospital bed for fifteen years... She wanted to run her hands through his hair, hug him, talk with him like anyone else.

"There was a cat at the house," Antonio said. "The potato cat."

"Brien," she said. "Potatoes O'Brien. He's still alive."

"He's a Ragdoll," Antonio said. "They told me that."

"Yeah, Dr. Capello got Brien for Deacon to replace his cat that died."

Antonio snorted like she'd said something stupid.

"You're an idiot," he said. "You don't know anything about it."

Allison tried not to let that comment hurt. Michael had warned her not to take Antonio's remarks personally.

"Tell me, then. I want to know. What about Brien?"

"He was a test," Antonio said. "Deacon's cat didn't die the way a regular cat dies—being stupid, getting hit by a car or whatever. He killed it."

"Who killed it?"

"Deacon killed it. Stabbed it with a knife, cut off its head,

skinned it. And the neighbor's cat. And the neighbor's dog...
Little asshole. Even I didn't kill dogs."

Allison couldn't speak at first. She'd been shocked into silence.

"Say something," Antonio said. "You look dumb just sitting there."

"Deacon killed animals."

"I just said that."

"How do you know all this?"

"They told me," he said. "Before they cut me. They told me it would make me better, said it worked before on other kids. Like Deacon." Antonio grinned. "He was a monster like me. Then he wasn't anymore."

"A monster? How were you a monster?" Allison asked. She pulled up a chair and sat in it right across from Antonio's face.

"I was bad..." Antonio whispered. "I hurt girls."

She tried to imagine what a child could have done to hurt other kids. "Hurt them? You kicked them? Punched them? Pulled their hair?"

"No, I had to do...stuff to them."

"What stuff, Antonio?" she asked.

"I started cutting off their hair when they weren't paying attention," he said. "And then I would rip it out." Allison watched his hand open and close into a fist and then he jerked his hand, jerked it hard as if yanking out a hank of hair. "And other things."

"Other things?"

"I was on top of one girl," Antonio said. "Caught her on the playground. Teacher got to me before I could get started."

"Jesus," Allison said, clapping her hand over her mouth in horror.

"You look stupid," he said. "Everything I say makes you look stupid. Not your fault. I'm tied up. I look stupid, too."

She slowly lowered her hand. Her head swam. Her stomach was lodged in her throat.

"Why did you hurt all those girls?"

"I couldn't stop," he said. "I don't know why. I wish I knew why. If I knew why maybe I wouldn't have had to go under the knife."

"You had brain surgery because you hurt people?"

"Nothing else worked." He didn't say those words so much as sing them. "Drugs didn't work. Doctors didn't work. Beating the shit out of me didn't work."

"Did you have a brain tumor?" she asked. She remembered Roland telling her about the famous patient with the brain tumor who'd turned into a sexual predator because of it and returned to normal once the tumor was removed.

"That's what they said. Maybe I did. Maybe I didn't. But they took something out of my head and, for a while, it worked, but then I had a stroke and all the wiring went..." He moved his fingers in a pattern of chaos, like a ball of yarn tangled up in a thousand knots. "Now I'm here forever."

"You said he fixed you like a cat," Allison said.

"The cat, I forgot the cat," Antonio said. "It's the drugs. I'm not as dumb as I look. The cat. It's a Ragdoll cat. They're nice cats. They breed them nice. Cats are killers, but with Ragdolls, they breed the killer instinct out of them so they don't bite. You can't breed people not to bite, but you can cut into their heads to make them not bite." He smiled at her. "Nice cats can't survive in the wild, you know. When you cut off a cat's claws or breed a cat to be tame, you're not doing it for the cat. You're doing it for the cat's owner."

Antonio's eyes fluttered. "I don't bite anymore," he said. "Except my own tongue."

He went silent and started to breathe like a man asleep.

"Antonio? Tony? You asleep?"

"No," Antonio said, rousing himself. "The cat was a test. A test to make sure Deacon wouldn't kill any more cats."

The article.

The article on the wall. What had it said? One of the kids Dr. Capello fostered compulsively harmed animals and children.

That was Deacon?

"I can't believe it," Allison said.

"Believe it," Antonio said. "I don't know how to lie. Maybe he cut that out of me, too."

She shook herself out of her shock.

"Who took you to Dr. Capello?"

"He found me," he said. "He was looking for kids like me. Fucked up. Violent. Incurable. A kid nobody wanted. A kid nobody would miss. That was me. Nobody wanted me. When we met...you know what he said?"

"No, tell me."

"He said I was very lucky he'd found me, because he knew how to cure my disease."

"What disease did he say you had?" Allison asked. "Tony, what disease did Dr. Capello tell you that you had?"

Antonio opened his eyes again.

"Evil."

Allison looked away from Antonio's wide, waiting eyes. She'd known that was what he was going to say. She might have known before she'd come here. Maybe she even knew from the day on the beach when Dr. Capello had said he hoped for the day it would be possible to cure evil. He'd spoken with such conviction, conviction that bordered on certainty. He was sure they could do it. He was sure because he had done it already.

He'd done it already.

To Antonio.

To Kendra.

To Deacon.

To Thora.

To Oliver.

And to Roland.

"Why are you crying?" Antonio asked. "You aren't as pretty when you cry. No offense."

Allison looked back at him and saw tears on his own face.

"Why are *you* crying?" she asked him.

"Because my head hurts."

"You have headaches?"

"All the time." Antonio's face screwed up in obvious agony. "Will you rub my head? Just a little?"

His voice was so pleading and his pain so apparent that she reached out to him in compassion. Antonio jerked forward toward her with a sudden lunge. The bed lurched as he lurched. Allison screamed and jumped back in her chair. The restraints had caught him but she'd seen the expression of animal rage in his eyes as her hand neared his head. It was there in a flash and gone in an instant.

Antonio beat his head against the pillow, tears streaming from his eyes.

"I'm sorry," he said. "I'm sorry, I'm sorry, I'm sorry..." He said it a dozen, two dozen, a hundred times, as Allison caught her breath. Antonio couldn't seem to stop apologizing and she couldn't stop weeping. She went to his hospital bed and walked around the side to stand behind him. This time, when she reached out to touch him he lay still. She ran her fingers through his shaggy dark hair and he quieted. The litany of apologies ceased.

"Are you okay?" she asked.

"You'll never come see me again now," he said.

"No, I'll come, I promise. You just gave me a little scare. I'm not mad. It's not your fault."

"I wish I was dead sometimes," he said.

"No, don't say that," Allison said. "Please don't say that. I'm so glad we met, Antonio. I like talking with you. And I do want to come see you again."

"You do?"

"I do, I promise."

His hair was so soft and Antonio so apologetic and helpless that she had to love him. She couldn't help but love him. To her he was the boy in the photograph, the child of eight in the stupid bucket hat, not the man of twenty-eight who had to live day and night chained up in this hotel he could never check out of, never leave.

"He was supposed to make me good," Antonio said. "He just made me sorry."

"Oh, Tony," she said, weeping with him. His back heaved with his sobs and she rubbed it as best she could, trying to soothe him. No one deserved this. No one. Not even a boy who'd hurt children the way he had. To be given a life sentence for crimes committed at age seven and eight...to be trapped in this place for decades with no hope of ever getting out, of ever getting well...no visitors and no one to touch him but doctors and nurses and orderlies. No one deserved this.

"Allison," he said, the first time he'd spoken her name.

"Yes?"

"Hit the buzzer."

"What's wrong?"

"Hit it. I'm going to have a seizure. Hit it."

She ran to the door and hit the buzzer. It wasn't more than ten seconds, though it felt like an eternity. Allison stood in the corner of the room watching Antonio's back rise off the bed like a scene from an exorcism movie. His face was contorted in agony and the sound that escaped his lips was that of a wounded animal or a terrified child. She wanted to help him but didn't know how. Two nurses, one male and one female, burst into the room and rushed to the bed. One of them forced a mouth guard between Antonio's teeth.

Allison slid down the wall to sit on the floor.

And she remembered what happened that day.

It played before her eyes like a scene from a movie. A horror movie. And she was the star.

Antonio seized, and Allison remembered. Everything passed by in slow motion, like the floor was covered in glue and the air in the room was as thick as molasses. Eventually time found its footing again and she came back to herself and to the present. The two nurses had finished with Antonio and now they stood calmly at his bedside, one wiping sweat from his face and neck and the other making notes in a chart.

The woman with the chart turned to her.

"You okay?" the nurse asked.

"Fine," Allison said. She had never been less fine in her life.

"We gave him another sedative. He's going to be out like a light soon."

"Do I have to go?" Allison asked, still sitting on the cold floor.

The nurse shrugged. "Visiting hours are till six. You can stay if you want. He'll be asleep, though."

"That's fine," Allison said. Her voice sounded different to her, like it had detached from her throat and it was speaking outside of her body.

"Take it easy, Tony," the male nurse said, patting Antonio's arm. He looked at her and furrowed his brow. "You a relative?"

"I'm his sister," Allison said.

"You never been here before?"

"I never knew he was here."

"Ah," he said. "That happens. Sorry."

They both left and Allison forced herself up to her feet. She returned to Antonio's bed, where he was on his side in the fetal position, a blanket over him, the shackles still on. His face was red and his lips looked swollen.

"Antonio?" she said softly. "Tony?"

"You still here?" he said.

"I am. They said you're going to sleep."

He nodded.

"Do you want me to stay?"

"Please."

"I'll stay." She fetched a washcloth from his bathroom and put cold water on it. When she pressed it to his face, he exhaled with obvious pleasure.

"I love you," he said.

"Can I get into bed with you?" she asked.

"God, yes."

She carefully climbed into his hospital bed with him, spooning up behind him and resting her arm as gently as she could over his side.

"You smell like the ocean," he said. "You smell like heaven."

She smiled. "What does heaven smell like?"

"It smells like…" He yawned hugely, which made her yawn hugely. "It smells like a girl when she kisses you."

Allison took the hint. She leaned up and over him and kissed him on the temple before lying down again a little closer.

"Allison?" He sounded half asleep already.

"Yes, Antonio?" she said.

"If I weren't drugged up I'd have a boner."

"I'll take that as a compliment," she said.

"Tits could be bigger, though."

"It's true," she said. "They could be bigger."

"You'll come see me again?" he asked.

"Yes, I will," she said, and it was a promise she fully intended to keep. "You were right, by the way."

"About what?" Antonio asked. He sounded so tired she wondered if he knew what he was saying.

"Dr. Capello did do something to me in that house."

"Ah," Antonio said. "Told you so."

CHAPTER 24

Allison stayed with Antonio until she was certain he was sleeping comfortably. She left her phone number with Michael, who seemed to be Antonio's closest, likely only, friend at Fairwood, in case of an emergency. She also put ten thousand dollars on Antonio's commissary account so he could make his room more of a home. It felt inadequate, but what would be? After, she got into her car and left to return to The Dragon. Why was she going back after all she learned? She could take her money and run. She could leave without saying goodbye. But she couldn't leave without looking Dr. Capello in the eyes and asking him one question.

As she drove she remembered it all again, remembered it fully, every minute, every moment. The second she'd seen the mouth guard being forced between Antonio's lips, seen his back rise off the bed like an electric shock had ripped through him...everything came back, came back like water filling an empty fountain. Everything she'd forgotten, everything she'd repressed, everything she hadn't remembered and hadn't wanted to remember, and everything stolen from her by someone who was supposed to be her savior... It bubbled up from the bottom, crept across the floor and rose and rose to the very edge where it threatened to spill over.

It had all started that day on the beach, the day she and Roland had kissed. She'd been wrong to tell him that the kiss and her leaving the house had nothing to do with each other. They had everything to do with each other.

Everything.

She'd skipped breakfast for the third morning in a row. That's the excuse Thora had used to come to her room, to check on her, to get inside when she'd refused entrance to everyone else in the house.

Allison wasn't even hungry. That's not why she let Thora inside her room. She didn't want the food on the plate. She just had to tell someone what had happened.

Thora thought it was something else. Thora, barely fifteen and as pretty as a *Seventeen* magazine model in her short khaki skirt and white knit top, sat on the side of Allison's bed and asked her if she'd finally started having her period.

Allison whispered a denial. She wished it were something like that.

"Then what is it?" Thora asked. "Please, tell me. I won't tell anybody. I can keep secrets."

"You swear?" Allison couldn't face her. She lay on her side under the covers, though the room was stuffy with summer heat.

"I swear to God," Thora said. "You haven't left your room in days. What is it?"

Allison told Thora what had happened.

The wave.

Roland carrying her to the beach.

Straddling him and how good it had felt.

Why did that feel so good?

The kiss.

That stupid kiss.

Roland's hands on her waist, on her thighs.

The sound he'd made when Allison had moved her hips.

She told Thora everything. It all came out in one long tortured monologue, whispered between gulping sobs.

The child in Allison had expected the worst, that Thora
would condemn her and mock her. The little bit of Allison
that was growing into a young woman thought Thora would
maybe tell her she was overreacting, that it was no big deal.

Thora hadn't done either.

"I have to tell you something," Thora said, and the tone
of her voice made Allison finally roll over in her bed to face
her. Thora was ashen. Even her lips looked white, bloodless.

"Tell me what?" Allison asked.

"You can't tell anyone I told you," Thora said. "I'll keep
your secret, you keep this one. You have to swear. I'm not
supposed to know."

Thora's mouth was such a tight line it would have taken a
pair of pliers to open it up.

Allison said the two words necessary to unlock Thora's lips.
"I swear."

Then Thora told her a story. Thora told her the story of
how she'd wanted to peek at Dad's medical files he kept under
lock and key in the closet in his office. She wanted to know
something—didn't matter what, Thora said, so don't ask.

Allison didn't ask.

Thora waited until a night when everyone was going to
see a movie in Astoria. And right before they were all about
to leave the house and pile into Dad's van, Thora had said she
changed her mind, had an upset stomach, didn't feel like going.

Everyone went without her.

And when she was alone in the house, she looked high and
low and in and out and finally she found the key to the closet

and the key to the filing cabinet. She found the files she was looking for and sat down in the closet to read them.

"What did you find out?" Allison asked, fascinated now, far more fascinated than scared or ashamed.

"You need to be careful around Roland," Thora said. "You need to stay away from him."

"Why?" That made no sense to Allison. Roland wasn't just nice, he was the nicest. He wasn't dangerous. She was the one who'd kissed him…

"He had a sister named Rachel," Thora whispered. "She's dead."

"Dead?"

Then Thora said the three ugliest words Allison had ever heard.

"Roland killed her."

Someone knocked on the door. Hard. Loud.

"Girls?" It was Dr. Capello. "Everything all right in here?"

Thora looked at her frozen on the bed.

"Don't be alone with Roland. Ever," Thora said, and that was all. Then she ran to the door and opened it.

"Hi, Daddy," Thora said. "Everything's fine."

"You missed breakfast again, young lady," Dr. Capello said to her. And Allison knew she needed to lie if she were going to survive.

"I had an upset stomach," Allison said.

Dr. Capello looked at Thora, who nodded, and Allison knew she had a partner in the lie. Thora was going to let Dr. Capello think it had been girl trouble and that's all this was.

"Let me know if you need anything," Dr. Capello said. "Feel better, doll. Come on, Thora. Allison's not feeling well. Let her rest."

Thora hadn't wanted to leave, but she wasn't as quick on

her feet as Allison had been. After giving Allison one last look of warning, she walked away.

And alone in the room in her pretty little blue bed, Allison's heart died.

Eternity passed while Allison rocked back and forth, her arms around her knees, crying and shaking, too scared to leave her room. Roland had killed a little girl. Roland had killed his sister. Thora was scared Roland would kill her, too.

The house's morning sounds faded to silence. Roland was at work at his new job at that fancy restaurant in Clark Beach. Allison knew Dr. Capello would be up in his office. Kendra was probably in her room reading. Deacon and Thora lived on the beach during the summer. Oliver had left two days ago. And from her bedroom window, she saw Dr. Capello walk out the front door and take his usual path into the woods for his daily ramble.

This was her chance.

She crept from her room into the hallway. When she walked past Thora's room she heard low voices murmuring—hers and Deacon's. That was all right. As long as they stayed in there and didn't try to stop her it would be okay.

Allison snuck up the third-floor stairs and slipped through the door into Dr. Capello's office. She found the key where Thora had said she'd found it the week before when she'd gone on this very same hunt. The key was to the closet door in the office where Dr. Capello kept his filing cabinet. Allison didn't know where to start. Thora'd had three hours to dig, but Allison might have half an hour, if that, until Dr. Capello came back from his walk. But it couldn't take that long to find out the truth, could it? All Allison wanted to know was that Thora was lying to her. She had to be lying to her. Roland? Kill his baby sister? Never. Never ever. Maybe Thora was in love with Roland. Maybe she made all that up because she was jealous. It had to be lies. All lies.

But deep down, Allison knew Thora wouldn't lie to her.

Allison had just begun digging through the first filing cabinet drawer when the closet door opened behind her.

There stood Dr. Capello.

He didn't look mad. He didn't even look all that surprised.

He gazed down at her—she was tall now at twelve but not as tall as him—and held out his hand.

"Come on," he said. "Let's talk about it."

With a hand gentle on her shoulder he led her from the closet to the sofa in his office. He sat facing her and gently smiled.

"What's going on here, doll?" he asked.

"I read your files," she said. "When everyone was at the park Sunday. Roland was outside. He didn't know what I was doing." Thora had taken a risk by telling her the truth. She wasn't about to pay Thora back by getting her into trouble.

"I see," he said, nodding. "How did you get into the closet?"

Thankfully Thora had told her that part.

"You lock your keys in your top desk drawer," Allison said. "But you can get in the desk drawer from under the desk with a coat hanger."

"Smart kid," he said. "I knew you were smart from the day we met."

Even then, she wasn't afraid of him. There was no reason to be afraid of Dr. Capello. It was Roland she had to fear.

"Have you told anyone?" he asked.

"Nobody."

"This is why you've been so upset?" he asked.

Two hot fresh tears ran down her face, answer enough.

Dr. Capello opened a drawer in his desk. He took out a bottle of pills, opened it and shook two pink ones out into his hand. He got up, went to the small half bath in his office and came out with a paper cup of water.

"Here, take these," he said. "You'll feel a lot better very soon."

"What are they?" she asked.

"They'll help you relax. You've been crying so hard you'll get sick if you're not careful."

She took the pills. They were little and it wasn't hard to swallow them. She would have swallowed anything he'd given her if it came with a promise to make her feel better. Dr. Capello sat down on the chair next to her. He faced her and smiled.

"What did you read in the file?" Dr. Capello asked her.

This, Allison didn't know. They'd been interrupted before Thora could tell her anything else about Roland.

"Just that...that he killed Rachel."

"He did kill his sister, Rachel. Yes. That's true. But you don't have to be afraid of him or anyone else in the house," Dr. Capello said. "It was just an accident."

"It was?" she asked, instantly relieved. Why had Thora scared her like this if it had been an accident?

"It was. And he feels very bad about it. And if you start talking about it you're going to upset him and everybody in the house. And we don't want that, do we?"

A simple question. Allison knew what answer he wanted from her.

"No."

"Good. I'm glad we're on the same page."

"Are you sure?" she asked him. "I don't think...I don't think it was an accident. It wouldn't be a big secret if it was an accident."

Dr. Capello sighed heavily and nodded his head.

"Too smart," he said. "You're just too smart." He tenderly patted her cheek, still wet with tears.

"I want to go home," Allison said.

"This is your home, doll. You leave and it'll break everybody's heart."

"I don't care. I don't want to stay here anymore. You're all liars. You and Roland and—"

"Shh…" He touched a finger to his lips. "Calm down. We'll talk about this, okay? I need to go check on something. I'll be right back. You just lie down on the sofa and rest. Then we'll figure it out. Together."

She wanted to figure it out. And she didn't really want to go home. How could she? She didn't have any other home except maybe her aunt in Indiana.

"Okay," Allison said. "I promise."

He stood up to leave, then bent over and kissed her on the forehead.

"You poor thing," he said. "This is what we call a much ado about nothing. Just rest now. You have to be so tired."

He left her in the office and shut the door behind him. Maybe it was the pills and maybe it was that she hadn't slept much the night before or the night before that, but she did lie down on the couch facing Dr. Capello's desk. Her eyes grew heavy and yet she refused to close them. She was afraid to close them, though she didn't know why. She locked her gaze on the drawing of the skull map hanging on the wall behind the desk. She wondered why there were little dragons in the center of the skull. When Dr. Capello finally came back into the room she asked him.

"Why are there dragons in the brain?" she said.

"You still awake?" he sat next to her on the sofa and brushed her hair off her forehead.

"Almost."

"You should sleep," he said. "When you wake up, you won't remember anything that's happened the past few days. I promise. Won't that be nice?"

Sleepily she nodded. It would be nice. It would be nice to forget it all happened—Roland's arms, the wave, the kiss, his hands on her waist, the tears, the shame, Thora telling her that Roland had killed a little girl... Yes, she did want to forget it all. But that didn't make any sense. She was twelve, a kid, but not stupid. You couldn't magically make people forget things.

She closed her eyes and started to fall into sleep, and when she was almost out, she felt Dr. Capello's strong arms under her, lifting her up and carrying her from his office. Was he taking her back to her bedroom? To his? No, they were going up. She heard the creaking of stairs under his feet and felt hot sticky air on her face. The attic. He had taken her up to the attic. But why?

She was too sleepy to ask. Those pink pills, they were the allergy pills Kendra had to take in spring, the ones that made her fall asleep and stay asleep for ten hours straight when she took two. Allison wanted to wake herself up but the pills had her. Even when she felt something cold on her temples, she couldn't shake free of her need to sleep. But she knew she had to try.

"What about the dragons?" she asked.

"You really don't want to sleep, do you?" He sounded almost proud of her for the way she could fight off sleep. "The hippocampus is a structure at the center of the brain. *Hippo* means horse. *Campus* means sea monster. They call it that because it looks like a sea horse or a water dragon. That's all."

"Oh," she said. "There's a dragon in my brain."

"There's a dragon in all our brains," he said. "And some of us have nice dragons and some of us have bad dragons. You know what I do sometimes?"

She shook her sleepy head.

"I slay the bad dragons," he said.

"Like a knight?"

"Just like a knight. How about you recite one of your poems to me," he said. "That'll help you fall asleep. And when you wake up you won't remember anything bad about Roland. Okay?"

"What poem?" Her body felt so heavy. Her brain like mush. But if someone wanted her to recite a poem, she would do it.

"Kubla Khan," he said. "That's a good dream poem. Maybe it'll give you good dreams."

"'In Xanadu,'" she began, "'did Kubla Khan / A stately pleasure dome decree…'"

She was almost asleep, one second from it, when she felt something hard, something that tasted of plastic being shoved into her mouth between her lips. She felt something cold on either side of her forehead. And then a shock tore through her, a shock like lightning had struck her. It lifted her into the air and ripped a hole into her brain.

And after that…nothing.

The next thing she remembered was waking up in the hospital in Astoria. The first face she saw was her great-aunt Frankie's. She was a tall thin lady with long white hair tied up in a bun. Her dark eyes sort of reminded Allison of her mom. Allison liked her immediately.

"What are you doing here?" Allison asked, after her aunt Frankie introduced herself.

Aunt Frankie answered very simply, "Little girl, I'm getting you the hell out of here."

Allison pulled into the long driveway to the house, parked and went inside. She went quietly, not wanting to draw attention to herself. Where Deacon and Thora were she didn't know, but she glimpsed Roland standing on the deck, staring out at the water. Praying? Maybe. She wanted to talk to him more than anything but she couldn't trust herself yet. Or him.

She went right up to the third floor. Part of her wanted to confront Dr. Capello but she didn't know what to say to him. She needed proof, first of all. She needed proof that what she remembered was true.

Outside Dr. Capello's bedroom door she paused and listened. Allison heard nothing. She peeked in and saw the room was dark. He must be sound asleep. It was late, past eleven, but Allison knew she wouldn't sleep for a very long time.

She went to the attic door. It was unlocked. She turned on the light and walked up the wooden stairs, going as slowly as she could. She didn't want a creaking footfall to telegraph to the entire house where she was and what she was doing. She made it up without a sound, no sound but her own shallow, panting breaths.

Allison knew what she was looking for, and she even had a good idea where to find it. She walked to the south wall, to the row of display cases where Dr. Capello kept his collection. She pulled down one white sheet and peered through the glass front doors. She saw bone drills and assorted ivory-handled scalpels, a metal mouth stretcher, a copper syringe and a sterling-silver catheter. But not what was she looking for. She pulled down the second white sheet on the second glass case and searched it top to bottom. Nothing again. Allison was starting to panic now. Any second Roland would come up and ask her what she was doing and why she was doing it, and she didn't have a good answer. She ripped the sheet off the third and final case and scanned all the contents.

Nothing.

She stood up and rested her head against the top of the case. It had to be here. Had to be.

"Where the hell are you?" she said to herself.

"Tell me what you're looking for," Dr. Capello said, "and I'll tell you where to find it."

CHAPTER 25

Allison spun around and saw Dr. Capello in his blue bathrobe standing at the top of the stairs.

"Fairwood called me," Dr. Capello said in answer to her silence. "They said someone came to see Antonio today. I knew it had to be you. You must be pretty upset."

"They called you?"

"I asked them to," he said. "I like to keep tabs on the poor boy. Michael said Tony had a seizure while you were there today."

"He did," she said. "It was...awful."

"Kid was dealt a bad hand at birth," Dr. Capello said. "I'm afraid I couldn't change his cards."

"You aren't playing cards," Allison said. "You're playing with kids and their lives."

"It wasn't playing, doll face. It was my job."

Now was Allison's chance to ask the question she'd come back here to ask.

"What did you do to your children?"

Dr. Capello didn't answer. He shuffled across the floor to a chair and sat down in it, hard and heavy. He looked sick and he looked tired. He looked just like what he was—dying. He took a few moments to catch his breath and then began speaking.

"There was a girl," Dr. Capello began. "A French girl. We studied her in med school. She had epilepsy. No drug could silence her seizures, no treatment could quiet her suffering. Day in and day out she suffered without hope. And then a surgeon proposed a rather radical treatment. Her seizures were seated in her hippocampus. Perhaps if he removed it, it would end her seizing. Of course, there was a great risk to this surgery. The hippocampus is also the seat of empathy, of inhibition, of memory. You can't just cut something like that out of someone's brain without consequences. But the girl was desperate. It was this or death by seizure. They performed the operation. She lived. Everyone held their breath to see what sort of person she would be once the organ of empathy was cut out of her brain. Would she be a zombie? A psychopath? Would it have been all for nothing? And then the most wonderful thing happened."

"What?" Allison asked, swept into the story despite herself.

"She stopped seizing. That they expected. What they didn't expect was that she developed hyperempathy."

"Hyperempathy?"

"Yes, it's a condition wherein a person overidentifies with the feelings of another. Hyperempaths are so sensitive to other people's moods and feelings they can seem almost psychic. It's the brain, you see. We call it neuroplasticity. A big word that simply means the brain has extraordinary powers of healing itself. Especially in children. Whole hemispheres of the brain can be removed and people can not only survive but thrive as the remaining hemisphere of the brain quickly takes over the job of the lost hemisphere. My God, Allison, it's like magic to see something like that happen. Keep the moon. Keep the ocean. Keep outer space, I don't want it. It's the brain that's the true undiscovered country."

"And you explored it," she said.

"I did indeed. Inspiration is a terrifying thing. Hits you like lightning and you're never the same again. I read that case study about the French girl thirty years ago and had the idea that this was it, this was the cure the world was waiting for. It's the common denominator among all psychopaths— the lack of empathy. And here was a way to create empathy, *hyper*empathy even, in a human brain. Remove part of the hippocampus. It'll shock the brain into rewiring itself. We already knew thanks to Phineas Gage that if you damaged the brain you could damage the personality. Well, it turns out if you sculpt the brain, you can sculpt the personality. Like Deacon with his glass, that was me with the brain. A sculptor. Dr. Jarvik created artificial hearts. I sculpt artificial souls."

"This sounds insane, you know," Allison said. He waved his hand in disgust.

"It sounds insane to break a child's jaw, doesn't? Sounds awful. But we do it all the time. If a child is born with an overbite, you break the jaw, you reset it and you let it heal correctly. That's all I did. I broke the brain, reset it, let it heal. And I'm not the first to do it, kid. It's called psychosurgery, and it's been around for decades. In the 1970s, a procedure was perfected in Japan to treat aggression. Cut out part of the amygdala—the seat of aggression—and violent people become less violent. My procedure simply went a step further. Or two."

"Or three?" Allison asked.

"Or three," he said.

"What did you do to these kids?" she asked again.

"I called it 'the Ragdoll Project.' A little joke. My mother kept Ragdolls until she died. Best cats there are."

"Because they're so tame they can't even protect them-selves?"

"What's wrong with being tame?"

"That's really what you did, isn't it? You 'tamed' violent kids?"

"Not any old violent kids. Psychopathic kids," Dr. Ca-pello said. "I found children who fit the criteria. I operated on them. The end."

"No," Allison said, shaking her head. "Not the end. Not even close to the end. You didn't always cure them, and that's only the beginning. Now tell me the rest. Kendra's on a dozen drugs and almost never leaves her house. Antonio's a wreck. Oliver's *dead*. You want to explain that to me?"

"What's to explain? It's experimental surgery. It's the risk we take."

"Antonio has to be restrained constantly. He's been chained to a bed for fifteen years! This isn't the risk 'we' take. It's the risk you took for him. He was a child."

"Yes, and had he been an adult they would have locked him up in prison and thrown away the key," Dr. Capello said. "Save your sympathy. If I hadn't operated on him, he would have been facing a death sentence long ago."

"How do you know? You can't see the future."

"You're a sweet young woman," Dr. Capello said, "and you'd make a lovely wife, a good mother and a wonderful friend. But you'd be a terrible doctor. The children were ill. No other treatment works for kids like that."

"Kids like Deacon," she said. "Right? Antonio said he killed his cat."

"Oh, Deacon killed lots of cats. And dogs. And birds. And anything he could catch. It was a mania. It was…sick. That was part of the Macdonald Triad, you know. The old criteria to diagnose future violent offenders—do they set fires, do they wet the bed, do they harm animals? Deacon had all three."

"And Kendra?"

"The newspapers called her 'the Firestarter,' like that old movie. Burned down her grandfather's house with her grandfather still inside. And Oliver—"

"Threw his baby brother against the wall," Allison said. Dr. Capello raised his eyebrow. "We went to see his mom."

"I see," Dr. Capello said.

"And Thora?"

Dr. Capello nodded.

"And Thora. Psychopath through and through. A pathological liar like most psychopaths are," Dr. Capello said. "Accused her first foster father of molesting her after he punished her for beating up one of the other kids in the house. He was arrested for sexual contact with a minor. His wife left him. He wasn't allowed to see his children. By the time Thora recanted, it was too late. His father-in-law had shot him and killed him."

Allison buried her face in her hands.

"Allison, listen to me. There was no hope for these kids. They were done for the day they were born, the second they were conceived. The same way some kids are born with bum tickers, these kids were born with bum brains. Unlike the heart, you can play a little with the brain. And that's what I did. Partial hippocampectomy, burn a few holes into the prefrontal cortex and then wait and see. If it all goes well, in six months to a year, you have a brand-new child with a brand-new personality. When it goes right you get Roland. If it doesn't go quite right, you have—"

"Antonio. Oliver. Kendra."

"Sadly, yes," he said. "I couldn't save them all. But I tried."

"They never had tumors, did they? Or cysts or anything?"

"When the procedure works, the kids all have healthy consciences. Too healthy. If they were going to be normal kids, they couldn't be walking around thinking they were born evil. Better to let them think it was a tumor, something foreign that had invaded their brains, something easy to fix. It's hard to heal when you're saddled with guilt. A tumor or a cyst—that was something they could point the blame at rather than themselves."

"And it gave you a reason to operate," she said. "Right? I'm sure you had to come up with an excuse to cut inside the heads of little kids. You couldn't just walk around saying you wanted to cure them of evil."

"You would think that, wouldn't you?" he said, shaking his finger at her. "You would think I would have to show the parents and guardians X-rays, test results, brain scans, treatment outcomes… You would think my nurses would try to stop me, residents, interns, the hospital brass. You would think. You want to know how it really happened?"

"You walked in, snapped your fingers and they gave you a kid?"

Dr. Capello snapped his thin old fingers.

"These kids weren't kids anymore to their parents or their social workers. They were problems. And you tell someone you can make their problems go away, they will roll out the red carpet for you and say, 'Be my guest.' Nobody wanted anything to do with these children. I said, 'Show me your worst kids and I'll take them off your hands.' It wasn't a hard sell. They gave me the kids with a sigh of relief and no questions asked. That's not a cliché, my dear. In all the years I was looking for children to help, not a single social worker ever asked to see the X-rays."

"Of course they didn't. You were a pillar of the community. People looked up to you, trusted you."

"That had nothing to do with it." He waved his hand, batting away the idea. "I promised to make their problems go away. They would have let the devil himself take those kids if it meant they didn't have to deal with them. What would you do with a boy like Antonio? A boy who stabbed a girl in the neck with a fork and tried to rape her on the playground? A boy who giggled when you tried to punish him for it? A boy who'd as soon set your bed on fire as look you in the eye? A boy who *did* set his own mother's bed on fire for trying to discipline him. He was remorseless as a snake. Allison, one of my own nurses looked at one of my Ragdoll patients on the table and said, 'At least if she dies, it's no big loss.' You know which kid that was? Thora."

Allison pressed her hands to her face. She couldn't believe she was hearing this.

"You love Thora?" Dr. Capello asked. "You can thank me anytime now because believe me, you wouldn't have loved her before I helped her."

"Don't pretend you're some kind of saint or angel. I know the truth."

"I never hurt a child on purpose in my life."

"Except me."

Finally she managed to land a blow hard enough to crack his self-righteous facade.

"Ah," he said. "You do remember everything now, don't you?"

"I remember."

Dr. Capello let out a long breath. His skeletal shoulders slumped. He pointed a bony finger toward the filing cabinet that had held all the medical records before he'd burned them. Allison went over to it and opened the second drawer. She'd already seen inside the top one.

"Bottom drawer," Dr. Capello said.

Allison bent down and opened the bottom drawer. She saw

something inside it covered in an opaque milk-white plastic cover. She pulled the cover away and there in the bottom of the drawer was a machine, no bigger than a four-slice toaster, that looked like a prop from a 1960s sci-fi film. It was white plastic with rounded corners, large dials and knobs, with black wires coiled around it.

"That what you were looking for?" Dr. Capello asked.

"That's it," she said. Once she saw the ECT machine, she knew that was the thing Dr. Capello had used on her. She went cold looking at it, nauseous. "Was this your grandmother's?"

"Oh, no. That one's from a mental hospital that closed down in the 70s. It's very safe, you know," he said. "It's not like the movies. You get the shock and you have a headache and some retrograde amnesia. That's about it. What's fascinating is that you remember anything at all from that day. It's usually permanent, you know. The amnesia from ECT." He spoke as if he wished he had the time to study her.

"I remember it all now. When I saw Antonio seizing today, it came back to me."

"Interesting," he said. "I wonder if it wasn't the ECT that made you forget. Good chance you simply didn't want to remember."

"I didn't," she said. "But I do. I remember that I was twelve. And I remember I wasn't sick. And I remember we weren't in a safe, sterile hospital," she said. "We were up here in a dark stuffy attic, and you drugged me and used thirty-year-old medical equipment on me."

He had the decency—or the cowardice, perhaps—to say nothing to that.

"I never did fall, did I? You made all that up," she said.

He raised his hand in surrender, the only admission of guilt she needed.

"How could you do that? You drugged me," Allison said. Her voice was small, scared, far away.

"Just Benadryl," he said. "A double dose."

"You made me recite a poem to help me fall asleep. *Kubla Khan.*"

"'A savage place!'" Dr. Capello recited, "'as holy and enchanted / As e'er beneath a waving moon was haunted / By woman wailing—'"

"'For her demon-lover!'" Allison completed the line, finally remembering it. She closed her eyes and whispered a name. "Roland..."

"Yes, Roland," he said.

"It wasn't an accident, was it?"

"No."

"He killed Rachel. Murdered her."

"I don't believe children, even psychopathic children, are capable of committing murder in the legal sense. But did he kill her on purpose? Yes," Dr. Capello said. "He did. Their mother was long gone, father wasn't home much. Roland would abuse Rachel, brutally abuse her. That's how she came to me. Through the ER. Roland cracked her skull against the sidewalk."

"Oh, God," Allison said. She didn't want to know any of this.

"She was too scared of Roland to tell anyone the truth about her injuries. The police assumed it was an accident and so did I. She was the sweetest little thing. I held her hand before the surgery, just to let her know I was taking good care of her. She didn't want to let my hand go," he said. "I can still feel those tiny little fingers. Her whole hand fit inside my palm. I told her she needed to be more careful playing outside. She said her accident wasn't an accident, someone had pushed her.

I assumed it was her father. Who would ever have guessed it was her brother? He was just eight."

He stopped speaking and for a moment it seemed he was somewhere else, somewhere he wanted to return to.

"She asked me to take her home with me," he said. "The sort of desperate hopeless wish children make, like wishing for wings. I never planned on having children. Work was my life. But I couldn't let her go back to her father. I thought I would die if something happened to her. I'd never felt like that before with one of my patients, like she was my own child. So I asked to take her and they gave her to me. Just like that. And I thought if the father was hurting her, he'd probably hurt Roland, too. I brought them home and we spent a happy week together. Five whole days in this house, the three of us. And on the morning of the sixth day, before I was even awake, Roland dragged her out to the beach, buried her in the sand and let her suffocate to death. My little girl. My poor little Rachel."

Though his eyes were dry and his body dehydrated, he still found a way to weep. Allison wept, too, but not with him. Their tears were for different reasons. He wept for what he'd lost. Allison wept for what he'd taken.

Finally, he calmed himself. He turned and opened the filing cabinet drawer, the third one, and riffled through some papers before bringing something over to Allison.

"There she is," Dr. Capello said, handing her the photograph of a little gap-toothed girl of five with brown hair and brown eyes and a smile to break anyone's heart. Allison stared at the photograph, the little girl killed by her own brother. Her brother, the man Allison loved.

"Master manipulators, psychopaths are," Dr. Capello said. "Even as children. And I fell for it hook, line and sinker. Rachel was too scared of Roland to tell me the truth. And she died for it."

In the photograph, the girl sat cross-legged on a bed, a blue bed, holding a stuffed toy puppy. She wore a floppy beach hat to hide the shaved part of her hair from the surgery. She wore a smile to hide how scared she must have been trapped in the same house as the boy who would kill her that week.

"I made Roland tell me why he did it and you know what he said?"

"I don't want to know."

"He said, 'Because you liked her better than me.' He killed her because I loved her. It almost makes me want to believe in hell. I could have wrung the life out of him with my bare hands. A boy of eight and I hated him. Do you know how terrifying it is to realize you truly want to strangle a child? But I didn't do it. I didn't hurt him. I fixed him. And I was right to do it, Allison. Instead of justice, I showed him mercy. They love to talk about mercy at his monastery. I say what I did *was* an act of mercy. I operated on him, and lo and behold, the old boy was dead and a new boy was born in his place. He was a work of art. Total transformation. Demon to angel… Yes, he killed her because I loved her, and I saved him because I hated him. God, I hated him. Until I loved him." He lowered his head and Allison knew he wanted to weep.

"I love him, too, you know."

"Love him? You'll destroy him if you aren't careful."

"Destroy him? How?"

"You don't know fragile these kids are. Before the surgery, they have no remorse. After, they're penitent as saints. You have to protect them from too much guilt. They're like sponges, especially in the beginning, soaking up everyone's feelings. If you hate them, they hate themselves. That's what did Oliver in. His mother's grief became his. And I saw the way she watched him, like he was a bomb about to go off. He was better here where no one knew what he'd done. He needed to be shielded. But she took him home and you know the rest. I didn't want to lose him. I didn't want to lose him like I'd..."

"What?"

Dr. Capello didn't answer.

"You lost another patient, didn't you?" she asked. "Another kid? A kid who killed himself like Oliver?"

He still didn't answer.

"How many kids?" Allison demanded. "Tell me how many kids died."

"Five."

CHAPTER 26

"Five," Allison repeated. "Five kids? Five of your patients committed suicide?"

"Two killed themselves within a year of the procedure. Two died during or right after the operation—brain bleeds. One lived but...she wasn't well. She ran away. I don't think she's ever turned up."

He paused and took a weak, shuddering breath.

"Oliver was the last one. After his death, I stopped the experiment."

"It took you that long?"

He raised his hand in a fist. "Dammit, Allison, it had worked. On Roland, on Deacon, on Thora—somehow I got them just right. I had proof right inside my own house the procedure was valid, that it had merit. Everything came together with them. The stars aligned. They were..."

"Lucky," Allison said.

Dr. Capello lowered his fist. "I was shooting arrows in the dark," he said. "Even a master archer will miss a target he can't see."

"You were shooting at children. It's not right."

"I never said it was right. Never! But it was necessary."
He nearly spat the last word out at her. *Necessary.* She'd never
heard an uglier word.

He rested against the filing cabinet.

"I never meant to love them, you know," Dr. Capello said,
quiet again. "I never meant to love those awful kids. Especially
not Roland. I planned on operating on him and sending him
back into the system. His father could have him if he wanted
him. Anybody could have him as far as I cared."

He paused to take a breath. He was angry and that alone
was keeping him upright.

"And then the damnedest thing happened," he continued.
"I went into his hospital room after the surgery and watched
him sleeping, a bandage on his head and bruises on his eyes.
He was just a little boy. That's all he was. This skinny twig
of a boy, just a little boy. He was in a coma for a week after
the surgery. Longest week of my life." Dr. Capello laughed to
himself, a mirthless sound. "The operation damages the memory. When he woke up, he didn't know his sister was dead."

"You didn't tell him the truth, did you?" Allison asked.

"I told him he killed her, but I told him it was an accident.
That's the memory he has now. Playing in the sand with Rachel, a hole opening up underneath, the sand covering her
face… I made sure that was how he remembered it. As an
accident."

Allison nearly fainted with relief. Roland hadn't lied to
her, after all. He'd hidden things, yes, but he hadn't outright
lied. He couldn't lie because even he didn't know the truth.

"I knew," Dr. Capello continued. "When I looked him in
the eyes, it had worked. I'd turned the lion into a lamb. I told
him Rachel was dead and that it had happened while he was
playing in the sand with her. I said he shouldn't blame himself,
but he did. He blamed himself and he felt remorse and guilt

and shame. And he cried. His little body shook so hard I had to sedate him before he hurt himself. First time in his life he ever cried real tears. Over and over, he said, 'I'm sorry, I'm sorry. Dad, I'm so sorry...' A miracle of science."

"Brave new world," Allison said.

"Call the social worker who investigated Rachel's injuries," Dr. Capello said, his tone sharp, his eyes blazing with the last fire of his life. "She's probably still got the pictures in her files. You want to see what Roland had done to her? You want to see the black bruises on the side of her face? You want to see her arm in a sling because he grabbed her so hard he yanked it out of the socket? You want to see the X-ray of her skull fracture? Do you?"

Allison didn't answer. She was weeping far too hard to speak.

"And for all that," Dr. Capello said with a ragged sigh, "I forgave him. I took him back home with me, and from that day ever after, he was my son and I was his father. I loved him and I protected him as best I could."

"You protected him from the truth."

"As he got older, he started asking me awkward questions. Kids are good at that. He wanted to know why he had to have brain surgery. He wanted to know why he remembered hitting Rachel and dragging her and throwing her against a wall. I had to tell him something so I told him that he had a genetic condition that caused lesions in his brain and those caused his violent outbursts. I told him I had cured him of it."

Dr. Capello took another labored breath. Allison knew she was looking at a man who was not long for this world.

"But deep down he knows...something doesn't add up. That's why I wanted to keep him out of that monastery. I thought for sure they'd break him with their talk of sin and guilt. I thought he'd end up like Oliver, with a gun in his mouth and a bullet in his brain. But that's not what happened. Instead, he finally forgave himself. He knew better than I did what he needed. And you...you fell in love with him," he said. "You know how well he's turned out."

"I was a test, wasn't I?" Allison asked. "Like Brien? You got Deacon a cat to make sure he wasn't violent toward animals anymore? Did you bring me into this house as a test to make sure Roland wasn't violent toward little girls anymore?"

His silence was answer enough for her. Allison nodded.

"And Thora?" Allison asked.

"Me," he said. "I put myself to the test with her, as well. She falsely accused her last foster father of molesting her. I took a big risk for these kids. And I did so willingly. I love children. I loved you, too. I did. I do."

She raised her hand to block out his words. She didn't believe him. She didn't want his lies anywhere near her.

"You can sit there and judge me all you want," he said. "But you have benefitted from my work. The man you love wouldn't exist but for me. And you would have destroyed it all with a temper tantrum."

"I was scared he was going to kill me."

"He'd die before he hurt a fly, thanks to me," Dr. Capello said. "And you were going put all that at risk. Our family. You were always safe here."

"You also gave a twelve-year-old girl electroshock therapy to shut her up. You could have killed me!"

"The machine was old," he said. "But I knew it worked. I had played with it. The extent of the shock—that wasn't meant to happen. There was a power surge, totally unforeseen. I never meant to harm you. I overreacted. I just wanted to make it all go away. For Roland's sake. For the family's sake."

"Well, you certainly made me go away. That solved your problems."

"Not my intention at all. You would have woken up a few hours later with a headache and no memory of what had happened the previous few days. That's how it works. That's what was supposed to happen. And now you're going to do it again, aren't you?" he asked.

"What do you mean?"

"You're going to tell them what you know. You're going to tell them what I did to you."

"I'm not going to lie to them."

"You'll destroy them if you tell," he said. "You have to realize that. None of them know they were born psychopaths. They all think cysts and tumors caused their violent behavior. You'll make them hate themselves, and me, too."

"I love Roland. Am I supposed to look him in the eyes and lie?"

"Yes," he said. "Of course you are. Lie through your teeth. Lie like your life depends on it. Lie like his life depends on it because it does, Allison. It does. It's what I've been doing all their lives. Because I love them. Because that's what you do when you love someone."

He was weeping again, but her sympathy for the man was long gone. She'd seen what he'd done to Kendra, to Antonio, to Oliver and his mother.

"Children are dead because of you."

"Don't you understand how it works? Someone has to be the first. Like them," he said, raising a thin arm to point to his cases of medical antiques. "The first to saw off a leg to save a soldier's life. The first to drill a hole in the brain to relieve the pressure. The first to cut a womb open to rip out a baby. Look," he said, shuffling over to the cases. He opened a door and pulled out a large steel object, something like a saw with some kind of hand crank on it. "You know what this is? Guess?"

She shook her head, too scared to speak.

"A rib-spreader. You cut open the chest and pry the ribs apart with it. This is one of the first ever used in a hospital in America. It's demonic. Look at it. It pries the chest open. It's a serial killer's toy. But it's saved lives. It's saved thousands and thousands of lives. Roland killed a little girl, Allison, and didn't bat an eyelash about it. Zero remorse. Zero empathy. Rachel would have been the first of many if I didn't help him. But I did help him. I helped all of them... I loved all of them..."

The rib-spreader fell out of Dr. Capello's hands as he collapsed onto the floor.

"Dad!" Allison cried out, and ran to him. She knelt on the floor next to his body slumped against the filing cabinet.

"Are you all right?" she asked him. He lifted his hands and put them on her shoulders as if he wanted to try to stand but couldn't.

"I saved them," he said. "I saved them and you're going to destroy them."

"You're losing it. I'm going to call 911."

"I can't let you," he said. "I won't..."

He wrapped his hands around her throat.

Allison let out a scream of utter shock before his hands clamped so hard on her throat she could no longer make a sound. She tried to jerk away but couldn't. He had little strength left in his body, but what he had left was concentrated in his hands clamped around her neck like an iron collar.

His face contorted in effort and his hands squeezed the breath from her body. She tried to scream but nothing came out. In the faraway distance she thought she heard someone calling her name, but she couldn't answer. Stars swam in front of her face. Her lungs ached and burned. She beat her fists against Dr. Capello's chest but couldn't get him off her. So she kicked against him, kicked against anything she could find. The filing cabinet fell over, crashing into the display cases. Glass shattered, wood splintered, but nothing would break Dr. Capello's vicious grasp from around her throat.

Frantically she grabbed at her pocket until she felt it, the can of pepper spray Deacon had given her. She pulled it out and let it fly, right into Dr. Capello's eyes.

He screamed and collapsed on the floor in agony. The whole attic shook like a great fist was beating against the walls of the house. Was someone trying to save her? Or was that sound nothing more than the final beats of her dying heart?

She heard the voice again, someone shouting her name, and she tried to answer. Once free of the death grip on her neck, Allison could breathe again, but she couldn't speak. She swallowed huge gulps of air, wheezing as she breathed, nearly vomiting in her panic and her pain. She fell onto her side. Through her watering eyes, she saw Roland yank his father to his feet and slam him back against the wall.

"She was going to kill you," Dr. Capello said, his eyes bloodred and streaming tears. He coughed so hard it sounded like he was trying to vomit. Roland pushed his father away and ran to her, broken glass cracking to powder under the soles of his boots.

"Allison? Allison?" Roland knelt in front of her. He touched her face, stroking it gently.

"I'm all right," she said, her voice barely a whisper.

She struggled to her hands and knees. Her neck ached and her lungs were on fire but she could breathe, she could move. She was alive. Everything that happened next was a blur. She heard Roland calling his father's name. She saw Dr. Capello trying to flee out the door. She heard the sound of a body falling down stairs. Allison grabbed the wall and used it to stand. She hobbled to the top of the narrow attic staircase and saw Dr. Capello at the bottom, sprawled on the ground, either dead or unconscious. Deacon appeared, falling to the floor, screaming, "Dad! Dad!" over and over, running his hands over his father's body, trying to find the wound or the heartbeat. Thora stood by Deacon's side, not touching her father, not touching Deacon. She looked up at the stairs and Allison met her eyes. Thora said nothing. She didn't have to.

Dr. Capello was silent.

Roland took her into his arms and held her. She looked past his shoulder and saw the door hanging off the hinges. Someone had taken an ax to it.

And close by and growing closer came the sound of sirens.

Allison closed her eyes and didn't open them again for a very long time.

CHAPTER 27

When Allison came to, she wasn't sure if ten minutes had passed, ten hours or ten days.

She lay in her bed in her room, a white afghan over her. She blinked herself into awareness and tried to raise her head.

"Don't move." It was Roland speaking to her. She turned her head despite the order and saw him sitting in the white wicker chair at her bedside, the little bedside lamp glowing softly.

"I'm all right," she said. "I think."

"The EMTs checked you."

"Am I okay?" she said.

"You fainted. The EMT said to let you rest. He said it didn't look like you had any pepper spray in your eyes. You have some bruises on your neck but nothing broken. I need to get him."

"No, stay. Please?"

"You were choked and you passed out. You need medical attention."

Allison started to sit up. "Later."

"Allison." Roland said her name like a plea or like a prayer. She couldn't say for sure.

"Is he dead?" she asked, suddenly remembering everything that had led her to this moment.

"Not yet," Roland said. "Soon. Tonight."

Allison closed her eyes, breathed, nodded.

"I don't know what he said to you. Or did," Roland said. "But—"

"Let's not talk about it. It doesn't matter."

She wasn't sure if that was true but she needed to say it, needed to try to believe it.

"So he's still here?" she asked.

"Yeah," Roland said. "The EMTs want to take him to the hospital."

"He wouldn't want to go."

"I know. I ought to let them take him. After what he did to you."

"No," Allison said. "He's just sick. Let him die here in his home in his bed like he wanted."

And let it be quick, Allison thought but did not say aloud.

"It won't be long now." Roland's voice was hollow, empty of emotion.

"Why aren't you with him?"

"Because I'm with you."

"I'm fine. Go to your dad." She lay back down again.

"No," Roland said. "I'll stay here with you."

Allison swallowed a hard lump in her throat. It hurt but not enough to scare her. She'd be okay. Eventually.

"I tried to do something nice for you today," Roland said.

"You do something nice for me every day," she said.

"I was going to finish the laundry you started yesterday," he said. "I threw your jeans in with mine. This was in the back pocket."

He held up a folded piece of paper. She didn't have to look at it to know what it was. The note about Roland's operation.

"Is that why you didn't wake me up last night?" he asked. "You found that?"

"I needed time to think. Do you blame me?"

"You could have asked me about it," he said.

"I wasn't sure if you'd tell me the whole truth."

Roland took the hit well. He nodded in agreement.

"The truth hurts sometimes."

"It does, yeah," she said. "But so do lies."

She rolled over onto her side, facing him. His hand was there on the covers and she could reach out and take it if she wanted. She wanted, but she didn't.

"I don't think I lied to you," he said. "Except by omission. It's not easy to talk about…"

"What? Tell me. You told me you were in love with me, so I know you're not a coward. I was with McQueen for six years and never told him I had real feelings for him."

"This," he said, holding up the page again with the notes on his surgery. "So, ah…when I was twenty, I met this girl in Astoria. We worked together. We went out on all of two dates, and I thought, yeah, she's the one. Dad asked about her and I told him that. I thought he'd be happy. He was but he said he needed to tell me something. He said that what I had as a kid, that condition that made me violent, it could be genetic. And I needed to be really careful. He said…he said I shouldn't have children. That is not an easy conversation for a twenty-year-old guy to have with his dad when he's madly in love. Dad knew a doctor, he said. He…"

"Tell me, Roland. Just say it."

"I had a vasectomy."

"What?"

"This is not a comfortable conversation for a man to have

with the woman he's in love with, either. It's humiliating. I know it shouldn't be, but that doesn't change that it is. So, you know, not the easiest thing in the world for me to talk about."

Allison took a heavy breath. She hadn't expected that, not at all.

"Is that why you joined the monastery?" she asked. "Because you can't have biological children?"

"Terrible reason, right? I joined for a lot of bad reasons. I didn't want to risk falling in love again. I felt tainted by what I'd done to Rachel. I felt like I maybe should go away for a long time. There were good reasons, too. I wanted to be forgiven. I wanted peace. I wanted to be a different person. But that doesn't work. You're still you no matter where you go."

Allison touched his face, the scruff on his chin, pale as snow on sand.

"I remembered something else today," she said.

"Like what?" Roland, she knew, was trying to sound normal but it wasn't working. He sounded scared, and for Roland that wasn't normal.

"The first time you and I made love upstairs in my room, which used to be your room, I remembered I tried to run my fingers through your hair. You pushed my arm down on the bed before I could. I thought you were being sexy..." Allison ran her hands through his hair and pulled the little black elastic band out of the short ponytail he always wore it in. Roland lowered his head. She dropped the elastic on the floor, and started stroking his hair. Under her fingers she felt a ridge of scar tissue under his hair. It was in the same place she felt the scar on Antonio's scalp.

"How long were you going to keep it a secret from me?" she asked. "The surgery, I mean."

"Which surgery?" He almost smiled, almost.

"Both."

"It wasn't a secret at first. Just private. Then I started falling in love with you. Then it was a secret because I knew you needed to know," he said. "I was scared I'd lose you if you wanted to have kids of your own."

"That's why you didn't tell me," she said.

Roland lowered his head again, exhaled.

"Sometimes I remember things," he said. "Awful things. Hurting Rachel. Doing terrible things to her." He swallowed hard and she saw his Adam's apple bob in his throat. "I used to try to talk to Dad about them, and he told me to forget it all. He said I hurt her sometimes but it wasn't my fault—I had a condition. But I think I did more than hurt her. Sometimes I think I…sometimes I think I killed her. And I don't think it was an accident, like Dad said."

He looked at her with pleading eyes and she saw him as the Roland he'd once been years and years ago. The little boy. He looked scared and young and innocent and sweet, just the way she must have looked her first time at the house when he'd changed her life for the better by asking her to help him turn the pages in the book they were reading.

"You were a kid," she said. "Whatever happened, you were just a kid."

Allison covered his hand with hers, and he grabbed it, gripping it so tightly it hurt. She sat up and pulled his head to her stomach and held him in her lap. She ran her fingers through his hair over and over again, ignoring the scar because the scar was nothing, it was old news, it was part of him but it wasn't him.

"It's okay," she whispered as she stroked his hair and his shoulders and his face. Her leg was damp with his tears. "I'm okay. Dad's got crazy poison in his system and it made him lose it. That's all. I'm fine and you're fine and we're fine."

"I'm not fine," Roland said with a shuddering breath.

"Why not?" she asked, smiling.

He looked up at her, his face open and honest and aching.

"Because my dad's dying."

Allison took his face in her hands.

"Mine, too," she said. Then they held each other and wept together for a long time. They stopped when Deacon came to the door and knocked to get their attention. They wiped their faces and looked at him.

"You okay, sis?" Deacon asked. He looked pale and haggard and haunted.

"I'm all right. Just had a rough moment there," Allison said. It was no time now to tell them the truth.

"I'm glad you're okay," Deacon said. He looked at Roland. "It's, uh, it's time."

"Is he awake?" Allison asked.

Deacon nodded. "For now. They gave him some meds for pain so he's calm. The EMTs said to hurry if you're coming. He's…he's going."

She looked at Roland and Roland looked at her. He stood up and held out his hand to her. She took it and let him help her to her feet. Allison found a light scarf in her suitcase and wound it around the bruises on her neck. When she was ready, they left the room and went upstairs. Outside Dr. Capello's bedroom, Deacon stopped them.

"The EMTs are just going to wait downstairs," Deacon said. "It won't be long now."

Roland and Deacon went inside. Allison stayed in the doorway, watching.

Dr. Capello lay on his bed, a blanket over him and his arms on top of the cover. His face was red from the pepper spray but he didn't seem to be in pain. Thora sat at his side on the bed, clutching his hand in hers. The hands that had nearly killed her barely an hour ago now lay limp and trembling on the bedcovers. The attack on her had taken the life out of him, she saw. She'd survived it. He would not.

Allison took a step into the room. She sensed Death close, hovering near the bed. Allison could feel him breathing down her neck. His breath smelled sour like old milk, and she had to crack open the window to let in the cleansing scent of the ocean. Sea air wafted into the room and over the bed. Slowly Dr. Capello's eyes fluttered. He must have sensed movement, felt the breeze on his face. Allison waited and he met her eyes and smiled.

"There's my doll…" He sighed. His voice was as thin as a Bible page.

"I'm here, Dad," Allison said.

It wasn't easy to put a smile on her face and call him "Dad" but she did it. She did it for Roland and she did it for Deacon and she did it for Thora. But most of all, she did it for the seven-year-old girl she'd once been, the girl who'd loved this man with all her little heart, and for the little piece of her heart that loved him still.

"I'm sorry," he said. "I didn't…"

"Don't say anything," Allison said to him. She crossed her arms over her chest and looked down at him in the bed. He seemed too small now, so terribly small and fragile and harmless. "You're sick and you had a spell. That's all."

His head moved like he was trying to nod.

"A good girl," he said.

He took a long shuddering breath, the sort of breath taken after a good long cry. It was excruciating watching him breathe like that, seizing up in momentary agony before relaxing again and going so still that Allison was afraid they'd lost him already. Yet he somehow managed to find the strength to speak again.

"Promise me, kids," he said, and each word cost him a

breath. The more he spoke, the quicker he would die, and yet he seemed to need to speak, anyway. "Promise me you'll always love each other. Promise me you'll always take care of each other."

"I promise, Dad," Deacon said. "Of course we'll take care of each other. You taught us how."

"Yes, Daddy," Thora said. "I promise."

"Roland? Allison?"

Roland said softly, "I promise, Dad."

And Allison, too, made the promise. "I promise," she said, though she wasn't sure she could keep it.

Dr. Capello nodded a little and closed his eyes again. They all stared at his face, waiting for that moment it went utterly still and slack when the spark of life would finally go out.

"So quiet," he said, and they all looked up in surprise. They'd thought he'd already spoken his last words. "Who died?"

He tried to laugh at his own joke, but the laugh quickly turned into a spasm of coughs. Thora soothed Dr. Capello with her hands on his chest.

"We're all here," Thora said. "I'm here and Deacon's here and Roland's here and Allison's here."

"My children," he said. "Don't grieve."

"Your children can't help it," Roland said. His every word sounded strained, like it was being dragged out of him against its will.

"Rotten kids," he breathed, then smiled again. "Dragons guard treasure."

It was an odd thing to say, odd enough they all looked at each other in confusion until Dr. Capello spoke again.

"That's you, kids," he said. "My treasure."

"Love you, Daddy," Thora said. It seemed to take everything she had in her to push those three words past the block-age in her throat. Tears streamed from her eyes.

"Too quiet," he said, and it was clear he was suffering in the silence. He was scared. He needed to hear his children's voices, but his children were mute. Their throats were tight as a miser's fists and their tongues heavy as sandbags. They loved him with their grown-up hearts and child's hearts combined.

Why Allison did it, she would never know for certain, but in the silence she began to speak, tenderly, like a mother speaking an old rhyme to her child.

"In Xanadu did Kubla Khan
A stately pleasure-dome decree:
Where Alph, the sacred river, ran
Through caverns measureless to man
Down to a sunless sea.
So twice five miles of fertile ground
With walls and towers were girdled round;
And there were gardens bright with sinuous rills,
Where blossomed many an incense-bearing tree;
And here were forests ancient as the hills,
Enfolding spots of sunny greenery."

"Ah," Dr. Capello said, a sound of bliss. His pupils were fixed and dilated. "I see it all. The trees. The garden. The river. I see—" he took one more labored breath "—my Rachel."

Roland's head snapped up, his eyes wide open.

"Dad?" Roland leaned forward and put his hand on Dr. Capello's face. "Dad?"

Allison placed her hand on Dr. Capello's chest. She felt nothing.

"He's gone," she said in a whisper, but in the silence of the room it sounded like she'd shouted it.

Allison looked at Roland. He shook his head, not in disbelief but in protest against the unfairness of it all. His tongue was loosened then, and at last he said all the things he'd been meaning to say.

"Dad, it's your son. It's Roland. Listen to me. I love you, Dad. I'll always love you. You loved me when no one else could. You loved me when no one else would. You took me in when no one wanted me. You didn't just forgive me, you called me your son. When no one else would have me, you gave me a home. You made me who I am. You made me a good man. I owe you everything. I owe you my whole life and everything I am and everything I have and everyone I love. Dad? Do you hear me? Dad?"

Thora and Deacon sobbed in each other's arms. They were lost in grief, drowning in it, choking on it. Roland had started his litany all over again.

"I love you, Dad. I'll always love you. You loved me when no one else could. You loved me when no one else would. You didn't just forgive me…"

Those words filled the room, filled it to the rafters and filled Allison to the ribs so that she thought they'd crack and splinter for how her heart swelled to bursting with love for Roland. Whatever sin Dr. Capello had committed against her, Allison vowed then never to hold it against Roland.

She reached for him, pulling him away from Dr. Capello's corpse, guiding him to the chair. Outside the window the moon was high and round, and in the bed, Dr. Capello's face went slack and his lips slightly parted in his death mask. And Allison knew she had to be the one to do it. Slowly Allison eased the covers down to free them from Dr. Capello's arms and pulled them up, up and over his face.

Allison knew she should say something then. Something profound and poetic and merciful, something about this man who'd done beautiful things and ugly things and was now standing at the gates of heaven waiting to find out if the beauty outweighed the ugly in the eyes of God. But for the first time in Allison's life, poetry failed her. She was left with only two words.

"Goodbye, Dad."

CHAPTER 28

The next two days passed in a blur. Allison helped make the necessary phone calls. She cooked, she cleaned, she brewed pot after pot of coffee while Roland, Deacon and Thora walked around the house numb with shock, acting almost normal, which always seemed the most abnormal thing people did after a death. Every night Roland slept with her in her bed, holding her and sometimes kissing her but that was it. They didn't make love or talk about their future together, if there was one. Nero might have fiddled while Rome burned, but not even he played in the ashes.

And there were ashes. Four glass urns that contained Dr. Capello's last remains were delivered to the house on the morning of the third day after he'd passed away. There would be no funeral, no visitation. Dr. Capello wanted none of that. He found it maudlin and strange and religious, which he wasn't. So the urns sat side by side by side by side on the floor of the sunroom next to the windows, waiting to be scattered. Allison caught Deacon staring at them. He stared so long and hard, Allison finally took a blanket off the couch and draped it over the urns.

"Thank you," Deacon said, and swallowed.

"Not a problem."

"I made them, you know."

"Did you?" she asked.

"Do you have any idea how hard it is to make urns for your own father while he's still alive?" Deacon asked.

"I can't imagine."

"I don't recommend it."

"You made four of them."

"One for each of us," he said. "But if you don't want to—"

He smiled at her, a pained smile.

She took him in her arms and held him. He didn't cry but that was no surprise. They were all cried out by the third day.

"You're going to stay, aren't you?" Deacon asked.

"You want me to?" she asked.

"Roland needs you. Sexually, I mean," Deacon said, pulling away.

"Deacon."

"It's part of the healing process," he said. "It's cleansing. Gotta get all the fluids out."

"You're hopeless."

"It's true. At least, that's what I keep telling Thora. She's not buying it, either."

Allison playfully shoved him and they laughed, the first laugh she remembered laughing in days.

"I have something for you," Deacon said. "It's up in my room."

"I'm scared."

"You should be," he said with a wink.

He took her upstairs to his bedroom and showed her a large box sitting on the floor tied up with twine.

"For you," he said. "Open it."

Allison gave him a look before untying the string and opening the lid. And there nestled inside the packing peanuts she found a glass dragon. Not one glass dragon but two. Not two but three. Not three but four. She pulled all four of them one by one out of the box. They were exquisitely sculpted, with detail so intricate her eyes could barely see it all. They were all different—one was black and laughing; one was golden and pensive; one was red, chin high, proud and smiling; one was jade green and held a book in its talons. Allison recognized them at once—a dragon for each of them. And even better, they weren't just dragons but bookends. Each one of them was situated on a heavy glass pedestal with a heavy glass back. Deacon had done this for her, made these with his own hands. She loved them in an instant.

"They're beautiful," she breathed, barely able to speak aloud.

"I like to make animals," Deacon said, and she glanced up at him. He looked a little sad, a little embarrassed. "You know when I was a kid—"

"I know," she said. "When I was a kid I stepped on every ant I saw because I thought they'd swarm and eat me. I think I had them confused with piranhas. Kids are dumb sometimes."

Deacon gave her a grateful smile.

"You can sell the dragons in your bookstore," Deacon said, his eyes bright and eager again. "I can make more, I mean, so you can keep these ones."

The bookstore. Of course. What a perfect idea. So much for Pandora's Books. She would call it the Bookstore at the End of the World. And the window would have a dragon painted on it and it would say under the name *Here there be dragon books...* She'd have a whole section on sea monster books, mythology and lore. And maps, too. Beautiful old maps with dragons at the edges of the known world. She'd work there all day and come home to Roland every night. What would he do? Start a children's charity with his father's money? They'd live at The Dragon, all four of them. Plenty of room, beautiful house, happy memories. No reason not to. And she and Roland would get married on the beach and maybe Thora and Deacon would have a private sort of ceremony so they could feel married at last, if that's what they wanted. And they'd all be happy together and Allison would never, ever be alone again.

A nice dream.

"They're so perfect," she said. "I can't even believe they're mine."

"I hope you don't mind I made them without you. I was afraid you'd try to pet them when they were still a thousand degrees."

"You're never going to let me forget that, are you?"

"Reminding people of their stupid mistakes is what family's for," Deacon said.

Allison carefully put the dragons back in the box and carelessly threw her arms around Deacon.

"Hey, yo," he said. "Calm down. I'm already sleeping with one sister."

Allison laughed. "God, you're terrible. I love you so much."

Deacon's arms tightened around her. She felt his chest heave with a breath.

"Dad would never hurt anybody, you know," Deacon said. "Not on purpose. Never hurt anyone in his life. His entire life all he did was help people, help kids."

"I know he did," Allison said, forcing a smile. "He was a very sick man. That's all. But thank you for the pepper spray. I didn't think I'd have to use it."

"I'm just glad you're okay, sis."

"You and me both."

Before Allison could say anything else, Thora stuck her head in the room.

"Hey," Thora said.

Deacon stepped back, far back, away from Allison.

"I wasn't doing nothing," Deacon said.

"Likely story," Thora said. "I need Allison for a minute."

"Girl talk?" Deacon asked.

"Yes," Thora said. She grabbed him by the collar of his shirt, kissed him good and hard and finished with a firm, "Out."

Deacon left smiling.

"Good to see him smiling," Allison said.

"He's trying to be okay," Thora said. "He's having a rough time with all this."

"I'm sure he is," Allison said, nodding.

"But we'll get there." Thora went and sat down on Deacon's messy bed. The whole room was a hurricane of clothes and computers and sketchbooks and dirty dishes. Just like when he was a kid. Minus the conspicuous box of condoms on the cluttered night table. Thora caught her looking at them and smiled sadly.

"We can't have kids," Thora said.

"Because legally you're siblings?" Allison asked although she knew already that wasn't why.

Thora was wearing faded jeans and an oversize Oregon State Beavers sweatshirt that Allison guessed she'd stolen from Deacon. She looked tired and small, but not as sad as Roland, and not nearly as sad as Deacon.

"Because psychopathy has a genetic component," Thora said. "Not that Deacon knows that's what he is—was. I just told him I don't want kids."

"So you know then?" Allison asked.

Thora lifted her empty hands. "I learned a lot when I broke in and read Dad's files. I learned what we were before Dad. I figured the rest out on my own."

"Are you sure? I mean, about what you are?" Allison asked, finding it impossible to imagine Thora as a psychopath. And yet...

"Can't take the risk," Thora said. "Deacon's biological father is as horrible as it gets. He killed Deacon's mom."

"I knew he'd killed someone but not Deacon's mother."

"Deac's scared he'll turn into his father one day."

Allison thought of the pepper spray Deacon had given her. Her and Thora. He needed to protect the two women in the house. From who? From himself.

"I did some research after I found out what we were," Thora said. "They don't even diagnose children with psychopathy anymore. They wait until you're eighteen. You know why?"

Allison waited for the answer.

"All adults diagnosed as psychopaths showed symptoms of it as kids," Thora said. "But not all the kids who show those same traits turned out to be psychopaths. Basically...some kids grow out of it. *We* might have grown out of it. But maybe not."

"I'm so sorry," Allison said. And she was truly sorry. The word *sorry* seemed far too small here, like giving a penny to a man who'd just lost a million dollars. Thora, Deacon and Roland had been subjected to an unethical, unlawful, untried and untested surgery on their brains that had completely and inalterably changed their personalities. And it had been their father who'd done it to them.

"You do want kids, don't you?" Allison could tell from the aching in her eyes.

Thora whispered a tortured, "Yes."

"There's always adoption," Allison said.

Thora smiled. "True. I'd like that. Maybe someday. But in case you were planning on kids with Roland, you should know—"

"I know," Allison said. "He told me."

"Good." Thora rubbed her face and pushed her hair back off her forehead. She looked exhausted. Allison wanted to send her to bed right that second but it seemed Thora was intent on getting everything off her chest.

"Deacon started having nightmares when he was twelve," Thora said. "Not nightmares, night terrors. He'd dream about animals attacking him, and he'd wake up crying."

Allison shuddered in sympathy.

"He didn't want to tell anyone but I got him to tell me. You know, since I'm his 'twin.' After everyone went to bed, I'd go to his room to sleep with him. He slept better when I was with him. If he woke up crying, I'd comfort him. One night he told me he was scared it wasn't the slug that did it."

"The slug?"

Thora smiled. "That's what Deacon called the brain tumor Dad told him he had. Apparently Dad said that the tumor looked kind of like a slug. Deacon blamed it for all the horrible things he'd done. But he was scared that maybe it wasn't the slug, he said. That's why I...why eventually I wanted to figure out if there was something wrong with him I didn't know about."

"That's why you broke into Dad's medical files?" Allison asked.

"That's why," Thora said. "And that's when I found this big file called the Ragdoll Project. I read it front to back. Didn't understand a tenth of it, but I understood enough to figure out that none of us ever had anything wrong with us. Not nothing. But you know what I mean. No tumors, no lesions, no cysts."

Allison said nothing.

"Dad told me, and I'd told myself, that all the bad things I'd done, the lies I'd told, that it wasn't really my fault, that it was this thing in my brain," Thora said. "It was my one comfort. But it wasn't a thing. It was all me."

"You were a kid, Thora. A little kid."

"I know," she said. "But it's still…" She shook her head. "Imagine being smart and being proud you're smart, and then finding out you're only smart because a doctor put a microchip in your brain when you were seven. Imagine thinking you're a decent person and then finding out the only reason you're not a monster is because a doctor screwed with the wiring in your head?"

"I can't imagine," Allison said.

"Pretend you just found out that the only reason Ro loves you is because someone rewired his brain. It is, you know. If he really was as bad as that file said, then he would never have been capable of real love. How does that feel?"

"Not great," Allison admitted. "But it wasn't his fault he was born…" What did she even call it? Born evil? Born wrong? Born broken? Born sick? She left it at that. It wasn't Roland's fault he was born, the end.

"Maybe your father was right," Allison said. "Maybe what we call evil is just a disease. Someone had to try to cure it, right?"

"Maybe," Thora said, but it didn't sound as if she believed that. "I never told Deac what I found in the file. I never told Ro. I think they both still believe what Dad told them. They need to believe it. I know how horrible it was for me to find out I wasn't who I thought I was."

"It must be hard keeping that secret," Allison said.

"It's not easy being the only kid in the family who knows there's no Santa Claus," Thora said.

"Am I supposed to lie to his face if he asks me what I know?"

Thora turned away and gazed out the window at the long

winding driveway that had brought each of them here once long ago.

"Sometimes," Thora began, "on clear nights, Roland will stand on the beach and look at the stars, and it's like he's looking to see if God's up there. When he does that, I love him so hard it hurts. I'm scared one day he's going to look up and see that nobody's looking back." Thora met Allison's eyes. "If you knew no one was looking back, would you tell him? Or would you let him keep looking?"

"Isn't it a waste of time to keep looking if no one is up there?" Allison asked.

"The stars are up there," Thora said.

"Tell me one thing," Allison said. "Did Dad do the right thing with you all?"

"Oh...who knows? He made us good," Thora said. "He didn't make us wise. I have no idea if it was right or wrong, good or evil. I know it would be considered unethical, the way he went about it. But I ask myself this—would I want to undo what he did?"

"No?"

"Never in a million years. I don't remember much about my life before Dad, but I do remember..." Her voice trailed off. She looked away out the window. A tear escaped her eye and all the way down her face where it fell off and landed on her thigh. "I remember enough."

Allison didn't ask for details. Thora deserved some privacy, even some secrets.

"I know there were others," Thora said. "I know he hurt them when he was trying to help them. But I know Dad loved us. To take the risks he took to help us, that's love, right?"

"It's a kind of love," Allison said. "Or an attempt at it, anyway."

"When you love someone, you sometimes make choices

you don't want to make. You do things to help them that you wish you didn't have to do," Thora said. She had been looking at the floor but she lifted her head and met Allison's eyes.

Allison knew then who it was who'd called her aunt that day.

"I had a feeling it was you," Allison said. "Though I could never guess why."

"I saw you lying there unconscious," Thora said with a shaking voice. "I saw Dad over you, panicking. And I watched the ambulance take you away. You looked so helpless. You looked so little. I knew what Dad had done to us and I thought... I was scared."

"You were scared he was going to do it to me, too?" Allison asked. "The operation?"

"He lied to people so he could do it to us. What if he was lying about you falling down the stairs so he could experiment on you? When Deacon ran to find Kendra and tell her what had happened, I called your aunt. I pretended I was you. I didn't know what else to do. I'm sorry."

"Don't be," Allison said. "Sisters protect each other."

"They do." Thora nodded, her face contorting as if she was forcing herself not to collapse into her grief. "But I was wrong to make you scared of Roland. I was so wrong about him. I love him so much. And you, I loved you and I still do. Can you love me?"

"Yes, I can love you. I can love you forever," Allison said. She took Thora into her arms and they wept together, held each other, shook and cried together.

Oh, yes, Allison could love Thora. Thora who had called her aunt to protect her all those years ago. Deacon who had given her the pepper spray to protect herself. And Roland who'd taken an ax to the attic door when he'd heard her scream. Dr. Capello, their "savior," had tried to kill her and the killers had saved her. Dr. Capello hadn't just made his children good. He'd made them even better than him.

"Thank you," Thora said, pulling away to wipe her face.

"No problem." Allison ran her fingers through Thora's wild hair, taming it. Like sisters do.

"I'll have to tell them," she said, shrugging. "Deac and Ro. They need to know it was me who called your aunt."

"I called my aunt," Allison said. "It was me. I called her because I was freaked out after Roland and I fooled around on the beach. I'd forgotten it was me because of my head injury. I was so upset about Roland, crying so hard that I tripped. That's what we tell them."

"Is that what happened that day? You were crying and you tripped? Or did Dad do something to you?"

Thora knew her father had lied to them about what they were. She knew he lied about the operations he'd performed on them. She even knew he'd harmed other children with his experiment. But Thora didn't know what he'd done to her sister up in that attic.

And Allison wasn't going to tell her.

"He caught me going through his files. I got scared and ran off. I fell down the stairs. But he didn't push me. No one pushed me. If your dad acted cagey about it, though, that's why. Because I'd run from him, and he knew I knew about you all."

"So he didn't…he didn't *do* anything to you?"

"No," Allison said. "Except catch me in his files."

Thora took a shuddering breath and, once again, she seemed ready to weep. This time, however, it was tears of relief. It hadn't been easy to lie to Thora, but she was glad she did it.

"I was worried," Thora said in a hollow voice. "I was… I don't think I could forgive him if he'd done something to you."

"Don't be worried. Not about that."

Thora took another long shuddering breath. A few seconds passed and she pasted on a smile. Thora gently tapped the large cardboard box on the floor with her bare toes.

"So...you liked your dragons Deacon made you?" Thora asked.

"Loved them. They're perfect."

"He worked so hard on them. I'm glad you love them. He told me he was trying to make up for all the Christmases and birthdays you missed here."

"Deacon's so sweet," Allison said. "My own personal dragons."

"You know, in China, dragons are considered lucky, not scary," Thora said. "And they bring rain. You're either going to have a ton of luck in your life or a ton of rain now."

"I'll be happy with either," Allison said.

"You won't tell them, will you?" Thora asked suddenly, panic in her eyes. "Everything I mean? About what they really are? About the other kids?"

It was a hard thing Thora asked of her. Dr. Capello had asked her the very same thing. To keep the secret would break her heart, Allison knew. To lie and lie to the man she loved... And yet to tell him the truth about his father, what he'd done to them, what he'd done to Kendra and Antonio and Oliver, and what he'd done to her, would hurt even more. It wasn't fair. As a kid she'd thought evil people had glowing red eyes and sinister smiles. She didn't want to believe that evil could look like a kindly old man with soft brown eyes and a snowy white beard who gave the best hugs in the world.

Allison started to answer, "I don't know," but before she could say it, a soft knock sounded on the door.

"Come in," Thora said. It was Roland. He stood, as he usually did, right on the threshold, not quite in, not quite out. His jaw was set and his lips were tight.

"What's up?" Thora said.

"It's time," Roland said. "If we're going to do it today, we need to go now. Sun's almost gone and weather says the temperature is dropping tomorrow."

Thora climbed off the bed.

"Yeah," she said. "I'll get Deacon. You're with us, right?" Thora said to Allison.

"For what?" Allison asked.

"The ashes," Roland said. "You'll come with us to spread them?"

The man had tried to kill her and now his mortal remains sat in jars in the sunroom. Time to empty the jars. Time to let it all go for good.

"Yes," Allison said. "I'm coming."

CHAPTER 29

Allison went downstairs with Roland to the sunroom to wait for the others. They didn't speak, but they did lean on each other. Allison leaned into Roland and he leaned into her. Between the two of them, maybe they could hold each other up just a little bit longer.

Deacon joined them and Thora arrived shortly after, holding something red in her arms.

"What's that?" Roland asked.

"I know it's dumb, but I thought Dad would like it," Thora said. She held up red hooded sweatshirts.

"What? No way," Deacon said, laughing. "He used to make us wear red on the beach so he could spot us easier. He was such a nag. I hope this fits."

"I got them yesterday," Thora said. "It'll fit."

Deacon pulled on the sweatshirt and Thora put on hers. Roland wormed his way into the sweatshirt. Thora put the hood up on his and nodded. "Now you're a red monk," she said.

Thora held out one last sweatshirt, a size small. Allison looked at it a second before taking it from Thora and pulling it on.

"We're wearing these in the picture I have of us," Allison said. "The one with the sparklers."

"That was a good day," Deacon said. "Any day when I get to play with fireworks is a good day."

"It was a very good day," Allison said. "Any day when I got to play with you all was a good day."

Roland kissed her on the forehead.

Once they were all in their red sweatshirts, Allison removed the shroud from the urns. Each of them chose one. They were pretty urns, leaded glass, and all different colors with lids to hide the contents. Walking from the house down to the beach as the last feeble rays of autumn sunlight faded and died was the hardest, longest walk Allison had ever taken. They set the urns down in the sand, took off their shoes and socks and removed the lids from the urns. Inside were white and gray ashes, and Allison studied them in wonder. All that was left of a man, his knowledge and his dreams, his nightmares and his hopes and his love for his children, looked like something you'd sweep out of the bottom of a cold fireplace.

They picked up their urns again. There was a pause, a long one, as all of them waited together for someone to say something. Allison feared they were waiting on her but she had no more to say.

Then Roland began to sing.

He sang in the way of the monks, in the ancient way of the Benedictines. He sang a Psalm to his father and to the ocean and to his Lord.

"Praise the Lord—
Praise the Lord from the Heavens;
Praise him in the heights!
Praise him, all his angels;
Praise him all his host!

Praise the Lord from the earth,
You sea monsters and all deeps,
Fire and hail, snow and frost,
Stormy wind fulfilling his command!
Praise the Lord..."

In her weeks at The Dragon she'd never once heard Roland sing or pray. If his Psalm of praise wasn't lovely enough to make her believe in gods and sea monsters, it was enough to make her believe in Roland.

In the holy quiet that fell after his Psalm, Roland finally took the first step into the ocean. Allison watched slippery silver water rush over his naked toes and his feet sink deep into brown sand.

They followed him.

The water was cool, not cold, but from the paleness of all their faces and the shaking of their bodies as they waded ankle-deep and then knee-deep and then hip-deep into the ocean, one might have thought they'd submerged themselves into ice water. In unison they tipped their urns and let the ashes fall into the sea. And when the urns were almost empty they dipped them into the waves to wash them clean.

Thora wept and Deacon's eyes were bloodred from trying to hold back his tears. Roland looked deceptively calm. How Allison looked she didn't know, but probably tired and probably cold and probably sad.

They turned and trudged out of the water quickly before a wave could catch them and knock them under. Deacon collapsed onto the beach. Thora sat at his side and then Roland at hers. Allison stood behind them, near them, and together they all watched the water scattering the mortal remains of their father.

"Once upon a time," Deacon began and Allison couldn't

say if he was speaking to them or himself or maybe even his father. "A Roman glassmaker figured out how to make glass that could never break. Even if you dropped it on the ground, it would dent, not shatter. This Roman glassmaker knew the emperor Tiberius would want to see his amazing invention. He got an audience with the emperor and presented him with a vase made of this unbreakable glass. Tiberius immediately threw it on the ground. It didn't break and the emperor was astonished. He asked the glassmaker if he'd shared the secret of unbreakable glass with anyone else. The glassmaker swore he didn't. The emperor pulled out his sword right there and cut the glassmaker's head off. You see, the emperor knew that if you could make glass that couldn't break, that could be worked by metal and that was as plentiful as sand, all his gold and silver and other precious metals would be worthless. Tiberius knew there were some secrets too dangerous for the world to know."

None of them spoke. And none of them asked Deacon what he meant. They didn't have to. They knew. They knew what their father had done. And they knew the secret of how it was done was now safely buried in the Graveyard of the Pacific.

Thora kissed Deacon's cheek and rested her head against his shoulder. Roland leaned back against Allison's legs and Allison stroked his hair. The four them watched the water and listened to the wind and the waves. And with her family right there all around her, together, Allison knew one thing: they were all very, very lucky.

"Stay here," Deacon said.

"What?" Allison said.

"Just stay. I'll be right back. One more tribute to Dad."

Deacon ran across the sand and into the house. He emerged a few minutes later with a slim box in his hand. He held it up and it rattled when he shook it.

"Sparklers," he said. "And my phone. Picture time."

"This is ridiculous," Allison said. "It's October."

"Then they're Halloween sparklers," Deacon said. "Come on. It would make Dad happy."

Deacon pulled a lighter out of his hoodie pouch as Thora distributed the sparklers. With a flick of his thumb, Deacon set a flame to blazing and the four of them brought the tips of their sparklers together until they were all brightly dancing in the twilight. The ocean breeze threatened to blow them out so they turned their backs to the beach and huddled together.

"Ready?" Deacon said as he held out his phone to take the picture.

"Not yet," Roland said. "We have to do this right. And it won't be easy. Allison doesn't weigh sixty pounds anymore."

"I weigh sixty-mumble," Allison said. She held her sparkler in her right hand. Roland held his in his left. Then with his strong right arm he hoisted her up, holding her against him, her legs wrapped around his waist. It was so awkward, so ludicrous and precarious, she started to laugh at the absurd pose of a grown woman being held like a child on the hip of a grown man. And that was the picture the camera captured, her openmouthed laugh, Roland's somewhat pained grin, Thora rolling her eyes at them in adoring disgust and Deacon sticking his tongue out because that's what Deacon did.

Roland set her down hard and she ended up falling onto her back in the sand. She stuck her sparkler in the sand to put it out and lay back.

"What are you doing down there?" Roland asked.

"Making sand angels," she said, waving her arms.

"That's not a thing," Roland said.

"It is now." Allison wallowed in the sand a moment longer, to get Roland to smile for her just once. And what a smile it was. A kind and loving smile. A good man's smile.

Roland held out a hand and she took it. He pulled her up and onto her feet.

"See?" she said, pointing at the shape her body had left in the sand.

"Goddamn," Roland said. "It is a sand angel."

"You shouldn't swear like that. You're still a monk, right?" Deacon asked.

"I am for now," he said. "I'd have to tell them I was leaving if…"

"Are you?" Thora asked. "Please?"

Allison tensed. Roland glanced at her as if waiting for her to speak up and answer the question for him. But she couldn't.

"We'll see," Roland said.

"What about you, sis?" Deacon asked. "You staying? Please?"

Allison glanced at Roland. He could no more answer the question than she could. She looked at Deacon and she looked at Thora. Up in her bedroom window, Brien sat perched looking down at his silly humans playing in what he must have thought of as the largest litter box in creation.

"We'll see."

They drifted back to the house and found a large white box on the porch. Roland took it inside and set it on the dining room table. It was addressed simply to "The Capellos" and they all gathered around as Roland opened it.

Inside were flowers. Dozens of flowers, all white. Roses, lilies, monte casino and carnations, but it was mostly one flower Allison didn't recognize.

"What are those?" she asked.

Thora grinned. "Snapdragons. Very fitting."

"Who are they from?" Deacon asked.

"I can guess," Allison said.

"You guessed right," Roland said. He opened the card, which contained a one-hundred-dollar bill, and read it aloud.

"I lost a part of myself the day I lost my father. Luckily I found it again when I looked in the eyes of my children. Your father lives on in the love you all have for each other. Thank you for taking good care of Allison. My deepest condolences,

Cooper McQueen.

P.S. Use the hundred to buy bourbon—Bulleit Barrel Strength if you can find it. It's what we call 'drowning your sorrows' bourbon."

No one spoke at first. Allison blushed a little as Roland put the card back in the envelope.

"Flowers *and* booze money?" Deacon said, nosing through the massive bouquet. "You must be a fantastic lay, sis."

"Deacon, I swear to God," Thora said.

"He's not wrong," Roland said. Allison elbowed him in the ribs.

"I'll take these," Thora said. "They're going on the mantel out of the way of Brien's reach."

"What about the booze money?" Deacon asked.

"I'm keeping that out of *your* reach," she said.

Thora walked away with the flowers, scolding Deacon all the while and leaving Allison and Roland alone in the dining room.

"That was nice of him," Roland said. She didn't argue—it was very nice of McQueen. She hadn't told him anything about what she'd learned other than that Dr. Capello had died and she was certain now she was safe. He hadn't pressed her for more. She had a good feeling these flowers would be the last time she heard from him. And that was okay. It really was.

"Once or twice every year he remembers he has a conscience." Allison picked up a loose carnation from the bottom of the florist's box and twirled it in her fingers. "Today's our lucky day."

"The day you came home was my lucky day. The first time and the second time." Roland took the flower out of her hand and tucked it behind her ear. "And it'll be my lucky day again when you come back for the third time. If and when you come back."

She looked up at him.

"What?" he said. "I can read you pretty well by now. You are leaving, aren't you?"

She smiled weakly.

"I was thinking of doing what I told myself I came out here to do. See the coast. All of it. Drive down the 101 until I hit the ocean or Mexico." She hadn't given away all of McQueen's money. She had plenty left for a long trip.

"Sounds like a nice drive," Roland said. "Want some company?"

She'd been afraid of that question.

"Yes," she said. "But…"

"Right," he said.

"I think I need to be alone," she said. "I've always been afraid of that, you know. I should get over it."

"Why?" he asked. "Seems like being alone is something worth being afraid of."

"You were a monk, remember?"

"And I lived with forty other monks. Monks aren't hermits. I'm scared of being alone, too. We can be scared of being alone together if you want."

"I signed up for six years of McQueen last time I got scared I was going to be alone in the world."

"Didn't turn out that bad, did it?"

"You're defending my ex?" she asked.

"He sent us flowers *and* bourbon money," Roland said.

"I guess he's not so bad," she said. "And we did have fun those sex years."

"Six years?"

"You heard me," she said.

Roland laughed. The laugh didn't last long, but it was a good laugh while it lasted.

"So…" he said, perching himself on top of the dining room table. A no-no in the old days but the old days were over. "You're leaving tomorrow morning?"

"That's the plan," she said.

He sighed. He didn't look surprised but he didn't look happy, either. Simply resigned.

"And you?" she asked. "Back to the monastery?"

"I suppose," he said. "But not right away. I don't want to leave Deac and Thor alone to clean up all the messes. Dad had money, lots of it. Lots of paperwork when there's lots of money."

Allison wondered what they would find when they went through the paperwork. Would he find out about the dead kids? The kids who hadn't been so lucky? Not likely. Dr. Capello had burned all the evidence.

"You all rich now?" Allison asked.

"We have trust funds," he said, and the tone implied they were substantial but not enormous. "But Dad's also donating a big chunk of his money to a few children's charities. He left a separate trust fund just for upkeep on the house, which is nice. I'll have more than enough money to buy your bookstore if that'll keep you here."

"Nice try," she said.

"Had to do it. Dad would have wanted me to."

"You want to," she said, raising a hand to his face. "Because you are the nicest boy in the world."

It was a teasing compliment but Roland took it hard. He lowered his head and stared at his hands clasped across his lap.

"Am I?" he asked.

"I think you are," she said.

"I didn't used to be."

"You used to be a kid. Now you aren't. Now you're a grown man, and a very handsome one at that."

She stepped between his knees and wrapped her arms around his shoulders, and she sensed him flinch.

"What?" she asked.

"You hit my sore shoulder," he said. "See?"

He pulled the collar of his shirt down and Allison saw the black bruise that mottled his entire shoulder. She stared at it, long and hard, and realized she hadn't seen him shirtless since the night before Dr. Capello died. And this was why.

"I thought you used the ax."

"I tried, but it was taking too long," he said. "Brute force did the trick."

"You plowed through a locked door with your shoulder."

"I heard you scream," he said. "What else was I going to do?"

Far more gently this time, Allison put her arms around Roland and held him to her.

"Thank you for saving my life," she whispered.

"Don't go," he said into her ear. "Tomorrow, I mean."

"Roland…"

"I know I'm making it harder for you. But I let you go the first time without a fight, and I'm not going to do that again. So let me fight."

Allison pulled back to face him and gave him a weak smile. "Okay, fight me then."

"I lied to you about one last thing."

"Huge surprise," she said. "What about?"

"Chopping wood. I told you I was chopping so much wood because it was relieving my stress about Dad. That's not why. I couldn't stop thinking about you being here this winter, and winter in Arrow Cape is why fireplaces were invented. I wanted to keep you warm all winter. I pictured you and me on the sofa in the living room with the fireplace going. I was dreaming about how I was going to read to you every night before bed, the fireplace roaring in front of us and you'd be lying in my lap half asleep. And I was dreaming about how you would hide with me under the covers when it rains. And it rains a lot out here so that's a lot of hiding. And I know you're leaving because we had to lie to you and you had to lie to us…but you lie when you love someone and you don't want to hurt them. Maybe those lies don't have to be a wall between us. Maybe they can be a bridge. Anyway, the truth is I chopped so much wood because I want to keep you warm forever."

It was the most beautiful thing anyone had ever said to her. How could she say anything back that was worthy of his confession?

"I…" she began.

"It's okay," Roland said. "I know you're still going. I just wanted to get it off my chest."

"I love you," she said.

His eyes widened.

"You can't say stuff like that to a monk," he said.

"Let's go have sex all night long."

"You really can't say stuff like that to a monk."

"I guess I can't," she said. "Too bad."

She started to drop his hand and found that she couldn't because a monk with a ponytail was hanging on to it.

"Maybe you can," he said.

"No, you were right. You're a monk and you're going back to the monastery."

He pulled her a little closer to him, a little closer still. He took the flower from her hair, McQueen's flower, and tossed it on the table.

"But not tonight."

CHAPTER 30

For the first time in all her days at The Dragon, Allison woke up before Roland. She got up and left him lying in the bed. In the dark room she dressed and by dawn she could see him and the bruise on his shoulder, a bruise nearly as blue and ugly as the bruise around her neck. She stared at it and wondered why Roland never asked her what she did the day she was gone, what she remembered about the "fall" that had taken her from them. Maybe he'd guessed? Maybe he decided he didn't want to know. Or maybe he did want to know but knew she would lie to him. And he loved her enough to spare her the lie. Allison wrenched her gaze from his sleeping form. She wanted to make Crescent City, California, by nightfall. That drive would take all day.

Since they were too valuable and too fragile to pack, Allison's glass dragons she'd left sitting on the bookshelf where bookends belonged. Thora had promised to pack them up carefully and mail them whenever Allison figured out the next step in her life. She'd miss them until then. In the watery light of morning they glinted like they were covered in dew. Allison touched them one by one for luck. Four glass dragons all in a row, with claws that didn't cut and teeth that didn't bite and fire that wouldn't burn.

And yet so lovely. So awfully lovely.

She picked up her purse and her suitcase. She decided to leave without kissing Roland goodbye because if she stopped for a kiss, even one, she'd never leave.

As she was walking out the bedroom door, Allison heard a sound, a sound she'd been missing, a sound she'd been waiting for since the day she arrived.

It was a dark and stormy morning.

She put her suitcase down on the floor by the door and walked to the window. Water was falling and falling and falling. It rained on the ocean and the ocean got wet. She put her hand on the glass and the glass steamed around it. The gold sand turned to brown and the sky glimmered a light black. It looked like Xanadu out there, like a magical kingdom. She thought of poor Coleridge, who wrote *Kubla Khan* after a vision he had while on opium. Some silly man knocked on his door and jarred the poet into waking. He never did finish his masterpiece. There was no going back to his dream. And for the rest of his life he was left to wander outside of Xanadu but never again pass through the gates.

But she had been allowed to come back to her Xanadu. Coleridge would chide her for thinking of leaving. It would be a shame to disappoint the great poet. *Eat the honeydew*, he would say, *and drink the milk of Paradise. No matter the price, pay it.*

Why was she leaving, then? Because of the lies, of course. Because of the secrets. Because she'd made this mistake before, traded her integrity for the promise of something like a family.

But they *were* a family, weren't they? And she had gotten

very good at lying. It didn't even feel like lying anymore. It felt like forgiveness, leaving the past in the past. It felt like mercy. It felt like moving on. The God Roland believed in said suffer the little children to come unto Him. In his sleep, Roland looked like a little child. If God was as old as they said He was, then they were all little children in His eyes, weren't they?

And what was one more secret in this house packed to the attic with secrets? Roland had secrets. So did she. It gave them something in common. Roland might be onto something. Maybe the secrets didn't have to be a wall between them. Maybe they *could* be a bridge.

And…she did have McQueen's money in her suitcase. She hadn't given it all away. It would be more than enough to live on for a while…

"I thought you'd be long gone by now," Roland said, his voice distant as if he were speaking from out of a dream.

"It started raining," Allison said. "I'll wait until it stops."

Roland raised his head off the pillow, pushed his hair off his face and gave her a bemused and sleepy look.

"You know the coast. It won't stop raining till June," he said.

That was true. It would rain until June. That's how it happened out here. And maybe she wasn't ready to sign up for an entire lifetime of lying to someone she loved, but maybe, just maybe, she could do it a week or two, or a month or two. Or three. Or four…

Allison slipped off her shoes and Roland held back the covers for her.

"Storms scare me," she said as she crawled back into bed. Roland pulled her to him as Brien hopped up on the pillow to supervise the new developments. "Maybe I better just stay here with you."

"Maybe you should," Roland said before kissing her like he wouldn't stop until June.

Allison had always loved the rain.

★ ★ ★ ★ ★

ACKNOWLEDGMENTS

I would like to thank my editor, Michelle Meade, and my agent, Sara Megibow, for their support and invaluable assistance during the writing of *The Lucky Ones.* I would be lost in the book world without you both.

Special thanks to the designers at MIRA for their beautiful work on my stunning cover. I can't stop staring at it.

I'm indebted to Dr. Kent A. Kiehl and Dr. Robert D. Hare for their published research on psychopathy. While their books are not easy reads, they were fascinating and informative, and made me very, *very* nervous.

I'm also deeply indebted to author and neurosurgeon Dr. Henry Marsh for his wonderful memoir *Do No Harm: Stories of Life, Death, and Brain Surgery.*

I would be remiss if I didn't thank the true muse of *The Lucky Ones,* the windswept, rocky and terribly Gothic northern Oregon coast. I will be back someday.